# MEANWHILE, BACK AT THE RANCH

## THE SECRETS THAT A ROCK CAN TELL

as told by

### KRISTINE MCGUIRE

Air Force Brat
Wildlife Biologist
Wife/Mother
Rancher/Cashmere Expert
Skeptic/Writer

# MEANWHILE, BACK AT THE RANCH

## The Secrets That A Rock Can Tell

# KRIS McGUIRE

**CITIOFBOOKS, INC.**
3736 Eubank NE Suite A1
Albuquerque, NM 87111-3579
www.citiofbooks.com

Hotline: 1 (877) 389-2759
Fax: 1 (505) 930-7244

Ordering Information:
Quantity sales. Special discounts are available on quantity purchases by corporations, associations, and others. For details, contact the publisher at the address above.

Printed in the United States of America.

ISBN-13:     Paperback     979-8-89391-417-7
                    eBook           979-8-89391-418-4

Library of Congress Control Number: 2024922552

# Table of Content

# Map of the West

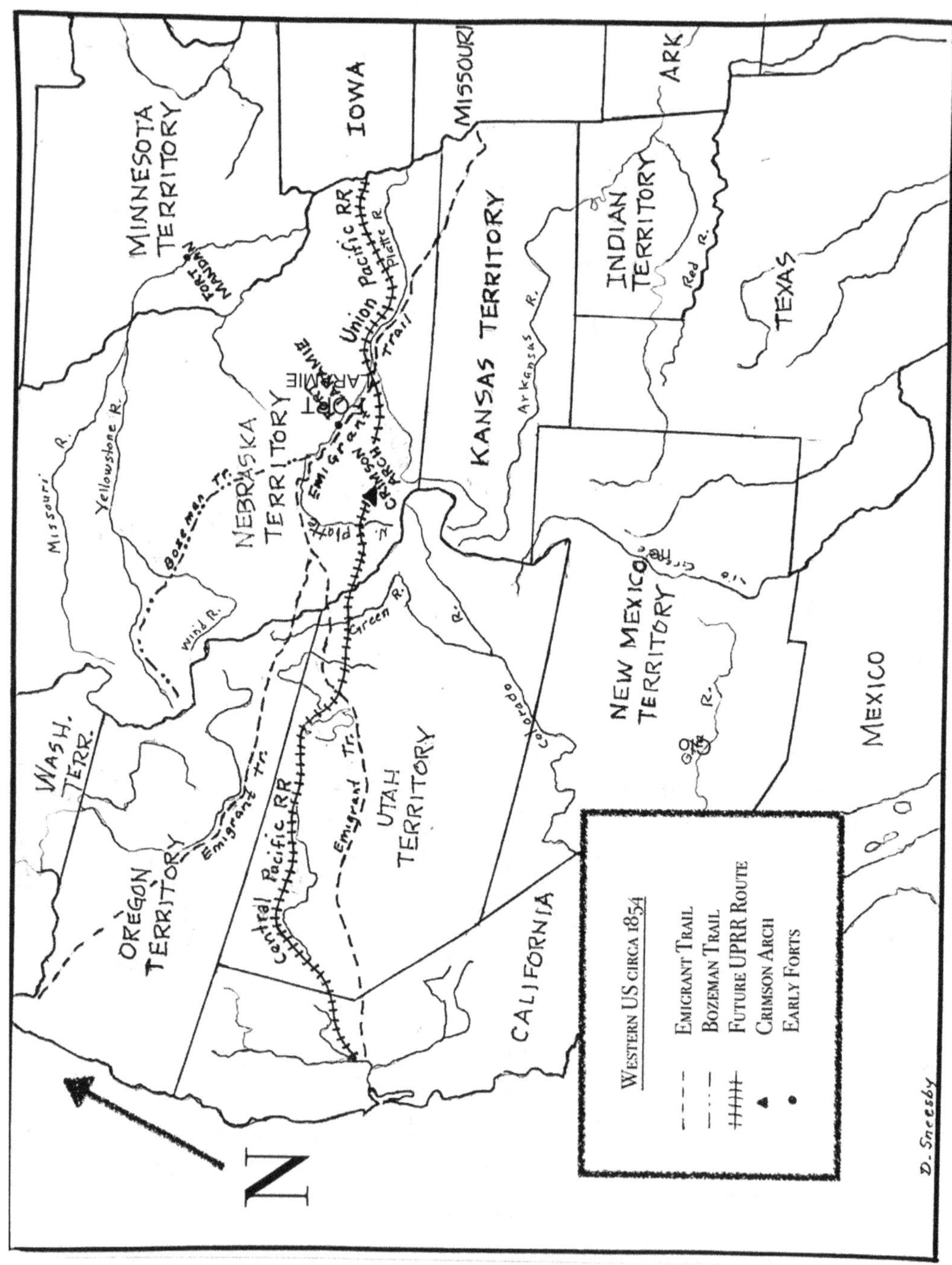

To my family who supported me, encouraged me, ignored me & loved me... no
matter what.
To my editors Barbara Love, Suzanne Scholton, Eileen Murray & Ginny Lee.
To my husband Richard McGuire, whose help & support were invaluable.
And to Greg.
To my Mother, Yvonne & to our friend, Amy Lawrence
who are partying together in Heaven.

North face of the Crimson Arch
(Photo by K. McGuire)

# Preface

As a novice rancher on the Laramie Plains, I was prepared to learn a thing or two about cows, cowboys, and ranching as a lifestyle. But historic preservation? My "new" historic barn leaned dangerously, although it seemed structurally sound. I had to know if it was worth saving. In the pre-Googleian age, my knowledge of the Dewey Decimal System was the ticket, so I immediately set about researching historic barn restoration techniques at the University of Wyoming's Coe Library. Happily, I got sidetracked by the ranch history. My mother, an British schoolteacher with a penchant for history, enthusiastically joined me in the task. She delighted in her discoveries.

Turns out, a pair of fellow Brits had owned the barn at one time, Scottish veterinarians named Stokes and Whitehouse who shared the given name of Arthur. More digging revealed that a local Swedish families of carpenters and horsemen had built and then managed the Oxford Horse Ranch. The discovery of a red sandstone signature rock hidden on the east side of the ranch brought new people to discover. Dozens of folks had scratched their names into the hard sandstone between 1812 and the present. Even though the rock signatories left only tantalizing clues as to their identity, sheer doggedness has revealed eighteen of them:

**BER 1812 = Ed Robinson, Trapper**
**TY 1817 = Thomas Young, US Army**
**GUNNISON 1849 = Surveyor, US Army**
**HJY 1851 = Joaquin Young, Western heir**
**WS Benton 1863 = Political grandson**
**CHH = Charley Hutton, Rancher***
**Nichols '68 = Western Union man****
**MCB 1875 = Melville C. Brown, Jurist***
**L.P. Bradley 1871 = Colonel, US Army**
**J.I. 1867 = John Iliff, Early cattle baron**
**John Daniels 1879 = Indian agent**
**J.L.H. '80 = John Hunton, Diarist**
**H.R. HAY = Cattleman**
**Belle Kuster 1883 = Young immigrant***

**Trabing = Laramie businessman***
**Travis + Tanner '92 = Local workers**
**MEP '95 = Mary Powell, Rustler***
**EM '95 = Esther Morris, Suffragist**
* buried in Greenhill Cemetery, Laramie
** abbreviated dates reflect the original signature.

Try as I might, I did not locate all the signatories back in 1996 when I started the research. I remember finding perhaps half of them. And then my computer crashed. At the time, I was busy managing the livestock on the Old Oxford Horse Ranch, overseeing the barn restoration, and governing the Cashmere Producers of America. On the home front, I had to keep track of three school-aged kids. So I relegated the original project notes to a dusty shelf, thinking the only copy of the complete draft manuscript was lost. Restricted by a miserly office budget, I had not printed it out.

Life has a way of intervening, and I avoided thinking about the project until Mother died. Miraculously, I found a complete paper copy of my manuscript among her papers, thirty pages printed front and back, albeit in tiny font. My late father was never one to waste paper, either. Two hundred years after Ed Robinson and Thomas Young scratched their initials on my rock, I sat down again, laptop computer, ink-jet printer, and online backup at the ready. Tremendously aided by the smartphone at my fingertips, I could search online databases. My favorite is Find-A-Grave (findagrave.com), followed closely by Albany County Library Wyoming.org (acplwy.org) and the Wyoming Newspaper Project (wyomingnewspapers.org).

My searches revealed a treasure trove of dull facts and fascinating trivia alike. As my research identified potential characters, the challenge was to place them within a few miles of my arch around the year of the inscription. Most times, I was successful. I watched as the stodgy portraits I first painted in my mind of each of my new friends fleshed out into authentic western characters. It was like a treasure hunt as one source led to another as if guided by a divine hand. The discovery of each new vignette made these characters part of my family.

The difficulty lay in the fact that while I knew almost everything about three-quarters of the signatories, I knew little to nothing about the rest. One may wonder how certain I am that these tales are true. The answer is that I am positive half the time and pretty sure about most others. There are a couple of wild guesses in there too. Each set of initials was explored in all of the available sources: census rolls, newspapers, indices, bibliographies of history books. Luckily, there were not many people in Wyoming during the 19th century (or the twentieth, for that matter). All the references I needed to access resided along the dusty shelves of the Coe Library on campus and the Albany County Library's Wyoming Room. The Wyoming Room, established by the late J. David and Jane Love is the perfect environment to enjoy Wyoming's history. The valuable volumes are close at hand, and there is a handy, comfy couch upon which to while away the hours enjoying a book too rare to check out.

To find references at UW, I used the newly digitized card catalog kiosk to find the locator number. At the time, the library staff was busy upgrading the printers from the old dot-matrix machines. Then a book cart, my mother, and I rode up and down the elevator, gathering oversized books from the FOLIO section on the top floor, theses that lived in the basement, and texts of all kinds in between. With students queuing patiently behind us in the check-out line, we became the custodians of a tiny slice of Wyoming history. The books were due three weeks later, and in that interim, I read every one. And I ran a ranch.

The ease of completing my research has been my impetus to finish this project. But it isn't easy to let go. Interesting facts fall off the shelf and hit me in the head every time I venture into the Laramie *Boomerang* database. And for this latest update, I have the pleasure of using Artificial Intelligence driven database searched.  What a joy; no more running stairs!

But I have to stop because haying season is upon us once again. Few joys exceed that of driving a John Deere 4020 tractor dragging a Vermeer R-23 twin rake around in circles for days on end. My goal to redirect the dancing light of these little-known episodes of Wyoming's history upon the face of today's State of Wyoming is complete.

~~~~~~~~~~~~~~~~

# Timeline of Western Events

(Rock protagonist's names or close associates are in bold)

- **1804** - The Lewis & Clark Expedition, including John Colter, departs for the Pacific Northwest following the Missouri River. That fall, Zebulon Pike explores Colorado, names Pike's Peak, but fails to summit it. He is captured by the Spanish and freed only after Aaron Burr intervenes on his behalf.

- **1807** - Manuel Lisa explores Nebraska and encounters John Colter after he leaves the Corps of Discovery. Colter returns to Wyoming to trap beaver and encounters geologic wonders. He is captured by Blackfoot and narrowly escapes. Naked, he crawls back to civilization, festering cactus spines in his feet.

- **1809** - Manuel Lisa departs St. Louis, builds Fort Lisa in Nebraska, and returns to St. Louis that fall. Nathaniel Pryor follows but returns to St. Louis immediately, defeated by restive Arikara incited by false promises made by Lisa. Meriwether Lewis dies. Louisiana Territory land opened to licensed trapping.

- **1810** - Lisa, William Clark, & Major Andrew Henry form the St. Louis, Missouri Fur Company. Lisa & Henry establish Fort Union in Montana. Three Kentuckians are employed mid-route and winter at Fort Henry.

- **1811** - Astorian Wilson Price Hunt departs for the Pacific Northwest and encounters Lisa descending the Missouri River. Hunt briefly employs the Kentuckians, **Ed Robinson**, Jacob Rezner, and John Hobart. They return to Wyoming and stay there.

- **1812** - Astorian Robert Stuart leaves Oregon, crosses South Pass, and encounters the Kentuckians in Wyoming. Lisa and Henry ascend the Missouri once again. They establish Fort Manuel and return to St. Louis.

- **1817** - Colonel Ashley & Major Henry lead a government-funded expedition and leave for Wyoming with Lieutenant **Thomas**
~~~~~~~~~~~~~~~~

**Young** in their employ. They encounter Jacques LaRamie at the Arikara Village in Dakota Territory and take him along as far as the Laramie Basin.

- **1819** - Major Stephen Long departs St. Louis in a fearsome steamboat and overwinters at Council Bluffs. A national economic panic prompts Congress to defund his grand expedition partially. Long is forced to walk to Colorado.

- **1820** – Long explores Colorado on foot, names Long's Peak, returns to St. Louis, and publishes a self-aggrandizing journal. Manuel Lisa dies young. Clark takes over the Missouri Fur Company.

- **1822** - Ashley & Henry again leave for Wyoming with Jedidiah Smith, Jim Bridger, Thomas Fitzgerald, and Hugh Glass employed. Glass is attacked by a bear in northern Dakota territory and is abandoned by Bridger and Fitzgerald. He crawls back to Fort Atkinson (present-day Kansas). Henry, Smith, and Bridger stay in Wyoming that winter. Ashley returns to St. Louis.

- **1823** - President James Monroe formalizes the Monroe Doctrine. The Doctrine commits the United States to militarily defeat all European attempts to control any part of the Western Hemisphere.

- **1823** - Colonel Henry needs horses in Wyoming after losing his to raiders, so he sends Jedidiah Smith back downstream to Major Ashley with the message to bring more. The up-river-bound Ashley expedition meets Smith while they are under siege at the Arikara Village that guards the ascent of the Missouri River. Jedidiah conveys Henry's message and returns to Wyoming without any horses. The Arikara disastrously turn back Ashley. Bridger explores Wyoming and Utah.

- **1824** - Major Ashley explores the Laramie Basin, takes celestial coordinates for South Pass, and overwinters in Wyoming. Bridger is invited to join Major Ashley & Colonel Henry's Rocky Mountain Fur Company. General Leavenworth attacks Arikara village in retaliation for the 1823 attack on Colonel Ashley's expedition.

- **1825** - Major Ashley discovers Utah Lake and establishes Fort Ashley. Leavenworth negotiates the Treaty of 1825, granting the Overland Trail Stage Company safe access across Kansas and Nebraska.

- **1832** - Major Benjamin Bonneville, a future commander in the Civil and Mexican-American Wars, explores and traps Wyoming, builds Fort Bonneville, and explores and traps Utah. Bonneville Flats are named for him.

- **1834** - Sir William Gore of Sligo, Ireland, explores Colorado and Wyoming with Bridger as a guide. The mountain man era peaks, and beaver become critically endangered.

- **1836** - Washington Irving publishes *Astoria*, a wildly popular novel about the Astorians and cannibalism.

- **1837** - Sir William Drummond visits Wyoming with Bridger as a guide. Washington Irving publishes his second novel, *Captain Bonneville*, an equally outlandish but wildly popular novel.

- **1842-** Captain John Frémont explores Wyoming with 22-year-old Kit Carson as his guide. He climbs and names 13,745-foot Frémont Peak, thinking it is the highest peak in the Rockies. The first version of the Homestead Act is enacted, granting forty acres to patent holders in the Eastern states.

- **1843** - Frémont travels to Oregon guided by Kit Carson and Thomas Fitzpatrick, unexpectedly overwintering in California after crossing the Sierra Nevada in January. Without his excellent guides, the expedition would have been lost.

- **1844** - Frémont returns triumphantly to Washington and publishes his self-aggrandizing journals.

- **1845** - A severe winter kills most large animals in Wyoming.

- **1846** - Frémont is in California for the end of the Mexican American War.

- **1849** - Captain Howard Stansbury maps Bridger's Trail ending up at Fort Laramie. **John Gunnison** is his second-in-command, with Jim Bridger as his guide. The gold rush in California attracts  thousands of emigrants. Frémont mounts a fourth private expedition to California, which costs ten lives.

- **1850** - The Fort Laramie Treaty (also known as the Treaty of 1851) negotiated by Tom Fitzpatrick, is signed in front of ten thousand Plains Indians; their encampments surround Fort Laramie. The chiefs agree to refrain from warring upon the emigrants, to accept tribal boundaries, and to limit wars among themselves. They are promised $50,000 worth of supplies annually for fifty years if they allow the whites to build roads and forts upon their lands and allow wagon trains to cross unimpeded. Fitzpatrick doubted this would prevent inter-tribal warfare but felt the annuity might work. When Congress ratified the treaty in 1851, they reduced the annuity to ten years. The full annuity was paid only for the first few years. Then it was held back to encourage "good" behavior. Thousands of Indians, faced with starvation, decide to fight to the death.

- **1851- Joaquin Young** travels from Taos to Salem, Oregon, to claim his inheritance, following a route recommended by his father's friend, Kit Carson.

- **1854** - The Grattan Massacre near Fort Laramie destroys that year's annuity. After wiping out Grattan's Company, the Sioux attack one stagecoach, killing three, but otherwise, emigrants are allowed to pass unchallenged that year.

- **1856** - General William S. "The Butcher" Harney comes out of retirement to retaliate for the Grattan Massacre. He discovers some Brulé Sioux camped along the Little Blue Water Creek in present-day Nebraska and attacks at dawn, killing half the warriors and taking all the women and children captive. The guilty warriors surrender and serve one year at Leavenworth Prison. Chief Spotted Tail, upon release, vow to cooperate with the whites so impressed was he with their firepower. The Little Blue Water Massacre was the twelfth-largest army engagement with Indian groups and is often cited as the action that drastically elevated the Indian Wars.

- **1857** - The first global recession depresses the economy.

- **1860** - General Reynolds overwinters in the Laramie Basin with Jim Bridger as his guide. His exploratory expedition was otherwise unremarkable.

- **1861** - Pressured by eastern tribes displaced from their tribal lands, Red Cloud unites his Lakota tribe with the Northern Cheyenne, Arapaho, and Northern Oglala to drive the Crow out of the Powder River Basin. Crazy Horse excels as a fearless warrior.

- **1862** - The Homestead Act is revised, granting 160 acres to any patent filer as long as they had never taken up arms against the United States. Gold is discovered in the Bighorn Mountains of Wyoming, and the illegal Bozeman Trail blazed.

- **1863** - **Stephen Benton** signs rock after escaping from Order Number 11 in Missouri. President Abraham Lincoln welcomes Southern Cheyenne Chiefs Lean Bear and Black Kettle to Washington, promising peace terms but warning that "some of his children might behave badly." He awards both chiefs bronzed copper Peace Medals.

- **1864 - May.** Colorado Governor John Evans confines the Southern Cheyenne to a reservation encompassing southeastern Colorado, but there is not enough game left there to feed them. Colonel John Chivington and his four columns of troops find Lean Bear's hunting camp near Smoky Hill, east of Denver. Lean Bear rides out to Chivington with a few warriors to parley, his Peace Medal on his chest and white treaty papers in his hand. Chivington opens fire at thirty yards, killing them all. He then decimates that camp and all others he encounters that summer.

- **1864 - November.** After a disastrous summer and fall, Chief Black Kettle sues for peace and seeks safety at the Arkansas River Indian Agency. His starving village encamps nearby and awaits the promised supplies. Black Kettle's Peace Medal, white flag, and Stars and Stripes hang upon his tipi. Chivington attacks at dawn, killing 200 Cheyenne, two-thirds of whom were women and children. Black Kettle is uninjured in the attack, but his wife was shot nine times. She also survives.

- **1865 - John Hunton** arrives in Wyoming. The Civil War ends, and the enlisted soldiers either quit the army or travel west to hunt for gold. The US Army Western Division is repopulated with raw recruits too young for the Civil War and are led by wet-behind-the-ears West Point graduates. Most have never ridden a horse or fired a gun. An over-active Eastern press influences all.

- **1865 - Peter Johnson** arrives in the Laramie Valley. He files a patent at Red Buttes, eight miles south of Laramie, and begins dredging irrigation ditches.

- **1866 - April.** General Sherman negotiates a treaty with Red Cloud, allowing passage across the Bozeman Trail. Indian Agent Edward B. Taylor promised that the travelers would not hunt game and the trail would not be garrisoned, effectively lying to both Red Cloud and Washington DC. Colonel Carrington's "Overland Circus" arrives with Lt. Col. **L.P. Bradley,** second-in-command, 700 troops, as well as their 300 wives and children, to build three forts. Infuriated when two innocent warriors were choked to death at the end of a chain at Fort Laramie, Red Cloud continuously harasses the troops and the travelers on the Bozeman Trail.

- **1866 - December.** Riding out from the newly completed Fort Kearny, Lieutenant Fetterman and eighty-one troops are baited by Crazy Horse and a few warriors. Tempted into a trap beyond the protective cannon of the fort, all are massacred by Red Cloud.

- **1867 - John Iliff** establishes himself as a cattle baron and the Goodnight-Loving Cattle Trail is blazed. In January, Congress publishes the Doolittle Report, calling for the war upon Indians to cease and desist. The generals in charge ignore it. Some tribes remain on their reservations, expecting to be fed. The renegade Red Cloud attacks a wood-hauling crew near Fort Phil Kearny and, a week later, a hay-cutting crew near Fort Smith, both along the Bozeman Trail.

- **1868 -** Union Pacific Railroad reaches Laramie. Western Union employee **J. Harvey Nichols** signs the rock. Judge **M.C. Brown** is elected mayor of Laramie. **Charley Hutton** settles on the Laramie Plains. Charles and Augustus **Trabing, Esther Morris** as well as **Belle Kuster** arrive in Laramie.

- **1868 -** Fulfilling a campaign promise, President Ulysses S. Grant orders General John Sherman to abandon Forts Kearny, Smith, and Reno. Red Cloud has won his war. In the Second Treaty of Fort Laramie, the Lakota are promised a reservation in South Dakota and hunting rights in northern Nebraska and northwest Wyoming. They are also pledged schools, healthcare, hunting rights, and rations for thirty years.

- **1868 -** Cheyenne Chief Black Kettle is killed by General George Custer in a dawn raid resembling the Sand Creek Massacre. Indian Agent John Wynkoop resigns in protest.

- **1869 -** Wyoming suffrage was established.

- **1870 - Esther Morris** is appointed Justice-of-the-Peace in South Pass City, Wyoming.

- **1871 -** Former Fort Smith commander, Colonel **L.P. Bradley**, takes command of Fort Sanders, south of Laramie. The Red Buttes Ranch becomes the Stokes Ranch.

- **1871 -** By an act of Congress, individual tribes are no longer recognized as entities with which treaties could be struck. Efforts to distinguish between peaceful factions of tribes from warlike ones are abandoned.

- **1872** - The Homestead Act is revised again, offering 160-acre parcels west of the Mississippi under the Desert Land Act and the Timber Culture Act. Individuals are allowed to develop water or timber in exchange for land ownership. There is little to no government supervision. The Territorial Prison is dedicated in Laramie.

- **1873** - Panic of 1873 depresses the economy.

- **1876** - The Battle of Little Big Horn. All-out war, including brutal winter campaigns, hunt down all remaining, free ranging, native warriors.

- **1877** - After being pursued relentlessly, Crazy Horse surrenders and is killed at Fort Robinson, where Colonel **Bradley** is in command. The remaining Lakota are forced onto their reservation.

- **1878** - Thomas Edison travels to Wyoming to observe the total eclipse of the sun using his new invention to measure the distance to the sun. Wyoming becomes a Territory. **John Iliff** dies.

- **1879** - **John Daniels** retires as the Red Cloud Agency Indian Agent.

- **1881** - Jim Bridger dies in Missouri.

- **1883** - The last Sun Dance is held in Wyoming Territory. **H.R. Hay** builds a ranch in Centennial, Wyoming.

- **1884** - Maverick Law is established in Texas. Severe winter kills most of the Swan Cattle Company's livestock.

- **1885** - **Charles Trabing** dies.

- **1886** - The Great Die-Up of 1886 kills most of the commercial livestock in southEastern Wyoming.

- **1887** - The Stokes Ranch is renamed the Oxford Horse Ranch after the death of Sir George Gordon. The University of Wyoming is dedicated.

- **1887** - Congress passes the Dawes Act decreeing that instead of reservation land being held communally by the tribe and governed by tribal elders, tribal members could privately own (and sell) their parcel of land. This also meant that a white man married to a Native American woman could inherit her parcel upon her death, even if he is suspected of killing her. J. Edgar Hoover's FBI got its start by investigating such murders among the fabulously wealthy Osage Indians of Oklahoma. The Dawes Act also opened up reservation lands to white settlement. If there were not sufficient tribal members to populate their land at the rate of one household per 160-acres, the "left-over" reservation land was opened to homesteading with the whites getting first choice. Think of the movie *Far and Away*. Those wagons were racing to stake out the best land on an Osage reservation.

- **1890** - Wyoming becomes a state.

- **1891** - Red Cloud is killed in the aftermath of the Battle of Wounded Knee. All free-ranging northern Indian groups are now subdued and confined to reservations under threat of starvation.

- **1892 - Travis** and **Tanner** sign the rock. Laramie's economy booms. The Johnson County War begins and ends a month later. The Langhoff Gang is tried in Laramie.

- **1893** - The Panic of 1893 begins and ends in 1897. Wealthy Republicans set out to doom Democrat Grover Cleveland's presidency by tanking the economy. There were five major economic panics in the 19th century; 1819, 1837, 1857, 1873, and 1893. The Federal Reserve was formed in 1913 to even out such swings and New Deal acts passed later had similar goals.

- **1895 - Mary Powell and Esther Morris** sign the rock. Augustus **Trabing's** business burns to the ground.

- **1898** - Teddy Roosevelt charges up San Juan Hill.

- **1899** - The Great Blizzard of 1899. Freezing temperatures and snow extend south into Florida.

- **1901 - H.R. Hay** signs the rock.

- **1903** - Tom Horn is tried for a murder he did not commit and hung.

# The Old Oxford Horse Ranch

THE BARN AT THE OXFORD RANCH, CIRCA 1995.
(PHOTO BY RICHARD COLLIER)

~ ~ ~ ~ ~ ~ ~ ~ ~ ~ ~ ~ ~ ~ ~

# *Chapter One*
# BUYING THE PROPERTY

When my husband and I purchased the Old Oxford Horse Ranch, it consisted of two-and-a-half sections of land, about 1,600 acres, small compared to the surrounding spreads. We had been hunting for ranch land for some time, but while there was good availability, the price was always too high. Finally, our realtor showed us the Oxford Ranch, allowing us to wander around the deserted property independently. It was late September, and the hay meadow was at its peak production. We became almost hypnotized by the 150 acres of sub-irrigated hay meadow at the heart of the ranch.

The smooth brome, red fescue, and wheatgrass were mature, and the heavy seed heads undulated gently in the wind like an enormous, deep green comforter. The land climbed towards the foothills east of the hay meadow, a mile-wide swath of low grasses, yellow daisies, and grey-green shrubs. Stark red and white rocky outcroppings punctuated the landscape as the topography prepared to mount the shoulders of the Laramie Range. A precious water right on Harney Creek belonged to the ranch, as well as the right to lease part of the school section to the south, 230 additional acres of land courtesy of the State of Wyoming.

Western school sections (usually sections #16 and #36) are federal lands granted to the new state governments to defray the cost of educating the citizenry. And back in the 1870s, before statehood, some 40,000 people, mostly men and overwhelmingly white, did, in fact, flood into the newly formed territory of Wyoming. When the state section "belonging" to the Oxford Ranch was defined, the quarter section occupied by the ranch headquarters was excepted and remained private. The right to graze, mine, or timber the land was leased out, generating an income stream for the local government.

Included in the deal were some tumbling-down log buildings and a modern pole barn/cow working facility. The old log barn was enormous: 160 feet long, 50 feet wide, and thirty feet tall. Its second story leaned dangerously to the east. We avoided standing too close. Old transmissions, abandoned farm implements, dead cottonwood branches, and the rubble from fifty years of inattention littered the barnyard. The old blacksmith shop had many missing slats and roof shingles, so the bright sunlight played daintily over the rusting anvil, tattered bellows, and dusty workbench. Upstairs, the main house had exposed patches of wooden lath on the ancient plastered walls, and all the woodwork languished under thick layers of yellowing, lead-based paint. Drab, brown indoor/outdoor carpet was glued firmly to the straight-grained birch floors. The house was freezing inside, even though the day was sunny.

The modern cattle facility just north of the original log structures was a more promising addition to our potential ranching business. The neat brown and white pole barn floor was deeply strewn with fresh sawdust, temporarily concealing the beginnings of rot at the base of the poles. A draft horse harness was carefully arranged atop the pristine sawdust as if a giant animal might suddenly appear to shoulder the heavy leather. A large, homemade sign leaned against the wall: "OXFORD RANCH" was spelled out in crude, block letters. The sign looked ready to hang on any sturdy gatepost. Was it waiting for someone to love the ranch enough to call it home?

Outside, spacious corrals surrounded the pole barn but were overgrown with a type of tumbleweed that overtakes disturbed areas. The dead plants are prickly, so we picked our way through the thigh high jungle to inspect the broken water fountain and the creaking pole gates. We could not see over the high pinewood slab barrier fence that defined the corrals on the lee side of the barn. These fences were designed to block winter gales, but that day was just-turned-fall perfect and the wind was warm and gentle. The sun seemed to smile upon our faces as we decided to buy the place.

We, the newcomers were so enchanted by the impending concept of ranch ownership that we did not notice the rotted barn poles until after we closed. However, we immediately noted the absence of all the good steel gates. Overnight, it became impossible to lock the place up. One by one, we listed the things present before closing that had since disappeared: the ranch sign, the horse harness, the old blacksmith bellows, the anvil, and half a dozen gates. With a wide Wyoming grin crinkling the crow's feet on his deeply tanned face, the realtor admitted he had "staged" the pole barn with the harness. He did return the sign ten years later, but I doubt that the anvil and the bellows were standard staging accessories. I was miffed; after all, they belonged to the original Oxford Horse Ranch, and I wanted them back. Despite my protestations, all I got was another wry smile. His new barn got the gates.

A few years before we went into the ranching business, the first Iraq war had raged briefly. Wyoming ranchers were affected economically in two ways.

On the positive side, grass-fed beef contracted to feed the troops overseas kept beef prices high until the war ended. The second way involved the House of Representatives. In 1993, they eliminated the wool and mohair price supports that had been in place since World War II. American tax dollars that had given sheep and goat ranchers a guaranteed income for many years finally dried up. An army of lobbyists from Wyoming and West Texas, the center of the Angora goat industry, testified before Congress, but the votes were not there.

The loss of this subsidy was the last straw. When added to the ongoing mini-recession, a familiar economic pattern emerged. The Wyoming economy has always been at the mercy of three unpredictable factors:

- The capricious climate

- The demand for agricultural products (beef, horses, hay)

- The demand for natural resources (timber, minerals, fossil fuels).

That trifecta makes or breaks those struggling to achieve the American dream.

Dropping cattle prices tempted the old-time ranchers to sell out, and I appreciate their position well. After operating a historic family spread on a fingernail budget, ranch patriarchs faced a grim retirement without a son or son-in-law to take over the workload. Ranch kids grew up spending weeknights in town so they could attend high school and there they remained after graduation and marriage. Ranching just was not profitable enough to support one modern family, let alone two. Plus, when a recession forced belt-tightening, consumers bought chicken and polyester from Walmart, not beef and wool. Throw in a random hay crop failure, a massive fuel cost increase, or a tightening credit market, and aging western ranchers become highly motivated to sell off their land. Suddenly, thirty-five acres with an air-conditioned modular home nestled among the Arizona cactus looks pretty good. Many a weatherbeaten face turned hopefully south.

The trend became a stampede as the market for Wyoming ranches plummeted because land was even cheaper in arid Arizona. The remains of the once magnificent Oxford Horse Ranch had been on the market for years, so the absentee owner accepted our meager offer. He even further discounted the price to incentivize us to purchase the derelict ranch buildings, which we had initially declined to buy. Delighted, we secured a Farm Bureau loan and went to work.

The first order of business was to clean the place up. We already owned a 1946 Chevy six-cylinder, two-ton beet truck. We had used "Big Red" years before hauling logs to build our mountain cabin twenty miles south of the new ranch. We found an old farm tractor inside the barn that my husband coaxed back into life. A visit to the local farm and ranch auction added a grapple loader to the Allis-Chalmers tractor, and we now had the means to dispose of the transmissions, trash, and tree branches that littered the barnyard.

We had never had a mortgage before, and the payment deadlines seemed to come quickly, so we decided to monetize the operation by renting out the old ranch house. It was huge: three bedrooms upstairs, an ensuite master on the main floor, and yet another spacious room in the basement. We laid new carpeting right over the old indoor/outdoor stuff, thinking it might provide some insulation from the winter cold. The plaster-and-lath walls upstairs were repaired and repainted. The 1970s-style walnut paneling on the main floor rooms brightened considerably with bright floral and blue stripe wallpaper. I put an extra layer of wallpaper lining underneath to hide the furrows in the paneling. To my amazement, adding two layers of wallpaper significantly increased the R-factor insulation value of the walls.

With the rent now carrying the mortgage, we considered saving the log outbuildings. The big barn was leaning about twelve degrees to the east, and all the chinking had deteriorated. Most of the shingles that once covered the massive roof were missing or damaged, so the sunlight traced dynamic, dappled patterns the massive but empty hayloft floor. Restoring a barn that size and age is a tricky proposition. The structure had few nails because the ingenious *pièce-sur-pièce* building technique slotted the carved, horizontal log ends into the massive, upright support beams.

Thick iron plates connected the second story to the first. Over the years, the barn became unstable in high winds, inching farther and farther to the east. Removing half the stallion stalls to make room for tractors also removed critical support beams. And since hay was no longer stored loose in the loft, its weight could not stabilize the structure. Luckily, there is a science that informs the restoration of log structures, so we engaged the services of an expert. He warned against suddenly jacking the logs straight again as the pressure would shatter the ancient wood. We had to put it back the same way it got there, slowly but surely.

Following his advice (with a grain or two of salt), we strung half a mile of old elevator cable from solid cement bollards sunk on the structure's west side to the barn's east wall. Securing the free end of the cables to large plates on the outside of the east side logs, we could begin to apply westward pressure to the structure as a whole. Industrial grade turnbuckles we bought at yet another farm and ranch auction were perfect for putting just the right amount of tension on the multiple cables. Inch by inch, the upper walls regained their stature without splintering the wood. This whole process took three years.

In the interim, we worked on replacing the barn's foundation. Built originally upon red sandstone blocks that had since turned to dust, we first excavated underneath each of the upright support beams along the walls. We dug down four feet after placing temporary supports for the structure above. Concrete block, rebar, and cement filled the excavations. Removing the temporary supports, one by one, we renovated the remaining support columns, twenty-six in all.

Next came the foundation under the horizontal logs that filled the space between the twenty-six columns. Our Mexican hired man, Espíritu "Speedy" Medina, did most of the grunt work. My husband was still gainfully employed at our environmental firm in Laramie. I was busy raising three human kids and 200 goat kids, to say nothing of the working dogs, cattle, and horses. Speedy dug a trench under the lowest log in each section and, using scrap lumber, framed out some 400 linear feet of form. After Speedy completed that project, he moved on, leaving us ready to pour the foundation. Advertising in the local paper, the Laramie *Boomerang*, I had just hired a new ranch hand. This guy (young, tall, and blond) was looking forward to a career as a cowboy on the Old Oxford Horse Ranch. His first day on the job was to help me pour two pre-cast mixer trucks full of cement into Speedy's forms.

It did not have to be pretty, but it had to be fast because concrete sets up very quickly in the high, dry air of a ranch half an hour from the batch plant. Eventually, the cement truck drivers took pity upon this crazy woman when the exhausted young man hit the proverbial wall. At sunset, we three finished shoveling the concrete into the last few yards of the foundation. The new ranch hand (I do not even remember his name) quit the next day. I cannot tell you how difficult it is to hire decent ranch help. The hard work on a real ranch does not correspond well with the fantasy of freely riding the range tending "dogies."

After more months of interior reinforcement, the barn was finally (mostly) square again and ready for the new roof. We hired a roofing contractor because working in the Wyoming wind, two stories above the red hard pan of the barnyard, was not at all appealing. Some $40,000 later, the barn had a new roof and could again stand proud, straight, and tall against whatever Wyoming's weather could offer.

## *Chapter Two*
# ALONG HARNEY CREEK

Skirting the ranch to the east is the meandering Harney Creek. The surrounding meadow is a brilliant patch of emerald green set upon a dominantly red landscape silhouetted against the cerulean sky. Guided by underlying geologic features, the Harney Creek watershed drains to the north along the western foot of the Laramie Range. The water slows upstream of the ranch, forming an elevated, marshy puddle impounded by the near-impervious red clay of the Laramie Basin. This surface water, the source of our water rights, is continuously fed by at least one hundred artesian springs. The springs keep the surrounding water table at ground level even during drought years.

This unique wetland perches incongruously at the feet of stark, red sandstone outcroppings that resemble oversized teapots and medieval castles. Collectively called Red Buttes, the runoff from the slick rock feeds the puddle and, in turn, our modern irrigation reservoir, Leazenby Lake. Because of the boggy ground, it is a problem to harvest the hay that grows thick among the hummocks. Additionally, the grass that prefers to grow in those marshy conditions is not palatable to most herbivores. When we bought the ranch, we had no idea that the State of Wyoming had condemned the deteriorating dam, although it was probably common knowledge. The dam had failed twice already in its history. We had to rebuild it again before we could fill the lake and effectively irrigate the hay meadow on the ranch. I thought a lot about Mr. Peter Johnson but more about our realtor as we began yet another restoration project.

My appreciation of Mr. Johnson peaked as we labored on the dam. He arrived in 1865, before the train and before General Ferdinand V. Hayden started his western land survey for the United States Geological and Geographical Survey (the precursor to the US Geological Survey). Johnson liked this well-watered stretch of Harney Creek surrounded by a relatively flat hay meadow, so he decided to homestead it. He labored alone for five years using horse-drawn dirt scoops to build the dam. His ditches still snake across the dry uplands, although they do not efficiently deliver water to the meadow. He filed his patent at the courthouse and went to work. It required five years to prove up, or complete, a patent, so Johnson built a sturdy log house near what is now the Red Buttes whistle stop on the railroad and settled in. He also built two large irrigation canals: one he called the Peter Ditch and the other, the Johnson Ditch.

The ranch at Red Buttes was established in 1870 with the completion of Johnson's patents. While no one can claim all the water in a stream as his own, water rights are distributed based on who first used the water for beneficial purposes. The senior right on Harney Creek was awarded based on the vision of irrigating yet-to-be-established towns. A local water development corporation secured that right just days before Johnson's junior right was filed and sold it years later to the town of Wheatland, Wyoming (founded in 1894). Wheatland is a major corn and alfalfa producing area, both irrigated crops.

With his patent proved up, Johnson purchased the land directly to his north from another homesteader for $1,000, about $110 an acre in today's money. Johnson lived on the ranch and was active politically, attending the 1878 Republican State Convention as the representative from Red Buttes.

According to Robert Burns in *Pioneer Ranches of Wyoming*, Johnson sold out to a Scottish veterinarian named Arthur Stokes in 1880. Dr. Stokes was more of an investor/adventurer than a vet. He bought the land with the purpose of developing it into a premiere horse property. By the end of 1887, the ranch was fully operational with its two large log barns, log ranch house, and brick mansion. Although the ledgers at the Albany County Real Estate Office are unclear, Stokes eventually partnered with Arthur W. Whitehouse and established the Stokes & Whitehouse Ranch, soon to be renamed the Oxford Horse Ranch.

Over the next few years, they presided over one of the West's largest and most impressive horse ranches, indeed Wyoming's largest. The Oxford Ranch was famous and well-visited by both English gentry and US government contractors seeking war horses, large numbers of war horses. The barn could securely confine fifty high-strung breeding stallions and thousands of broodmares. Since southeast Wyoming crawled with horse thieves, every stall door had a padlock.

In the early 1890s, Arthur Stokes turned over his share to Arthur Whitehouse for ten dollars and departed. Whitehouse also soon departed, leaving the ranch in the hands of his able ranch foreman, Axel Palmer. Whitehouse had decided to attend veterinary school in Ontario, Canada. His first stop was New York City, where he married Sara S. Digges in a ceremony at her Manhattan home on January 26, 1892. Upon their return to Wyoming in the summer of 1894, Sara began painting watercolors while Whitehouse hung out a shingle as a veterinarian. Until the end of the century, this unique country vet traveled far and wide, visiting remote ranches and tending to their livestock. Known for his witty conversation, he listened to many a tale of the American West. His sharp memory and ability to spin these tales later made him a popular professor of animal anatomy at Colorado A&M and later at Glasgow Veterinary College in Scotland.

GUS PALMER BREAKING A HORSE.
PAINTING BY SARA WHITEHOUSE.
(PHOTO COURTESY OF AMY LAWRENCE)

~ ~ ~ ~ ~ ~ ~ ~ ~ ~ ~ ~ ~ ~ ~

Sadly, the extravagant lifestyle of the Gilded Age was short-lived. While Whitehouse was in school, a crop failure in far-away Argentina and a political coup here in the States precipitated a global recession that affected even the remote Laramie Plains. This downturn, coupled with over-enthusiastic railroad expansion (more than 100,000 miles of track laid in twenty years), destabilized the railroads' financial backers. Then bank instability undermined public confidence, leading to a run on the banks. The Panic of 1893 reined in the Oxford Horse Ranch's economic carousel. All the family money keeping the ranch afloat was suddenly at risk.

While the 1893 Chicago World's Fair amazed millions with its fabulous Ferris wheel and glimmering White City, the global economy faltered. Over the next four years, seven hundred American banks failed. The US government itself came close to failure. Even the mighty Union Pacific Railroad (UPRR) declared bankruptcy, but not the Union Pacific Corporation. Protected by its straw corporations, the corporate stockholders survived. Unfortunately for Wyoming horse ranches, the budding age of the automobile followed the end of this recession, so the Oxford Horse Ranch turned to commercial cattle ranching.

The need to double-track the transcontinental railroad track became apparent as the economy picked up again. This expansion (granted in 1900 and completed in 1905) cleaved the Old Oxford Horse Ranch in half. Eventually, Dr. Whitehouse abandoned the section of deeded land upon which sat his treasured ranch headquarters, land to which I now hold title. Stokes & Whitehouse had taken their families' fortunes and ranched until the money was all gone.

~~~~~~~~~~~~~~~

The Oxford Ranch was unique because it was originally established as a horse ranch, not a cattle ranch. Most Wyoming ranchers embraced Hereford cattle after the Texas longhorn cattle drives ended. The switch happened when the famous Swan Land & Cattle Company imported the red and white cattle from their native Scotland. The Swan Ranch ran from Ogalala, Nebraska, to the top of the Laramie Range and from the Colorado state line to the Platte River. They ran hundreds of thousands of livestock; most starved in the terrible winter of 1888, but that is another story.

After 1910, the Oxford Ranch's title chain became more complex. Tracing the ownership changes in the massive leather ledger at the Albany County Clerk's office was challenging. After Stokes & Whitehouse dissolved their partnership, the title briefly passed to Axel Palmer. Palmer ran the ranch until 1910. It is unknown if the cruel winter of 1910-11 contributed to Axel Palmer's demise as a ranch owner. By 1915, Palmer had moved on to manage **Charley Hutton**'s ranch. Palmer worked for Hutton for a few years and then moved on to manage the Millbrook Ranch up on the Little Laramie River. Eventually, he built a sturdy cabin down near Philip Mandel's stage station.

By 1913, a Chicago lawyer named Daniel C. Buntin and his partner, investor E.R. Talmadge, owned the ranch. Buntin then partnered with a man named Maclay to purchase and manage sheep. Maclay immediately stocked the land with over one thousand purebred Hampshire sheep brought in from Idaho at eighteen dollars each. Because they needed two grand residences, Buntin remodeled Axel Palmer's ranch house. They added a large living room with a grand fireplace and moved the main entrance to the south side.

The following year, they added cattle to their pastures. In the fall of 1914, the newspapers reported a "nasty fire" on the old Oxford Ranch. When an automobile engine exploded one windy night, a major conflagration began that consumed the garage, the carriage barn, a shed, and Daniel Buntin's mansion house. It must have been a devastating loss, more than the stated monetary value of $15,000. Buntin had a checkered investment history and was deeply in debt. Confronted with increasingly bad winter weather alternating with
~~~~~~~~~~~~~~~

summer drought threatening his ambitious irrigation projects, Buntin returned to Chicago and committed suicide.

Three years later, after complex title swapping between local investors, John Leazenby purchased the ranch. Leazenby ran thousands of sheep and imported Basque sheepherders to tend them. The bad winters and droughty summers continued through the 1920s, but Leazenby hung on. During the winter of 1933, a Siberian Express swept down from the north, again burying the plains. The record low temperature documented in Yellowstone that season stands today, negative sixty-six degrees Fahrenheit. In 1948, Leazenby sold out when US Highway 287, which marks the ranch's western border, was rebuilt, cutting off the Johnson Ditch. The infusion of cash the government paid to secure the new highway right-of-way was enough to spur Leazenby and his wife into retirement. Good thing, too; that winter of 1949 brought the "Storm of the Century," and all activity in southeastern Wyoming and the Nebraska panhandle ground to a halt for weeks. Military helicopters air-dropped feed to stranded cattle and sheep.

On his way out, Leazenby split the once magnificent ranch even smaller, this time into four 1,600-acre parcels. The remains of the Oxford Horse Ranch headquarters were sold to a retired UW botany professor, Dr. Otto Lembke. The University of Wyoming bought the second quarter, which surrounded the UW fish hatchery (built in 1911 upon the state land), to protect the water right. They needed an endless supply of artesian water to flush through the fish tanks. The all-important Oxford Ranch winter grazing ground is now UW's property and is under-used to this day. The third quarter of the Oxford Ranch was sold to a local developer who split it into thirty-five-acre parcels. Wisely, he designed the development to preserve the open space necessary to support the resident antelope herd. An Irish homesteading family bought the southernmost quarter, which was contiguous with their existing land. They bred top-quality black Angus bulls, which grazed there each summer as yearlings.

Black Angus cattle originated from Scotland but are more compact than the rangy Herefords preferred by the Swan Company. They are also pure black, with no white spots. Recently, a brilliant marketing campaign by the beef industry has led to a nearly 80% shift of Wyoming ranchers to running black cows, not red and white, not longhorned. My husband and I were no exception. When we lived in the Colorado mountain cabin, we had always invested in cows of no particular color or breed. As we learned about ranching, we bought only black cows and leased black bulls from the Irishman's ranch. They sell only pedigreed bulls, and they guarantee them. If one of their bulls will not breed, you return him.

Running cattle at high altitudes brings its own challenges, no matter the color. Ranchers above 6,000 feet have to worry about factors that lower-elevation producers do not. High altitude cattlemen cannot just go out and buy any bull; they must go to a reputable breeder. Why? All reputable breeders certify that their bloodlines do not harbor the dreaded livestock disease called "brisket." Brisket is a genetic disorder carried on the his Y chromosome. A bull carrying the gene and raised at high altitude will die. Pastured at a lower altitude, it will survive to pass his genetic disease on to his offspring. So smart bull breeders ensure that all their bull calves enjoy the clear cold air of the Laramie Plains for their first season. After surviving that first summer of freedom, medical testing results for pulmonary sufficiency will go on their pedigree.

<div align="center">~~~~~~~~~~~~~~</div>

Before we bought it, the last person to run livestock on the Oxford Horse Ranch was a retired car dealership owner, Keith Burman. In 1980, he built a beautiful home overlooking Hundred Springs, abandoning the log ranch house. He did not know that 2,500 acres is insufficient to support 200 mother cows. On this ranch and all over the Mountain West, the range carrying capacity is about one cow-calf unit/year per thirty-five acres. The metric used to define this number is the AUM (animal unit month is the number of acres required to support one 1000-pound cow for three months). For the Oxford Ranch, that number was seventy head; not enough to break even. The truth is that even with luck, ranching is not a reliably profitable pastime.

In Stokes and Whitehouse's time, the heart of Harney Creek was a looping, meandering maze of foot-deep channels and grassy hummocks. They did not mind that the horses inefficiently grazed that grass; more palatable grass species were readily available. When left to choose freely, cattle are also remarkably picky eaters. The luxurious-looking grasses in the marshy areas are rarely consumed. Over the winter months, they tend to get trampled by water-seeking animals or a thick layer of ice. In the winter, the meadow was flat enough on the edges to support a tractor. But down near the productive stream bed itself, the ground was dangerously boggy for a heavy machine. The underground puddle effect that characterized the Red Buttes area also dominated the stretch of Harney Creek that ran through the ranch. But there were still grasses to harvest and stack in the loft of the great barn. Early fall was generally harvest time.

So Mr. Burman channelized Harney Creek, hoping to eliminate those unpalatable native grasses. He planted smooth bromegrass *(Bromus inermis Leyss)*, a popular exotic species. He also thought he could seed the far north end of the meadow and bring water to it along the largely abandoned Peter Ditch. About this time, as my husband and I commuted past the Old Oxford Horse Ranch, we could see a single tractor plowing under the fragile soils on the north end of the meadow. We couldn't figure out why anybody would do such a thing - the Dust Bowl proved that rain does not follow the plow. Soil scientists have also established that deep plowing disrupts the fragile soil profile supporting plant growth.

We did not know that the owner was dynamiting a more direct route through the meadow for Harney Creek's waters. He did not know that the underlying geology dictates the course creek water will always follow, and that runs much deeper than his dynamite reached. While he diverted the surface water in places, the groundwater followed the ancient stream bed. His efforts allowed him to run heavy machinery right up to the edge of the new channel. However, his hay production was vastly decreased because the groundwater was now below the reach of the grassroots. We knew none of this when we signed the purchasing contract. To our untrained eye, the meadow looked beautiful. Later, as we labored to get water to the north pastures in a drought year, we appreciated the wisdom of letting Mother Nature take her course. After twenty years of trying, we have never gotten Burman's ditches to run water to their ends. The same can be said about Peter Johnson's two main ditches.

Throughout the 1990s, the Mountain West experienced drought conditions. The typical heavy snowfalls and regular summer rains became less frequent. The Wyoming wind continued to sap moisture from the newly disturbed soil. Then, the usually reliable Wyoming winds became unpredictable. The water tanks on the pastures, customarily filled using wind power, were not kept full due to lengthy periods of calm. Cattle are typically very thirsty animals. They are willing to walk up to ten miles to get their daily requirement. And they need a lot of water, up to twenty gallons a day in the summer.

The truth was that the ranch did not have enough water or grass for 200 cows. Frustrated by the inability to tame Harney Creek and beset by health problems, Burman retired to a smaller ranch near Greeley, Colorado. He put the Oxford Ranch up for sale once again. The sale bill offered four parcels: 1,600 acres of ranch land with a pole barn, 860 acres of development land with his modern home, and the old ranch headquarters. The Old Oxford Horse Ranch dwindled to a mere 100 acres plus half a grazing lease. Things were looking pretty grim for the old barn.

~ ~ ~ ~ ~ ~ ~ ~ ~ ~ ~ ~ ~ ~

SOME OF THE ORIGINAL 50 STALLION STALLS INSIDE THE OLD BARN. NOTE THE WHEELBARROW (IT HAS SKIDS, NOT WHEELS). (PHOTO COURTESY OF AMY LAWRENCE).

## The Buckhorn Bar

The famous watering hole next door to the Kuster House is now called the Buckhorn Bar. The long, mahogany bar of today's Buckhorn is original; a bullet hole mosaics the back bar mirror. Gus Palmer of the Oxford Horse Ranch was a well-known customer. He had the habit of riding his horse directly into the bar to order a drink. The bar owner did not complain, claiming it was good for business.

One Saturday morning, as Axel Palmer was delivering his wife's eggs to market, his green team bolted through the doorway of the Buckhorn Bar. Tempers flared over the best method to extract the thrashing horseflesh from the entranceway. Eventually, the cowboys unhitched the horses; one was brought inside the bar, and the other taken out to the boardwalk. Axel bought the bartender a drink, and they parted amicably.

~~~~~~~~~~~~~~~~~~

## *Chapter Three*
# STOKES & WHITEHOUSE

When my husband and I decided to buy a ranch, our experience was limited to running a few mother cows on eighty acres in Colorado. For a few years, we had picked up individual bred cows at auction houses in Fort Collins, Colorado, or Torrington, Wyoming. Older cows are often a good investment, especially if you are more interested in selling the calf than building a quality herd. Mostly though, I needed more pasture for my cashmere goats. Goats are wily characters, always wanting to leave virtually any confinement. As goes the old joke; if you seal three goats in an oil barrel, one will die, one will escape, and one will be just fine.

The front pasture at the Old Oxford Horse Ranch had been securely fenced along the right-of-way for Mr. Leazenby and was, I thought, ideally suited for my goats. I was desperate for a place to put my growing herd. After we bought the run-down place, the goats were the first to move in. I quickly learned that while sheep-fence will confine goats, it can also trap a goat by her horns, requiring extra vigilance. Because of this time requirement, the family moved in, occupying the ancient and still drafty ranch house. The school bus ride into Laramie was only fifteen minutes. Suddenly, after-school activities such as soccer and 4H were possible. It was tricky to juggle leisure time because I needed my human kids to help me work the goats, sometimes under slave-labor conditions. My visions of escaping to our remote mountain cabin provided some incentive, but the reality was there was just too much work scheduled on the weekends.

My herd numbered about 150; all descended from twenty-one Australian cashmere goats I had imported in 1989. I resolved to save my little four-footed investments from a torturous death entangled in Mr. Leazenby's sheep fence. With those fences though, my $30,000 was definitely at risk. We had crunched the numbers repeatedly and felt that an alternative approach to ranching might just turn a profit. Running both goats and cattle on the range can increase your bottom line because the two species like to eat different plants, augmenting the traditional carrying capacity calculation. The fact that goats were automatic weed-control agents was a blue-sky advantage. But our
~~~~~~~~~~~~~~~~~~

business plan's spreadsheets assumed a three-percent mortality rate, and I could not afford to exceed that parameter.

At the time, I had no idea that there was a population of red fox denning nearby, courtesy of the British gentry that had once offered fox hunting as a pass time. The cute and fuzzy mammals' great-great-great-great-grandparents arrived from the old country so the doctor's guests could pursue them. The head horse trainer, Axel Palmer, draped any nearby wire fences with sheep fleeces or cowhides. The hides made the wires more visible and predictable so that the thundering steeds could leap them confidently in their pursuit of the fleeing fox. That must have been an entertaining sport, but I lost a fair percentage of that first kid crop to descendants of those foxes. In self-defense, I started breeding Great Pyrenees guard dogs.

~~~~~~~~~~~~~~~

During the reign of Queen Victoria, the aristocracy of England, Scotland, and Wales enjoyed a thriving economy throughout their empire. Confined to a small island and with the most modern forms of transportation at their fingertips, many Brits struck out to explore the world; Wyoming was a top-rated destination. Arthur Whitehouse and his best friend, George V.H. Gordon, were two such adventurers. Whitehouse and Gordon were third-year students at Oriel College, Oxford University, anxious to experience the American West. Both were twenty-two years of age and second sons of landed aristocrats. George's father was the Fourth Earl of Aberdeen, former Prime Minister of the United Kingdom, the British ambassador to Canada, and the owner of a large ranch in Texas. In Victorian England, this meant that neither Whitehouse nor Gordon would inherit an estate, assuming the survival of their older brothers. Freed from the familial and social responsibilities of governing their family estates, both had generous trusts that assured their absence from the family home.

Howard Wyndham of Laramie, Wyoming, had been visiting his family back in England in the summer of 1887 when he befriended both Whitehouse and Gordon. He invited them to his ranch forty miles southwest of Laramie. Wyndham needed help to bring in the hay, and the Brits were experienced horsemen. Elated, the pair planned to survey the area for suitable land to purchase for their families. After the hay was stacked, Gordon spotted a couple of antelope running past Wyndham's ranch house. He proposed an antelope hunt, even though the daylight was beginning to fade. Both dressed in light-colored clothing, Whitehouse and Gordon set off after the elusive antelope. They pursued them onto Bull Mountain in the fading light, splitting up to track them through a narrow draw; Whitehouse traversed the bottom of
~~~~~~~~~~~~~~~

the draw, and Gordon followed on the ridge above. Stealthily advancing for some time, Whitehouse spotted what he took to be a mountain lion crouched upon a ledge some 120 yards ahead of his position. He stared at the still form for some minutes before carefully aiming and firing. Whitehouse fired three more shots at the lion to be sure of the kill; lions were notoriously dangerous if merely wounded. Elated, he fired two more rounds to signal his friend Gordon but got no response. Imagine his agony when he approached the high ledge and found his best friend shot cleanly through the temple; Whitehouse's other three shots had missed.

It took some time to remove the body in the dark, and it did not arrive in Laramie until evening the next day. Whitehouse had arrived earlier and spent the rest of his day at the sheriff's office, detailing his account of the tragedy. He was not charged, and the body was prepared for transport back to England. But that did not happen, and George Vincent Hamilton Gordon was buried in the Greenhill Cemetery of Laramie, Wyoming.

Distraught and unable to leave his friend behind, Whitehouse withdrew from Oriel College and remained in Laramie. Later that year, he fulfilled part of their shared but shattered dream. Arthur partnered with Arthur Stokes, and the property was locally referred to as the Stokes & Whitehouse ranch. The partners were notorious for their skills at racing horses. Stokes, in particular, jockeyed many horses in the famous races over in Cheyenne and as far south as Denver, Colorado. He once bet a man from Nebraska $500 over a match race. I still wonder if he won or not. Wearing white and salmon silks, Stokes piloted many horses to victory, including Endebar and Jack the Jumper. He was aboard Fireball during a match race in Laramie with a $1,500 side bet on the outcome. As Stokes rounded the homestretch curve, Fireball took the bit in his mouth and hurdled the perimeter fence, racing six miles towards home before he pulled up. Fireball returned to the track, but the bet was lost.

Arthur Stokes and Arthur Whitehouse dissolved their partnership in 1889, listing $10 as the amount of money exchanged in the bargain. Stokes moved to Canada and fifteen years later, joined the army, fighting on behalf of the British Commonwealth. He was killed on March 18, 1917, while serving in Greece as an artillery caisson driver.

Meanwhile, back in Wyoming, the grand log ranch buildings became very popular with the flocks of friends and family visiting from Britain. Arthur Whitehouse and his visitors were typical British gentlemen, avid hunters, polo players, and steeplechasers. They scheduled elaborate events with their wealthy neighbors once or twice a month. They played polo in the new Oxford Ranch racetrack's infield or streaked across hill and dale to another estate where the party would continue. Three race meetings every year were held at the Oxford Ranch racetrack and were very popular and well-attended. According to write-ups in the Laramie *Republican*:

> *There were at least two hundred conveyances from town alone, [with people] hanging from hacks down to Studebaker wagons, while a number of people took advantage of the special train which left Laramie at noon.*

There were grandstands and special tents for the ladies. The grand buffet was elegant and well-served. All were abuzz in anticipation of the upcoming eight events. Whitehouse came close to being seriously injured when his favorite mount, Musk Plant, struck the hurdle post and fell. According to the Laramie *Boomerang*, Cocotte, the fourth race favorite, was "the finest bred horse in this western country." Unfortunately, Cocotte was a scratch that day.

The Oxford Ranch stabled many high-powered stallions: Busy Bee, a registered American thoroughbred; Galliard, another thoroughbred who commanded a stud fee of $1,000; and the famous $1,500 imported stallion, Fireball, to name three. Other registered breeders in the barn were Viscount, Blue, Jack the Jumper, Creole, and Wyoming. The Percheron breeders were Nellie Bly (the mare) and Endebar (a stallion). Brilliant (a stallion trotter), Mirthful (who cost $7,000 and died at altitude because he had but one lung), and Dutch Skipper rounded out the field.

AXEL PALMER WITH HIS FAMOUS THOROUGHBRED STUD HORSE "BUSY BEE" (PHOTO COURTESY OF AMY LAWRENCE).

The Oxford Horse Ranch headquarters originally included a carriage barn capable of sheltering a dozen or more wagons and carriages. It housed the elaborately decorated and suspended coaches and an automobile or two in the end. Whitehouse loved horses and allowed his herd, which eventually numbered 3,000, to graze the 16,000 acres they controlled. "Control" had a different connotation back then. Control was not about legal papers. It was about physical presence. Those who arrived in the country first bought the best land and used the marginal sections surrounding them for free. No one questioned that at first; there was plenty of land available. But the ranch was dangerously overgrazed at this rate. One horse is eighty percent of an AUM, meaning it takes twenty-eight acres to support a single horse. Sixteen thousand acres should support 570 horses, using modern carrying capacity metrics to calculate carrying capacity. They had to have used nearby land without permission.

Oxford Horse Ranch soon became legendary as purveyors of fine horseflesh. Racehorses were the crowning glory, but the sale bills included carriage horses, cavalry mounts, polo ponies, and draft horses. The barns and houses on the ranch had modern conveniences: running water, sewer, and electricity. Whitehouse initially rode high on the crest of early tourism to the Laramie Valley. Scores of distinguished British gentry, all well-connected friends and family, were eager to leave the dreary English winter behind and book passage to New York on a luxury liner. From there, after enjoying the sights and sounds of the most modern city in the world, they could board luxury Pullman sleeper cars on the transcontinental rails and head west to Wyoming.

AXEL PALMER COMPETING IN SADDLE BRONC RIDING AT THE FALL ROUNDUP/RODEO AT THE ALBANY COUNTY FAIRGROUNDS. (PHOTO COURTESY OF AMY LAWRENCE).

~ ~ ~ ~ ~ ~ ~ ~ ~ ~ ~ ~ ~ ~ ~ ~

## *Chapter Four*
# THE CRIMSON ARCH

I sight down the north-side fence line of my new land. It runs straight up towards the geologic break called the Laramie Range for two-and-a-half miles. These mountains are the easternmost feature of the massive Rocky Mountain complex to the west and tower nearly a mile and a half high into the clear blue sky. Section fences are a fixture in the West. They always run in the cardinal directions, describing specific parcels of land that can be otherwise indistinguishable. Amazingly, the section lines published back in 1869 and 1871 by the Hayden Geologic Expedition come very close to modern standards.

My fence runs straight as an arrow over slick rock and crevasse alike until it takes a dramatic dogleg to the north about halfway to the summit. Along the way, and especially in mountainous territory, the surveyors made corrections to account for the curvature of the Earth. Usually, it was a Section 6 that was adjusted because they occupy the northwest corner of every township's boustrophedonal pattern. A township is a surveyor's geographic unit of measure and is six-miles square. Each square-mile section is numbered one through thirty-six. Section 1 lies in the northeastern-most corner. If one proceeds right-to-left for six sections, the northwestern-most corner holds Section 6. Moving down one row, and proceeding left-to-right for six miles, the numbers are consecutive. Section 36 is always in the southeastern corner. The word boustrophedon refers to the opposing direction of some ancient text script on alternating lines.

Today's chore is to check the seven miles of fence on the east side. Fence pliers at the ready, I turn my attention to the task. Fixing fence is a cowboy's dominant and least-liked pastime. It is the one ranching chore that has changed little over the years. The truth is, the skills displayed at the local rodeo are no longer necessary in the modern era, but fixing the fence is. Ancient fences have extra staples stuck in the crown of the occasional post, available to make repairs. It is common for elk to drag the top wire as they bound across the landscape. Every once in a while, loops of rusting wire hang on fence posts. They are not forgotten. They are stashed in case a cowboy has to patch a broken fence without the aid of a bulky fence stretcher. Ever on the outlook for time- and energy-saving methods, the everyday cowboy needs only to pack a pair of fencing pliers while riding miles of fence. This chore is as easily done when riding a utility vehicle as a horse. Ironically, if a cowboy is driving a ATV, he may as well pack the fence stretcher.

~~~~~~~~~~~~~~~

My fence has evolved over the years into a full seven-stranded barrier. It can prevent the passage of sheep, cattle, and horses. It is clear that these pastures held sheep at one time; many rock cairns were built by Basque sheepherders either out of boredom or industry. Such a fence impedes the native pronghorn antelope population in their annual migration. Elk and mule deer naturally jump fences, but antelope will always try to go under or through a fence, even though they can jump perfectly well. Mother Nature did not quite get that one right; the open prairies had few vertical obstacles. Deer and elk, typically forest animals, jump downed trees in their natural habitat. Because I am tired of seeing antelope racing along even four-strand fence seeking escape, I have never been a big fan of fences.

Educated as a wildlife biologist, I learned mitigation techniques designed to minimize the impact of fencing and other man-made influences upon wildlife populations. As a curious observer, I have noticed that male pronghorn have learned to use fences to corral their chosen harem during mating season. A secure flank makes it harder for rival bucks to sneak up and steal his females. As a wildlife professional, I spent countless hours peering at stereo pairs of aerial photographs, carefully drawing lines around different types of wildlife habitats. At the time, the technology was very early Google Earth, and I loved the bird's-eye views of Wyoming's vast landscapes. I grew to appreciate fences; they helped me to orient my lines drawn on the transparent overlay to the topographic map. From above, parcels belonging to "good" ranchers are often obvious. The grass can indeed be greener on the other side of the fence, depending upon the management practices of the landowner.

Standing there on my new land, fencing pliers in hand, I am determined to be a responsible "steward of the land," as ranchers are fond of calling themselves. So, I set out to fix fence. This fence has been damaged by floods, falling trees, trespassers, and passing elk herds. It has been patched back together so many times the patches have patches. Judging from the twist and gauge of the wire and the configuration of the barbs, I could tell that some of my wire was very old, probably dating to 1871 when the Fort Sanders
~~~~~~~~~~~~~~~

boundary was expanded, an effort overseen by commanding officer **L.P. Bradley**.

The thin air was crisp in the bright sunshine in the early summer. The land generally faces west, exposing the steep cobbled drainages and brushy slopes to the summer sun. Mule deer had crossed the dusty road the evening before, leaving their tracks and scat for me to ponder. The two-track followed a small gully past a short windmill, its blades turning lazily in the light breeze. The water in the stock tank was clear and cold; I sipped a double handful as it poured from the outlet pipe. It was delicious, unlike the water at the Oxford Ranch headquarters down below, which is dark with iron and sharp with the slight odor of sulfur.

As I climbed into the rarified air at 8,200 feet of elevation, the surrounding vegetation became compact, conservative, as if saving its energy for the coming winter. Various grasses interspersed with clusters of yellow daisies blanketed the level ground. A mixture of mountain mahogany and serviceberry shrubs, head-high and greenie-grey in color, were dense on the steep slopes. The vegetation is prime winter habitat for big game and excellent summer-grazing land for livestock. The dense slope makes a great place to hide a newborn calf. Most of the large predators that naturally cull the wild ungulate herds (elk and deer) no longer inhabit this area. No wolves or grizzly bears patrol the steep escarpments. Occasionally, young mountain lions will explore the river drainages, but humans will force them to withdraw to their remote mountain refuges in the nearby forest.

The greatest risk is coyotes. An exceptionally large family can threaten young calves, bovine and cervine alike. However, Mother Nature has provided a fix for this dilemma. Newborn elk, mule deer, and antelope are essentially scentless, allowing them to be safely left alone, sequestered in the tall grass or shrubs by their mothers. If threatened, the mother will draw attention to herself and move away from her newborn, who will instinctively drop and remain motionless. Until the young can keep up with the herd, usually just overnight, they hide from danger. When they are up and running, safety is in numbers for the wild herds grazing my uplands.

My cattle, though, were not really safe. I leave them to fend for themselves, providing only minerals, salt, and, of course, water. I am forever on the lookout for feral dogs and wandering coyotes. The fact that I could ask the US Wildlife Control Program to kill any coyote I deemed threatening was of some comfort. Another government program pays bounties for predator ears or pelts, even past the time when the large predators have disappeared into the forests, helping them to vanish altogether. In yet another anti-predator program, if a large predator kills livestock, the government steps in and compensates the rancher for his loss and removes the offending predator, dead or alive. Although I lost scores of goat kids to Dr. Whitehouse's foxes over the years, it never occurred to me to bill the government.

But I was anxious to complete my fencing work, so I pressed on, following the still-life parade of ancient pitch posts that march up the mountainside. When a cedar tree dies in this part of Wyoming, it never rots. It just stands there, slowly turning as hard as a stone. These pitch posts are persistent, impervious to the raging winds and the driving snows punctuating a Laramie Basin winter. They will even withstand fire. My fence stands in silent testimony to those who built it long ago.

~ ~ ~ ~ ~ ~ ~ ~ ~ ~ ~ ~ ~ ~

I stop halfway up the fence line to appreciate the view to the west. The Laramie River watershed spreads out before me like a cat's eye, sixty miles long and thirty miles wide. All the moisture that falls on the landscape surrounding me winds up in the Laramie River, flowing past the foot of Laramie Peak, the northernmost apex of the watershed. At 10,276 feet, the peak stands sentinel over miles of empty, high plains beyond that stretch far away to the east. The remnant ghosts of the Emigrant Trail pass silently on the other side, out of sight but not out of mind.

The floor of the Laramie River watershed forms a relatively flat grassland called the Laramie Plains. A full 7,200 feet in elevation, it snuggles between the feet of mighty mountains. The Laramie River meanders lazily north, joining with the Little Laramie near Philip Mandel's ranch, the first one established on the Laramie Plains. In the shadow of Laramie Peak, this previously unassuming river still takes a hard turn to the east, flowing in the west side of the Laramie Range, through a steep, rugged canyon and thundering right out the other side. This unique phenomenon occurs nine times in Wyoming: the Laramie, the Bighorn (twice), the North Platte (twice), the Snake, the Wind, the Shoshone, and the Belle Fouche rivers bisect intervening mountains. As glaciers melted and hurricane-force winds blew, their silt-laden waters ground down the buried mountains like a bandsaw.

From my perch high on the eastern rim of the watershed, the broad Laramie Basin looks like an ancient stage, complete with stunning backdrops. Indeed, it has hosted a variety of pageants including ferocious geologic uplifts, centuries-long windstorms, ancient glaciers grinding to a halt, mastodon migrations, aboriginal people celebrating life, mountain men harvesting beaver, military expeditions in precise formations, dusty freighters, railroads, ranchers, water developers, and finally, real estate agents.

Looking west, the white peaks of two wilderness areas and a national forest decorate the western boundary of the watershed. On the southern rim, northern Colorado's mighty Never Summer Range divides into a pair of lesser mountain ranges. Lofty Cameron Pass guards the headwaters of the Big Laramie River and anchors the southern apex of the watershed. The rugged mountains cradle the river's V-shaped womb. Only in the spring does this river spread her raging floodwaters across the flat Laramie Basin, delivering their lifeblood to the plains.

By 1994, it was clear we needed even more pasture. My husband was fixing to retire from his desk job. He had been building up his cow herd, investing in younger, more closely bred mother cows. There was land for sale that adjoined the sections we already owned; areas perfect for summer grazing were just on the other side of the railroad tracks. Some ranches hold the right to lease federal or state grazing lands where they pasture their herds in the summer. It is a little-known federal welfare program; I call it food stamps for cattle. Typically, those leases change hands only when the ranch sells; the price per acre is equivalent to the adjoining lands. Those who hold them are either very wealthy people or folks who settled in the area first and managed to hang on. Technically, grazing leases have no resale value.

We were neither wealthy nor original settlers, and leasing private grazing land is expensive, about ten times more than US government leaseholders pay. So we started looking seriously for more property to buy. The Cheyenne developer offering land for sale to our east still needed to own that land. After a year on the market, he grudgingly accepted our cash offer because he needed that money for his down payment on the larger purchase of the old XX Ranch.

Once again, realtors were playing fast and loose with land titles. They divided the land up, manipulated the water and grazing rights, and resold it before the ink on the register book at the county clerk's office was dry. I was not surprised to learn from the title chain that this new land had once been part of the Old Oxford Horse Ranch. Given how difficult it is to drive our herd across the double set of mainline UPRR tracks to reach the rich grazing lands on the other side, I now appreciate why the railroad impediment may have spelled the demise of the historic ranch. It is complicated to cross the herd.

So it came to be that we owned another 1,600 acres directly east of the first purchase. As we explored its narrowing gulches and enjoyed the broad vistas, we came across a small red sandstone arch delicately balanced on three legs. It brimmed with abandoned mud swallow nests, stuck firmly beneath the arch's smooth mushroom cap. The fact that the little arch remained where it formed is a testament to the hardness of the stone. I had to wonder why it did not erode as its neighbors had. And then, upon the flanks of this outcrop, we discovered numerous inscriptions, peoples' names but mostly sets of initials, some with dates, all scratched deep into the hard sandstone. The earliest date I found was 1812, really early for a white man in Wyoming. The first known white incursion into Wyoming was in 1807 by Lewis & Clark Expedition member John Colter. No one believed his tales regarding the geologically active area.

I slowly realized that literate people stood in the same sparse shade of the tiny arch almost two centuries ago. Not only did they locate the arch, but they were also there for an extended period, carving the hard, red sandstone. I could not help but wonder who they were and where they were going. The little Crimson Arch, hidden away as it is, had somehow attracted a score of travelers over the years. The first faint signature, **BER 1812**, or the more prominent **TY 1817**, must have inspired subsequent travelers to scratch their names or initials deep into the hard sandstone. Their stories and those of people close to them turned out to be a closely connected web of circumstances that aptly traces how Wyoming evolved into our 44th State.

## *Chapter Five*
# BER 1812 - ED ROBINSON
### *& the Birth of the Robber Barons*

(PHOTO BY K. MCGUIRE)

Some signatures on my rock were easy to identify. For example, Colonel **Bradley's** name was quickly associated with Fort Sanders, the ruined fort located five miles north of the Oxford Ranch. **Trabing** was the well-known name of early Laramie businessmen brothers. We bought a grand Trabing home in Laramie as an office for our environmental consulting business in 1985. The rest of the names remained a mystery as I hefted hundreds of books in Laramie, Cheyenne, Greeley, and Denver libraries. I leafed through each index looking for names that matched the initials left on my rock, and then I read thousands of pages of often conflicting accounts of historical events. The quintessential Wyoming historian, Charles G. Coutant, published his *History of Wyoming* in 1899 when many protagonists were still alive. But even his version is contradicted elsewhere.

My life at the time (1992 through 2000) consisted of keeping the livestock fed through a couple of particularly vicious winters. I watched as the driveway between the house and the barn slowly filled with a snowdrift twice my height. When I got stuck trying to plunge my Suburban around its edge, the vehicle stayed there for two weeks. I passed it nightly as I inspected our heifers every two hours as calving season peaked. Comet Hale-Bopp and I got to know each other quite well as I checked for impending deliveries in sub-zero temperatures. I knew it was just a matter of time before I froze.

Wyoming ranchers typically calve in February, meaning their market steers will be ready for shipment in the fall, the traditional calf-selling season. This paradigm incorporates the theory that February will bring the Chinooks, winds that are warmed by the friction of blowing at near hurricane force down the mountainsides. While our Chinooks are still famous, the February respite theory is slowly circling the drain.

The calves that hit the ground during those freezing nights could miraculously bounce up and nurse for the first time. Just hours old, they led me on a wild scramble the following day as I tackled them to ear tag, vaccinate, and castrate the bull calves using a strategically placed heavy-duty rubber band. In the evening, I curled up by the fire, reading the history volumes. Even bundled up, it still sent shivers through me to learn about mountain men wading into icy ponds to check their traps in the middle of winter. Ever sensitive to revealing their position to hostiles, they might then have to spend a snowy night in wet clothing, cautious about making a fire. These men, and they were all men, were incredibly hardy and brave. I cannot imagine myself doing what they had done. But how did these guys get so far away from home, and why would they do that? Literature and film have immortalized the era of the mountain man. My son's favorite movie is *Jeremiah Johnson*. My husband often states he was born 200 years too late. The magic and mystery do not add up when little research describes the actual day-to-day conditions under which these men labored.

It is incredible that a fashion craze sparked an entire historical era. Indeed, if a Parisian milliner had not shaved the hair off a thick pelt and fashioned it into a tall, stovepipe hat, there might still be beaver in the mountains, working hard to preserve the watershed. Still, the fad continued, and the beaver paid with their lives, first in the eastern mountains. The fur companies had no choice but to expand into the Louisiana Purchase Territory when it became available.

Once purchased, the trans-Missouri lands needed definition, so President Thomas Jefferson sent Lewis & Clark out to do just that. The area was little known; indeed, Clark thought he might observe mastodon. Their crucial economic discovery turned out to be the beaver population. The year following the triumphant (and miraculous) return of the Corps of Discovery, fur companies organized and began sending men into the wilderness to collect the pelts, first from willing natives. When that source dried up, they fielded private trapping expeditions, and the Age of the Mountain Man was born. **BER** must have been one of those mountain men, and I was determined to find him.

~~~~~~~~~~~~~~~

Because of my English mother's penchant for reading, I was well aware of the West's history. As a child traveling by car from one Air Force posting to another, the family habitually stopped at all historic site markers. We called them "hysterical markers," and they afforded a much-needed opportunity to climb out of a packed car and stretch cramped legs. My mother's obsession with the Lewis & Clark Expedition caused us to visit the Tennessee cabin where Meriwether Lewis had committed suicide.

On subsequent trips, we stopped at all the historical markers along the Missouri River in Missouri, the Dakotas, and Montana relating to the Corps of Discovery's incredible odyssey in 1804. Other hardy explorers followed their blazed trail, some populating these lonely roadside markers. We stopped at every single one of them.

A large roadside display in Nebraska concerned Manuel Lisa, the Father of the Mountain Man Era. Lisa was from New Orleans, born to a wealthy Spanish merchant family. Interested in harvesting beaver, he first ventured into the West in 1807, encountering John Colter at the Mandan encampment (near present-day Bismarck, North Dakota). Colter was fresh from the Pacific Northwest as a Lewis & Clark expedition member. Sitting around the campfire at night, Lisa pumped Colter for information on beaver populations. He ignored Colter's report of scalding hot water shot into the air at odd intervals. Likewise, the pools of bubbling mud and sulfurous gasses seemed unbelievable.

~~~~~~~~~~~~~~~

By 1809, Lisa organized the Missouri Fur Company, partnering with the new Territorial Governor William Clark and Major Andrew Henry, who had orders to find another route to Oregon. It was a partnership made in heaven; Lisa needed a license to trade in the West, and Clark was just the man to procure it for him. Major Henry was the muscle of the expedition. His government appropriation financed the armed guard that would protect them while he mapped the largely unknown Louisiana Purchase lands. The trappers were along to make money for the company while under government protection. Lisa was the logistics guy, the entrepreneur, the businessman. And Lisa was ruthless; to him, it was tooth and nail to reach the beaver hunting grounds first.

As my family drove north along the Missouri River, we found yet another roadside marker. This one memorialized the site of Fort Union, established by Major Henry and Manuel Lisa on that first expedition in 1809. Beyond there, the Three Rivers area of southern Montana crawled with beaver, buffalo, and bears. The human residents did not much appreciate the incursion either. The new fort was the intended rendezvous point for teams of company trappers who ventured into the wilderness, returning with baled pelts ready for transport back to St. Louis. They traveled in heavily armed groups across the High Plains. It was too dangerous to attempt to traverse the wilderness alone.

Later, as I read through volumes of history books, I picked up some names I recognized from the roadside markers of my childhood. Three friends from Kentucky were included in the Missouri Fur Company roles: John Hoback, Jacob Rezner, and Edward Robinson. I automatically visualized J.H., J.R., and E.R. Could E.R. be **BER**? Would Robinson's travels place him within striking distance of the Crimson Arch? I hungered to know more.

~ ~ ~ ~ ~ ~ ~ ~ ~ ~ ~ ~ ~ ~

The best thing about early history is that expedition leaders habitually kept detailed diaries. If the journals (or their authors) survived, local newspapers often published them. Soft-bound pamphlets might be archived in a library basement somewhere. It took some digging, but eventually, I discovered that these three Kentuckians set out together from Fort Union to trap the Gallatin, Jefferson, and Madison Rivers in Montana.

Major Henry's journal aptly describes his journey up the Yellowstone, following Lewis & Clark's route. The Kentuckians, however, were hounded mercilessly by the Blackfoot; revenge for the two braves killed by Meriwether Lewis two years before was on their minds. They harassed the trappers relentlessly, attacking them repeatedly. Finally, the tribe drove them right across southern Montana, over the mountains, and into eastern Idaho, which was Shoshone country.

Somehow, Hoback, Rezner, and **Robinson** managed to rendezvous with Henry and his troops. How they found each other in that vast landscape is unimaginable. Together, they built Henry's Fort somewhere in southeast Idaho to protect them from a long, cold, and hungry winter. They left the fort the following spring and, traveling by night to avoid attracting the Blackfoot's attention, descended the Missouri towards "civilization." The fort itself has turned to dust and is not eligible for a roadside marker.

Near Fort Union (in present-day North Dakota) on the Niobrara River, the Kentuckians encountered Wilson Price Hunt and his Astorians on their way up the Missouri. Their destination was the Pacific Northwest. Hunt had already consulted with John Colter, who was back in St. Louis, dying from syphilis. John Jacob Astor sent two expeditions westward that year: one by land and the other by sea. The goal was to exploit the rich peltries of the Pacific Northwest. After talking to the Kentuckians, Hunt resolved to avoid the Blackfoot entirely by taking a more southerly route across Wyoming. Hoback, Rezner, and Robinson's area knowledge could prove invaluable, so he engaged them as guides, but only as far as Henry's Fort. Guide Edward Rose would take it from there. Manuel Lisa and Major Henry returned to St. Louis with their harvested pelts. The Kentuckians' share would be credited to their Missouri Fur Company account. In the West, a company store account was golden. Credits could be used to reimburse anyone who presented a signed draft at the company headquarters in St. Louis. Actual money was rarely exchanged. Resupplied by Hunt, they headed back to Wyoming.

~~~~~~~~~~~~~~

When they left the Mandan villages in the Dakotas that spring, they struck out overland, generally following the Little Missouri River. The river was a water source but too shallow to navigate, so they left the longboats behind. They entered Wyoming from the northeast, missing the giant monolith of Devil's Tower. They crossed the Powder River near present-day Buffalo, Wyoming. From there, Edward Rose, ignoring the Kentuckians' warnings of the steep mountain terrain ahead, decided to lead them across the rugged Big Horns. **Robinson** might have counseled a more southerly route around the range had he not been a trapper at heart. There were more beaver in the mountains than in the foothills, so up they went.

By the time they reached the Wind River Mountains in west-central Wyoming, they had been traveling for five months, and the going was getting tough again. Co-investor Joseph Miller and party-leader Hunt had a falling out in their fatigue. There is another placard along Wyoming Highway 26 leading south out of Jackson, Wyoming. It marks the spot where they last camped together, a place now called Hoback Junction, after trapper John Hoback. The party agreed to split up there because they were nearing Henry's Fort. Miller, a man named Martin Cass, and the three Kentuckians, freshly released from their guiding duty, elected to stay in western Wyoming. They anticipated spending another winter harvesting the abundant supply of beaver. Hunt and Rose continued to Oregon with the main body of the expedition.

Over the next six months, the group of five mountain men roamed far and wide, trapping beaver. By many reports, the Kentuckians discovered the Great Salt Lake that winter, eleven years before Jim Bridger or Major Bonneville ever saw it. They plied the entire Colorado-Wyoming border, traveling west to east, exploring the Uinta Range in Utah.

Remember that every pelt they harvested had to be cleaned, rubbed with diluted beaver brains, and dried, stretched tightly on a circular frame fashioned from a willow branch to dry flat. A fresh buffalo hide packaged the
~~~~~~~~~~~~~~

accumulated, pressed beaver pelts. As the robe dried, it shrank, sealing the furs within a reasonably waterproof bale that would float. The men had to transport the bales from location to location as they traveled, caching them here and there. Finally, rafts of bales were floated down the river to St. Louis.

Hunt continued to Oregon and connected with their seagoing compatriots. Together, they harvested the rich bounty of sea otter bound for the lucrative Japanese market. Unfortunately, the Astorian's flagship *Tonquin*, their only seagoing vessel, was overrun by the Pacific Northwestern natives and burned with significant loss of life. In dire straits, the Astorians regrouped and decided to send a tiny contingent of men back overland to St. Louis to summon help. Since they could spare precious few supplies, the return party was sparsely provisioned and led by Robert Stuart. In keeping with explorers of the day, Stuart kept a neat and complete diary that described his daily activities.

His journal reports that he successfully retraced Hunt's steps across Oregon and southern Idaho to Hunt's Fort. From there, he struck a more southerly route, traversing central Wyoming very near, if not through, South Pass, the low pass key to travel to California. Stuart noted in his journal that he scratched his name on what would be named Independence Rock along the Sweetwater River, just southwest of Casper, Wyoming. His signature does not survive, but many others do because the rock lies along the later route of the Emigrant Trail. Engraving rock outcroppings was a popular pastime.

~ ~ ~ ~ ~ ~ ~ ~ ~ ~ ~ ~ ~ ~ ~

Meanwhile, Miller, Cass, and the Kentuckians had spent the winter of 1811 trapping along the Colorado-Wyoming border. According to David Lavendar, an early Wyoming historian, the group holed up near the Medicine Bow mountains to pass the inclement months of March, April, and May 1812. In Wyoming, spring is a season known for furious floods and blizzards, bringing everything to a standstill. There is single superior camping spot in the Laramie Basin along the Big Laramie River, eight miles southwest of present-day Laramie. There they built a rough cabin. It was the prime spot along the Laramie, high enough not to flood and within sight of my Crimson Arch.

Spring is too late in the season to trap beaver commercially. Their pelts are past prime because all animals begin to shed their winter coat's dense underdown in February. So the trio only had to hunt to feed themselves. That would have taken them to the nearby summit of what was then called the Black Hills, right past the Crimson Arch. A signature, **BER 1812**, the earliest inscription, was scratched in the hard rock almost certainly by Kentuckian B. Edward Robinson. To think that this man, unimportant in the grand scheme of things but instrumental in opening up Wyoming, had stood right there, knife in hand, scratching out his initials? That thought stirs my heart.

They may have intended to pass the summer in their cozy cabin and strike out once again the following fall in search of more prime beaver pelts; I am just guessing. I do know that historian Lavendar reports that they were robbed of their possessions by a band of Arapahoe sometime that summer. So in the fall of 1812, the group set out on foot, following the Laramie River. When the river suddenly disappeared into its unnavigable canyon, they struck out overland, again to the north. Their only hope was to encounter another expedition.

Still eastbound on what was to become the Emigrant Trail route, Astorian Stuart encountered the starving group of trappers. After much back-clapping and celebratory whooping, Stuart inquired about the fate of the fifth group member, Martin Cass. A lengthy silence prevailed. When further questioned, the Kentuckians bowed their heads and mumbled that he had taken a horse and left them the previous fall; Miller remained silent. Stuart immediately doubted this version of events and made notes to that effect in his journal. In 1895, American author Washington Irving sensationalized Stuart's diary by publishing his first novel, *Astoria*. He postulated that Cass was unlikely to venture out on his own, especially riding an edible horse. The book portrayed the group as drawing lots and eating the unfortunate Cass to survive.

Righteously mortified that the story would get out, the Kentuckians declined to return to civilization with Miller and Stuart. Robinson, Rezner, and Hoback accepted an outfit offer from Stuart and set off again for the mountains. They had not seen civilization for almost five years and wanted none of it. Miller accompanied Stuart as he continued towards St. Louis, but they did not get far.

Trapped by September's early snows, the Astorians built a cabin on Bessemer Bend on the North Platte, near present-day Casper, Wyoming, to pass the winter. They did not realize they were within striking distance of Fort Atkinson, Kansas. It was early, and the weather was likely to clear into a famous Indian summer. Unfortunately, they did not know that, so they prepared for winter. They had just moved into their cabin when a band of friendly Arapahoe found them. Stuart, following Western tradition, smoked a peace pipe with them and they feasted together for three days, parting peacefully with their new friends.

Miller was sure it was the same band that had robbed him and the Kentuckians before as they camped along the Laramie River. Afraid the Arapahoe would return and massacre them, the party repaired to far eastern

Wyoming near the future site of Fort Laramie to pass the balance of the winter. There, they constructed a sturdy structure out of stone and called it the Gratiot House, named after the Astorian's Chief Financial Officer, Charles Gratiot.

Until 1822, large fur companies obtained beaver pelts by trading for them with the well-acclimated natives. After securing a government license to trade in the West, fur companies would typically buy trinkets, beads, woven cloth, food, and arms to exchange with the native peoples for beaver pelts. One dollar's worth of trinkets would purchase a pelt worth ten dollars in St. Louis. Even though indigenous cultures revered beaver as spirit animals, they could be tempted to exploit them. Beads, especially blue beads, were highly prized trade goods.

Nevertheless, trading with the whites was problematic for the natives. Disease swept through the Native American camps, "firewater" was dangerous and addicting, and many fell victim to unscrupulous white men. When the Indians finally refused to trade with the fur companies, the continuing demand for pelts dictated that the whites field private trapping expeditions, and the Era of the Mountain Man blossomed.

~ ~ ~ ~ ~ ~ ~ ~ ~ ~ ~ ~ ~ ~

Whatever happened to Robinson and his friends has been lost to history. I feel honored that he took the time to inscribe his name upon my rock, and I hope his spirit has found peace. He and his compatriots suffered gravely in the pursuit of their lifestyle. This dogged determination to make a living under such dire circumstances is a real eye-opener. I wonder how many men today could complete such a task given the physical toll that the weather and other intrinsic dangers took upon them? Still, they have left their mark, evidence of their passing, upon my rock, and I am forever thankful for knowing their story.

## *Chapter Six*
# TY 1817 - THOMAS YOUNG
### *& Jacques LaRamie*

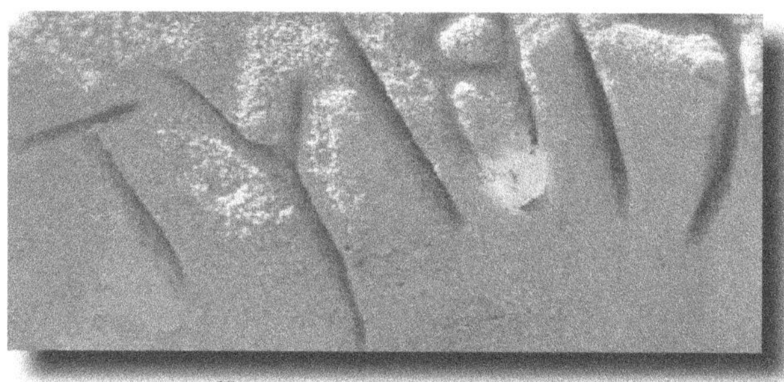

(PHOTO BY K. McGUIRE)

Hands down, the most eye-catching inscription is that of TY 1817. It dominates the eastern face of the hard rock mushroom cap of the red sandstone arch. It should have been easy to locate a TY in the historical record; few literate men traversed the Laramie Plains so long ago. My first tactic was to scan the indices of every large volume I checked out of the library under "Y." No luck. I found only Ewing Young, a noted trapper and cattleman who came into the country in 1820 and died in 1834. There was not anyone else.

Thinking about it, I realized that French surnames beginning with "Y" are non-existent, and Spanish ones are very few and far between. So, TY had to be an American, but my searches were unproductive. It was my mother who located a tiny notice published in the St. Louis newspaper listing members of Ashley & Henry's 1817 US Government expedition. One man was named Lieutenant **Thomas Young**. Without any alternative, I decided that Lieutenant Young was the most likely candidate. I imagine that Young was an educated man, fluent in French, perhaps a trained surveyor, drawing the maps that Ashley needed to bring back to Washington.

Ordered by President James Madison to map an overland trail across Wyoming, the expedition followed the familiar route up the flooding Missouri to the Arikara camps near present-day Council Bluffs, Nebraska. Ashley and his men departed St. Louis in three longboats crewed by the hard-drinking men who hung out in the bars near the docks. The weeks-long row against the swift, snag-infested Missouri took all hands.

The War of 1812 brought its own set of changes to the economy of the largely unexplored continent. Having emptied eastern Canada's tributaries of beaver, Hudson's Bay Fur Company suddenly claimed all the territory in the reaches of the upper Missouri Basin, a clear violation of the Louisiana Purchase Treaty. Concurrently, their primary competitor, the XY Company, staged a hostile takeover of the struggling Astorians in Oregon. The guns of a British warship persuaded the American Fur Company to sell for pennies on the dollar.

Then, inexplicably, the British fur companies fell upon each other. Hudson's Bay, led by English traders licensed by the Crown, and the XY Company, a French-Canadian company, began a trade war. Religious differences (Anglican versus Catholic) fueled the conflict, but so did the drastic reductions in the beaver population. The war saw them both employ guile, deception, and outright violence to gain the advantage. XY employee Jacques LaRamie and a few other like-minded trappers quit Canada and joined the 1817 Ashley & Henry expedition as they departed the Arikara Village in Nebraska. Connected by a common language, I can imagine Young and LaRamie becoming fast friends. Was this the link to the Crimson Arch signature?

Every expedition the US Government fielded during this era picked up people wanting secure passage across unknown lands. Thusly, Jacques La Ramie went west. Major Ashley was hunting for a navigable pass across the Rocky Mountains, so they followed the Platte River across western Nebraska and into Wyoming. There, the expedition split up; Ashley continued west along the North Platte to officially map South Pass, the key to opening the West. Young and the trappers followed Chugwater Creek into the eastern ramparts of Wyoming's Black Hills, where they scattered over the available beaver habitat they found there.

When LaRamie took up residence in the isolated Laramie Basin, he was the first white person to intend to live year-round in the windswept valley. In charge of mapping the watershed of the Laramie River for Major Ashley, LaRamie and Lieutenant **Thomas Young** might have looked out over the plain, perhaps from the vantage point of the little Crimson Arch. Young deliberately carved his initials almost on top of the only other signature there, that of **Ed Robinson**. Cutting the letters deeply, the Lieutenant intended his initials to last millennia and eclipse Robinson's. He succeeded in both.

~ ~ ~ ~ ~ ~ ~ ~ ~ ~ ~ ~ ~ ~

What greeted a mountain man's eye when he crested the summit of the Black Hills and looked out over the Laramie Plains in the 1820s? Vast herds of buffalo must have darkened the plains. The mule deer and elk were unafraid of the travelers, ignoring them as they passed. Skittish antelope would have jerked their heads high as he emerged onto the plain. If startled, their white rumps would bristle as they bounded off at speeds approaching thirty-five miles per hour. Beaver, forever busy in their ponds repairing leaks, would have disappeared underwater after a thunderous slap of the lookout's great tail. Beaver populations that numbered in the millions in 1700 were almost extinct by 1830.

Beaver play an essential role in their environment. They instinctively build long, sturdy dams that are effective flood and erosion-control devices across narrow streams. Alder, willow, and ash bushes might choke a deeply eroded stream bank without beaver to control them. Access to the available water would be difficult and dangerous. The surrounding land would be dry, perched above the water table. Enter a pair of beaver, and the situation changes. Natural engineers, beaver always choose an advantageous location to begin their construction, and if the first location washes out, they persevere and build another dam.

The Crimson Arch is within a few miles of prime beaver habitat. The upper reaches of Harney Creek are just over the next ridge. Three miles to the east, Dale Creek flows south, joining the Cache la Poudre, which flows into the South Platte near present-day Greeley, Colorado. Ten miles west of the arch, the Big Laramie River arises near Cameron Pass. The Little Laramie, thirty miles west, drains the mighty Snowy Range. The drainages teemed with beaver at the time, their dams flooding the bottomlands. These natural engineers kept the groundwater table high so the surrounding land was well-watered and lush. Like all rodents, beaver productivity is very high. Trappers could count on harvesting a bale's worth of pelts in a short period. Beaver pelts were prized for their thick, glossy, winter coat. Once shaved, the thick fur was felted and fashioned exclusively into tall hats for men to wear in high society city life. Trappers like LaRamie practically wiped beaver off the face of the earth, so efficient were they in their harvest.

~~~~~~~~~~~~~~~

Not much more information exists about the life and death of Laramie's namesake, Jacques LaRamie. Most histories are content to report that he was a mountain man in Wyoming almost 200 years ago. I imagine him riding past the Crimson Arch, heading back to his cabin along the Laramie River after a successful early morning deer hunt. He must have known every inch of this
~~~~~~~~~~~~~~~

territory and witnessed the massive herds of bison roaming freely across the plain.

As a ranch owner, I learned that hay meadows need to flood seasonally to sustain production. Without beaver, the Laramie Basin meadows must have been in pretty bad shape by the 1860s. Beaver activity had ceased almost fifty years previously, and without constant maintenance, the dams failed. With nothing to stem the spring floods, the main channels of the Big and Little Laramie Rivers eroded, leaving the grass high and dry. During the spring floods of 1867, when railroad tie hacks floated tree trunks down the Laramie River, some trunks got away and created a log jam. Accidentally dammed, the river flooded as it had not done in decades. The following year these flooded areas produced twice the hay.

As much as I would like to introduce beaver to my land, I cannot. There are no remnants of historic beaver activity. To be fair, my ranch faces south and east; most of the willow-lined creeks occur on north- or west-facing slopes. The exposure on the Oxford Ranch is just too harsh to support the vegetation necessary for the beaver's existence.

~~~~~~~~~~~~~~~

By 1817, the Missouri Fur Company received $35,000 worth of pelts a year (3,500 dead beaver) from the Rocky Mountains. Those were just the ones that made it down the thrashing, turbulent rapids of the Missouri River. Manuel Lisa visited the region frequently to gather the harvested pelts from his far-flung employees, such as Jacques LaRamie. In addition to his white wife in St. Louis, Lisa had a second wife, a Pawnee, with whom he had a family. They lived on the South Platte River near present-day Denver. He would have been LaRamie's pipeline to market the pelts he collected in the Laramie Basin watershed.

When Lisa's first wife died in 1816, he remarried as soon as he returned to St. Louis the following spring, this time with a young Spanish boy in tow. The Pawnee had captured the lad on a raid on the Spanish near Santa Fe. Lisa traded some pelts for the boy's freedom, and he lived with Lisa and his new wife in St. Louis. He attended school along with Clark's Shoshone guide, Sacajawea's son, Pomp, whom Clark had adopted after the Lewis & Clark Expedition returned.

His third wife was none other than William Clark's recently widowed cousin, and they established a grand home near that of Clark. Lisa's next expedition took him back to his Pawnee family. On his return trip with the last season's harvest of pelts, Lisa escorted the Arikara and Mandan chiefs to St. Louis to sign a peace treaty with Governor Clark. Theoretically, the Treaty
~~~~~~~~~~~~~~~

of 1825 established a "safe" route to the beaver resources in Wyoming and Montana, but it only lasted seven years.

~~~~~~~~~~~~~~

Over the next few years, LaRamie became a trusted member of the local Arapahoe and Cheyenne tribes. He and his Arapahoe wife lived in harmony with their surroundings. The mountain men plying their trade at this time were a rare breed. Normally solitary, they usually maintained a very low profile. However, when in peer groups, their behavior altered drastically. When Ashley & Henry organized the first mountain man rendezvous in 1824 along the banks of the Seedskedee River in far southwestern Wyoming, the gathered Americans spent most of their communal time drinking, eating, gambling, and engaging in friendly gunplay. Six of the sixteen major rendezvous occurred along the broad river valley now called the Green River near Fort Bridger.

When Jacques LaRamie did not show up at that first rendezvous, his friends went looking for him. **John Hunton** recorded in his journal that Jim Bridger told him that he had been along on that mission. They found a half-completed cabin on the banks of the Big Laramie and a partially clothed skeleton, respectfully laid out at the cabin door. Bridger sought out the local tribes for an explanation. The Arapahoe band he encountered described how LaRamie had drowned crossing the swollen river. An Arapahoe chief stated,

> *Why would we kill him? He was our friend. He always gave us more for our furs than any of the big companies did* (**Hunton**, 1920).

Jacques LaRamie is memorialized throughout Wyoming. In addition to the city and county, apartment buildings, businesses, mountain ranges, geologic events, and epochs all carry this one man's name. LaRamie is one truly immortal man. His profession, though, indeed his entire way of life, is no longer possible. While hunting and trapping are still practiced (with concurrent licenses), the ability to trap unencumbered throughout the mountains is impractical and illegal. Today, only films and books can capture the era of the mountain man. The fate of **Thomas Young** is not recorded, as far as I can tell. His name does not again appear in the annals of history. Young, LaRamie, and their way of life are gone forever.
~~~~~~~~~~~~~~

~~~~~~~~~~~~~~~



## *Chapter Seven*
# GUNNISON 1849
### *& the Wisdom of Jim Bridger*

From my perch up near the Crimson Arch, Laramie City, the "Gem City of the Plains," is just out of sight to the north. I often sit and contemplate the many people who inscribed my rock. This tiny arch was discovered by a good number of travelers between Laramie and Cheyenne in the mid-19th century. Given that the vast majority of pre Civil War men in Wyoming were illiterate, the fact that there are any early signatures on my rock is impressive.

In 1849, Jim Bridger departed Fort Bridger guiding an expedition led by Major Howard Stansbury, United States Army Corps of Topographical Engineers. Second in command was Lieutenant John W. **Gunnison**. They were heading east along Bridger's Red Buttes Trail. Stansbury's orders were to map a suitable railroad route through the Rocky Mountains, and Jim Bridger was the only man capable of directing him. Bridger knew Wyoming like the back of his hand, and he knew local tribes, what they were thinking, and where they would be. Bridger had come into the county in 1822, aged nineteen. He survived a rough childhood in Missouri and took this first chance to escape an abusive father who prevented him from attending school. Jim was illiterate, unable (or perhaps unwilling) to make even an X.

As he led the expedition over Bridger's Pass and into the Laramie Basin, Stansbury made meticulously accurate descriptions of geologic formations. He also kept complete celestial-based observations of their location. On the evening of September 27, 1849, Stansbury camped near the Little Laramie River on what is now known as the Millbrook Ranch. He wrote in his journal:

> *Today we entered the Laramie Plains, and traveled over a beautiful rolling country, covered with grass, with here & there a small lake or pond, formed in the low grounds by the drainage from the neighboring hills.... Buffalo have been very numerous and tame.*
~~~~~~~~~~~~~~~

The next morning, they broke camp and headed southwest, descending into a sizable blown-out valley along the foothills of the Medicine Bow Range. Later that day, Stansbury described what is now known as the Big Hollow. As they approached the Big Laramie River, they noticed the presence of several hundred natives. Fearing attack, Stansbury retreated to a grove of narrow-leafed cottonwoods and fortified their position as best they could. The natives turned out to be friendly Oglala Sioux in the area only to harvest the "good medicine" wood that grows high in the mountains. In keeping with Plains Indian etiquette, Stansbury, Gunnison, Bridger, and the Sioux smoked the peace pipe and feasted all evening, but by morning, a couple of axes, a blanket, and a rifle turned up missing.

Not wanting to appear intimidating, Stansbury sent the bulk of his soldiers, including Bridger and Gunnison, up into the Black Hills, past the red rock formations. Stansbury spent the next few hours unsuccessfully negotiating for the return of the stolen goods. Near a small tributary of the Laramie River (now called Harney Creek), Gunnison and Bridger halted at mid-morning to wait for Stansbury to catch up. To pass the afternoon, Bridger and Gunnison scouted the best route up and over the Black Hills, now known as the Laramie Range. Would it be present-day Sawmill Gulch? Or Gilmore Gulch? These gulches bracket the Crimson Arch, and the buffalo trails were distinct. During this excursion, Gunnison encountered the signature rock.

Jim Bridger was right there with **John Gunnison** as they waited for Captain Stansbury to arrive. They were passing the time as Gunnison casually carved his full last name in block capital letters: ***GUNNISON 1849***. The rock on the mushroom cap is incredibly hard, much harder than regular sandstone. That is why the arch is still there; it takes a long time to scratch letters deeply enough to withstand a hundred years of Wyoming wind. Making curves is practically impossible, although some adventurous souls even undertook that lengthy task. Gunnison understood geology; he knew that where the hard cap meets the arch's spindly legs is much softer. Unfortunately, his name is one that has eroded over the decades since I first discovered the arch.

Stansbury wrote in his journal some time mid-day on September 28, 1849:

> *Ascending the western slope of the Black Hills by a very gentle rise, we followed the trail of our party, passing between low cliffs and detached masses of red & grey sandstone, worn into isolated pillars, hillocks and other forms by the action of the elements.*

Decoding the geographic notations recorded by Stansbury in his journal proves that Bridger and the expedition camped that night near the Gangplank, the future route of the UPRR. Stansbury wrote:

*Passing over an undulating and gradually rising country, for seven or eight miles, we at length look over the train which had halted at noon on a small tributary of the Laramie River. Aspen, fir, pine & cedar here occurred in sheltering clumps, and the grass has been abundant. From this point, we continued our course more to the north-east for four or five miles, over ground considerably cut up by ravines, when we reached the summit of the ridge, which gives rise to the head of Lodgepole Creek, an affluent of the South Fork of the Platte...*

Stansbury just described the eastern half of the Old Oxford Horse Ranch to a "T."

The name of the drainage that parallels the Gangplank is Lone Tree Creek. In his official report, Stansbury called it Lodgepole Creek just like General Granville Dodge did in his report. Nevertheless, Dodge is credited with the discovery of this money-saving path to California. He was richly rewarded with UPRR stock, which he lost when the market crashed in the Panic of 1893. Bankrupt, Dodge moved on to Argentina to build more railroads.

~~~~~~~~~~~~~~~

In 1853, having never visited the Rockies, Secretary of War Jefferson Davis sent Lieutenant **John Gunnison** on an impossible mission: to find an easy route across Colorado. The modern railroad that bisects Colorado today took a decade to build. The best route, the one surveyed earlier by Stansbury, passed through too many free states for the likes of the southern slave states. Jefferson Davis ordered two more surveys that might bisect potential slave states. Davis's preferred route passed through far southern New Mexico Territory, so he affected the Gadsden Purchase, named for James Gadsden, an influential North Carolina senator and a former ambassador to Mexico. US taxpayers paid ten-million dollars for the 30,000 square miles called the Gadsden Purchase. That is fifty cents an acre, the most expensive cactus- and sand-choked real estate that America ever bought. Davis never saw either of his railroads built. A positive, if unintended, consequence of these surveys was a thorough examination of southern Rocky Mountain flora and fauna. The multiple volumes produced contain detailed lithographs of every tree, every flower, and every animal the scientist/military explorers encountered.

Thinking that Colorado and Utah might also enter the Union as slave states, Davis ordered Lieutenant Gunnison on another surveying expedition. Gathering a small team that included second-in-command Lieutenant E.G. Beckwith, a topographer, an artist, an astronomer, a botanist, a geologist, and a surgeon, Gunnison embarked on Secretary Davis' surveying expedition. Gunnison climbed the formidable Rockies west of Denver and carefully
~~~~~~~~~~~~~~~

surveyed the entire landscape. They exited Colorado by following what is now called the Gunnison River down to its grand junction with the Colorado River. He continued across the Utah desert and crossed the Wasatch Range in central Utah Territory, generally following the route of present-day Interstate 70. The notes and observations from these three expeditions filled volumes. The expedition costs ran into the hundreds of thousands of dollars.

Unfortunately, Gunnison was more a surveyor than a military man. Ignoring warnings of Indian unrest, he split his troops into two groups and continued working. Gunnison was inside his tent making calculations when he was attacked. Unarmed, he scrambled for his horse and led six of his cavalrymen in a suicidal counterattack. Only four of the eleven expedition members survived; Gunnison was not among them. When Jim Bridger learned of his friend's death, he suspected that the "Utes" were Mormons in war paint. They had employed this tactic before to discourage incursions of American government expeditions into Deseret, the Mormon homeland. Mormons did kill two members of the John Wesley Powell expedition as well as fifty migrant Gentiles during the 1854 Mountain Meadow Massacre. Still, official history affirms that Paiutes killed Gunnison because the tribe was angry over the recent killing of their chief by Mormons.

~~~~~~~~~~~~~~~

I am a staunch anglophile because my mother was born in north London. I have visited England and Scotland and am fascinated by the frigid castles that spring up at every turn. I toured several with my mother and sister long ago, including a particularly cold castle in Scotland. Murthly Castle is near Edinburgh, Scotland, and I wish I had taken the time to admire the famous paintings which hang on the cold, stone walls. Murthly was the ancestral home of Sir William Drummond Steward, a wealthy Scot who, in 1837, traveled for two years throughout the American West with a huge entourage. His guide was Jim Bridger. As an industry, tourism made its first inroad into the Wyoming landscape.

To capture a pictorial history of his adventures, Steward employed a struggling young artist as he passed through New Orleans, Louisiana, and commissioned him to record the scenery. The artist turned out to be Alfred Jacob Miller, who today ranks as one of America's leading 19th century artists. Miller spent the two years making hundreds of sketches of Western life, which later transformed into full-scale, oil-on-canvas portraits of the mountain man era. Some still hang in Murthly Castle, well preserved by the chill.
~~~~~~~~~~~~~~~

Steward and Miller attended the 1834 rendezvous, and there Miller captured the scene: native Americans in full ceremonial regalia, fur-clad men engaging in gunplay, drinking, and gambling. He sketched the abundant wildlife, the spectacular mountains, as well as thirty-four-year-old Jim Bridger riding about the scene full-tilt, wearing Steward's suit of armor. The West, immortalized by Miller and his contemporaries, disappeared almost before it became known to the outside world. The way of life for the mountain men disappeared forever, never to return.

~ ~ ~ ~ ~ ~ ~ ~ ~ ~ ~ ~ ~

Jim Bridger was a famous guide, well-known to whites and natives alike. He had his finger on the pulse of western life. After Jim quit trapping, he and his life-long partner, Louis Vasquez, pursued other endeavors. In 1842, they purchased a Spanish land grant and established Fort Bridger in the shade of the long-leafed cottonwood trees along the Black's Fork of the Seedskadee River in southwestern Wyoming, now called the Green River. This trading post soon became an important stop along the Emigrant Trail.

Indians considered Jim Bridger a family member, especially the Shoshone and Ute tribes. He first married a Flathead princess who bore him two children, but she died in 1848. His second wife was a Ute named Cora, who died in childbirth in 1849. Mary Ann, the infant, was raised on buffalo milk, and Bridger later sent her to the famous Dr. Marcus Whitman's school for her safety.

Dr. Whitman first befriended Bridger at the 1835 rendezvous on the Seedskadee. The doctor cut an old arrowhead out of his new friend's hip, where it had lodged five years previously while Bridger was in Montana. Whitman returned to Wyoming the following year along with his wife, Narcissa, the first white woman in Wyoming. They continued towards Oregon and established a mission near present-day Walla Walla, Washington. When Dr. Whitman failed to stem a measles outbreak, angry and suspicious natives attacked. The doctor, his wife, his three adopted sons, and all other male residents of the mission were killed. They took the surviving women and girls captive. Mary Ann Bridger was among the girls rescued by Peter Ogden the following spring. Weakened by her winter of captivity, she died soon after. Only one child, Virginia, survived her father and was with him when he died in Missouri in 1881.

~ ~ ~ ~ ~ ~ ~ ~ ~ ~ ~ ~ ~

During the prime of his life, Bridger explored Wyoming. He could identify a stream by its particular taste and knew the route of every major game trail in the territory. His eyesight was exceptional; he could see a campfire smudge from sixty miles away; he was the most sought-after guide in the West. Bridger must have walked or ridden across my land scores of times. Illiterate, he would not have left a mark. Someone surely forged his signature on another rock outcropping in western Wyoming which was discovered and photographed by General Hayden's survey crew in 1869. He never even learned to write his initials.

In his old age, he drew a map that guided General Granville Dodge from Omaha, Nebraska Territory, to the spot where the railroad would traverse its highest point. The year was 1865, Bridger was sixty-one years old and semi-retired in Missouri, but he never forgot a landscape. The path Bridger indicated went up the Gangplank west of Cheyenne.

General Dodge took Bridger's map in hand and explored the Black Hills of Wyoming. His company of armed soldiers began searching the hills west of Fort D. A. Russell looking for Bridger's Gangplank. Stories differ about what happened next. Some say Dodge was surprised by a small band of Indians and defeated them in a heroic standoff. Others say that Dodge staged an organized retreat from the summit, fighting a running battle. Still others say that Dodge saw the Indians at a distance and beat a hasty retreat.

Whichever story is true, the bottom line is the Gangplank, which connects Cheyenne to Laramie, Wyoming, finally appeared on a white man's map. This route was too narrow to support the livestock associated with passing wagon trains, but it was perfect for the Iron Horse. The low, long slope increased in elevation only 100 feet in a mile. Construction began out of Cheyenne in 1867, and today, a major highway shares the Gangplank with the railroad. At the summit, a bronze bust of Abraham Lincoln marks the highest point on Interstate 80 and Highway 30. Also called the Lincoln Highway, it was built in the 1930s and was superseded by Interstate 80 in the 1960s.

After the railroad was completed, the US government called on Jim Bridger once again. Bridger responded, venturing for the last time into the West. Under the Second Fort Laramie Treaty of 1868, the army agreed to remove three forts in the Powder River Basin in north-central Wyoming. The forts had been built illegally on Sioux hunting lands to protect the Bozeman Trail, and Red Cloud hated them. But even without the protection of the forts, whites continued their rush for gold and silver in Montana and present-day South Dakota. Both areas were legally Sioux sovereign land.

Meanwhile, Fort Bridger had fallen into the hands of the Mormons. Threatened, Bridger sent his single surviving daughter east. Bridger left government service for good in the fall of 1868 and retired to Missouri, never to return to his beloved Wyoming. He died in 1881, unheralded by the press and unknown to his neighbors. General Dodge wrote a lovely biography and published it in 1905. He also had Bridger's bones exhumed and moved to their present-day location in Independence, Missouri. At his own expense, Dodge placed a stone monument to the greatest mountain man that ever lived. Dodge wrote of Bridger:

> *Unquestionably, Bridger's claims to remembrance rest upon the extraordinary part he bore in the explorations of the West. As a guide he was without equal and this is the testimony of everyone who ever knew him. He was a born topographer; the wild West was mapped out in his mind, and such was his instinctive sense of locality & direction that it used to be said of him that he could smell his way where he could not see it. He was a complete Master of plains & woodcraft, equal to any emergency, full of resources to overcome any obstacles afforded in that wild region.... Bridger was not an educated man, still any country that he had ever seen he could fully and intelligently describe, and he could make a very correct estimate of the country surrounding it.... He understood thoroughly the Indian character, their peculiarities & superstitions.... As a guide I do not think he had an equal upon the Plains* (Dodge, 1905).

Isolated and blind at the end, Bridger took most of his knowledge to his grave. Jim Bridger stands as the foremost mountain man, and as a valuable military guide and interpreter. He was the one who located an overland trail and railroad route across Wyoming. He was the one white man who thoroughly appreciated the native culture in which he lived. Sadly, Bridger's friend **John Gunnison** died too early. Even so, Gunnison is among the most famous of Western explorers, ranking above John C. Frémont, Zebulon Pike, and Stephen H. Long. He contributed his name to some of the coldest, most scenic places in Colorado. And, of course, he added his name to the Crimson Arch. The West will never see the likes of either of them again.

# *Chapter Eight*
# HJY 1851 – JOAQUIN YOUNG
## *& the Siren Call of the West*

(PHOTO BY K. MCGUIRE)

When I started researching the rock inscriptions, my primary motivation was to identify TY 1817, the most prominent inscription on my little arch. So, I first searched the index of each volume I checked out from the library, hoping for a stroke of luck. None materialized. No one had a last name starting with "Y" and a given name beginning with "T," but there were plenty of listings for an Ewing Young, no relation to Thomas. On a lark, I followed the thread and read about him.

Ewing Young settled in Taos, New Mexico Territory, in the early 1820s. He took as his common-law wife María Josefa Tafoya, the daughter of a prominent Mexican land grant family. Together, they had a son whom they named José Joaquin. Mexicans sometimes spell things phonetically, and a common mistake is to change the "J" to an "H" for the name **José. Joaquin** was not well-educated like his father, and he probably made this mistake.

Locally famous for trapping beaver and exploring the southern Rockies, Young was nonetheless restless. The quality of the pelts from the far south Rockies was not prime, and as the cash value dwindled, so did the number of available beaver. So, in 1830, Young followed the route pioneered by Jedidiah Smith three years earlier, employing a 21year-old Kit Carson to guide him into California. The desert crossing took a mighty toll upon them, and they limped into San Bernardino, ghosts of their former selves. In passing, they blazed a new route across the desert, over Cajon Pass, and into the Los Angeles Basin. They stayed at a Spanish land-grant hacienda near present-day San Bernardino, California, until they regained their health.

After recuperating their strength, they left to trap beaver and trade for more pelts until they reached San Francisco. Along the way, they assisted a Spanish mission foreman in the recapture of eleven runaway indigenous converts. The Spanish mission system was forcibly converting California Indians to Catholicism, and some did not take kindly to the incarceration. Young returned to Taos enriched, but he did not stay long.

Leaving his Taos family behind in 1834, he moved to Oregon's Willamette Valley. He was the first settler there and built a large and prosperous cattle ranch along the river. He owned fifty square miles, some 32,000 acres, between the Willamette River and Wapato Lake. He immediately formed a cattle cooperative and bought 700 head of cattle in California. It took the herd nine months to make the trek to their new home, and he lost 200 head along the way. Ultimately, he established the most extensive and farthest west ranch in the United States until Hawai'i became a state more than one hundred years later. In the prime of his life, he ranched and operated a sawmill until the winter of 1840-41. Tremendous rains soaked the valley that season and flooded his properties. Young contracted pneumonia and died even though a friendly neighborhood doctor, Sydney Smith, dropped everything to attend to his sickbed.

When Young died in 1841, he left a large estate with no apparent heir and no will; the wife and family in Taos were unknown to his peers. Dr. Smith bought Young's claim and cattle for about three hundred dollars and became Young's estate administrator. It was he who planted the acorn on Ewing Young's grave. Today, Oregon celebrates Ewing Young Day at the base of that tree. The trunk now measures almost fifteen feet in diameter, spreading its branches over eighty feet into the Oregon sky.

Apparently, Young was the first person of influence and property to die in Oregon without a valid will. So, the good citizens of Oregon organized a judicial infrastructure to probate his estate. These same gentlemen oversaw the budding state government and became the leaders of the new State of Oregon a decade later.

News travels slowly in the West, so it took some time for Young's New Mexican family to learn of his death. His wife suspected there might be a substantial estate to settle. So his only son, **H[J]osé Joaquin Young**, set out for Oregon to claim his inheritance. Traveling the American West at that time was difficult and dangerous. Indians still roamed freely and could be openly hostile to unarmed transports.

Joaquin's route would have taken him from Taos up the Santa Fe Trail to Bent's Fort in southern Colorado. At the time, there were no white settlements in the territory besides Pueblo, Colorado. So Joaquin called upon his father's friend and former guide, Kit Carson. Carson had established himself as a famous trapper, buffalo hunter, Indian scout, Indian fighter, and western statesman. He was a frequent visitor to Bent's Fort. John C. Frémont had hired Carson in 1842 to guide him across Wyoming, and he was familiar with the territory. I can imagine him instructing Joaquin about the best route and its pitfalls. Indeed, two years later, Carson followed this same path, driving 5,000 sheep from Taos to Oregon.

Beyond Bent's Fort was Indian-controlled territory; Joaquin could only follow the Trapper's Trail between the Arkansas River and Salem, Oregon Territory. I do not know, nor does history record, exactly how he made his way to Oregon in 1851. Frémont was finished making biannual treks across the continent, so that opportunity was lost. But the Mormons were in full flight to Salt Lake City following the murder of their leader Joseph Smith, so there were many caravans to follow; I doubt Joaquin traveled alone. The favored handcart route followed the shortcut up the Gangplank and past the Crimson Arch; they did not the acres of night pasture afforded by the Emigrant Trail.

I am confident that Joaquin paused in his travels long enough to carve his initials and the date, ***HJY 1851***, into a humble, red sandstone outcropping that Carson would have also described to him. Known as Bridger's Trail, the route followed Lone Tree Creek up a gentle slope now known as the Gangplank. The path continued into the relatively peaceful valley of the Laramie River, right past the arch.

<div align="center">~~~~~~~~~~~~~~~~</div>

A steady stream of wagon trains used the Emigrant Trail on their way to Oregon in 1843. The indigenous tribes would call it "the Holy Road," referring to that holy document, the yet-to-be-negotiated Treaty of 1851. Americans called it the "Emigrant Trail," and most of the wagons that passed westward headed towards British-held Oregon. The travelers knew little about the West, the hardships they might encounter, and next to nothing about the natives, except for what they read in sensationalized newspaper stories. About nine hundred wagons passed through Wyoming that year.

In the 1844 election, presidential candidate James Polk ran on a platform that openly antagonized the British to the north. He had underpinned his campaign with a war-like platform, hoping to create a common enemy, unite his divided Democratic party, and appear "presidential." Polk had a catchy campaign slogan, "Fifty-Four Forty or Fight," referring to the location of the Canadian-American border, which had yet to be determined. The 54th parallel runs from the southern end of the mainland Alaska archipelago through Edmonton, Alberta. Clearly, this was an impossible campaign promise. After Polk was elected, the British wanted their western territories and compromised on the 49th parallel. But this was the first time the Eastern press spotlighted Western politics in a presidential campaign.

Polk's opponents were Henry Clay (representing the Whig Party), James G. Birney (of the Liberty Party), and Joseph Smith (King, Priest, Ruler Over Israel on Earth, and head of the Lord's One True Church, the Church of the Latter-Day Saints, then located at Nauvoo, Illinois). Being guided by the Hand of God was not enough to win the election. Polk won 48.1% of the vote, only 38,367 votes ahead of Clay, meaning that Birney and Smith hardly registered at the polls. Having settled his election year argument with northern neighbor Canada, President Polk turned his aggressions upon the neighbor to the south, Mexico. Frémont was sent to claim California for the United States. About one thousand families passed the Emigrant Trail that year.

In 1845, the weather was so cold that not only the livestock but most of the deer, elk, and buffalo in Wyoming perished in the deep cold, estimated at -60 degrees Fahrenheit. The lack of ponies the next spring prompted Jim Baker, the famous mountain man, and some friends from Utah to journey to Los Angeles, California, to steal horses from the Spanish. They succeeded in driving a herd of 4,000 stolen ponies to Utah, where they divvied them up. Baker continued into Wyoming alone. The Wyoming tribes, desperate for new ponies, attacked his camp on the shores of present-day Battle Lake and drove off about half of his stolen ponies.

~ ~ ~ ~ ~ ~ ~ ~ ~ ~ ~ ~ ~ ~

By 1846, about three thousand emigrant wagons streamed westward, three times the number the previous year, and shortcuts to California were needed. One new route turned southward after passing the newly established Fort Bridger, Wyoming. This route, first traversed by Colonel John Frémont the year before, cut across the flat hard-pan of the Bonneville Flats near Salt Lake City and over what is now called Donner Pass. Frémont barely completed that crossing in 1843 due to heavy snow, but that was not common knowledge. The route was extolled but indeed not mapped by Lansford W. Hastings, a newly arrived Mormon. A group headed by William Donner decided to take this shortcut to California, expecting to arrive ahead of the larger train.

Delayed by miles of impassable muddy flats and trackless basins broken only by steep, rugged, and waterless mountain ranges with uncharted passes, the Donner party struggled on. They found early snows accumulating when they reached the final barrier, the high Sierra Nevada. Trapped by the deep snow near what is now called Donner Lake, the survivors famously consumed their dead comrades. They were saved only after James Reed and several strong women struggled through head-high snow to a logger's camp on the other side of the divide. When Reed reached Sutter's Mill, he begged Colonel Frémont to mount a rescue party, but Frémont was otherwise engaged. His priority was to lay siege to the Spanish at the mission in Monterey, California. He could spare only three men. Four months later, when the relief party reached the Donner's hastily constructed cabins, half of the eighty-seven emigrants were dead. Their stripped skeletons remained frozen in the snow outside.

Donner did not know that the Central Pacific Railroad would follow his path twenty years later. Jim Bridger also took note of Donner's progress. Since the Sublette cut-off on the Emigrant Trail was established, many Oregon-bound trains were bypassing Fort Bridger. Another more southerly route would have made his trading post the jumping-off point, guaranteeing more traffic past his doors. By this time, Mormon emigrants were also avoiding Fort Bridger, preferring to patronize Fort Supply, a Mormon-owned business just twelve miles from Bridger. With the livelihood of Fort Bridger in jeopardy, a new route to California was just what Bridger needed.

The peak years for westbound wagon trains were 1847 through 1852 when about five thousand emigrant wagons crossed Wyoming annually. A pioneer's diary records that during an eleven-day period in 1850, 933 wagons and their associated livestock passed Fort Laramie. Included in the count were over 3,000 humans, 7,000 oxen, 1,500 horses, 2,000 cows, and 544 mules (quoted in Lageson & Spearing, 1988).

The race west was on in earnest after they discovered gold in 1848 at Sutter's Mill, California. The passing wagon trains created a series of parallel ruts along the Platte River across Nebraska, frightening the buffalo and laying waste to miles of grasslands on either side of the ever-widening trail. Wild game disappeared from the river bottoms, and the buffalo failed to complete their annual migration for the first time in memory. The tribes were starving. Unvaccinated and without prior immunologic insult, they succumbed to smallpox by the hundreds. Plagues of measles, influenza, syphilis, and typhoid decimated the western populations, especially the starving natives. The 1849 cholera epidemic was notably bad, killing equal numbers of whites and natives.

The emigrants came in all colors. What is now known as the Cherokee Trail was blazed in 1849. It ran from Bent's Fort (near La Junta, Colorado) up through present-day Cherokee Park, Colorado, and into the Laramie Basin of Wyoming. It was named for a band of Cherokee escaping their Oklahoma reservation after being banished from their ancestral homelands in Appalachia by President Andrew Jackson and enduring the Trail of Tears. They headed west to Oregon Territory, where they thought they were far enough away from the whites to be safe. They were wrong.

Other groups labored westward along the Emigrant Trail that year following the Platte River. Fort Laramie was a welcome rest stop after traversing the flat expanse of Nebraska Territory. The nearby Register Rock records many names of weary travelers and is part of a red hematite outcropping named "Rawhide Buttes." The term originated after an unknown wagon train member vowed as he left St. Louis that he would shoot the first Indian he saw. When the train encountered a peaceful encampment at the foot of these buttes, the man, true to his word, shot himself a young squaw (Hafen, 1984).

The enraged natives promptly besieged the wagon train and demanded the unfortunate man be surrendered for Indian-style trial and punishment. The surrounded wagon master complied, and the train members watched in horror as the murderer was slowly flayed in the warm sunshine. He died a horrible death after the wagon train moved on. About a week later, his mother succumbed to grief and was buried near Independence Rock along the Sweetwater River. The name "Rawhide" refers to the flayed emigrant's condition.

This story illustrates the fundamental clash between civilizations. In the West, there was no such thing as trial by jury, but the native Americans knew murder when they saw it and exacted their revenge. Whites, however, saw no difference between shooting an Indian and a stray dog.

~ ~ ~ ~ ~ ~ ~ ~ ~ ~ ~ ~ ~ ~ ~

Ten years after his father died, Joaquin Young arrived in Oregon Territory to claim his share of his father's estate, a sum exceeding $4,500 (about $125,000 today). Young's peers in Oregon had no idea that he had a family in New Mexico, and they looked upon Joaquin's arrival with considerable skepticism. But the youth carried with him copies of census and birth records. After three years of litigation, Joaquin won a settlement.

After that, **Young** returned to New Mexico Territory. What he did with the fortune his father's estate bestowed upon him is unknown. The census lists him as a resident of the Costilla District in 1860, unmarried at age twenty-eight. He would not receive his inheritance until 1861. He moved after that to San Bernardino, California. He died in 1903 at age 70 and is buried in California.

# Tree Rock Point of Interest

In the median of Interstate 80, about halfway to Laramie from Cheyenne, there grows an ancient limber pine (Pinus flexilis), seemingly out of solid rock. While the illusion is not accurate, the presence of the tree was a source of distraction for the hard-working but unimaginative railroaders. Impressed with the little tree's perseverance, they christened it "Tree Rock" and changed the route to spare it.

Of course, the stream nearest to the location is called Lone Tree. The railroaders were not the first to take note of this natural phenomenon, even though it marks the dead center of the I-80 corridor. Limber pines can live for two hundred years, and they seem to prefer harsh conditions. J. David Love once likened the weather on the Gangplank, the spot where Tree Rock survives today, to that in the Arctic. The same little tree that lives there today was probably an unmistakable road sign for folks following Bridger's Trail; people like Joaquin Young.

~~~~~~~~~~~~~~~~

<div align="center">

*Chapter Nine*

# W. S. BENTON - 1863

*& the Pathfinder*

</div>

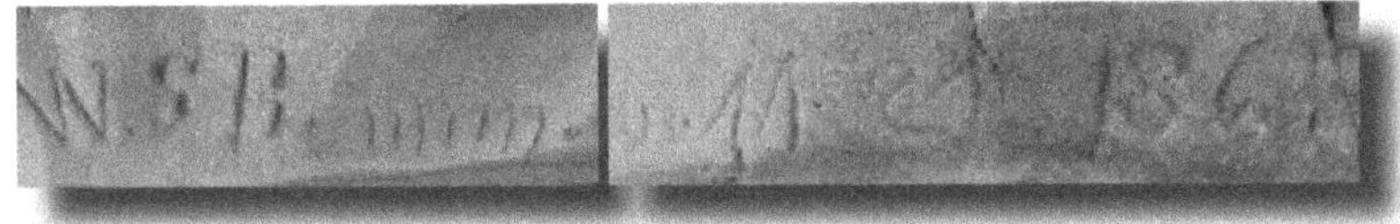

W.S. BENTON. SEPT 24 1863 INSCRIBED UPON THE
CRIMSON ARCH.

B F B 1863. A POSSIBLE BENTON COMPANION.
(PHOTOS BY K. McGUIRE)

Sometimes, people with famous last names find that their reputations precede them, unlike W.S. Benton. There were plenty of references to Thomas Hart Benton: Benton County, Benton City, Benton this, and Benton that, but not one was for a W.S. Benton. It took plenty of digging (especially using the Find-A-Grave site) to piece this little mystery together.

Young **William Stephen Benton** grew up in Missouri. He was a child of privilege, but a melancholy boy, never knowing exactly where he fitted in his bustling household. His favorite uncle, Randolph, was always on his mind, the only son of the powerful senator from Missouri, Thomas Hart Benton. A frequent household guest was John C. Frémont, the Pathfinder. Frémont had married Jessie Benton (named for her Uncle Jesse), Randolph's older sister. Stephen's grandfather Benton was the central figure of the Democratic political machine whose stronghold was Missouri. Stephen heard all about the West from his Auntie Jessie's husband, John, as he prepared for his latest expedition.

The senior Benton had served as Andrew Jackson's aide-de-camp during the War of 1812. Jackson, allied with millionaire steel magnate Andrew Carnegie
~~~~~~~~~~~~~~~~

and southern statesman John C. Calhoun, attracted a populist following who worshipped him. During his presidency (1829-1837), he fought openly with Congress, vetoing twelve bills, more than all of his six predecessors combined. Jackson spoke directly to the people through newspapers, circumventing the stodgy and deferential relationship between Congress and the White House. He demanded blind loyalty from his cabinet members, going through four secretaries of state and five secretaries of the treasury. He and his "Kitchen Cabinet" circumvented Congress and embraced a *laissez-faire* approach to economic policies. His opponents called him "King Jackson" because of his authoritarian style. They even resurrected the name "Whig Party" to represent their opposition to his tyranny.

With the Democrats temporarily controlling the White House, Congress, and the Supreme Court, the party began planning to dominate the entire continent and populate it with slave states. Thomas Hart Benton tried to secure US government funds to send his son-in-law west to claim Oregon and California territory. His efforts were unsuccessful, but Frémont was able to secure private funding. In June 1842, Frémont left St. Louis on his first expedition west, bound for Oregon. His young brother-in-law, Randolph Benton, and Henry Brandt, Jessie Benton's nephew, accompanied Frémont, expecting to visit California. They only made it as far as Fort Laramie. Frémont writes in his published journal:

> *In addition to these [party members], Henry Brant, son of Colonel J.B. Brant of St. Louis, a young man nineteen years of age, and Randolph, a lively boy of twelve, son of Mr. Benton, accompanied me, for the development of mind & body which such an expedition would give. We were all well-armed and mounted, with the exception of eight men, who conducted as many carts, [and wagons] in which were packed our stores, with the baggage and instruments, and which were each drawn by two mules. A few loose horses, and four oxen which had been added to our stock of provisions completed the train. We set out on the morning of the 10th, which happened to be a Friday – a circumstance which our men did not fail to remember and recall during the hardships & vexations of the ensuing journey* (Frémont, 1845).

Frémont left the boys at Fort Laramie because Randolph was Benton's only son, the youngest of six children. Randolph was well liked by the expedition members, providing a boisterous and jolly counterpoint to the rigors of expedition life. But he was so young. His first guard duty assignment came during a tremendous downpour with sheets of lightning and rolling thunder.

His trembling falsetto could be heard throughout the camp, asking Kit Carson if all was safe. Upon reaching Fort Laramie, Frémont writes in his journal:

*In case of misfortune it would have been thought, at the least, an act of great imprudence; and therefore, though reluctantly, I determined to leave them [Brandt & Benton]. Randolph had been the life of the camp, and the petit garçon was much regarded by the men, to whom his buoyant spirits had afforded great amusement. They all, however, agreed on the propriety of leaving him at the fort because, as he said, he might cost the lives of some of them in a fight with the Indians.* (Frémont, 1845)

The fort embraced the lads, taking them on excursions up into the Black Hills, perhaps past the Crimson Arch. Randolph met Jim Bridger, who was by then building Fort Bridger on the Seedskadee River in western Wyoming. He waited patiently for his uncle to materialize.

Randolph returned to St. Louis with Frémont the following spring, but it was a lonely existence. Sister Eliza, the oldest of the Benton children, was in New Orleans with her famous lawyer husband, William Carey Jones. Sister Jessie Frémont now lived in California arriving by packet ship. Traveling with their 6-year-old daughter, Lily, she had negotiated the dangerous overland portion of the Panama Gap. Sarah was in Kentucky with her husband, Richard T. Jacobs, the lieutenant governor. Sister Susan was in Peru with her French ambassador husband, Joshua Brandt. Randolph's father, Senator Thomas Hart Benton, spent most of his time in Washington. His chronically ill mother remained in St. Louis, unable to join her husband in the nation's capital. Randolph and the youngest Benton sister, Katherine (or Kate as revealed on her tombstone), nursed their mother together, alone in their St. Louis mansion. Mss. Benton died in 1851.

~ ~ ~ ~ ~ ~ ~ ~ ~ ~ ~ ~ ~ ~

Katherine herself is rarely mentioned in official Benton lore. Her pregnancy, out of wedlock and by a father she refused to name, resulted in a son whom she christened **William Stephen Benton**. During this period, Randolph delighted in telling little Stephen about Jim Bridger's West, and Colonel Frémont continued using the home as a staging area for his California-bound expeditions. But soon, Randolph began frequenting the bars along the St. Louis waterfront to listen wistfully to the tall tales of the French watermen. These rough types had been the boatmen for many Western expeditions. He longed to return to the West, but his father strictly forbade it. He had converted to Catholicism at some point, much to the dismay of his strictly Protestant family. He attended a Jesuit college for two years, but the family sent him away as discouragement. He returned in 1852, intending to re-enroll and finish his degree, but instead met his unexpected and untimely death. The St. Louis *Union* published his obituary:

> *We regret to announce the death of this young gentleman, the only son of Colonel Thomas H. Benton. He was but twenty-two years of age, and was cut down in the very bloom of health & manhood, giving out every promise of a long & distinguished future... On Tuesday, the 10th, he was one of the myriad who met Kossuth [a popular Hungarian philosopher who was touring the West, lecturing]; on Thursday, the 12th, he was at the St. Louis University, arranging with the president for some branches of study of which he was eager to enter; that night he was taken ill - at sunrise on the 17th he had breathed his last* (St. Louis *Union*, 1852).

Randolph died of alcohol poisoning, much to the shame of his powerful father and four successful sisters. Jessie and Frémont were in London at the time; they did not cut short their visit. Her diary does not mention his death. After a full-blown Catholic Mass, John Randolph Benton was buried in the Bellefontaine Cemetery in St. Louis. His father did not attend. Kate and Stephen were the lone family mourners. Kate died in 1860, leaving seventeen-year-old Stephen alone in a big, empty house.

~~~~~~~~~~~~~~~~

When he turned eighteen, Stephen left home and joined a company of rowdy young men. Together, they became full-fledged members of the Quantrill's Bushwhackers, a band of irregular, pro-Confederate rangers. They habitually crossed the state line into free state Kansas to tear up the countryside randomly. Quantrill himself wore the Confederate uniform, thinking he would avoid immediate execution if captured by Union forces. Jefferson Davis recognized a terrorist when he saw one and consistently rejected his requests for a commission.

In August 1863, Quantrill and about 300 men, including Benton, undertook a daring raid. They rode through the night and crossed Missouri into sleeping Kansas. By noon, they had burned Lawrence, Kansas, to the ground and killed 100 men and boys as they escaped their burning homes. During the long ride back to St. Louis, the pursuit by Union troops was half-hearted. They were out-gunned, out-manned, and out-mounted.

Criticized by the press and his superiors for his tepid response to this bold and bloody incursion, Union General William Schofield issued Order
~~~~~~~~~~~~~~~~

Number Eleven, a blatant infringement upon the civil rights of the people of Missouri. All families were required to report to the nearest military post. They remained there until the male family members could provide an alibi for that night, proving they were not raiders. Guilty until proven innocent, hundreds of men left the state and headed west to California. Facing certain imprisonment under Order Number Eleven, Benton and his group fled up the Platte River, traveling by night to avoid the Union patrols.

Galloping hard, they reached the safety of Wyoming in early September. There, he found the journal of his Uncle John's 1842 expedition and the recollections of his Uncle Randolph to be precisely correct. Riding towards the verdant Laramie Basin, Stephen located the tiny Crimson Arch. There, the group decided against heading to California and instead set a course for Canada, the only safe refuge available. During that brief stay, ***"W.S. Benton. Sept 24 1863"*** was inscribed on the delicate Crimson Arch. Benton chose to place his name just below that of ***TY 1817***. There is another inscription close by that reads ***BFB 1863***. It is of similar age and style, but I could not identify it further. It could well be another of Quantrill's raiders escaping justice.

Then, they rode into the sunset to disappear from history forever. My only clue to his whereabouts was a lonely and unremarkable grave in Ontario, Canada. The headstone read **William Stephen Benton**, but no birth or death dates were listed. The tombstone was sufficiently old to qualify as a potential final resting place for this mysterious rock signatory, but we will never know.

~~~~~~~~~~~~~~~
~~~~~~~~~~~~~~~

# A Geology Lesson

"The Gangplank" is a unique geologic formation. It is a slab of sandstone anchored to the top of the ancestral Laramie Range as it rose out of the plains sixty-five million years ago. Its edge was elevated intact and remained attached and unbroken. The Gangplank formed a gentle, smooth confluence from the Great Plains to the top of a mountain range, another Wyoming geological first. It is the perfect route for the UPRR over the Laramie Range (McPhee, 2000).

At one time, loose debris blown in from the geologic events to the west buried the Laramie Mountains to a depth of five miles. The underlying red sandstone and white limestone were compressed and hardened by the great weight of this debris. Eventually, the overburden was eroded by melting glaciers or blown eastward during an event referred to as the "deroofing" of Wyoming. The soil that covers the Great Plains to the Mississippi River and as far east as Cape Hatteras might have once been in the Laramie Basin.

So fierce are the winds in Wyoming that in that one spot out on the Laramie Plains, the wind alone displaced some four million acre-feet of soil. Today, they call it the Big Hollow.

## *Chapter Ten*
# CHH - CHARLEY HUTTON
### *& the Wild Wyoming Weather*

(PHOTO BY K. McGUIRE)

The Laramie Basin has long been a difficult place to live year-round. Even the tribes came here only in the fall to harvest ash tree branches from which they fashioned their "good medicine" bows and arrows. Some early explorers trekked through, commenting on its rich grasses and spectacular scenery as they moved on. When winter snows closed the pass leading into the basin, things ground to a halt. Because of a volcanic eruption in Iceland in 1845, the weather in Wyoming was so cold that most horses, deer, elk, and buffalo perished in the deep cold. Scientists estimated the temperature in Wyoming at sixty degrees below zero Fahrenheit.

As significant numbers of Americans established themselves a thousand miles to the east and west, it was natural that a communication line must come to exist between California and the more settled Midwest and East. That first line went right past the Crimson Arch in the form of an oxen freighting trail. By 1858, few freighters operated between Omaha, Salt Lake City, and distant San Francisco. Edward Creighton, a millionaire owner of a wagon manufacturing company, pioneered one such company. Creighton later established Creighton University in Nebraska and the First National Bank of Omaha. **Charley Hutton**, Philip Mandel, and Hiram Kelly worked for Ed Creighton as bull-whackers. These freighters were familiar with the verdant and violent nature of the Laramie Basin, having traversed it many times. They traveled only five to ten miles a day, depending on the gradient and the amount of available fodder. At the end of each day, the unhitched oxen were allowed to graze and water freely.

I know that early freighters went right past my crimson rock because, in 1863, Creighton employees Thomas Alsop and Philip Mandel were caught by a December snowstorm while toiling up Bridger's Red Buttes Trail. They were headed east over the Black Hills on the way back from Salt Lake City to Omaha. It had been a long summer, and Alsop and Mandel had been on the trail since early June. On this trip, they commanded fifty wagons, each laden with one ton of goods. Canvas covered each conveyance securely stretched over arching poles to prevent snow from accumulating and weighing down the load. The bull-whackers typically entrained four wagons. The first in line was hitched to as many "yolks," or teams, of bull oxen necessary to pull the load across level ground. At times, there were up to twenty yolks in a hitch. Individual wagons were hitched to four yolks of bull oxen going up an incline such as that near the Crimson Arch. At the top, Creighton's drivers would have unhitched the oxen and returned down the hill to help bring another wagon up. Extra oxen, typically driven alongside the wagon train, were pressed into use as replacements.

With the weather worsening, Creighton's wagons got stuck in the steep, snow-filled draw near the Crimson Arch. The situation looked hopeless, so they unhitched the teams and set them free, never expecting them to survive the winter. The whole crew made it safely to Omaha on their long-legged horses to wait out the season. The following spring, Mandel and Alsop returned to retrieve the abandoned wagons. Finding the wagons was easy, but there was no sign of the oxen. They scanned the sky; there were no circling turkey vultures potentially feasting on rotting oxen carcasses. So they went looking for the bulls. After all, they were worth five dollars each, and 250 head were missing.

After several fruitless days, Alsop came across some fresh tracks and, a week later, found the bulls, fat and happy, grazing on Sand Creek near the Chimney Rock, some ten miles away from the Crimson Arch. It was nothing short of a miracle in Alsop's eyes, and, like any resourceful Swede, he wondered how they did it. There must be something about the grasses, he thought. And he was right.

Creighton soon went into the grading business for the UPRR, sending teams out to grade the road under the direction of his new partner, **Charley Hutton**. When they finished the grading contract in 1868, they partnered with Phillip Mandel and started the first commercial ranching business on the Laramie Plains. Their headquarters, called the Hart Ranch, is on the Big

Laramie River, where **Ed Robinson** and Jacques LaRamie had built their cabins.

**Charley Hutton** became the Overland Stage station manager and later turned to ranching. The decision to locate Fort Sanders on the higher ground east of Harney Creek became expensive when Hutton & Creighton built a bridge over the river. They charged troops a fee of two dollars fifty per wagon and a dollar per horseman every time they used the Overland Stage Company bridge to cross the Laramie River, even if they were pursuing Indians who might attack the stage.

The stage station was rarely attacked as the proprietor was known as a source of guns, ammunition, and, most importantly, alcohol. But Hutton must have stopped at one time to engrave his initials, *CHH*, upon the little Crimson Arch that marked the spot of Alsop's eureka moment. **Hutton** died in 1899, well-loved but penniless, and is buried in Greenhill Cemetery, Laramie. The lake just south of the Hart Ranch is named for him.

~~~~~~~~~~~~~~~

The view Hutton and his compatriots enjoyed from my Crimson Arch would resemble what it is today. There were more trees, though, towering ponderosa pine and sinuous limber pine. Today, only their pitch pine stumps remain. By 1868, every tree within miles of the transcontinental railroad route was cut, hewn, shipped, and laid out like dead soldiers to support the track-building effort. That worked out to be 2,500 trees per mile of track. The Oxford Ranch rail crossing is 557.1 miles from Omaha, Nebraska, the eastern terminus of this railroad. Well over a million trees were cut, not counting wood for the prefabricated trestles, which were shipped in from Chicago. Only the cottonwoods survived because this species sends suckers out that continue to grow after the main trunk is cut. Plus, they make terrible ties; the wood is just too soft. They were used anyway, all across Nebraska, but I am sure they were among the first ties to be replaced once the race to Promontory Point was complete.

Otherwise, Hutton's view would be the same as mine. Today, I can pick out copses of cottonwoods that mark the location of the Old Oxford Horse Ranch headquarters and, farther south, the Willow Creek Ranch. An Overland Stage transfer station used to be there, and Charley might have seen the dust raised by a passing stage as he scratched his initials upon my arch. In 1862, the Overland Stage had been rerouted to respect the treaty prohibiting white trespass upon lands north of the Platte River. The new policy brought the main stage line across the Laramie Plains right below the arch.
~~~~~~~~~~~~~~~

From the vantage point of the Crimson Arch, Hutton could also trace the course of the Big Laramie River. A narrow band of cottonwoods snaked across the grassy plain, clearly marking its path. The plains appear as a pristine wonderland, calm, welcoming, and serene. Good building sites are few and far between out where the rivers come together; the old oxbows make terrific hay meadows but terrible home sites. **Hutton**'s partner, Phil Mandel already owned land in the Laramie Basin. He was the first person to officially file a patent establishing a ranch where the Overland Trail crosses the Little Laramie River, about ten miles from the Hart Ranch.

Both the Hart and Mandel ranches became stage stations. Mandel became a station master and began buying exhausted stock from westward-bound travelers. He would turn them out, and by the next spring, they were recovered and ready for travelers in need of fresh stock. Mandel put up no hay, provided no shelter, and built no fences. Wyoming stockmen did nothing towards husbanding their animals until after the Great Die-Up of 1886. Philip Mandel lived until the ripe old age of eighty-three and is buried in Greenhill Cemetery.

~~~~~~~~~~~~~~~

As Wyoming worked to achieve statehood, it braced for an expected onslaught of settlers. Unfortunately, most post-war emigrants had their sights set on Oregon or California. They did not even get off the train when it stopped in Laramie. Stephen Long's 1820 description of Wyoming as the Great American Desert had stuck. Long explored northeastern Colorado in 1819 after steaming up the Missouri in a special paddlewheeler designed to intimidate the resident Indians. The exhaust from the engines could be routed through tubes making the ornate and colorful dragon on her bowsprit appear to breathe smoke. Entering northeastern Colorado on foot, Long climbed and named Long's Peak and then retreated to St. Louis. He turned a tidy profit from this disastrous expedition though, selling the hides of buffalo his men slaughtered during his return. Another source of income was his self-serving, descriptive but inaccurate journals, popularly published upon his return. These pamphlets discouraged a generation of travelers from settling on the Great Plains.

The scenery out the window as the trains lumbered past miles and miles of empty, golden brown prairie was no help. The over-active press heralded reports of continuing Indian depredations and cattle rustling. Keep in mind that Wyoming receives an average of twelve inches of precipitation per year, mainly in the form of snow. The mean temperature is thirty-eight degrees Fahrenheit, and the elevation of arable land ranges from 3,600 feet to 7,000
~~~~~~~~~~~~~~~

feet at a latitude between 41 and 45 degrees. Generally speaking, the farther north and west portions of Wyoming's arable lands are lower in elevation than the Laramie Basin by some 2,000 feet. The growing season is, at most, ninety days, sixty in the Laramie Basin. According to J. David Love, a former USGS Geologist,

> *Conditions are about the same in [the 8,600-foot gangplank of] Wyoming as at the Arctic Circle* (quoted in McPhee, 2000).

Even with an average of two hundred plus days of sunshine each year, average temperatures hover dangerously near freezing. It is challenging to grow any vegetable crop in those conditions. The worst part is the wind. The wind takes on a whole other dimension with the chill factor, howling across the open prairies at a regular twenty-five mph. A windless, sunny day at minus twenty-five degrees Fahrenheit is comfortable weather. Add the Wyoming breeze, and productive working time outside becomes severely limited. It is no wonder that wind and solar energy have become attractive sources of energy throughout the state.

Wyoming had taken the first step toward statehood, but it needed to attract population. Enter the pamphleteers. Pamphleteers published wild and unimaginable stories at will because no one fact-checked their assertions. Their misinformation led many a naïve immigrant to their death on the Wyoming frontier.

United States Army Surgeon General Dr. Hiram B. Latham was probably the most infamous pamphleteer. Ostensibly employed by the UPRR, he occupied a small house on the grounds of Fort Sanders near present-day Laramie. The commanding officers consistently complained that Latham's home's untidy appearance was detrimental to post morale. The military maintained only the highest standards, policing the grounds regularly. The good doctor, however, remained unmoved. He was peculiarly incapable of making money, but his silver tongue and pleasant disposition gained him entrance into society. He eventually made his way to Washington to plead Wyoming's case for statehood.

His publications were popular and widely distributed. It seems that the weather had been relatively mild since the first "die-up" of 1845 when a winter-long blizzard killed almost all wild and domestic hoofed animals in the state. In 1870, Dr. Latham wrote about the possibilities of stock grazing in the "trans-Missouri" area, meaning Wyoming. The pamphlet is titled, *The Pasture Lands of North America: Winter Grazing, The sources of the future beef & wool supply of the United States*. He claimed that grasses are "self-curing" and that:

*Sheep & cattle live and thrive the year around without food or shelter [other] than afforded by Nature* (Burns et al.,1950).

Technically he was right. It was possible to overwinter a few cattle on the High Plains, but it was risky. The grasses self-cured because the dry winter wind swept away any trace of moisture that might allow the stems to rot. If left untrammeled by large herds of bison, Laramie Basin grasses remained upright as they desiccated in the cold, dry wind. They also protruded through the snow cover, signaling the hidden presence of feed. Bison and horses will paw away the accumulated snow to expose precious fodder. They will also eat snow to slake their thirst. Horses *(Equus caballus)* are non-native species, but their ancestors evolved in Wyoming so they are equipped with these life-saving habits. Cattle and sheep, both exotic species, will not perform either of those lifesaving techniques. Wyoming snow tends towards the dry side; during the cold winter months, it takes a full foot of snow to equal one inch of precipitation. Water was, and is, the limiting factor for survival on the Laramie Plains. For cattle and sheep in the winter, finding open water is hit or miss. They have to keep drifting with the wind to survive.

In his pamphlets, Latham went on to support his thesis, citing letters received from upstanding ranchers in the West. Alex Majors of Soda Springs, Utah Territory (now Idaho) reported:

*...as of May 1869, he grazed cattle on plains & mountains for twenty years and had wintered 15,000 work oxen on the plains and that they became fat by spring with no feed except grass with 33.5% body fat, sold as beef in the spring* (quoted in Burns et al., 1950).

This quote was disinformation specifically aimed to mislead anyone contemplating settlement on Laramie's high plain. Soda Springs, locally regarded as an oasis, is a full 2,000 feet lower in elevation than Laramie and is not subject to a constant wind of twenty to thirty-five miles an hour.

Hart Ranch partner Edward Creighton, who had since moved to Omaha, is quoted in a Latham pamphlet:

*During the present winter (1869-70) I have wintered about 8,000 head (on the Laramie Plains). They have done exceptionally well, no shelter but bluffs & hills and no feed but wild grasses. We have had 3,000 sheep the past winter and they are in the best of order and many were sold for mutton. The West has a great future in livestock raising... at half the present prices of Eastern-produced stock* (quoted in Burns et al.,1950).

Creighton had left **Charley Hutton** and Thomas Alsop in charge of the day-to-day operations at the Hart Ranch. During the winter of 1871-72, most of Creighton's sheep died in blizzards. Territorial Governor John Campbell was also excerpted in Latham's pamphlet extolling the future of sheep-raising on "the dry and gravelly soils" and the "richest of grasses." He went on to say:

> *not only sheep but other wool-bearing animals like cashmere & alpaca goats [sic] could be raised and their importation should be encouraged* (quoted in Burns et al., 1950).

Cashmere goats are just about the perfect animal to survive the conditions on the Laramie Plains. After all, they evolved in the Himalayas. While my goats arrived by jet plane, historically, Laramie's wooly sheep were trailed in from Oregon and Illinois by the thousands. William Collins imported 500 Angora goats from Texas in the fall of 1870. He had corrals, but they did not confine the goats. Most escaped to the heights of Boulder Ridge and survived for several years in the wild, fair game for sure-shot cowboys or hungry mountain lions.

In early 1871, spurred on by Latham's flowery publications extolling the quality of the Laramie Plains as rangeland, a flock of 10,000 sheep left LaGrange, Oregon, and began to walk east. They arrived in Laramie in September. Worth a dollar-fifty a head in Oregon, they were sold in Laramie for three dollars each. William Rogers, who lived in the Iron Mountain country northeast of Laramie, bought $15,000 worth. Latham, a resident of Fort Sanders, must have known that frost could strike as early as August, and snow was not unusual in September. On October 13, 1871, a strange series of snowstorms commenced. Blizzard after blizzard raged across the Laramie Basin until April 1872. In all, over five feet of snow fell that winter. The coldest temperature recorded on January 15, 1872, was negative twenty-five degrees Fahrenheit.

The soldiers at Fort Sanders suffered mightily. Sheep rancher Robert Homer at the Flag Ranch, just west of the Oxford Ranch, had imported over a thousand sheep from back East that summer. The flock included pedigreed Cotswold and Hampshire rams, bringing his herd to 2,100 sheep. He had no fences, no hay, and no shelter for them; they were all dead by the following spring. Mr. Rogers' recently purchased sheep suffocated when the relentless wind filled his unchinked barns with snow. He could not navigate between his house and his barn for five days, but neither gave up. Bob Homer restocked and sheared 2,000 head the following fall, working his way up to 4,691 sheep shorn in 1881.

In this part of Wyoming, we always joke that March comes in like a lamb and out like a lion. February is known for the warm-but-wicked Chinook winds that melt the accumulated snow. I always had to resist the temptation to let down my guard, knowing that winter still had weeks of life left, no matter what the calendar said. March is the month of the heaviest snowfall, and March 1879 proved no different. A blizzard moved in after weeks of mild and balmy weather. Five newly arrived railroad workers had taken their fishing gear in some wagons to Coopers Lake, twenty-seven miles north of Laramie. Caught by the sudden storm, their open tents provided little shelter. Their campfire blew out, and their horses froze to death, tied to the wagons. Only three bodies were ever found; the others must have tried to walk to safety.

~~~~~~~~~~~~~~~~

Over the next six years, the number of livestock on the range far exceeded the record set by buffalo, and they were all turned out on the already overgrazed range to fend for themselves. By May 1887, Swan Land & Cattle had failed. Alexander Swan was out as ranch manager, replaced by John Clay. Out of the 120,000 head they listed in 1884, the spring roundup could only account for 30,000 animals. That season, snow began to fall on September 20, 1886 and continued unabated until January 1887. Then in February, the warm Chinook winds began to blow, melting the accumulated snowfall. The streams quickly became clogged with ice, and the flooding waters spread over the hay meadows inundating the available grasses. Then it froze again, locking all available forage under a sheet of impenetrable ice. Unlike snow, ice does not blow away, and the cattle had nothing to eat.

These conditions resulted in an eighteen-million-dollar loss for British investors in Wyoming that year alone. They said a man could walk from Laramie to Casper, stepping only upon the carcasses of dead livestock. The Oxford Ranch, with its sturdy barns and smart leadership, reported no more than the usual losses.

Winters continued to dog the flagging Wyoming livestock industry, large and small, for the rest of the century. In 1899, one continuous blizzard raged from January 19 through April 15. Small homesteader John Whittaker lost 500 head of cattle. He had over 2,000 tons of hay available, but he could not get the cattle to the hay or the hay to the cattle. His neighbor, William Richardson, lost 100 cows, 30 horses, and 1,100 head of sheep in that same storm. The storm took its toll on livestock and wildlife alike; many antelope suffocated in the blinding snow. A hundred-twenty years later, an unexpected mid-May snowstorm hit the Oxford Ranch. We lost six calves and ended up
~~~~~~~~~~~~~~~~

with five bottle babies when the heifers refused to recognize their half-frozen offspring after we had warmed them up.

~ ~ ~ ~ ~ ~ ~ ~ ~ ~ ~ ~ ~ ~

**Charlie Hutton**'s name will live on as a pioneer rancher on the Laramie Plains and in association with endangered species. Hutton Lake National Wildlife Refuge is located just south of the Hart Ranch. The University of Wyoming has been trying for years to save an endangered species of toad, appropriately called the Wyoming toad. Efforts to breed them in captivity and release them into Hutton Lake, Creighton Lake, and the nearby Mortenson Lake are increasingly successful. The refuge is a popular birding spot from March through October. Despite a barb-wire gate, pedestrian traffic is welcomed as long as people close the gate.

~ ~ ~ ~ ~ ~ ~ ~ ~ ~ ~ ~ ~ ~

# Growing Tasty Beef

The average ranch in Wyoming is about 2,500 acres and markets 100 calves a year. These all go to feedlots for fattening and are slaughtered at two years old. Cattle on feedlots produce excessive methane in part because they are supplemented with corn. Ruminants are not well suited for digesting corn because it is a very "hot" feed, meaning an animal may die if given too much. Toxic gases produced by a proliferation of Escherichia coli in the gut build up, and the overfed animal bloats, dying a painful death.

Feedlots use corn because it forces the steers to put on a lot of weight fast. The excess energy is stored as intramuscular fat, which is what gives a cut of beef its flavor and tenderness. Some breeds, such as American Wagyu, naturally store fat intramuscularly, relieving the necessity to feed corn.

Bovine digestion also produces methane gas, produced in the rumen and released into the atmosphere when cattle regurgitate their "cud" and rechew it. There are measures that stockgrowers can take, such as adding kelp to the diet, to minimize methane production.

~~~~~~~~~~~~~~~~

## *Chapter Eleven*
# J.I. 1867 - John Iliff
### *& the Loving-Goodnight Trail*

(Photo by K. McGuire)

Historically, the short-grass prairie biome is populated by nutritious, lush, and deeply rooted perennial grasses. Due to the unbroken sod, adequate moisture (mainly in the form of snow), and the high elevation, Laramie's grasses were plentiful and unusually high in protein (almost twelve percent), even after curing naturally on the stem. By 1980, higher-producing species, such as smooth brome *(Bromus inermis)*, a true rhizomatous grass native to Europe, replaced the native grasses in the Oxford Ranch's meadow. It thrives where water is abundant and is especially lush just downstream of the septic tank behind the ranch headquarters. It grows well in damp and saline soils and forms a solid mat, choking out undesirable grass species. It is a coarse grass, palatable to cattle but not so much to horses.

We have since replaced the brome with a species known as Garrison's creeping meadow foxtail *(Alopecurus arundina)*. Do not confuse the foxtails. Foxtail barley *(Hordeum jubatum)* is an irritating grass species native to Wyoming. I recently learned that the "bad" foxtail is commonly used in civilized landscaping projects as an ornamental. I can only shake my head and trust that squirrels do not eat grass.

Foxtail barley produces thick, brushy seed awns whose terminal barbs are designed to lodge in the gums of animals unwise enough to eat it. Cattle, horses, and goats will not eat foxtail barley in the field unless it is very young and they are very hungry. After it matures, even hungry cows will avoid it,
~~~~~~~~~~~~~~~~

spitting out the shallow-rooted clumps if accidentally cropped. If they end up in a hay bale, the seed awns can cause chronic wasting when the gums become inflamed due to hundreds of awns stuck in the tender tissue. Affected livestock can quickly lose condition and even die of starvation. Desperate for hay after a dry summer, we once bid on thirty tons of baled hay from a ranch north of Laramie. It was dark when the auction ended, and we knew not what we had purchased. Foxtail contaminated the bales and we fed them, unknowingly, to our cattle and goats. Not only did I have to clean the teeth of 100 cows and 300 goats with a Water Pic, but we also managed to infect our pristine meadow with this horrible grass. To this day we fight foxtail barley.

~~~~~~~~~~~~~~~

The first grass-fed Wyoming beef steer intended for the slaughterhouses of Chicago was weighed as soon as a scale arrived at the railroad stockyards. John Iliff owned the steer and held the lucrative contract to supply beef to the UPRR. Born in 1831 in Ohio, **Iliff** attended Wesleyan University. Upon graduation in 1859, he accepted $500 of seed money from his father and started a mercantile business in Denver. When he had the opportunity to buy a herd of starving cattle cheaply, he sold the business and invested. Iliff had to rest the exhausted animals before he could butcher them and market them to the hungry gold miners in the mountains above Denver. Seven years later, Iliff owned 25,000 cattle, which ran on his numerous scattered ranches in northeastern Colorado. He held title to nearly 16,000 acres of bottomland but controlled two million acres of public ranch land in between. Iliff's ranches covered such a vast area it was almost impossible to keep track of the cattle that stocked them.

But he was always in the cattle market and rode all over northeast Colorado and southeast Wyoming, looking for cattle to buy. I speculate that he stopped in the shade of the Crimson Arch on one trip to inscribe his initials, **J.I. 1867**. I say this because my research yielded few surnames beginning with the letter "I." The only other candidate was James Irwin, an Indian agent in the mid-1870s, too late to be my signator. Iliff was just the sort of man to travel along the Red Buttes route on horseback. The inscription is very early, and I know John Iliff moved to Cheyenne in 1868.

**Iliff** became associated with Texans Charles Goodnight and Oliver Loving (of Goodnight-Loving Trail fame). They got into the cattle marketing business in 1866 quite accidentally. After the end of the Civil War, returning Confederate soldiers found that most of their longhorn cattle had escaped to the wilds of West Texas while they were off fighting the Yankees. Five years' worth of calves and grand calves were with them, all unbranded and,
~~~~~~~~~~~~~~~

therefore, free for the taking. That some might "belong" to a rancher in Mexico or some Mescalero Apaches was immaterial. They literally rode out into the West Texas plain, gathered a herd, and struck out for Wyoming, just like in the novel and associated television series *Lonesome Dove*. But the novel was well-researched. West Texas was a veritable pool of unbranded cattle. Longhorns, descended from the Criollo cattle of Spain (think bull-ring bulls), were notoriously wild, and their meat was stringy and tough. But it was what white men were used to; they never did develop a taste for buffalo meat. The arrival of these "spotted buffalo" on the northern plains was eerily similar to a vision quest had by Plenty Coups of the Apsàalooka tribe. Their appearance was indeed the forbearer of an ancient curse that prophesied the end of Indian civilization.

In 1866, Goodnight and Loving assembled a herd of 2,000 of these wild cattle and drove them first towards Fort Sumner, New Mexico Territory, and then on to Denver. To reach Colorado, the drovers had to cross the feared Llano Estacado or staked plain. As the herd neared Fort Sumner, the US government sutler found them and began to parley. About 8,000 captive Navajo families had been marched across the freezing desert to a temporary reservation called Bosque Redondo, 100 miles south of Albuquerque, New Mexico. The US government suddenly realized they had nothing to feed them, so they bought all the steers in the herd for eight cents per pound (Haley, 1981).

The remaining 800 mother cows were not for sale, so Loving continued north towards Denver. Splitting up, Goodnight returned to Fort Worth with his $1,200 in government gold to put together another herd. As Loving crested Raton Pass in southern Colorado, he encountered a very long chain stretched across the narrow trail. Chain owner Richens Lacey Wootton stopped the herd in its tracks, demanding a ten-cent per head toll for every cow that crossed the line. Loving paid the toll and continued to Denver, where he sold the herd to **John Iliff**, the local cattle dealer. Iliff, in turn, hauled the beef to the hungry mining camps in Leadville and Central City.

The following year, 1867, they repeated the cattle drive. Unfortunately, as the herd was fording the Horsecreek Crossing on the Pecos River, Comanche attacked and scattered the longhorns, delaying their progress. Loving and "One-Armed" Wilson left the group to complete the negotiations with Fort Sumner. Unwisely traveling by day, they skirmished with the Comanche again, and Loving was shot, receiving a wound that should have required the amputation of his leg. Refusing the surgery, he died of gangrene. Unaware of his friend's predicament, Goodnight continued into Denver to sell the herd to Iliff.

In 1868, Goodnight rerouted over Trincheras Pass, bypassing Wootton's toll, delivering the herd straight to Cheyenne. The next year, Loving's remains were exhumed by his friend and relocated to Weatherford, Texas. This sounds eerily similar to *Lonesome Dove*. Charles Goodnight later introduced some buffalo from the depleted Yellowstone herd onto his ranch in the panhandle of Texas. Descendants of these animals now populate the Caprock Canyons State Park and roam freely throughout the park. He died in 1929 at age ninety-three.

But back to the cattle drives. **Iliff** owned the contract to supply the US government with beef for the indigenous peoples confined to the reservations in Wyoming and Dakota. Between 1867 and 1876, Iliff purchased $40,000 worth of cattle each year, a total of 300,000 longhorns. Every year, Charles Goodnight drove a herd of cattle through the streets of Cheyenne and filled the stockyards, where they awaited distribution to the Indian agencies and army outposts. Unfortunately, there's many a slip 'twixt the cup and the lip, as my Cockney grandmother used to say. Indian agents were notorious for siphoning off and reselling US government supplies to the miners or, worse yet, to the reservations, which should have gotten them for free.

Eventually, the Laramie Plains began to produce enough cattle to fill railroad cars en route to Omaha to be trans-shipment to the slaughterhouses of Chicago. All the early Laramie Basin ranchers, **Charley Hutton, Augustus Trabing**, Hi Kelly, Thomas Alsop, and Phil Mandel, shipped their cattle by rail. Thousands of cattle would arrive daily at the Chicago stockyards to await their fate. But **John Iliff** was the accepted "Cattle King of the Northern Plains." Wyoming's first cattle baron died at age forty-six of obstructive jaundice and is buried in an elaborate mausoleum at the Fairmount Cemetery in Denver, Colorado.

~~~~~~~~~~~~~~~
~~~~~~~~~~~~~~~

# The Blue Grass Well

When one of Thomas Alsop's steers was four years old, it weighed 980 pounds. Today's yearling steers weigh at least 1,200 pounds. Alsop also had a steer that was over seven feet tall and weighed over 2,300 pounds. The animal had to graze while standing in riparian washes because his mouth could not reach the ground to crop grass. The press report did not mention how he drank the fifteen gallons of water a day he required.

The only explanation is that he must have had access to the famous Blue Grass Well. This geologic anomaly resulted from a blowout during a glacial interval one million years ago. Subsequently, a pool of clear water formed that was large enough to water thousands of head of livestock simultaneously. Shaped like a perfectly round silver dollar, the Blue Grass Well was 125 feet in diameter and fifteen feet deep. Alsop's steer could have waded in to slake his thirst.

Unfortunately, the creation of the water diversion project that brought Laramie Basin water to Wheatland changed the hydrology of the area, and the Blue Grass Well, once the largest water hole in the world, disappeared forever (Burns et al., 1955).

~ ~ ~ ~ ~ ~ ~ ~ ~ ~ ~ ~ ~ ~ ~ ~

# *Chapter Twelve*
# NICHOLS - '68
## *and the Union Pacific Railroad*

(PHOTO BY K. MCGUIRE)

The railroad dominates the Oxford Horse Ranch today. As I slumber in the ranch house, I can count on hearing a lonesome whistle announce that a train is approaching the Red Buttes crossing. I do not mind. It is reassuring in some ways. That said, the double set of tracks that bisects the ranch uplands present a clear and present danger to my cattle as we drive them over to the summer pasture. The crossing grade is steep and unforgiving, filled with sharp, two-inch crushed rock. My cows have a problem with the tracks; the unfamiliar sights and smells frighten them, just as they frightened the buffalo herds, short-circuiting their migration. We must cover the rails with yards of old carpeting scattered with straw to get them to cross. Their reluctance is frustrating.

Coming back across in the fall is another matter. The old girls know that the fresh-cut hay meadow is waiting for them, and, ignoring the carpet-covered tracks, they rush the gates, trying to get home. It is the calves that are a problem in the fall. They inevitably get separated from mom in the milling herd and end up racing up and down the right-of-way, searching for their mothers who are already hoofing it down to the meadow. One year, an old cow got one set of front hoof cleats stuck between the rail and the crossing decking. It took twenty minutes of prying with a long crowbar to free her. Luckily, she cooperated; had she gone wild, she could have broken some legs, either hers or ours. I am sure the UPRR employee in charge of holding all the trains while this rodeo takes place twice a year is more than amused.

Our interactions with the UPRR are, shall we say, less than satisfactory. In exchange for slicing the ranch in half, Sara Whitehouse signed over forty acres of land in exchange for livestock crossings every three-quarter mile. The crossing never did materialize. Another problem is arranging for UPRR personnel to show up as scheduled to cross the herd. Always, we wait by the gate for the railroad guy to arrive. The 200 milling cows and calves are not happy, and neither are we. Communicating with UPRR officials on any subject is a lengthy exercise in futility. The bureaucracy can be excruciating. It is as if the UPRR is an opaque behemoth that deems it trivial to deal with adjacent landowners on unimportant topics. I should not be surprised; the UPRR was America's first monopoly, and they continue to have that same entitled attitude.

That said, I found the history of the railroad fascinating. After reading through volumes and volumes, I postulated that one of the rock signatories, **_Nichols '68_**, was employed as a surveyor by the UPRR and was killed by Indians near my Crimson Arch. Surveyors were the backbone of the effort to build the railroad. Along with the grading teams, they ranged far ahead of the track builders, beyond the protective guns of the military attachment assigned to protect the rails.

Although H.K. Nichols' diary is housed at the Bancroft Library in San Francisco, I could not access it. I kept looking and found **J. Harvey Nichols**, the Western Union Telegraph operator in Cheyenne. This Mr. Nichols is a much better candidate for my rock as he was responsible for constructing and maintaining the telegraph lines that crisscrossed the region before the railroad came through. Following the route of the original Overland Stage trail across the Black Hills, the telegraph poles came directly through my ranch. I am confident that Mr. Nichols did, too.

Telegraph lines were first installed in 1862 by the Western Union Company. They let it be known that the wires were magical and that Indians were well-advised to leave them alone. This admonition was reinforced one day when a band of braves stole a mile-long section of wire. They were enjoying dragging it along behind their ponies, each holding tightly to the line. Unfortunately for the riders, a thunderstorm blew up suddenly, and a bolt of lightning hit the trailing end of the wire, some distance behind them. The shock dismounted all of the riders. News of this "magic" spread far and wide, temporarily guaranteeing the safety of the telegraph lines. As time passed, the Indians grew wise to this tale and realized that if they cut the line and removed the poles, the army would soon send out a contingent of soldiers to repair it. Their wagons, heavily laden with seventeen-foot-long poles and miles of coiled wire, were an easy target for an ambush. **Nichols** located and reported all problems to the troops at Fort Sanders so troops could repair them.

~ ~ ~ ~ ~ ~ ~ ~ ~ ~ ~ ~ ~ ~

When presidential candidate Abraham Lincoln met with a young surveyor named Granville Dodge in 1859, they discussed the route of a transcontinental railroad west to San Francisco. The public wanted a railroad, and they wanted it yesterday; that much was clear. The telegraph lines across the country were fairly humming with news of far-away gold strikes as well as Indian attacks. Still, the public clamored for more. So, Lincoln traveled by steamship to Council Bluffs, Nebraska Territory, to meet with Dodge. Lincoln and Dodge stood together on the same bluffs that Lewis & Clark might have used to survey the land that stretched endlessly to the west. Lincoln correctly predicted that either Council Bluffs or Omaha would be the hub for the great westward migration. His meeting with Dodge left a great impression on them both.

A newly married Dodge immediately filed on two homesteads adjacent to the Elkhorn River, where he and Lincoln had met. As Dodge staked out his claims, he encountered two ragged, starving men trekking slowly eastward. One turned out to be his great friend and mentor, fellow surveyor Frederick Lander, name sake of Lander, Wyoming. Lander had survived a harrowing surveying trip across Wyoming territory. They were returning to St. Louis on foot, having lost four of the six-man survey crew in Indian fights. After he recovered his composure, Lander looked at Dodge's land and remarked that the railroad would surely pass there. And it did. Dodge sold his property at a tidy profit, even though the railroad was rerouted a year later, leaving his land high and dry.

Early cost estimates to build the railroad varied between one and two million dollars, and hard cash was needed fast. The US government agreed to pay $16,000 per mile across the plains and $48,000 per mile in the mountains. The UP Railroad Corporation was created to meet this demand, the first corporation chartered by the government since 1816. A twin corporation was formed to fund the Central Pacific Railroad (CPRR), which would begin at Sacramento and build eastward to join the UPRR somewhere west of Salt Lake City.

As stipulated by the 1862 Railroad Act, the government loaned the UP and CP the credit of the government, not actual cash. It was more like a thirty-year mortgage bearing six percent interest with the government as the first lien holder. CPRR lobbyist, Collis P. Huntington, secured $200,000 cash immediately when he approached millionaire mining shovel manufacturers Oakes and Oliver Ames, the so-called "Kings of Spades." The UPRR and the CPRR were direct competitors and were not involved with each other financially. However, they both maintained powerful lobbyists in Washington, offering sweet deals to members of Congress and other powerful men to raise money, promising a ninety percent return on their investments. Brigham Young, an early UPRR board member, was the first and only person to buy bonds outright. He paid in full for five shares at $1,000 a share. UP Corporation major shareholders Thomas "Doc" Durant and his partner George Francis Train purchased twenty shares apiece but put up only ten percent in cash.

The builders did not have the time to wait until the land grants could be liquidated to raise cash, so they resorted to other means to raise money. They used the future sale of the land as collateral to raise money, sold US government bonds, and sold stock in their respective corporations. After the CPRR burned through their first million dollars on a very few miles of track above Sacramento, they knew they would need more cash. So, in 1864, Senator John Sherman came through and introduced a revised Railroad Act. Under the new legislation, the dollars per completed mile of track were increased, and the frequency of payment was doubled. Money was paid for every twenty miles of completed track instead of forty.

As an extra incentive, they cushioned the right-of-way width, offering both surface and mineral rights for a twenty-mile swath of all even-numbered sections in every affected township. The price of the stock was also reduced to ten dollars a share. The most significant result of this legislation was to subordinate the US government's position on the mortgaged land. The railroad corporations were now the primary lien holders. For his efforts, John Sherman was paid $20,000 worth of UP shares for "professional services rendered" (Ambrose, 2005). That was the second time the lobbyists got to write the legislation.

Competition between the UPRR and the CPRR provoked gambling joints and market speculators alike to go wild. They gave odds on which would get the farthest the fastest. The pressure to succeed was enormous, and the opportunities for fraud were too great to ignore. After CP lobbyist Huntington secured financing from Ames, he brought in two more investors, Leland Stanford and Charles Crocker. Stanford was the Republican Governor of California, and Crocker was his righthand man. When Stanford became the CEO of the CPRR, he came into conflict with Collis Huntington when Stanford's ego prevented him from making rational decisions. He once signed off on a million-dollar bank draft without bringing it to the board of directors for approval. He lived lavishly on his CPRR expense account, much like Thomas Durant, and rubbed elbows only with the elites of his day. Rules and norms clearly did not apply to this man. When Stanford's young son,

Leland Junior, died from typhus in 1884, the family was touring Egypt. In his anguish, Stanford Senior did not hesitate to divert CPRR funds and resources to endow a small, private educational institution in his memory. The Leland Stanford Junior University is better known today as Stanford. No wonder parts of the campus resemble the Cheyenne, Wyoming train station.

Collis Huntington also enriched himself while employed by CPRR, but he was never sanctioned either. He claimed the CPRR's books detailing the illegal stock transfers were lost when the company offices burned. Implicated in 1883 for bribing congressmen, Huntington became the most hated railroad man in the country. He defended himself saying:

> *The motives back of my actions have been honest ones and results have rebounded far more to the benefit of California than they have to my own* (Ambrose, 2005).

Huntington's wealth was significant and later in life he turned to philanthropy, helping the Rockefeller's establish Colonial Williamsburg, Virginia and a grand museum in Huntington Beach, California. He died in 1900 and is buried in a fabulous mausoleum in The Bronx, NY.

~ ~ ~ ~ ~ ~ ~ ~ ~ ~ ~ ~ ~ ~

When Abraham Lincoln agreed to fund a railroad to California, he enlisted some of the most powerful men in Washington. Besides Durant, he turned to George Francis Train. Mr. Train was an entrepreneur known for "creative" financing. He once traveled around the world in eighty days and is probably the basis for the fictional character Phileas Fogg.

"Doc" Durant judged himself to be the Union Pacific Corporation. Durant was a vicious and vindictive competitor, used to living in the lap of luxury and calling all the shots, no matter how ill-advised. He was given to fits of temper; he once physically attacked a fellow board member during a meeting. When the board tried to dismiss him, he buried them with litigation. Durant and Train had amassed their fortunes by smuggling cotton out of a blockaded American South. Both used their ill-gotten wealth to buy most of the Union Pacific Corporation stock when shares were first issued and became the controlling stockholders.

Even with surveyors risking their lives to survey the route and grading crews working around the clock, progress was slow. In 1865, only forty miles of track was laid by the UPRR. The CPRR was way ahead, having begun work eleven months earlier. Special trains ran on those forty miles of UPRR track west from Omaha at the fantastic speed of thirty-five miles per hour. At Durant's invitation and expense, congressional junkets enjoyed dining cars serving raw oysters, lobster, fresh vegetables, confections, and libations of all stripes. The Congress members were all duly impressed with the railroad's progress, and they authorized an additional $640,000 worth of bonds as soon as they returned to Washington. In exchange, they received free, lifetime, unlimited family railroad passes.

Meanwhile, the flooding Missouri River, the shortage of usable timber for ties, and the lack of manpower vexed General Dodge's efforts to move forward. So far, Indians had left them alone because heavily armed soldiers protected the surveying and grading crews. When Dodge made his final report to UPRR, he decided to route the railroad up and over the Gangplank from today's Cheyenne to Laramie. The track would not run south through Denver or Santa Fe nor north through Casper.

The winter of 1865-66 was locally severe. In April, rains and floods washed away twenty miles of track west of Omaha, half a year's progress. Faced with financial ruin, UP Corporation financiers Train and Durant sought a way to limit their liabilities. They quietly paid $50,000 for an obscure Pennsylvania corporation called Pennsylvania Fiscal Agency and renamed it Credit Mobilier. Credit Mobilier became UP's construction company and, as such, was in a better position to attract investors. They were able to sell shares in the new shell corporation to themselves and to their friends. Ben Holliday, the owner of the Overland Stage Company and holder of the lucrative US Mail delivery contract, bought $100,000 worth, Train held $150,000 worth, and Durant, $300,000 worth. America's first trust was born.

Oakes Ames solicited subscriptions to the highly lucrative Credit Mobilier from his fellow members of Congress. Eventually, the Ames brothers and their friends owned over half of Credit Mobilier's 25,000 shares. Durant owned only 6,000 shares and was held in increasing disfavor as he manipulated the stock market using insider trading. When Congress finally investigated him for violating the 1862 Railroad Act, Durant was convicted and fined, effectively a slap on the wrist.

On June 4, 1866, the tracks reached the 100-mile point in eastern Nebraska. Three-quarters of a mile of track had been laid each day since spring. In late July, General Dodge invited retired Brevet General John Casement and his brother, Daniel, to help with the railroad construction. John, called Captain Jack by his workers, ran the grading crews while Daniel financed the project. Together, they increased the rate to one-and-a-half miles per day.

A total of 153 miles of track was completed that year. Workers were paid two-fifty to four dollars per day, depending upon their task; room-and-board was five dollars a week. When the race to meet the CPRR was at its peak, over

7,000 graders labored in the hot sun. The only important factor was speed. Fine sand was used to ballast the ties instead of crushed rock, softwoods such as cottonwoods were "Burnettized" (their water replaced by zinc in a pressure chamber to make them last longer), and the rails were minimally spiked to allow the slow passage of the supply trains. The Eastern press sensationalized the progress as the two railroads labored towards each other.

By the fall of 1866, the UPRR had laid almost 300 miles of track. Durant and the Ames brothers were continually bickering over the excess spending Durant had authorized. Train regularly charged the corporation $4,000 every time he traveled from Omaha to Washington. As a gift to President Lincoln, Durant built a luxurious Pullman car with expensive paneling and fixtures. It was finished in time to transport Abraham Lincoln's coffin to Springfield, Illinois, after which Durant quickly converted the car to his personal use. Durant continued interfering with the railroad's route, ordering changes in Dodge's absence that benefitted him or his cronies. Dodge was tired of changing it back.

As the Ames brothers worked to take over operations, they managed to remove Durant from every official position in Credit Mobilier. Nevertheless, Durant continued with the Union Pacific Corporation. He knew that when the amount of the US government loan jumped from $16,000 per mile (across the plains) to $48,000 per mile (through the mountains), the value of UP stock would soar, and bond sales would increase. So, Durant worked around the clock to advance the completed tracks across Nebraska's high plains.

In the last six months of 1866, $3.8 million worth of UPRR bonds had been sold. The US government accepted 240 miles of track at $16,000 per mile, which equaled $8.1 million in loaned US government bonds. In 1867, the UPRR's construction company made over two million dollars in profit, and Credit Mobilier paid its first dividend. Each block of ten shares got $600 of the first mortgage bond money and six additional shares of UP stock. The return totaled seventy-five percent on the original investment. Train, Durant, and Oakes had gotten nine United States congressmen and two senators to accept stock as "gifts," some 160 shares. Everyone was happy!

After the Civil War, *Harper's Weekly* reported that prewar American railroads actually cost $40,000 a mile to construct. The UPRR was paid in bonds that yielded six percent interest biannually and land grants valued at a dollar and quarter an acre. Compare this to $100,000 a mile in England and $170,000 a mile in France during the same time frame in Europe. American ingenuity had conquered the West, but today's European trains can run at high speeds on the original rail beds. American trains cannot although roadbeds have been rebuilt multiple times.

~ ~ ~ ~ ~ ~ ~ ~ ~ ~ ~ ~ ~ ~

The logistics of supplying the transcontinental railroad were mindboggling. As the rails advanced, the survey crews worked farther and farther out ahead of the main workforce into increasingly dangerous country. Dodge, a surveyor himself, depended upon his crew's skill to locate the grade before work could begin. With ever an eye for opportunity, Dodge began selling lots cut from the land he homesteaded back in 1860 near Council Bluffs, Nebraska.

In the spring of 1868, workers labored at a fevered pitch. After a very long, cold winter, survey crews were repeatedly attacked, and their stakes pulled out by marauding Arapahoe. Deep snow drifts filled the previous years' crudely graded cuts. Two of Dodge's survey crew chiefs were discovered and killed by Sioux near Bridger's Pass in central Wyoming, the leading edge of the mammoth project. One, Robert Brown, was Dodge's good friend and chief surveyor; Dodge stepped in to fill his shoes.

Ahead of the tracks was the highest point on the route (more than 8,600 feet in elevation), the imposing Sherman Hill. The ascent up the Gangplank went quickly, but waiting at the top was Dale Creek. This obscure, meandering waterway was barely a trickle in the fall, frozen solid in the winter, and a stream capable of watering a passing herd of buffalo in the summer. However, in springtime, torrents of water coursed down the watershed. The rails could follow a route that Silas Seymour, assistant chief engineer to Dodge, proposed. Durant supported Seymour, but it meant crossing five separate Dale Creek tributaries.

General Dodge had another idea: build one grand bridge instead of five smaller ones. The descent from the summit was easy once the creek was bridged, and time was of the essence as the CPRR pushed eastward. All he needed was one bridge. More than two miles of solid granite had to be removed to form the eastern approach and the western egress to the bridge. The span would be 750 feet long and 127 feet high, soaring above the waters of Dale Creek. It was built of prefabricated Howe trusses manufactured in Chicago and shipped west on special train cars. Each truss was made from twelve-by-twelve lumber and was forty feet long. Once on-site, they were hoisted into place using miles of cables and heavy pulleys. A new town called Dale City came into being in the valley below the bridge site. Six hundred workers called the rambling sprawl of tents, cabins, and stone outbuildings home for thirty tumultuous days. It took only a month to build the most significant engineering marvel of the 19th century. At 8,200 feet above sea level, it was the highest and longest bridge on the entire railroad and, for a while, in the world.

DALE CREEK BRIDGE
(AMERICAN HERITAGE & GOOGLE MAPS)

The Dale Creek bridge proved so rickety that it was rebuilt in 1872 and replaced entirely with steel trusses in 1876. The brakemen, who ran nimbly along the roofs of the cars to apply the brakes, could not keep their balance as the bridge swayed beneath the weight of passing trains, even at a stately pace of only four miles per hour. Many brakemen fell to their deaths or dismemberment. The bridge was abandoned in 1901. Only the solid concrete footers mark the spot.

Today, near a windswept stretch of Interstate 80, west of Cheyenne, just before the road descends Sherman Hill into Laramie, a lonely pyramid stands off by itself. Completed in 1882 and designed by the famous architect H.H. Richardson, it is nevertheless dedicated to the contributions made by Oliver and Oakes Ames. It is an impressive reminder of these brothers' monumental effort and personal expenditure to build the railroad. Without them, the project would have been delayed a decade. With them, America prospered. In a classic case of the ends justifying the means, Oakes Ames was eventually censured by Congress for gifting stock to willing members. After they both were implicated in the massive fraud surrounding the railroad building, Oliver died bankrupt but not disgraced; ask anyone from Ames, Massachusetts, or Ames, Iowa. Oakes Ames returned home to Massachusetts, where he died of a stroke in 1873.

In July 1868, eleven generals and Doc Durant met at Fort Sanders, Wyoming. Future president Grant was campaigning for election throughout the West; Generals Sherman and Sheridan accompanied him on the campaign trail. Generals Harney, Kautz, Dent, Slemmer, and Potter, who were in the area, are also immortalized in the group photo taken at the meeting's conclusion. General Grant had taken a fast stage from Salt Lake and arrived in time for lunch.

During the meeting, Durant questioned Dodge's capability to continue as Chief Engineer. Dodge was still heavily involved in surveying the line because of the death of surveyor Robert Brown. Durant asserted that Dodge was wasting time and money, routing the tracks badly, and that his duties as Chief Engineer should go to someone who could devote himself entirely to the job. Grant heard him out and then looked around the room.

He said,

> *The US government expects General Dodge to continue as Chief Engineer* (Homsher, 1965).

The meeting ended, and the work to build the transcontinental railroad continued.

By December 1868, the UPRR had run up $10 million in debt, primarily to its number one contractor, Credit Mobilier. On the other hand, Credit Mobilier had paid out $3 million in dividends to its stockholders that month alone. The total dividends paid in 1868 was $12.8 million in cash and $4 million in UP stock at $100 a share. Total dividends paid since December 1866 were $28.8 million. The subscribed congress members were pleased.

~~~~~~~~~~~~~~~~

**Harvey Nichols** played only a minor role in the taming the continent. His constant attention to the telegraph wires and their critical messages allowed troops to be deployed to stem Indian attacks. Each cavalry movement included
~~~~~~~~~~~~~~~~

a contingent of wagons loaded with telegraph poles and wires. Even during the Battle of the Little Bighorn, Custer's rear commanders were in telegraph contact with General Crook. Telegraph communications enabled the army to track Crazy Horse's movements and keep him on the run throughout 1877.

After the Indian Wars ended, Harvey **Nichols** retired from Western Union and started a life insurance business. He represented the Equitable Company; advertising in the local Cheyenne newspapers claimed the company had $7 million in assets. He encouraged readers to secure the future of their loved ones should something unforeseen happen to them. The West was changing fast, and Nichols was on the cusp of development until his death in 1895. He is buried in Indiana.

~~~~~~~~~~~~~~
~~~~~~~~~~~~~~

# Public Land For Sale?

Utah's Sandy Ranch, near Capital Reef, owns 7,000 acres, and runs 1,000 head of cattle. The desert has a carrying capacity of 100 acres per head, so that is not enough land. The ranch survives because they lease 242,000 acres from the US government. Without those leases, the ranch could not run enough cows to make a profit. If the Sandy Ranch ever sells, the price paid per acre would be multiplied by 249,000 acres, not 7,000.

The cost to graze these public lands has just been reduced to a mere $1.35 per unit per month. Compared to the cost of private leases (about $10 to $15 per unit per month) that is quite the bargain. Is the continuation of this grazing subsidy used as a bargaining chip when a Western Congressman's vote is needed on a more significant issue?

You betcha!

~ ~ ~ ~ ~ ~ ~ ~ ~ ~ ~ ~ ~ ~ ~

*Chapter Thirteen*

# L.P. BRADLEY - 1871

*& the Death of Crazy Horse*

NOTE THE SCAR FROM AN APPARENT BULLET RICOCHET.
(PHOTO BY K. MCGUIRE)

I always felt a particular connection with the inscription of L.P. Bradley. His is the most carefully excised inscription on the rock. His letters are measured and precise. He knew he was leaving evidence of his passing and he wanted to ensure his legacy was neat. The future Fort Sanders commander, **Luther P. Bradley**, was born in Connecticut in 1822. He volunteered for the Civil War and received a commission as a lieutenant colonel in the 51st Illinois Infantry. Bradley was wounded at Nashville and was decorated for valor. He served with distinction at Chickamauga along Missionary Ridge. Under fire, his troops reversed formation and engaged the advancing Confederates in heavy hand-to-hand combat. Bradley made an orderly retreat and was brevetted to brigadier general for his courage. The Confederates won the battle but they were so bloodied by Bradley's orderly withdrawal that they could not defend Atlanta when Sherman regrouped. Sherman marched into the city with Bradley by his side and burned it.

After the war, Bradley resigned his commission and enlisted in the regular army with the rank of lieutenant colonel. He marched into sacred Sioux hunting grounds under Colonel Henry Carrington, with Major Jim Bridger as their guide. Their charge was to build a chain of three forts to guard the Bozeman Trail, an

LP BRADLEY
(WIKIPEDIA)

86

illegal route from Cheyenne to Montana's goldfields. The trail cut directly across Sioux Treaty lands, dangerously close to the revered Medicine Wheel near present-day Lovell, Wyoming. The Medicine Wheel was built above timber line and dates at least from 1100 AD. It consists of a central stone cairn surrounded by a stone ring. It has astrological significance in the celebration of the summer solstice as well as the rising of significant stars Sirius, Aldebaran, and Rigel. Other similar complexes date from 3200 BC. Red Cloud, the leader of the tribes, was furious.

Bradley was second in command at the new Fort Phil Kearney, near present-day Buffalo, Wyoming. That winter, Captain John Fetterman responded to a Sioux attack on wood-cutters near the fort. Crazy Horse led a small band of decoys over the low hills north of the fort, tempting Fetterman to disobey orders and pursue him. Fetterman and eighty other troops were killed after riding directly into the middle of thousands of hidden warriors. This action prompted "Portugee" Phillip's 286-mile ride to Fort Laramie to ask for reinforcements.

In July 1867, Bradley was promoted to colonel and took command of Fort C.F. Smith, Montana territory. There, he took delivery of modern, breech-loading Spencer rifles. Instead of firing three shots a minute, they could get off ten shots in a minute. In theory, the bullets would be better aimed as the rifle was lighter. This advanced military technology allowed the troops to repel the increasing attacks more effectively, even when surrounded and outnumbered. And that was happening with increasing frequency.

On the morning of August 1, 1867, at least one thousand Sioux warriors from the inter-mixed encampment on the nearby Little Big Horn River engaged a hay-cutting contingent from Fort Smith and their military escort. Later known as the Wagon Box Fight, twelve civilians and twenty soldiers retreated, sheltering behind fourteen abandoned wagon boxes. They were armed with the new Spencer repeating rifles. The wet-behind-the-ears lieutenant in command felt it was undignified for army men to fire from a prone position. Unaware the Indians had a few rifles, the lieutenant was standing, arguing his point, when a sniper felled him.

A more practical civilian took command as wave after wave of attackers stormed their position. Withering fire from the Spencer rifles repeatedly repelled them. The fight continued for six-and-a-half hours, out of earshot and sight of Fort Smith. Although Colonel Bradley was aware of the situation, inexplicably he did not send a relief column until later that afternoon. By then, three soldiers were dead (including the proud lieutenant), and two were wounded. One report claimed that 400 dead bodies surrounded them, although other estimates vary.

The Wagon Box Fight closely resembled the Hayfield Fight, which occurred the next day outside Fort Phil Kearney. Colonel Carrington was the fort commander. The armed guards and the lumbering wagons of the woodcutting crew were strung out along the trail returning to the fort when attacked. Many made it to the fort while others sought refuge in a corral; several were caught in the open and died. According to some reports, the attackers lost about 150 braves that day. As a result of these engagements, Red Cloud grew alarmed about the change in armaments.

Both colonels came under critical official review from Commanding General William Crook for their conduct. Officially, the failure to mount a relief column resulted in unnecessary deaths. But Crook's hands were full directing America's ultimate solution for her indigenous peoples. He felt this was not a reason enough to blemish the otherwise outstanding record of **L.P. Bradley**. After the inquiry, Bradley wrote to his fiancée. He questioned why the Indians

> *...would give up the best hunting ground they have. I do not see that we need it for ten or twenty years at least. So for the sake of the economy, if not for the sake of humanity, it were better to withdraw even our own pride* (Cozzens, 2018).

After two more years of fighting, General Crook pulled Colonel Bradley off the front lines. He was engaged to be married and needed some time off. In April 1869 he became the commanding officer of Fort D.A. Russell near present-day Cheyenne, Wyoming. Fort Russell was solidly constructed from red brick, probably manufactured on-site, and is surrounded today by F.E. Warren Strategic Air Command. The brick barns were capable of housing hundreds of horses. After living in the wilds of the Powder River Basin, this seemed like heaven to the Colonel. Joined by his new wife, they lived a relatively normal life.

Bradley was in charge for three months until two companies of the Ninth Infantry, headquarters staff, and band arrived from California to relieve him. Bradley remained on staff. On April 1, 1871, the Colonel assumed command of Fort Sanders, just north of the little Crimson Arch near Laramie, Wyoming. Laramie was not Cheyenne; Fort Sanders was built of manure-chinked rough logs, although the commanding officer's quarters were well-finished and equipped with wood stoves. Mss. Bradley, with their son, chose to live in Colorado Springs.

Fort Sanders was Bradley's home for the next eighteen months. He served as commanding officer and was responsible for 140 men. The enlisted man's pay was less than fifty cents per day. Out of that, each man had to buy his uniforms, underwear, and boots. The enlisted men's quarters were built along the south boundary of the fort near Soldier Springs Creek. Each cabin had a plank door opening onto the parade grounds. Unfortunately, opening that door would fill the room with icy, wind-whipped snow. Each troop was issued a thin woolen blanket and slept on a rough plank shelf cushioned by a lumpy, fur-ticked mattress, fourteen to a cabin. Each cabin had three small tin pot stoves to ward off the bone-chilling cold. Across the parade grounds, the officer's quarters were considerably more comfortable. Their doors opened away from the prevailing wind.

There was no running water for the troops. The outhouses were out the back and down the slope along the banks of Soldier Springs Creek. The creek was also the only place to bathe unless soldiers could get into town, where a bath might cost a week's pay. Morning muster was at 0600, and the troops assembled on the parade grounds in all weather to march about until dismissed. The food consisted of hard biscuits and salt pork augmented in the summer by a sparse selection of cold weather vegetables, such as onions, which the men grew themselves in the wet area south of the armory, downstream of the privy.

Payday was every three months, depending on the weather and the intensity of Indian raids along the Overland Trail. Laramie City was close and featured many popular attractions. Boarding houses featured beer saloons on the first floor. Soiled doves were available upstairs, as were a selection of more potent alcoholic beverages, mostly grain alcohol cut with a variety of toxic substances. A typical concoction consisted of one part grain alcohol, one part water, a stick of tobacco, and a dash of hot pepper sauce. All were designed to separate the trooper from his pay quickly.

As soon as Colonel Bradley assumed command in 1871, the military reservation was increased from nine to eighty-one square miles by order of the Department of the Army. Bradley spent much of the summer of 1871 overseeing the construction of the new reservation boundary; rock cairns and fences were erected along the new line at regular intervals. The southern boundary of Fort Sanders ran along the border with Arthur Stoke's new ranch, the future headquarters of the Oxford Horse Ranch.

Bradley must have spent considerable time resting in the shade of the Crimson Arch. From there, he supervised his men working along the ridge line, half a mile to the north. His initials are carved deeply, and he used lowercase, rounded letters for his last name. Curves are very hard to cut into the solid rock, but Bradley did an admirable job.

Eighty men deserted their posts that first winter, 1871-72, one of the more bitter on record. Fort Sanders recorded sixty-three inches of snow that winter and temperatures regularly reached negative twenty-five degrees Fahrenheit in January. Livestock carcasses littered the plains. One officer and three enlisted men died from disease, one soldier froze to death, and one officer committed suicide. No one was wounded in battle or skirmishes with Indians.

Fort Sander's troops under Bradley's command had but one fight; LaBonte Creek on May 2, 1872. The natives had become rather bold in stealing horses along the eastern foothills of the Laramie Range. In one raid, the brother of rock signatory **John Hunton** was killed, and fourteen horses were stolen. Hunton later applied for and received government compensation, as stipulated by the Treaty of 1868, for his dead brother's loss of livestock.

~~~~~~~~~~~~~~~

After L.P. Bradley completed his elaborate signature on my Crimson Rock, he left the Laramie Plains. By December 1872, he was serving once again at dangerous outposts in Wyoming and Montana. Small bands of "insurgents" who refused to take up residence on the reservations were being hunted by the US government in a concerted effort to end the "Indian Problem." After five years, Bradley became commandant of Fort Robinson, a small post in far northwestern Nebraska. From there, he monitored the chaos of the aftermath of General Custer's spectacular defeat.

Also referred to as Custer's Last Stand, this was Sitting Bull and Crazy Horse's most glorious victory. Five of the US Seventh Cavalry's twelve companies were annihilated. Custer was killed along with two of his brothers, his brother-in-law, and a nephew. The US casualty count was 274 dead with forty-nine severely wounded. About thirty Indians died. This debacle accounted for twenty percent of all US troop losses during this time. In the fifteen years of the Indian Wars on the northern plains, about 3,000 settlers were killed, and some 1,200 troops died. Estimates of Indian losses range from 45,000 to 70,000, from both disease and warfare.

Custer's defeat was the last straw. Central Command in St. Louis feared that the reservation tribes would rebel and try to join their victorious brothers. Commanding General Pope ordered General George Crook to stop at Fort Robinson and meet with the Oglala leadership. When Crook heard incorrectly that Crazy Horse intended to kill him, he unilaterally canceled the upcoming council and ordered Crazy Horse's arrest. Crook then departed, leaving the
~~~~~~~~~~~~~~~

military action to Colonel Bradley. Additional troops were brought in from Fort Laramie for the final assault.

On the morning of September 4, 1877, two columns of Bradley's men moved against the Sioux village only to find it abandoned. The starving Sioux had fled north towards the Spotted Tail Agency led by Crazy Horse and his sick wife. If they were going to die, they would do it as close to home as possible. Intercepted by the troops near Camp Sheridan, an exhausted Crazy Horse and his entire band agreed to return to Fort Robinson with Lieutenant Jesse M. Lee, the Indian agent at the Spotted Tail Agency, and a Cheyenne chief called Little Big Man.

After surrendering, Crazy Horse intended to ask Colonel Bradley for permission to live on the Brulé Sioux reservation instead of with the Oglala. Bradley avoided confrontation, offering through his adjutant a place to rest. Crazy Horse did not realilze that he was under arrest.

Bradley's official report states that Crazy Horse was escorted to the jailhouse at Fort Robinson by a soldier and Little Big Man. As the adjutant paused to unlock the door, Crazy Horse realized he was betrayed and attempted to escape. The soldier stabbed at him with a mounted bayonet. It goes on to say that Crazy Horse died several hours later in the arms of the army doctor, Valentine McGillicuddy.

There is another account of Crazy Horse's death based on an interview with Little Big Man, which took place over a year after the event. Little Big Man's description is summarized:

> *As Crazy Horse was being escorted to the guardhouse, he suddenly pulled two knives from under his blanket and held one in each hand. One knife was fashioned from an army bayonet. Little Big Man, standing behind him, seized Crazy Horse by both elbows, pulling his arms up behind him. As Crazy Horse struggled, Little Big Man lost his grip on one elbow and Crazy Horse drove his own knife deep into his own lower back* (Cozzens, 2018).

Crazy Horse fell, mortally wounded; it took him several hours to bleed to death. Little Big Man confirmed that the guard had indeed thrust with his bayonet, but that action missed entirely. The blade embedded instead in the frame of the guardhouse door. As they waited for Crazy Horse to die, Colonel Bradley suggested altering the story to conceal Little Big Man's role in Crazy Horse's death, thus avoiding any potential inter-clan reprisals.

Whatever the truth, that fateful night marked the end for his tribe as free-ranging citizens of the earth. When the news of Crazy Horse's death was announced to the waiting tribe members the following day, an eerie silence fell over the armed and mounted warriors. Without a sound, they turned and rode out of the compound. Bradley buried Crazy Horse on the parade grounds of today's Fort Robinson, and a stone monument marks the grave.

Contrary to popular opinion, Crazy Horse was neither a chieftain nor a sub-chief. His immense popularity was because he had never once been wounded in battle. This extraordinary record for a mature Sioux warrior convinced those around him that he was protected. They secretly hoped some of that protection would rub off as Crazy Horse led them into battle.

Like many male Native American youth, young "Curly" (his youthful nickname) had gone upon the high buttes of central Wyoming to seek a vision. This was the only way to transition to warrior status. But Crazy Horse was more than a warrior. He befriended Jim Bridger, Wyoming's pre-eminent mountain man and Indian scout. He had helped massacre Custer, Fetterman, and Collins. Although Crazy Horse and Chiefs Washakie, Spotted Tail, and Sitting Bull could have been the white man's best hope of preventing the impending genocide, their council was never sought. Indigenous people had been deceived, cheated, and hunted like animals. Crazy Horse watched his people's traditional culture collapse into a burning circle of misery. I can only imagine his tears falling as he died, a man weeping for his people and their lost way of life.

~~~~~~~~~~~~~~~

Ten years before Crazy Horse's death, Wisconsin Senator James Doolittle released the findings of his Committee on Indian Affairs. Rabid press reports vividly describing the various massacres and military actions in the West had raised public awareness, and they wanted answers. The report caused a firestorm of controversy regarding the beleaguered Andrew Johnson administration's management of the war effort. As impeachment proceedings against President Johnson began, the generals in charge (Grant, Sherman, and Sheridan) continued prosecuting the war effort as they saw fit.

The Doolittle Report concluded that most Indian hostilities were due to white provocations. Also, suffering among the native populations was due to disease, loss of suitable hunting grounds, and alcoholism. The report launched a peace initiative in Congress that flatly contradicted the efforts of the War Department. Additionally, a Congressional commission formed to investigate the Fetterman Massacre in 1866 concluded that:

- The Northern Plains tribes wanted peace.
~~~~~~~~~~~~~~~

- The Bozeman Trail and the three forts erected to protect trespassing gold-seekers should be immediately abandoned.

- Military operations should be confined to protecting emigrant trails along the Platte and Sweetwater Rivers.

- Parts of the Missouri River Basin, including the entire Yellowstone Basin and the Powder River Basin, should be set aside exclusively for Indian occupation.

Immediately, there was a loud public outcry for a final, peaceful solution to Indian War. The Congressional response was the Taylor Peace Commission. The new commission was to negotiate an end to the hostilities once and for all. The resulting Medicine Lodge Creek Treaty (signed in October 1867) and the Fort Laramie Treaty (signed the following April) guaranteed the six major Indian groups (the Arapahoe, Cheyenne, Blackfoot, Crow, Sioux, and Shoshone) annual annuities, schools, agricultural education, and support. Red Cloud, suspicious of this new overture, decided to wait to sign the treaty until he determined if the whites might uphold their end this time. They did not.

~ ~ ~ ~ ~ ~ ~ ~ ~ ~ ~ ~ ~ ~ ~

Bradley remained in the regular army for another nine years, crisscrossing the Powder River Basin. In 1878, his orders marched him north to the Little Missouri River. His commanders felt the upcoming total solar eclipse was bound to rile up the Indians, so Bradley was sent to be sure they remained on their reservations.

Thomas Edison was also in Wyoming for the celestial event. He set up his newly invented tasometer to measure the distance to the sun from the top of Battle Mountain. Fishing for his dinner in Battle Lake, a sudden thunderstorm temporarily trapped Edison on the lakeshore. Lightning fell all around him, electrifying the air, the lake surface, the trees; even the ragged fibers of his bamboo fishing pole vibrated with electricity. A certain candidate for a eureka moment, Edison realized that non-metal fibers conduct electricity. He returned to his Menlo Park, New Jersey, workshop and later replaced the metallic filament in his newly invented but stubbornly short-lived electric light bulb. It worked, and the mass production of light bulbs swung into action.

Bradley retired on December 8, 1886, his 64th birthday. He had served all over Wyoming but was not popular among his troops. He was considered reckless and pompous, too willing to send soldiers riding to their deaths. Pamphleteer Hiram Latham, a well-known propagandist for Wyoming statehood, considered him a wise counselor. He solicited Bradley's written testimony and published it in 1886. Bradley regaled the possibilities of ranching in the soon-to-be state. Much of his testimony is misinformation when applied to conditions in Wyoming.

Nevertheless, many Wyoming towns, including Laramie, have streets named for him. Bradley retired with the rank of Colonel, Thirteenth United States Infantry, and moved to Oregon Territory to start a ranch. He lived there until he died at the ripe old age of eighty-seven. He is buried at Arlington National Cemetery in Washington.

~~~~~~~~~~~~~~
~~~~~~~~~~~~~~

# Crazy Horse

The following is a recollection by Black Elk, Sioux chieftain and Crazy Horse's cousin, regarding Crazy Horse's vision quest:

When I was a man, my father told me something about that [Crazy Horse's] vision. Of course, he did not know all of it; but he said that Crazy Horse dreamed and went into the world where there is nothing but the spirits of all things. That is the real world that is behind this one, and everything we see here is something like a shadow from that world. He was on his horse in that world, and the horse & himself on it and the trees & the grass & the stones & everything were made of spirit, and nothing was hard, and everything seemed to float. His horse was standing still there, and yet it danced around like a horse made only of shadow, and that is how he got his name, which does not mean that his horse was crazy or wild, but that in his vision it danced around in that queer way.

It was this vision that gave him his great power, for when he went into a fight, he had only to think of that world to be in it again, so that he could go through anything and not be hurt. Until he was killed at the Soldiers' Town on White River, he was wounded only twice, once by accident and both times by someone of his own people he was not expecting trouble and was not thinking; never by an enemy (Cozzens, 2018).

~ ~ ~ ~ ~ ~ ~ ~ ~ ~ ~ ~ ~ ~ ~

## *Chapter Fourteen*
# MCB 1875 - JUDGE BROWN
### *& the Early History of Laramie*

Sometimes, when I want to cross the tracks, a coal train is rumbling past, clashing, groaning, delaying my passage. While waiting one day for the southbound train to complete the long, uphill pull, I noticed that the ground for a quarter-mile on both sides of the tracks was black. Coal particles blown from passing coal cars had aggregated with coal ash from the belching steam engines of yesteryear. I would later discover that what looks like two parallel roads on both sides of the tracks were originally fire breaks. The railroad's intent was to prevent fires along the tracks at all costs, a policy that led directly to the founding of the US Forest Service with its no-burn policy.

I can imagine a burly engineer, his head stuck out of the open cab of a chuffing locomotive, cheeks black with coal ash. "More coal," he calls, more power to mount the crest of the Laramie Range. In my mind, I can smell the cloud of steam released in a hissing rush. I turn just as the alpenglow lights up the slope behind me, and my heart fills with joy. Then, I carefully read the familiar sign at the railroad crossing:

PRIVATE PROPERTY
NO TRESPASSING
Right to Pass by Permission
Subject to Control of Owner

What on earth does that mean? Aren't I the owner? Talk about reading the fine print!

The only way to resolve the conflict was to visit the historic Albany County Courthouse in Laramie. All the title information exists in a set of dusty old ledgers within the real estate office, hidden away on the second floor of the grand old stone building. The ladies staffing the desk there were tremendously helpful. I looked for the earliest volumes and pulled out a thick, heavy ledger. A quick search revealed that the first person recorded as the owner of this particular section of land was Judge **W.C. Brown**. Brown had filed on the section in 1871 and must have discovered the nearby Crimson Arch. He carved his initials and the year MCB 1875 into the hard stone surface.

Brown was elected mayor of Laramie on May 2, 1868, the summer the railroad came through. In the two weeks before the election, 400 lots sold in Laramie. After the tracks departed, 500 structures were erected using the suddenly available dimensional lumber that arrived weekly at the depot. The mayor's salary, $400 per year, was paid by the downtown businessmen he and the sheriff pledged to protect.

Unfortunately, most downtown businesses were run by outlaws, specifically Steve Long and his half-brothers Ace and Con Moyer Moore. Long gunned down at least thirteen men in gunfights, fights that he incited with the idea of robbing his victims before the smoke cleared. The brothers ran profitable brothels with names like Bucket of Blood, Diana, Blue Front Saloon, and most of the breweries. They refused to pay a cent of tax, so Judge Brown and the other elected officials resigned three weeks after the election. Judge Brown published the following announcement in the *Frontier Index:*

> *To the People of Laramie City:*
>
> *In consideration of the fact of the incompetency of many of the officers elected on the 2d [sic] of May, A.D. 1868, in conjunction with myself, and the incapacity & laxity of said officers in the discharge of their duties, I find it impossible for me to administer the city government in accordance with my views of the necessity of the case, and therefore thanking the people of Laramie for honoring me with the highest position in their gift, and for their co-operation and all in the somewhat difficult administration of a provincial city government, I respectfully tender my resignation.*
>
> *I am very Respectfully, your obedient servant,*
>
> *M.C. Brown, Laramie City, June 12, 1868*

That statement must be among the longest run-on sentences ever constructed. It is unclear why his fellow officers were held in such low esteem, but the lack of a paid salary must have influenced Brown's decision to resign. Laramie City's Front Street was wide open to gambling, prostitution, public drunkenness, pistol play, graft, corruption, extortion, and murder. Meanwhile, the respectable people of Laramie began building homes, churches, banks, and civic offices, sometimes encountering bodies of unfortunate drifters buried in shallow graves. The remains were quietly removed to the potter's field, which later became the Greenhill Cemetery, along with scores of others. The official accounting of their names is incomplete.

Downtown Laramie sidewalks today offer a charming, friendly walk through time. Replace the cars with horse-drawn buggies and the scene could be in the century before last. It has retained its frontier-town style, minus the frequent gunplay that punctuated the evening air. Now called First Street, the former Front Street still fronts the tracks. Today's locomotive engineers thrill at their ability to deafen everyone along the block by leaning on their train whistle as they thunder past. Back in **M.C. Brown's** day, most Front Street businesses were legal brothels. My son-in-law purchased an architectural gem of that era a few years ago, so I felt compelled to research the history of that building.

Christened "the Tivoli," the foundation was built by the Bath brothers, German stonemasons. In that basement, Sheriff Nathaniel K. Boswell gathered the respectable businessmen of Laramie, including Judge Brown, to plot the arrest of the three outlaw brothers. On October 18, 1868, Steve "Big Nose" Long attempted to rob an itinerant prospector named Rollie "Hard Luck" Harrison. Goaded by insults, Harrison drew his pistol, and a shoot-out commenced. Long was wounded, and Harrison was killed.

Later that day, Sheriff Boswell activated his posse to take Long into custody. The plan was poorly executed and resulted in a wild exchange of gunfire up and down Laramie's Front Street. The wounded Long was eventually apprehended and was hung alongside his brothers inside a cabin under construction near his Blue Front Saloon. Long asked to be hung barefoot so his mother's prediction that her sons would die with their boots on would not be realized.

The Tivoli was eventually rebuilt as a hotel with a first-floor saloon and eight tiny bedrooms to rent upstairs. It also served as a gaming house and a legitimate boarding house. During the heyday of the Oxford Horse Ranch, an import shop two blocks from the Tivoli claimed to be licensed to the Queen of England, as contended by proprietor Peter Holt. Mss. Whitehouse indeed shopped there for confections from the home country suitable for her English guests. While excavating the new leach field at the ranch, I unearthed old jars that once held marmalade, laxatives, ink, washing bluing, and beer. All were imported from England and probably purchased in Peter Holt's shop.

As goes the cattle market, so go the downtown shops. The British proprietor failed as both a businessman and a husband. The adorable cottage he built, dubbed "Holt's Folly" by his neighbors, was intended to lure a reluctant wife to Laramie. She never came, but the house still stands near the corner of Eighth and Grand Avenue in Laramie, a monument to one man's heartfelt wish to house a family far from home.

As the years passed, the remaining respectable men of Laramie still felt the need for a brothel. Since the rest of the Front Street brothels were all out of business, the Tivoli eventually took up the slack. It remained a shady business until 1964, perhaps because an underground tunnel connected it to the perfectly respectable establishment across the street. Many shops' basements accessed storage rooms that extended under the street in front, and there is a door there today. Alas, it is walled off so the mystery remains.

~~~~~~~~~~~~~~

Once the first train rolled across the Dale Creek span in April 1868, travelers could travel quickly over the Laramie Range. Freight wagon trains pulled by oxen would no longer labor past the delicate stone legs of the arch, although horseback cowboys and a few local freighters would still take that route. Laramie City burgeoned as the construction project approached the town. Local businesses had been at work for months servicing the construction crews. A mark of progress, a large tent, the famous "Big Tent," went up on the corner of South A (later Ivinson Avenue) and Second Street. The tent was a 110 feet by forty feet (about the footprint of the barn at the Oxford Ranch). The lot remained the center of celebratory life (replaced by another tent) for years after the construction crews departed. The entourage that followed the construction crew was called "Hell on Wheels." Zane Grey, a popular Western novelist, described the Big Tent:

> *[I]t had been brought complete from St. Louis * * * It seemed a huge, glittering, magnificent monstrosity in that coarse, bare setting. Wide mirrors, glistening bottles, paintings of nude women, row after row of polished glasses, a brawny, villainous barkeeper, with three attendants, all working fast, a line of rough, hoarse men five deep before the counter--all these things constituted a scene that had the aspects of a city and yet was redolent with an atmosphere no city ever knew. The drinkers were not all rough men. There were elegant black-hatted, frockcoated men of leisure in that line--not directors and commissioners and traveling guests of the U. P. R., but gentlemen of chance. Gamblers!* (Ambrose, 2005).
~~~~~~~~~~~~~~

The celebration was short-lived, as the track-layers were out of sight over the horizon the day following the arrival of the completed tracks, thanks to the efforts of the Casement Brothers. The next stop for the Big Tent was Benton, Wyoming, some eleven miles east of present-day Rawlins at UP milepost 672.1. Benton's existence very short-lived, only three months. Before the tracks moved on in September 1868, Benton had attained a population of 3,000 souls even though it was smack dab in the middle of a dry, barren, typical Wyoming desert basin. John C. Frémont had been an early visitor to the place and, later in life, described the area that surrounded the town named after his father-in-law:

> *In some respects, it is a desert - barren of wood - sprinkled with sandy plains - melancholy under the somber aspect of the gloomy Artemisia [sagebrush] - and desolate from volcanic rocks, through the chasms of which plunge the headlong streams. But this desert has its redeeming points - much water, grass, many oases, mountains capped with snow, to refresh the air, the land & the eye - blooming valleys - a clear sky, pure air and a supreme salubrity. It is home of the horse found there wild in all the perfection of his first nature - beautiful & fleet - fiery & docile - patient, enduring & affectionate. The country that produces such horses must also produce men and cattle and all the other animals; and must have many beneficent attributes to redeem it from the stigma of desolation (Ambrose, 2005).*

Benton, Wyoming, was three miles from the closest water source. Water for bathing cost ten cents a pail, while the local alcoholic drink, called "forty-rod," cost twenty-five cents a glass. Forty-rod is homemade whiskey, warranted to kill at forty rods distance. Briefly, Benton City had twenty-five saloons and five dance halls, including the relocated Big Tent.

Eight months later, the Big Tent pulled up its stakes for the last time. On May 10, 1869, the Golden Spike was driven at Promontory Point, Utah, marking the spot where the UPRR and CPRR tracks met. The world went wild. The bridging of a continent was big news. Indeed, there was nothing like it in the world. **J. Harvey Nichols**, the lowly telegraph operator in Cheyenne who signed my rock, was on duty that day. A full twenty-seven minutes after the golden spike was struck, Nichols conveyed the joyous news to the people. Cheyenne erupted in celebration.

~~~~~~~~~~~~~~~

It was evident from the get-go that making a living at Laramie's latitude and altitude would require some measure of genius or luck. Many get-rich-quick schemes flared and faltered quickly, but others took much longer to
~~~~~~~~~~~~~~~

fail. Indeed, I was doing the same thing: trying to introduce a non-traditional livestock enterprise, cashmere goats, and pursue a ranching lifestyle. In 1888, **M.C. Brown** had been trying to start a horse ranch called the Buffalo Ranch. Brown spent $5,000 in capital to buy and stock the new ranch with two Percheron stallions imported from Holland. The ledger book tells me that his property was later sold at a sheriff's auction for $2,400 after one of the two stallions died. Section 11 eventually transferred to Sara Whitehouse, and it was she who signed over the ROW to the railroad.

Jay Gould ran the UPRR for a few years around this time. Gould was the wealthiest man in America, worth some $80 million, but he died of tuberculosis in 1892. Again, rock signatory **M.C. Brown** entered the scene. A Wyoming woman hired Brown to represent her in a suit against the Gould Estate; she claimed to be Gould's biological daughter and partial heir. When Brown determined that her claim was illegitimate, she sued Brown for defamation and lost.

After the UPRR went bankrupt for the second time in 1893, Edward H. Harriman took over management. He rerouted the southeastern Wyoming stretch of track to eliminate the dangerous Dale Creek Bridge crossing and double-tracked the line. Eventually, he extended the UP to Los Angeles. Of course, the UP had to fence the new tracks. It was just too dangerous otherwise. Animals often congregated in the lee of a road cut, trying to hide from the ferocious Wyoming wind. To minimize the threat to the trains, the company fenced both sides of the tracks using specially manufactured barbed wire so it could be traced if stolen (Liu, 2009). They had learned the hard way on that one.

~ ~ ~ ~ ~ ~ ~ ~ ~ ~ ~ ~ ~ ~

Judge **Melville Cox Brown** died in 1928 and is buried in Laramie's Greenhill Cemetery. Kim Viner authored an obituary that can be found on the website, www.WyoHistory.org.

## *Chapter Fifteen*
# JOHN DANIELS - 1879
### *& Indian Reservations*

(PHOTO BY K. McGUIRE)

In 1840, Wyoming was occupied by forty- to fifty-thousand Indians, specifically the Shoshone in the northwest, the Crow in the northcentral, and the Cheyenne, Ute, and Arapahoe in the southeast. The Comanche had already taken their stolen Spanish mounts and moved out onto the Great Plains, becoming the most successful and warlike Plains Indian group. The Wyoming tribes had various sub-groups such as the Bannock, Lakota, Oglala, Blackfoot, Ute, Kiowa, and Snake, also called Shoshone.

Alliances waxed and waned regularly as these tribes moved throughout the area on a seasonal basis, gathering what was necessary to see them through the cruel winters. Generally speaking, the tribes were constantly at war with someone. Living conditions were harsh enough to dangerously depress the birth rate. Slaves were needed to have enough hands to sustain the tribe. So, raiding parties made frequent forays to capture women and children, who were then incorporated into the tribe.

It was not an idyllic way of life but in pre-Columbian times, it was sustainable. After the Spanish brought their livestock to the New World, some animals escaped. This caused the Indian world to change dramatically; horses made all the difference in the history of the West. Although they evolved on the high plains of North America during the Eocene, they had disappeared from the continent until the Spanish Conquistador, Hernán Cortéz, brought them back to Mexico in 1519.

To Western tribes, horses became an essential to survival and served as currency. Eastern tribes had no such advantages and were quickly subjugated; the few who withstood the pestilence brought by early white settlers were horseless. The Plains Indians had the means to move swiftly away from danger and stage lightning strikes on the invading white armies. Like their Eastern counterparts, they were armed only with arrows and spears. However, their mobility allowed them to hunt buffalo efficiently and become effective fighting forces.

In 1869, newly elected President Ulysses S. Grant fulfilled his promise to the American electorate to make peace on the Great Plains and created the Bureau of Indian Commissioners. This new agency, part of the Department of the Interior, would be charged with distributing the Indian appropriations required by the treaty. It replaced the highly corrupt Bureau of Indian Affairs under the Department of War. Two years later, most Indian agents were Christian Evangelicals, especially Quakers. As of July 1884, Indian agents were to compile and submit an annual census of their charges. The *Frontier Index* reported on April 24, 1873, that,

> *J. Daniels the Indian Agent for the Red Cloud band & the agent for the White Clay Reservation have both resigned for fear of losing their hair.*

He must have reconsidered because in 1876, when the Red Cloud Agency was near Fort Laramie, rock signatory **John Daniels** still served as the Indian Agent. Daniels was responsible for enforcing the rules and delivering the tribes' share of the $50,000 worth of supplies as stipulated in the 1851 Treaty.

The following year, Daniels retired, and the agency moved closer to Fort Robinson. Because of the increasing corruption amongst the Indian agents, the quality of the tribes' supplies was unacceptable, so the Lakota murdered Daniels' successor. In 1879 the agency moved to South Dakota, and the name changed to the Pine Ridge Agency. The tribes rebelled against being forced to move away from their traditional hunting grounds, and skirmishes continued.

~~~~~~~~~~~~~~

Sitting by the arch, I imagine I am Arapahoe.

> *Fall is upon the earth, and the urge to head east, downhill towards the safety of the Mother River, is heavy upon my tribe. There, we can camp safely, huddling down in the driving snowstorms that regularly ravage the open prairie. Today, my family must set up camp for our stay near the place of the medicine bow. From here, we can hunt, fish, gather*
~~~~~~~~~~~~~~

*medicinal barks, and harvest the wood we need to make the tipis and weapons. These things allow us to sustain our way of life.*

*I can see the towering peaks of sparkling white mountains thirty miles due west from the gently sloping, hard rock terrace where we camp. Some days, the air is so clear that my mind's eye can easily touch those sparkling rocks. The slopes below those peaks are dark with lodgepole pine. Because they are tall, straight, and slim, with only small, twig-like branches, lodgepole pines trunks are perfect as replacement tipi poles. Our poles get broken, or sometimes we use them for firewood. Those doubling as travois poles dragging behind my horse over miles of rocky soils get pretty short as we follow the buffalo herds. The pines growing high in these mountains are the best source of lodge poles for my tribe.*

*On the lower slopes of the mountains, a riot of color marks the aspen stands growing in unseen drainages. Along the streams we find willow leaves to use for headaches and sore muscles. My tribe has come to this place to hunt for branches of the ash tree. Each fall, many groups congregate peacefully to celebrate healing rituals. The journey over the summit of the mountain to the place of the mountain ash takes days. When the warriors return with the special branches, the pow wows begin. The rituals endow the wood with special powers to protect our tribe during winter. Then we fashion them into medicine bows and arrows.*

Suddenly, I return to reality and frown. Sadly, that way of life has disappeared forever. Only rare artifacts remain. When I worked as a wildlife biologist, our firm employed several archaeologists. It was up to me to draw the detailed maps required for inclusion in an environmental impact statement. I learned the technical terms "feature" and "firepit". I saw the detailed drawings of the more significant shards and specimens the crew dug up all over Wyoming. Our archaeologists once found evidence of an ancient "pit house," confirming that some indigenous people were somewhat sedentary in Wyoming thousands of years ago. At the time, it was the oldest and highest archaeological site of that type ever found. Many more pit houses occur at lower elevations. Wisely, the ancient architects buried their living space beneath the earth's surface. Recovered pollen samples from the pit house floor provide a fascinating window into how these early populations sustained themselves 7,000 years ago.

~ ~ ~ ~ ~ ~ ~ ~ ~ ~ ~ ~ ~ ~

One afternoon I decided to hunt around on the partial BLM section, or government-owned and managed land that adjoins our ranch to the north. There I found twenty-one tipi rings, all in a single area. I imagined a large bonfire on the hard, slick sandstone just north of the Crimson Arch. Below the relatively level area hosting the tipi rings, there is a steep ravine. Piles of old brush and a sapling skeleton or two block the exit routes, making a clandestine corral for the most treasured of the tribes' possessions, their horses. Also, the path from the encampment to the horses offered many large bushes. Privacy, when nature called, provided needed fertilizer and moisture to the vegetation. A rough lean-to provided rude shelter for those individuals assigned to guard the horses at night. I have never found an artifact in all my miles of walking.

The favored wood for long bows is Greene's mountain ash *(Sorbus scopulina)*, a member of the *Rosaceae* family. It is commonly distributed in the Pacific Northwest. Only small, isolated populations occur in Wyoming and western Colorado. One such population exists high in the Sierra Madre mountains of Wyoming. Ash is the preferred wood for making long bows although mountain mahogany *(Cerocaropus montanus)* and alder *(Alder tenuifolia)* can also be used.

The tribes were there to gather the necessary things for survival, but they always counted on the Indian summer weather conditions. Tribal members took this time to make new bows from the newly acquired ash boughs. The branches had to be peeled and dried in a specific manner to give them the required recurve shape. Green-cut arrow wood was treated to ensure true flight. Eagle feathers were gathered to make the strong fletches that guided the arrow's flight. Everyone sitting around the campfire spent every waking moment doing something useful. Young men were practicing striking new points for their new arrows, plus there was a need for sharp hand knives to fashion the bows. As chips and shards piled up, the deerskin parfleches of newly finished arrowheads decorated the belts of many young warriors.

~~~~~~~~~~~~~~~

Just over the hill to the east is Vedauwoo, a spot on the map about five miles from the Crimson Arch. If I were to walk along my easement to the very top of the Laramie Range and look over, I would see the jumbled stacks of enormous granite tors next to the Interstate 80 corridor. "Biito'o'wu" is an Arapahoe word meaning "earth-born spirits," and was anglicized by UW professor Mary Lou DeKay into Veedauwoo in the 1950s. The soft pink and crumbly Sherman granite is naturally decorated with quartz inclusions, grey-green mosses, and brilliant, dark carrot-colored lichens; loose boulders are
~~~~~~~~~~~~~~~

a popular garden ornament nowadays. People can proudly point to one and state, "That rock is 1.4 billion years old." Furthermore, they would be right.

Just to the south of Vedauwoo is a peculiar arrangement of circular outcroppings. At the center of the inner ring, the topography is so rugged that no one goes there. The heart of this wild area harbors populations of mountain lion, bear, moose, and perhaps a wolf or two. On the second ring from the center lies Virginia Dale, twenty miles south of the Crimson Arch, tucked into the ancient curve of a valley like an infant in a mother's arms.

The local waterways, Dale Creek and Fish Creek, both carve deep and rugged canyons over a mile long. Fish Creek Canyon is only 400 feet wide at the top, narrowing to ten or fifteen feet at the narrowest spot at the bottom, the definition of mountain lion heaven. The rings form a partial set of concentric circles, like a bulls-eye with a quarter of it torn off; its orogeny is a mystery. I still have the stereo photos that J. David Love, USGS, gave me. Since this ancient set of rings can be seen from outer space, some believe it is a signal to approaching aliens. Although my neighbor is a fervent believer and waits to be transported up to a hovering spaceship, I think that geologic activity created the topography. However, when the sunset lights up Table Mountain, the aura is somewhat mystical.

<div align="center">~~~~~~~~~~~~~~</div>

Men like John Daniels presided over a tiny part of the country as the Indian Agent at the Red Cloud Agency in 1871. He resigned briefly in 1873, and then retired in 1876. What does his name, ***John Daniels 1879***, carved upon my rock tell me? Only that he survived the Indian War. While many Indian agents were dishonest, selling substandard goods to starving Indian tribes, I hope that Daniels was not one of these. It was clear by then that the whites had won the war.

## *Chapter Sixteen*
# JLH '80 - John Hunton
### *The Grattan Fight & Sand Creek*

Travelers on the road between Cheyenne and Laramie in the late 19th century used a route past the little three-legged, red sandstone arch, my Crimson Arch. There are many red sandstone buttes of this nature in the area. Their symmetry was shattered during the Laramie Orogeny when the buried Laramie Range shouldered five miles into the sky. Eventually, the ubiquitous Wyoming wind whittled them down to fantastic shapes. Many men and a few women have signed this particular arch. Perhaps it was a place to rest after fixing a broken wagon wheel. Alternatively, they might let the stock graze in the hearty grass before attempting to climb the mountain pass. They might have stopped to clean up a bit if they were bound for Laramie City. John Hunton did not stop on his way over to Laramie. On May 14, 1880, as noted in the detailed diaries he kept for almost fifty years, he rode to the county courthouse in Laramie to file some papers. He stopped on his way back to Cheyenne to scratch his initials into the sandstone of my Crimson Arch, **JLH'80**.

Hunton was a Civil War veteran who came west sometime in 1864. He had enlisted in General Robert E. Lee's Army of Northern Virginia at the outbreak of the war and was the only surviving member of his regiment after Pickett's Charge. Lee ordered General Pickett to attack the well defended stone wall in the center of the Gettysburg battlefield. Pickett's regiments attacked the far line while taking fire from the troops behind the wall; they died almost to a man. Some Confederates did make it to the stone wall and engaged in bloody hand-to-hand combat with the defending federal troops. Hunton was one of these courageous souls. After he recovered his health, Hunton became a galvanized Yankee, a captured Confederate soldier willing to pledge allegiance to the US Army, and he served five more years in the West.

Hunton's first posting was to Fort Halleck, guarding the Emigrant Trail in Wyoming. In 1865 he was assigned to guard the Platte River Bridge and watched as Lieutenant Caspar Collins rode out to his death at the Battle of Platte Bridge. As a fresh West Point graduate, Collins served alongside his father, Lieutenant Colonel William Collins. Jim Bridger had befriended the young lieutenant on a trip from Fort Laramie to establish Fort Halleck in the Laramie Basin. Collins wrote to his mother in 1862:

> *We had Major Bridger as our guide. He knows more of the Rocky Mountains than any living man.... He is totally uneducated but speaks English, Spanish & French equally well besides nearly a dozen Indian tongues* (Coutant, 1899).

Collins was eager to learn about the West, so Bridger drafted a detailed map of Wyoming drawn with charcoal on a finely tanned buffalo hide. Collins left the map behind when he rode out with Jim Bridger to confront the infuriated Oglala Sioux at the offending bridge. The structure belonged to the Overland Stage Company. It spanned the North Platte River, crossing the line established by the 1851 Treaty, the farthest point north white men could tread. The Indians were angry with the increasing number of whites trespassing wherever they wished.

One version of the events recounts that Chief Sitting Bull, a friend of Bridger, intercepted Collins and tried to get him to return to the fort. Just then, Collins' green horse bolted, carrying him beyond the area controlled by Sitting Bull and to certain death at the hands of Red Cloud's warriors. Other accounts differ. Present-day Casper, Wyoming, was named for Caspar Collins, and Fort Collins, Colorado, was named for his grieving father. Bridger's map survived and is archived at the American Heritage Center in Laramie.

After the required five years, Hunton mustered out of the army. He immediately began filing patents upon the fertile hay land flanking the banks of Chugwater Creek, north of Cheyenne. Two of his brothers followed him out from Virginia, and together, they were able to amass a significant landholding. Hunton purchased the Bordeaux trading post near present-day Chugwater, Wyoming. He set up a road ranch, a place to rest horses and refresh oneself, to service the increasing traffic between Cheyenne, Fort Laramie, and Fort Fetterman to the north. Hunton also owned a "milk" ranch (a dairy farm) on LaPrele Creek. Every fall, he would drive hay wagons over the divide into the Laramie Basin to Harney Creek and harvest the meadows there. He was a prosperous, busy man. Always circumspect and aloof from his peers, Hunton obsessively recorded his activities in small, black leather-bound books.

On Friday, May 14, 1880, Hunton wrote in his journal:

*Cheyenne. Paid all accounts owed in Cheyenne. Went to Laramie City to have mortgage of Williams & Smith recorded* (Flannery, 1967).

Hunton's journal continues on Saturday, May 15:

*Laramie City. Left the Williams & Smith mortgage with county clerk to be recorded. Went to Fort Sanders and paid a very pleasant visit to Gen Flint & family. Republican convention met and elected delegates to Chicago convention* (Flannery, 1967).

Hunton returned to Cheyenne on May 16, spending the next three days "doing nothing." What his diary fails to mention is the fact that John L. Hunton paused at the Crimson Arch. He scratched his initials and the date, J L H '80, on a rock formation just east of the little red arch.

When Hunton bought Bordeaux's relocated road ranch north of Cheyenne, he was married to a Sioux squaw named LaLee, who was devoted to him. They did not have children. As his wealth and influence increased, Hunton entered the nearby Cheyenne's social circles. He knew that "squaw" men were not accepted, so Hunton sent LaLee back to her people on the Wind River reservation. She schemed and begged, offering to run his road house business for him, but he would not have her back as a wife. Polite circles required a white wife on a man's arm when attending the grand balls hosted by the Cheyenne Social Club. So Hunton reached out to his family in Virginia to find himself a suitable one. After a long period of correspondence, Hunton married a Virginia belle, some years his junior, and went on an extended honeymoon in Florida. He found the damp air agonizing and longed to return to his high plains. He had built a substantial cement house near the trading post, and he and his new bride returned there in 1886.

The road ranch was doing well, and Hunton also held contracts with the US government for hay, wood, and beef. He could borrow what cash he needed on his good name alone. So he built a fine house in Cheyenne, befitting his wife's expectations. Mss. Hunton, a sickly woman, spent her time in Cheyenne in their stately residence as Hunton traveled up and down the Laramie Range, attending to his many business interests. They never had children either; perhaps Hunton's war wounds prevented that which he desired most. When his surviving brother Tom and his wife, Mora, gave birth to a son in 1883, John journaled:

*Sat, July 7 - Bordeaux. All hands branding the Grant cattle. Letter from Tom. Mora has a child* (Flannery, 1967).

Typical for John, his terse and cryptic text did not reflect the joy he must have had in his heart. His brother named the lad after his uncle, John L. Hunton, and the elder Hunton always referred to him as John Junior. His nephew went to school in Chicago and became an accomplished musician. In 1910 he moved to Laramie and taught music at the University of Wyoming. Hunton Junior composed Wyoming's only piano sonata; the "Song of the Plains" was published in 1934 but was not financially successful. The sheet music to this sonata is available at the American Heritage Center in Laramie, Wyoming. John L. Hunton, Junior died in 1934 and is buried in Wheatland.

After his wife died, Hunton declared bankruptcy. Business at the road ranch was declining due to the railroad. He was also under prosecution by **M.C. Brown** for illegally fencing federal lands, along with his friends and neighbors Hiram "Hi" Kelly, "Portugee" Phillips, and the senator who represented Wyoming, F.E. Warren. As his debts came due, securing additional financing to pay them off became difficult. So he sold his land, paid off his loans, and moved to Fort Laramie, becoming the sutler or general mercantile man. The heyday of the Emigrant Trail was long gone, but the army maintained the outpost until 1899. As an old man, Hunton befriended the young daughter of his neighbor, L.G. Flannery, and his wife. Hunton writes in his journal:

> *[Flannery's daughter] turned eight today. Mrs. [Flannery] baked her a cake and they had a party for the neighbors. I was not invited* (Flannery, 1967).

Hunton would receive a piece of cake later, and the friendship continued.

One hot summer day, Mr. Flannery emerged into the blinding sunlight from his home. Squinting, he spotted his daughter playing with her dolls near the well, over 100 yards away. His ears told him that there was a large and dangerously blind rattlesnake near her. Snakes shed in August, loose skin can cover their eyes, impairing vision. Flannery panicked and went for his rifle, but a shot rang out as he drew his bead. Startled, he looked over to see John Hunton, age eighty-five, leaning against a wall, a smoking rifle in his hands. He had not only seen and heard the snake from some 200 yards away but also shot its head off, saving the little girl. Even after Fort Laramie closed, Hunton continued to live there and had many neighbors, including Flannery, with whom he entrusted his collected diaries. Flannery lovingly edited and published them; the result is a touching and sincere view of Wyoming.

John Hunton and his wife are probably buried in the Hunton family cemetery in New Baltimore, Fauquier County, Virginia. Both of Hunton's parents are there, but the cemetery is in such poor repair it is not possible to identify all the individual gravesites.

~ ~ ~ ~ ~ ~ ~ ~ ~ ~ ~ ~ ~ ~

**John Hunton's** road ranch was the most popular meeting spot on the plains of Wyoming north of Cheyenne. Travelers heading to the goldfields of Sioux territory would convene daily with local ranchers amid a congenial mix of beer, tale-telling, leather, and gunpowder. The fierce competition often elevated the already tall tales. Far and away, the most storied event began with a dying cow. Hunton, the habitual diarist, occasionally wrote longer segments about exciting topics. In *John Hunton's Diary, 1883-84* Volume 5, Hunton describes at length what has come to be called the Grattan Fight. The following recalls that event based on Hunton's narrative.

The cow in question belonged to a member of a Mormon wagon train approaching Fort Laramie from the east on a hot August day in 1854. Gathered on the north bank of the Platte were thousands of indigenous Americans, mostly Sioux, patiently encamped, awaiting their annual distribution of $50,000 worth of goods and supplies as agreed in the Treaty of 1851. The supplies had arrived weeks before and were under guard in the Gratiot House, located on the grounds of Fort Bernard, a few miles from Fort Laramie. Fort Laramie was practically deserted; most troops were away cutting hay.

Indian Agent Whitfield had been detained in Denver and was long overdue. The supplies could not be distributed without him, so the tribes waited patiently. Each day they had to drive their horses farther and farther away from the camp to find sufficient feed. Each week, braves had to venture farther and farther away into the Black Hills to hunt game to feed themselves. They were hungry and hot as they watched miles of wagon trains rumble slowly past on the Emigrant Trail, appropriately on the south side of the river.

When a Miniconjou Sioux brave named High Forehead found a downer cow that had wandered across the river, he promptly slaughtered her. A downer cow is one near death and she was unable to rise. She might have been lost or left to die either intentionally or unintentionally. Either way, he and his Sioux friends enjoyed an unexpected feast. When the Mormon owner heard that Indians had consumed his cow, he decided to claim compensation from the US government. When he reached Fort Laramie, he reported the cow as being stolen to the young commander, Lieutenant Hugh B. Fleming, a fresh West Point graduate. Lieutenant Fleming was unsure of what to do next, so he waited. Conquering Bear, the Sioux leader, knew that the slaughter of the cow would mean trouble. So, he took one of his ponies to Fleming, offering to trade it for the dead cow. A lovely pony versus a ten-dollar cow? Not bad.

Fleming immediately refused the offer. Conquering Bear returned to his camp and conferenced with his Brulé sub-chiefs. The following day, Man-Afraid-of-his-Horses returned to the fort to renew the offer, but Fleming left him cooling his heels for hours. Later that afternoon, Fleming made the fateful decision to reject the offer and arrest High Forehead. He sent Man-Afraid back to Bear, demanding that he surrender the culprit immediately. Bear refused, citing the fact that High Forehead was a Miniconjou and, therefore, not subject to his authority.

Thousands of Indians surrounded Lieutenant Fleming; he was shorthanded and inexperienced but pledged to uphold the Treaty of 1851, which guaranteed government compensation for all Indian deprivations. Fleming decided to send his last platoon into the Indian encampment to make the arrest. The platoon commander was Lieutenant John L. Grattan, a hot-headed, brand-new West Point graduate anxious to make a name for himself. He succeeded.

Grattan included his mixed-blood interpreter, Lucien Auguste, as the troops gathered and prepared to depart the safety of the fort. Auguste and some others had fortified themselves with alcohol for the upcoming mission at the post canteen. The orderly column formed up to cross the bridge over the Laramie River. Grattan, Auguste, a wagon full of twenty-five soldiers armed with single-shot rifles, two drummers, and two horse-drawn caissons, each loaded with twelve pound cannon, rode forward and passed into history.

Watching this obvious show of force, Bear hurried to intercept Grattan before he reached the encampment. They met inside at the Bordeaux trading post, a trail-side store run by a French ex-fur trapper and his Sioux wife. Bordeaux was a respected member of the Sioux Nation, fluent in French, English, and Sioux. Grattan's interpreter, Auguste, hated Indians and, being drunk, was riding wildly around outside, hurling insults in French and Sioux to anyone who would listen. He was making a bad situation worse.

To defuse the tension, Bear offered an additional mule as compensation for the cow, a generous offer indeed. However, Grattan was not authorized to make such decisions and focused on fulfilling his orders on this, his first military expedition as a commander. He demanded that High Forehead present himself. When Bear left without producing High Forehead, Grattan responded by advancing his tiny column deep into the encampment. The lieutenant surrounded Bear's lodge, training both cannons on his tipi. The white traders at the post, incredulously watching this turn of events from the trading post roof, urged Bordeaux to intervene. So he took off on his horse but returned quickly. He was too late to stop the madness.

When High Forehead saw the cannon, he jumped out of hiding and began hurling insults at Grattan, insults only roughly translated by Auguste. Grattan calmly reached over and pulled the lanyard on the nearest cannon. However, it was aimed too high to hit the lodge. The explosion sparked a volley of nervous gunfire. When the smoke cleared, Conquering Bear lay mortally wounded. An eerie silence pervaded the scene as the soldiers held their ground. Then, the second cannon was discharged, tearing through nearby tipis.

Without Bear to keep the peace, 1,000 Sioux warriors fell upon the soldiers with knives and bows. Grattan was hit by twenty-four arrows almost simultaneously. Grattan's private, who was left holding the horses, tried to mount and ride out but was chopped to pieces when his ponies' legs were cut from under him. Meanwhile, the rest of the soldiers piled back into the wagon. They retreated to a small sagebrush covered hillock, abandoning their commander's body and the cannon. The soldiers held off the attackers for a time, but they were overrun and slaughtered when they ran out of ammunition.

Intoxicated by the fight, the Oglala Sioux contingent of the encampment were intent on exacting more revenge at Bordeaux's trading post. Finding only Bordeaux and his wife, they spared them and failed to discover the badly frightened white traders still crouched on the roof. The Sioux raced off towards the Gratiot House located nearby. Breaking down the wooden door, they looted and burned the structure, scattering most of the supplies.

In the meantime, the Mormons had retreated to the safety of Fort Laramie. For several hours, the Indians raced their ponies along the south side of the Laramie River, driving off all the loose livestock. They found and attacked a lone stagecoach, killing both drivers and a passenger. Then they left. When Lieutenant Fleming retrieved Grattan's body several days later, his pocket watch was the only available identifying object. Fleming buried the officer on the grounds of Fort Laramie, and the men occupy a grave on the sagebrush hillock where they fell.

Disturbed by this turn of events, the other Sioux tribes, the Cheyenne and the Arapahoe, moved their camps farther away from Fort Laramie but remained in the area. The place was tense and quiet when Agent Whitfield finally arrived at Fort Laramie the following week. He immediately called the remaining tribes to council. At the meeting, they presented Whitfield with a most unusual demand. The leaders requested $4,000 in cash immediately, the balance of their annuity in guns and ammunition, and that all travel cease on the Emigrant Trail. They also demanded one thousand white women for wives. The requests were refused, and the tribes dispersed without any agreement or supplies.

When news of the Grattan Fight reached St. Louis, General W.S. "The Butcher" Harney was recalled from his vacation in Europe. The following spring, Harney attacked Little Thunder's band of Brulé Sioux along the Little Blue Water Creek in the panhandle of Nebraska, very near Fort Laramie. Little

Thunder had been an observer during the Grattan Massacre and knew not of Harney's approach. Harney killed eighty-six Brulé adults, wounded five, and captured seventy women and children. Discovering a nearby cave, he fired his cannon directly into the chasm in case more warriors were hiding there. It was filled with tribal elders, women, and children. Crazy Horse, coming later upon the still-smoldering scene, wept for his people and resolved to fight to the death. The Blue Water Battle was the twelfth largest engagement during the Indian Wars and marked the beginning of a collaboration between Indian groups that otherwise might have been enemies.

Official Washington DC's reaction to this tragedy was detailed in a letter written by Superintendent of Indian Affairs D.D. Mitchell:

> *Great blame is very justly attached to the conduct of the inexperienced young officer [Grattan] in command of the detachment; but that is not the question.... The miserably mistaken policy which the Government has pursued in establishing petty little forts, along the Arkansas and Platte, for the purpose of protecting traders and travelers, and the same time overawing the Indians, has been worse than a useless waste of public money. These little forts are generally garrisoned by the fragments of a company of infantry, a forse [sic] that could be of no more use in protecting travelers or chasing Indians than so many head of sheep* (Nebraska State Historical Society, 1922).

~~~~~~~~~~~~~~~

The ability of Indians to range freely across the plains came to an end ten years later. Enraged by the overactive press' detailed descriptions of Indian depredation along the Emigrant Trail, the military took matters into their own hands. They began an organized and consistent campaign to wipe all Indians from the face of the earth. In an attempt to distinguish between hostiles and friendlies, Governor Evans, son of UPRR surveyor Colonel John Evans, ordered his Indian agents to offer sanctuary to all Indian groups who would report to the Indian agency and surrender their arms. In turn, Evans promised to feed them and protect them from harm.

That fall, a band of Cheyenne led by Chief Black Kettle, starving after multiple fruitless hunts across the scorched plains, showed up at the Upper Arkansas River Agency and surrendered. The agency could not feed them, so Black Kettle was ordered to stay within thirty-five miles of the fort and try to fend for himself. Black Kettle assumed he was under military protection and flew the obligatory American flag and white flag of surrender from his tipi. Hanging next to the stars and stripes was the peace medal he had received from President Millard Fillmore.
~~~~~~~~~~~~~~~

Defrocked Methodist pastor and Grand-Master of the Denver Masons, Colonel John M. Chivington, was anxious for action against an Indian, any Indian. Early in the frosty morning of November 13, 1865, Chivington's men attacked Black Kettle's slumbering village. He had 700 men under his command, and they fell upon the half-starved, lightly armed village of 550 Cheyenne camped along the Sand Creek. Most of the men were out hunting.

Chivington killed more than 150 people, mostly women and children, and lost seven soldiers. He and his men brought home as trophies male and female genitalia as well as fetuses to share with their friends. The Eastern press widely condemned him and later, a military tribunal formally criticized him. He was not removed from command by Governor Evans. This choice was recently sanctioned when Mount Evans, the highest peak in Colorado, was renamed Mount Blue Sky.

When Chivington's son, James, died that Christmas, Chivington hightailed it to Nebraska to administer the estate. Wisely, he remained there, trying to start a freighting business. He seduced and then later married his former daughter-in-law, fathering another son. They divorced in 1871, after which Chivington skipped to Canada.

~~~~~~~~~~~~~~

The State of Colorado has recently placed a marker commemorating the site of this war crime and created the Sand Creek Massacre National Historic Site to protect this sacred ground. Although no motorized vehicles can desecrate the blood-soaked soil, the final insult to Native Americans is that at the gateway to the site sits a town named Chivington.

In 1875, the chiefs recalled their bands to the Powder River and Big Horn Basins. They planned to stage a coordinated effort to finally defeat the army and stop the endless influx of whites into their territory. The whites, however, were well entrenched. Present-day Deadwood, South Dakota, was already a bustling town, complete with saloons and hotels. In 1876, "Wild Bill" Hickok was shot to death as he played his hand of aces and eights, his back to the saloon door. The stage was set on the plains for the Battle of Little Bighorn, yet another military debacle.

The remaining Sioux chiefs had either been killed in battle or would surrender by the following year. They would watch their people die of starvation, humiliation, exposure, and infection if they retired to their agencies. More than once, blankets potentially infected with smallpox were distributed by the agents. The maggot-infested beef delivered to the agency was all there was to eat.
~~~~~~~~~~~~~~

Biological Warfare. Scorched Earth Policies. Buffalo Extermination. Genocide. Let history books reflect that American men on American soil perpetrated these atrocities. One can only hope that the era that allows such insults has passed forever. Never again.

~~~~~~~~~~~~~~~
~~~~~~~~~~~~~~~

# War by Defoliation

In 1864, the US Army tried to burn the Great Plains by sending out the cavalry armed with firebrands. Their instructions were to ignite the remaining dried summer grass between the Platte River on the north and the Republican River on the south, from Denver to Fort McPherson, Nebraska, some fifteen million acres. Without grass, there could be no wildlife. With no wildlife, there could be no Indians. They would be forced to retreat south into Comanche Territory in Oklahoma or north, back into an everdwindling circle of Indian occupation on the High Plains.

On the appointed day, late in the winter, hundreds of riders departed their forts, heading in both directions, firebrands at the ready. They rode ponies dragging lighted branches for miles in either direction, late into the night, setting millions of acres of grassland on fire. Although they failed to burn the entire target area, they forced hundreds of families to abandon their winter camps. The survivors trekked across the frozen plains, seeking refuge in hostile territory.

## *Chapter Seventeen*
# H.R. HAY
### *& the Johnson County War*

(PHOTO BY K.MCGUIRE)

There are several inscriptions on the Crimson Arch that I had identified as local cattle ranchers. **John Iliff** fell into this group. Another inscription was WAG, the brand a local Laramie family, the Waggoners, have used for generations. There was a Miley '36 and a Clyde Liter '36, both long-time Warren Livestock employees; the date is 1936, not 1836. Paine was another ranching family that remained in the area. PAT and Rocking JM were also local brands for ranchers Patrick Carrol and Joseph Alford. All appear upon the flanks of the Crimson Arch. Indeed, whenever I visit the arch, I see new inscriptions by trespassers who sometimes ruin the underlying historic carvings. The ravages of time and temperature have also taken their toll. The date on Colonel Bradley's inscription has eroded. Gunnison's inscription has entirely disappeared, as have **M.C. Brown's**, **John Hunton's**, and **Esther Morris'**. **H.R. HAY** remains, dominating the south face of the arch.

The search for **H.R. Hay** was frustrating. There was Abraham Lincoln's private secretary, John Hay and Henry G. Hay, an associate of J.M. Carey, the father of Wyoming statehood. John never travelled to Wyoming but Henry was the head cashier at the Wyoming Stock Grower's Bank. He became bank president (with Mr. I.C. Whipple as the head cashier) and his activities are well documented in the press. H.G. Hay served in various official positions appointed by Territorial Governor F.E. Warren. Additionally, Whipple & Hay had a grand mercantile business located on the corner of 17th and Carey Avenue in Cheyenne and made a fortune shipping supplies to Deadwood, Dakota Territory. I guess they needed a bank to safeguard their money.

Later, Hay purchased the F.M. Phillips ranch on the Laramie River north of Cheyenne.

My Mr. Hay, however, was more low-key. He registered his brand "HAY" in 1880, identifying himself as **H. Hay**, no middle initial. His ranch was located in the Centennial Valley west of Laramie. By the end of the Indian Wars, stock growers and the railroad had divided Wyoming between their various interests. Open range policy dominated, meaning the large ranchers turned their stock loose to intermingle and go wherever the wind carried them. Natural barriers (with the occasional fence, mostly along the tracks) were the only things confining their movements.

Enter a third protagonist, the homesteader. Local synonyms for homesteaders were "nesters," "squatters," or "grangers." They were looked upon with disdain by the cattlemen. Both felt it was their right to graze the government-owned lands that often surrounded their private lands in a checkerboard pattern. They were both correct. The grazing allotment system had not yet been proposed. Nevertheless, it soon became clear that the government needed to regulate the livestock allowed on federal land.

The unclaimed parcels were, on the whole, marginal sections, not well-watered or well-vegetated. The encroaching homesteaders were mainly refugees from the economic wreckage of Europe, striving to breathe free. The new arrivals were German sod farmers, Swedish carpenters, Irish laborers, and Italian shopkeepers determined to earn a living. As naturalized American citizens, they believed their government when it said 160 acres were enough to make a living in Wyoming, a proposal that had long been debated in Washington. The UPRR lobbyists had convinced Congress that John Wesley Powell's scientific assessment of agricultural potential in the West was incorrect. Powell calculated that the number was more like 2,500 acres per homestead, which is the average size of a Wyoming ranch today.

By 1889, the tension between the large stock growers and the homesteaders peaked. The 1884 Maverick Law allowed any unclaimed or unbranded livestock discovered at either biannual roundup to be sold at auction. The Stock Grower's Association held the proceeds in escrow until ownership could be established. So, not only were small homesteaders required to occupy their claims, but they were also required to fence them because Wyoming was a "fence out" state. The Wyoming Territorial legislature decided Wyoming would be a fence out state for cattle but a fence in state for sheep. It was the cattlemen who could use private and public land at will. Incoming grangers would have to fence cattle out.

The last straw was that the grangers had to apply to the Wyoming Stock Grower's Association for a brand in order to market their livestock. More often than not, this critical paperwork was delayed or denied outright. Without a registered brand, small stockmen could not legally brand their livestock. Furthermore, if they used an unregistered brand or no brand, the animals would be confiscated if they ever made it to the sale barn.

Cattle tend to wander off occasionally, but it was not unknown for a small herd to mysteriously stampede, ending up sold at auction. Small stockmen were outraged by this situation. The large outfits and their straw man associates had already claimed the most desirable bottomlands. The grangers were frustrated, so they resorted to an insurgency.

It was expensive to fence 160 acres, so the grangers usually built sturdy corrals near the ranch house and allowed their livestock to wander, generally under their watchful eye. Then, they exacted their revenge on the cattlemen by stealing and immediately slaughtering as many range cattle as they could as they roamed freely across their land. Not only did the small stockmen battle the large stock growers, but they also fought each other in a cattle *versus* sheep debate. There was an increasing number of sheep growers in the Horse Creek area like Bill Lewis, who had purchased $15,000 worth of sheep in 1871 and watched them freeze to death the following winter. Low-level feuds were rife between these groups.

In 1882, sheepman Etherton P. Baker swore out a warrant for the arrest of small cattleman Fred Powell, accusing him of stealing some fencing supplies. Two years later, Powell was released on his own recognizance after he was charged with setting fire to Baker's sheep camp. Powell blamed the conflagration on Baker's Basque sheepherder. That December, while Baker and his wife were back East, someone poisoned thirteen of his horses.

Courts of the day were sympathetic to the cattle rustlers because grangers made up the majority of voting citizens responsible for the reelection of local judges. They also made up the majority of the jury pools. It is of little wonder that the Wyoming Stock Grower's Association took matters into their own hands and meted out justice as they saw fit.

The Cheyenne Social Club was a real organization founded in the 1880s. Membership was restricted to the elite cattlemen of eastern Wyoming. It was a partly social club, wholly political, and partly insurgent. Members tended to wear white cowboy hats and earned the moniker the White Caps. They were firmly in control of all political affairs in Wyoming, and among their members were rock signatories **John Hunton** and **H.R. Hay**. When the grangers in Johnson County began to make trouble, the White Caps reacted.

~~~~~~~~~~~~~~~~

The legacy of the Cheyenne Social Club is dark. Notary Public and Justice of the Peace James Averill, was also the postmaster of a small community in central Wyoming. A widower, he had filed on a homestead on the road between Rawlins and Buffalo along the lovely Sweetwater River. According to author John Davis' WyoHistory.org article, *The Johnson County War: 1892 Invasion of Northern Wyoming*:

> *Buffalo was "the most lawless town in the country," or a haven for "range pirates" who "mercilessly" stole big cattlemen's livestock. The cattle barons planned, organized & financed the invasion, declaring beforehand & afterwards that they had no choice but to take drastic action to protect their property. They said they were the victims of massive cattle stealing in Johnson County, and local authorities were doing nothing to protect their herds. They further declared that Buffalo was a rogue society in which rustlers controlled everything— politics, courts & juries. Those juries, the cattle barons said, refused to convict on cattle rustling charges no matter how strong the evidence* (Davis, 2014).

He was right. Small businessmen like James Averill populated the juries, and elected judges. The rural folk had valid homesteading claims surrounded by federal land. The grangers and the stockman locked horns without federal regulations defining whose cattle are and are not allowed to graze public land. The stockmen's only argument was that they had always grazed their cattle upon those lands, which gave them legal precedence. The homesteaders disagreed. This fight went on for twenty years until the passage of the Grazing Allotment Act in 1913.

Jim Averill was an educated man, a surveyor by trade, and he watched as the neighboring rancher tried to sell residential lots in a nonexistent town just downriver from his road ranch. He wrote to the editor of the Casper *Weekly Mail*, reporting that the town of Bothwell, Wyoming, was a scam. He had also been quite public in his published criticisms of the Wyoming Stock Grower's Association, of which Albert Bothwell, town founder, was a member. Averill and his common-law wife, Ellen "Ella" Watson, complained about their inability to get a registered brand. They had applied five times in three years and were denied each time. Averill and Watson's homesteads ran along ten miles of Johnson County's Horse Creek, and Bothwell wanted that land. In fact, he wanted the whole of the Sweetwater Valley.

Not to be intimidated, Watson purchased a registered brand from a sympathetic neighbor, fenced her property, and bought twenty-eight
~~~~~~~~~~~~~~~~

scraggly cows. While her husband ran the store at the road ranch, she and two young, adopted boys ran the cattle ranch. At the next seasonal roundup, Watson branded forty-one cows and calves. The stockmen assumed that her remarkable calf production rate was due to her stealing maverick calves, not that she might be a good animal husband.

The battle in the newspapers continued. As Justice of the Peace, Averill wrote long articles on the stockmen's illegal homesteading practices. Meanwhile, Watson was about to file on a water improvement project to take water out of Horse Creek, just above Albert Bothwell's ranch. She also removed the illegal fencing that guarded his irrigation ditches as they crossed her land. Both she and her husband were large thorns in Bothwell's side.

Enraged, he redoubled his efforts to catch them rustling, hiring a stock detective named George Henderson. Unable to gather any real evidence, on July 20, 1889, Henderson and some cattlemen, including Fred Hesse of Laramie, kidnapped Watson and Averill and spirited them away from town. The Carbon County sheriff and deputy sheriff looked on as the pair were hanged from a dead tree; the stockmen were judicially challenged no more. Not only did the stockmen lynch Averill and Watson, but they also poisoned one of her two adopted boys who had witnessed their kidnapping. The other disappeared, never to be seen again.

It might have ended there, except that Watson was a woman. Defensively, the stockmen took once again to the newspapers, reporting that Averill had been running a "Hog Ranch," meaning a house of prostitution, and that his wife was like the mythical "Cattle Kate," trading sexual favors for rustled stock. Nothing could have been farther from the truth. The reality was that Watson offered a clothing repair service to local cowboys. The existence of Cattle Kate is a construct. The White Caps used the newspapers to spread malicious lies about Watson after her death as a means of justifying their actions. According to a WyoHistory.org article by Tom Rea, headlines back East had read, "A Blaspheming Border Beauty Barbarously Boosted Branchward." The stigma of the label stuck to Ella Watson in the history books until 1965 when the truth about her was revealed.

Incited by Watson and Averill's deaths, the grangers' revolt gathered steam, and cattle rustling increased. The stockmen retaliated again, assassinating the granger leaders individually, sometimes in pairs. Those suspected of rustling were ambushed or "dry-gulched," murdered by their neighbors or agents of the Stock Grower's Association. The term dry gulch stems from the fact that it was easier to ambush a rider while he rode through a dry gulch. The echos of the shot off the sheer walls would conceal the shooter's position from any witnesses.

These tactics precipitated a mountainous wave of cattle rustling and murders. The Johnson County Invasion is probably the most notorious example of white-on-white violence in Wyoming history. The fact that it punctuated the entrance of Wyoming politics upon the national scene did not reflect well upon the cattlemen and the controlling politicians of the day. They did not care, nor did it have a lasting effect on their legacies.

On April 6, 1892, the Cheyenne stockmen launched the invasion, an abortive effort to punish the offending grangers. Major Frank Wolcott enlisted the support of thirty prominent stock growers and their employees, plus he hired twenty-three gunmen from Texas. Along with their horses and a few hangers-on, the army boarded a special UPRR train in Cheyenne. They rode to the end of the tracks near Casper, Wyoming, without charge. There, they set off towards present-day Kaycee, Wyoming, looking for any of the seventy grangers on their kill list.

They rode northeast for a while and finally found small ranchers Nate Champion and Nick Ray in a remote cabin; Nate and Nick were on the kill list. The cattlemen shot Nick from ambush and planned to burn the place. Nate held them off for hours, killing three or four and wounding a few more, hoping that reinforcements riding from Buffalo would arrive in time. Nate kept a detailed journal, writing:

> *Boys, I feel pretty lonesome just now. I wish there was someone here with me so I could watch all sides at once.*

When Nate heard the fire licking at the cabin walls just before nightfall, he ran for it, armed with a Colt pistol and a Winchester rifle. Nate was hit almost simultaneously by 28 bullets. When found, a note covered his bullet-riddled chest:

*Cattle Thieves Beware*

Johnson County Sheriff Red Angus and posse arrived too late to save him, but they continued to pursue the White Caps. The invaders rode another thirty miles north to Crazy Woman Creek, taking refuge at the TA Ranch, owned by former Laramie basin resident, Mr. Harris, who was sympathetic to their cause. They hunkered down, and were soon surrounded by the Sheriff and his two-hundred-strong, armed, angry posse.

The siege lasted three days with much expenditure of ammunition before Federal soldiers rescued the Cheyenne elite. When Republican acting Governor Amos W. Barber caught wind of the disaster, he reached out to the newly installed Wyoming Senators J.W. Carey and F.E. Warren. Carey raced to the White House and awakened President Benjamin Harrison from his bed. Harrison immediately called out the Sixth Calvary and sent them to save the invaders. An extremely well informed Carey kept track of the unfolding drama.

Miraculously, there was only one fatality among the invaders during the TA Ranch siege; one of the Texans eventually died from a self-inflicted wound to his foot. Sixty-five of the Cheyenne Social Club members and their cronies ended up in jail after being rescued by the Federal troops. Then, their lawyers, Laramie's own **M.C. Brown** and Willis Van Devanter, went to work. They used sixty-five preemptory challenges to eliminate the entire jury pool during the pre-trial proceedings. The Johnson County authorities faced the prospect of maintaining the inmates (at one dollar per day) while they recruited more potential jurors.

Discouraged, the Johnson County authorities quickly ran out of money, so Brown requested a change of venue back to Cheyenne and promised that justice would be served in the end. Everyone piled back onto the train, but he culprits were released as soon as it pulled into the Cheyenne station. A platform crowded with cheering women, colorful bunting, and brass bands greeted the returning White Caps. Brown returned to Laramie and Van Devanter went on to bigger things.

In the early 20th century, Van Devanter became one of the "Four Horsemen" of the United States Supreme Court, who dominated rulings for two decades, primarily defending states' rights. In his most remembered decision, which dealt with alcohol and Indians, he famously wrote:

> *[New Mexican Pueblo Indians were] intellectually & morally inferior and easy victims to the evils & debasing influence of intoxicants.*

Meanwhile, back in Washington, Senator Carey obstructed justice when he destroyed all correspondence with his ranch foreman. Secretly, the foreman had cut the telegraph wires from Buffalo to Cheyenne during the invasion. Wyoming Senator Warren claimed ignorance of the association's plans, even though he was an officer. He spent the next few years vigorously and publicly defending the accused Association members. **John Hunton** was aware of the plans but did not accompany the invaders because he was being sworn in as Laramie County commissioner that week. His journal entry reads that he "wished" he could have "gone along."

Vigilantism was rampant in the West due to a lack of effective policies and policing. It was not until the end of the 19th century that organized police forces began to make a difference. Everyone was armed to the teeth during that era, and Laramie had a fair percentage of law enforcement officers killed in the line of duty.

~ ~ ~ ~ ~ ~ ~ ~ ~ ~ ~ ~ ~ ~

Wyoming is the state that sports the highest average number of guns per household of all fifty states. United States citizens, as a whole, own somewhere between 200 million and 350 million guns. Using the lower estimate, that is still more than one-third of all privately owned firearms worldwide. A poll conducted in 2000 by the University of Chicago puts United States gun ownership at thirty-five percent of all households, down from almost fifty percent in 1975. Today, estimates are more refined, with most states (excluding the northeast) ranging from thirty-three to forty-four percent. Wyoming's 2017 percentage of households was around forty percent (University of Chicago, 2000). It has since skyrocketed to 66.2%.

According to Wyoming state law, people released from a mental institution are prohibited from gun ownership. Unfortunately, the state does not share this list of people, even with itself. However, Wyoming's homicide rate is extremely low. In 2010, there were only eight murders, five involving shootings. That is less than one murder per hundred thousand residents. In California, by contrast, only twenty-one percent of households own guns, but their homicide rate is almost three-and-a-half times higher for homicides per hundred thousand residents.

By 2024, Wyoming's murder rate more than doubled, and the rate per 100,000 people tripled. Wyoming also has the highest suicide rate by firearms (23.2 per hundred thousand people in 2017 and 29.4 in 2024), double the national average. These deplorable statistics are probably due more to the shortage of mental health care options outside of the five major cities than the availability of weapons. In the face of this crisis, the Wyoming legislature just defunded the 988 mental health help line in Wyoming.

Wyoming's concealed carry laws state that any adult legal Wyoming resident may carry a concealed weapon without applying for a permit. Concealed or not, firearms can legally be taken into any building in the state, be it a theater, grocery store, or rodeo. Open and concealed carry is legal everywhere except the University of Wyoming, courthouses, and the state capitol building, although those sanctuaries are now threatened by the ultra-conservative Freedom Caucus.

Dave Freudenthal, former governor of Wyoming, thinks that Wyomingites do not see gun ownership in the same light as other citizens:

*It is deeply ingrained, not only from the right to use but the idea of doing it responsibly. We do not like people who are cavalier with firearms.*

Freudenthal continues:

*My father would blister my butt if I was swaggering around with a firearm. That is not what you're supposed to do.*

However, legislators passed the Wyoming Firearms Freedom Act under Freudenthal's tenure. The law decreed that any state or federal official who enforces any federal gun law on a firearm "made or sold in Wyoming" could face a $2,000 fine and up to a year in prison. It is the arresting officer who would be fined and imprisoned, not the gun owner.

Many Wyoming kids are gifted a firearm when they are young, and most kids do not have to go far outside to find a place to practice. They soon discover it is surprisingly difficult to hit a ground squirrel at twenty yards. The straight-bore .22 caliber rimfire rifle is a popular gift for twelve-year-olds and is intended for shooting squirrels and other edible small game. If an AR-15 was used, there would be little left to eat. The high-velocity bullets fired from an AR-15 tumble as they fly through the air. As the bullet enters flesh, it rips and tears soft tissue as opposed to passing cleanly through. The AR-15 uses a larger, center-fire case with a much higher velocity copper-jacketed bullet than the .22 caliber rimfire. Due to the high velocity and modern construction, the bullet expands upon entering flesh, causing more tissue damage than the older style, solid lead bullet (Kling, personal communication).

In Wyoming, guns have a practical purpose and a place which is not on public display. Most Wyoming gun owners have a locking gun cabinet that is rarely opened except during hunting season. Anyone in the market for skilled labor in the fall needs to book ahead. During hunting season, any business is likely to be either closed or on restricted hours. It is not unusual to see rifles displayed in the back window of a passing pick-up. Six-to-one, a fluorescent orange vest will also be stashed behind the seat. Wyoming hunters take their sport very seriously. They practice ensuring their rifle or bow is sighted-in so they can hit their target with the first shot. The single-shot kill is the mark of a real hunter.

~~~~~~~~~~~~~~~

In 1907, **H.R. Hay** sold his ranch in Centennial to Fred Miller of Laramie and Issac Van Horn of Boston, Massachusetts, and left the country. Miller had grand plans for the Centennial Valley, naming it for the 100th anniversary of the signing of the Declaration of Independence. Miller and Van Horn built
~~~~~~~~~~~~~~~

the Mountain View Hotel, a fish hatchery, and an exclusive country club for wealthy city dwellers. The hotel remains the center of Centennial's social life and was placed on the National Registry of Historic Places in 2007. Miller and Van Horn even built a railroad. The Hahn's Peak and Pacific Railroad was intended to transport the tons of gold ore expected from seemingly rich deposits in the Medicine Bow mountains. Unfortunately, the claim played out before the railroad could be completed. Not to be deterred, the line was continued over to Walden, Colorado, to haul lumber, beef, and coal. The rails were removed in the 1990s and are now part of a popular "Rails to Trails" project.

**Hay** is not well remembered in Wyoming's history. His name does not appear in any textbooks. If his name did appear on the 1890 census, it burned along with thousands of other state records in 1921. Apparently, after ranching in the Centennial Valley for twenty years, Hay signed the rock and then retired to places unknown seven years later. His signature is unique in that he attempted to correct his typographical error. He accidentally began the date as 1801, when the century had just turned. So he attempted correction, changing the "8" to a "9." He is not buried nearby, nor did his name appear in the Laramie *Boomerang* whenever he visited, as do the names of other prominent ranchers. This only means he opted not to register at one of the downtown hotels. The *Boomerang* identifies him as riding the UPRR "Fish Special" down from Centennial to attend a grand gala sponsored by the railroad accompanied by C.L. Wanamaker (the editor of the Rock Springs, Wyoming, *Rocket*) and J.R. Billmeyer (a wealthy New York investor). Given the company he kept, it is safe to say he was a successful stockman and a member of the Cheyenne Social Club in its heyday.

## *Chapter Eighteen*
# GUS MUELLER & BELLE KUSTER - 1883
## *& the Travails of the Bath Family*

G. MILLER[SIC] & BELL[E] KUSTER SEPT.23, 1863. THERE IS
A HEART ABOVE THE SPACE BETWEEN THEIR NAMES.
(PHOTO BY K. MCGUIRE)

When Gus Miller and his girlfriend Belle Kuster were resting in the shade of the Crimson Arch, I imagine it was a beautiful fall day, the flowers faded from an early frost, and their pollen transformed to seed, consumed, or fallen. No longer did pine pollen fill the air with billowing yellow clouds. Because the nighttime temperatures were reasonable, the nearby rocks would still be warm. Add the direct rays of an overhead sun, and passions might stir. The most decorative signature on the Crimson Arch is **G. Miller & Bell[e] Kuster, September 22, 1883**. Their names scrawl across about two feet of the rock face. An artistic curl embraces both names from above, entwining in the middle to form a small heart. How sweet. I imagine they fell in love that day because they married a few years later.

In 1869, Laramie City was still a dusty, dry, ramshackle collection of tents and hastily constructed clapboard houses. The numerous projects underway foretold the coming civilization. By this time, the roughest components of its citizenry had either been hung or railroaded out. The downtown area was a collection of brothels, saloons, liquor stores, hotels, livery stables, merchants, and a single bank. Edward Ivinson became the *de facto* banker because he owned the only vault in town.

Immigrants like Ivinson were arriving daily on the newly established rail service. Others, such as the Bath family, soon followed. Belle and her extended family had left New York City after the Civil War ended. She was almost ten years old, and her brother, Theodore, was eight. Both had been born in New York City and raised in the filthy streets of upper East Manhattan. Belle's grandparents, Herman and Hanna Bath, emigrated from Germany in 1845, bringing their four children: Henry, Theodore, twelve-year-old Mary Marie, and the baby Louisa. Both grandparents had been hatters in the Old Country, probably felting the closely shorn beaver pelt underdown into stiff top hats. Making hats was the only trade they knew, so they opened another millinery shop. Son Henry opened a livery stable, and Mary eventually married a German sea captain named Gorie, who fathered her two children.

Unfortunately, the streets of New York were not kind to the Bath family. Mary's husband was lost at sea in 1863 during the opening salvo of the Civil War. Both of her brothers were drafted into the Union Army. They spent most of their time in the notorious Libby Prison, a Confederate prisoner-of-war camp in Richmond, Virginia. When Henry and Theodore were released, they came home to discover that the millinery shop was failing. Henry determined then and there to go west.

In the spring of 1866, Henry Bath, his wife Anne (and their children), his widowed sister Mary (and her two children), and his ailing parents set out from New York City by ox cart. Henry's youngest son, Albert Henry, was only six months old. They made it as far as Boone, Iowa, where they ran out of cash, so they opened a boarding house. It took two years for Henry, Anne, and Mary to make enough money to set out again. After the birth of little Fred C. Bath in April 1868, they left Iowa as soon as the weather cleared. Anne, Mary, Herman, Hanna, and all the kids rolled into Laramie on the train. The following month, Henry followed with the ox cart.

Belle's Uncle Henry immediately set out to establish the family. He put his cart to good use and went into the freighting business. The family filed multiple patents on homesteads north of Laramie, a place they called Poverty Flats. The surrounding land was alkaline, rocky, and dry, so the enterprising family used the only available resources. They built a stone barn and home that are now on the National Register of Historic Places. Two-foot thick stone walls in the house feature slots through which rifles could be discharged to defend the homestead.

After completing their family home, Henry and little Theodore Gorie began hauling stone to town. The Bath brothers built substantial stone edifices to replace the tents and flimsy frame structures hastily thrown up as the railroad came through. Most Bath buildings are still in use today and remain architecturally unique. Being a good German, Henry also founded Laramie's first brewery.

On April 10, 1870, Belle's mother, Mary Marie Gorie, then aged thirty-three, married Charles Kuster, aged thirty-two. Charles was the proprietor of one of the more successful liquor stores in Laramie City. Their union was made in heaven, given Mary's brother's interest in the next-door brewery. Intending to expand the ranching side of the business, Charles and Mary filed on some land thirty miles north of Laramie on Sybille Creek, but they could not prove up. They returned to the city and opened the Kuster House right in the center of town, half a block from the railroad depot. When she started working at the hotel, Belle stopped using the last name "Gorie" and became a "Kuster."

The Kuster House was a respectable business; there were no upstairs girls to entertain the stream of cowboys and merchants who entered the front doors. Charles and Mary Kuster were very popular with their clientele and with the business community as a whole. The economy was booming, and the Bath family was prospering. The youngest brother, Theodore Bath, emigrated from New York in 1872 with his family, followed by the last of the extended Bath family, Louisa. They arrived just in time to witness the birth of Charles Kuster, Junior, on November 6, 1875. Belle now had a half-brother.

~~~~~~~~~~~~~~~~

In 1883, the most tragic event occurred in the Bath family. Herman Bath, the patriarch, had died in 1880, leaving Hanna, his wife, in the care of Mss. Parsons, a dependable cook and housekeeper. On one of those glorious September days, the twelfth to be exact, Mss. Parsons and Hanna set out on a morning walk. They went south out of Laramie along the Soldier Springs Road. Irritated by her new shoes, Hanna Bath kept stopping to remove them. Mss. Parsons would have none of that and kept Hanna moving. Perhaps a bit weak in the eyes at age seventy-seven, Hanna was still a strong-willed woman, very fit and lean. On the other hand, Mss. Parsons was plump and prone to fainting spells.

When Hanna decided to head for the hills, shoes in hand, there was little Mss. Parsons could do to stop her. The Laramie *Boomerang* estimated that from the time Mss. Parsons abandoned her efforts to restrain Hanna and returned to town to spread the alarm, the old lady had about a three-hour head start. Numbering 100 riders, the search party split up and scoured a ten-mile radius of the spot where Hanna was last seen. Searchers most definitely rode
~~~~~~~~~~~~~~~~

the trails going past the Crimson Arch but Hanna Bath was nowhere to be found. That evening, a $100 reward was offered for any information leading to Mss. Bath's recovery.

There were no takers, but there were plenty of rumors. One man said he had seen a figure near Red Buttes. Others thought she might have been abducted, presumably by Indians. The next day, the entire city emptied to search the Harney Creek watershed for any sign of Mss. Bath, but to no avail. The Laramie *Boomerang* ran the following story:

> *September 19, 1883. One week ago today, Mrs. Bath disappeared and there is still no trace of her. Her sons have telegraphed to Denver for Bloodhounds, and if they can be procured, it is proposed to use them if possible in tracking her to the spot where Mrs. Bath's body now lies.*

During that bright and sunny fall, many people joined in the search, including, of course, Hanna's own family. Belle, her granddaughter, had just turned twenty-one that year. She had a beau, Gustave (Gus) Mueller, a cowboy at **Charley Hutton**'s ranch. On horseback, Gus and Belle rode slowly up the trail toward Sawmill Gulch. Needing to stop and rest the horses, they paused in the sparse shade of my Crimson Arch. They spent a lot of time standing by that rock, scratching at the surface. The date was September 23, 1883. They must have been out looking for Hanna. Why Gus Americanized his last name to "Miller" is not known. I would guess that a single "i" is much easier to carve than a "ue." He misspelled Belle's name, too.

The Laramie *Boomerang* continued on October 20, 1883:

> *Almost every carriage, wagon or saddle horse in the city was in use, men searching for the body of Mrs. Magdalene Johanna (Miller) Bath. The reward for the return of the body was raised to $500.*

The search for Hanna ended on November 3, 1883, when Caspar Hines discovered the much-decomposed remains in Evans Canyon, the route of present-day I-80, about six miles from the Crimson Arch. The *Boomerang* continued:

> *Funeral services took place at the Episcopal Church. It was one of the largest most imposing ever seen in Laramie, betokening the esteem in which she was and her relations are held in this community. Mrs. Bath is listed as dead on September 19, 1883.*

Belle and Gus were married in 1885 and lived in Laramie for the next twenty years in a little house on Second Street. After Mueller died in a railroad switching accident in 1906, Belle relocated to southern California with their daughter Vera. Their son Andrew remained in Laramie and worked at the electric light plant. Belle died in Los Angeles in 1930 from influenza. Her half-brother Charles Kuster immediately took the train to Los Angeles to arrange for her body's return to Laramie. She is buried beside her husband in the IOOF (International Order of Odd Fellows) block at Greenhill Cemetery. Her children, husband, mother, father, grandfather, grandmother, and a multitude of Bath cousins are nearby.

~~~~~~~~~~~~~~~

The Baths prided themselves on their fine horseflesh as did many ranchers on the Laramie Plains in 1896. Belle's cousins, Herman and Fred Bath, along with their father, Henry, decided to take a band of horses to Oklahoma to trade them for cattle. They trailed the horses south to Fort Collins and then on to Denver, driving the herd straight through the main downtown street. Then, it was on to Pueblo, Colorado. The quality of the horseflesh attracted spectators as they grazed the hungry herd on the banks of the Arkansas River. That year's drought had reduced the surrounding upland range forage to dust, so there was little hope of continuing to Oklahoma. The Baths were out of money, out of food, and low on hope.

Brilliantly, Herman had the idea of putting on a bronc riding display and serenading the crowd with their cowboy ballads. It was a remarkable success. They earned over six dollars, mostly in pennies donated by the appreciative crowd. In possession of enough money to see them back home, they abandoned their plan to go to Oklahoma; there was no grass along the way to feed the stock.

So, they set off from Pueblo, back along the trail through Denver. South of Fort Collins, a huge thunderstorm blew up suddenly. Large hail began pelting the camp, so Herman mounted his favorite horse and rode off to prevent the herd from stampeding. Just then, a bolt of lightning struck him. When the smoke cleared, Herman and fifteen horses lay dead in front of his brother and father. A wagon from Laramie was dispatched to retrieve the body. His mother, Anne, was inconsolable when she heard the news, falling immediately ill. She died the following year. Both mother and son are buried in the Greenhill Cemetery.

Henry Senior, Fred, and the rest of the Bath clan continued to be enthusiastic bronc riders. Along with the crazy Swedes at the Oxford Horse Ranch, they began the tradition of breaking horses at the annual July roundup in the Laramie Basin. The first bronc riding competition was held in Cheyenne on September 23, 1887, in conjunction with the Stock Growers' bi-annual roundup. Eventually, the event grew into Cheyenne Frontier Days. Louis Bath
~~~~~~~~~~~~~~~

emigrated to California, and because of his accomplished horsemanship, he was featured in the 1925 silent film production of *Ben Hur*.

That is pretty much how the typical Wyoming cowboy is pictured today: straight, polite, strong, and liable to have tragic events befall him. Wyoming culture is stuck right there at the end of 19th century.

It did not help that two Eastern writers published wildly popular dime novels, causing a wholly imaginary Cowboy Image to be seared into the readers' brains, never to be sullied. Ever. Owen Wister's *The Virginian* (1902) was preceded by Ned Buntline's *Buffalo Bill, the King of the Border Men* (1869), a fantasy based loosely upon 23-year-old Bill Cody's imagination. Cody was welcomed by adoring crowds when he attended a play based on the novel. After ten years of local fame showing off his equestrian and shooting skills, he organized The Greatest Wild West Show on Earth and wild it was. The entire population of Europe and America was captivated, if misinformed. Fifteen years after the Wild West Show closed in 1918, John Wayne cemented the cowboy image in his first cowboy talkie. Twenty-five years later, in his first full-color movie, *The Searchers*, Wayne's character puts two plugs into the dead body of an Apache warrior. The audience loved it. The most successful advertising campaign ever was for Marlboro cigarettes and it featured a ruggedlooking cowboy. When advertising tobacco products was outlawed, Philip Morris aired a mounted cowboy riding the western Montana range, and the unnamed cigarettes sold themselves. Only when Annie Proulx published Brokeback Mountain was the cowboy character altered from Bill Cody's image.

Cowboys circa 1880. Note the chaps made from Angora goat hide.
(Photo courtesy of Amy Lawrence.)

~ ~ ~ ~ ~ ~ ~ ~ ~ ~ ~ ~ ~ ~ ~ ~ ~

## *Chapter Nineteen*
# CHARLES & AUGUSTUS TRABING
## *& the Era of Fence Builders*

TRABING, IN A SQUARE, OVERWRITTEN BY RODOLFO.
(PHOTO BY K. McGUIRE)

Like most of Laramie's early residents, Charles and his brother Augustus "Gus" Trabing wore many hats. They came into the country in 1868 after their store in North Platte, Nebraska, was burned by hostiles. They bought the old Blue Front Saloon, which was on the market after the citizens of Laramie cleaned out the outlaws that used to dominate Front Street. The brothers had many business ideas, including freighting cordwood for the railroad. So they leased out the Blue Front and moved operational headquarters to Medicine Bow, Wyoming, about 60 miles north of Laramie. Gus was elected coroner of Carbon County and was known as a kind but driven man. An anonymous woman placed the following announcement in the Laramie *Daily Independent* in 1874:

> *A. Trabing called on us today and we had a pleasant chat and he paid us up on an old account like a little man. Trabing is a stirring, energetic business man, who is always bound to come out on top his share of the time.*

On September 4, Charlie and Gus opened the Trabing Brothers store in Medicine Bow and sold (both wholesale and retail) boots, shoes, hardware, crockery, glassware, fancy goods, drugs, and patent medicines. Gus promised "to defy the competition" by offering a thirty day same-as-cash settlement with customers who paid their bills promptly. By the following week in

September, he was offering groceries, wines, liquors, cigars, clothing, and dry goods. Seeing marketing opportunities in the fast-expanding economy, the **Trabings** branched out, freighting to Rawlins, White River, and Fort Washakie. They opened a store in Crazy Woman, Wyoming, where the Bozeman Trail crossed Crazy Woman Creek, but the notorious James Gang kept robbing them. So they leased out that location and moved once again to near present-day Buffalo, Wyoming. The freighting company employed one hundred men to transport goods all over Wyoming. They sent sales clerks to places like Saratoga, Baggs, Douglas, and Hanna, Wyoming. Charlie and Gus traveled to Cheyenne frequently, and they must have stopped next to a small red sandstone rock to carve the family name. A neat box surrounds the inscription but is undated. Unfortunately, the carving is partially obscured by another name, Rodolfo, whom I can only surmise was a Basque sheepherder.

The Trabings returned to Laramie in 1877, reopening the Blue Front as a grocery store. Over the next few years, they liquidated their farflung holdings and began to build new residences and businesses in Laramie. They also went into the cattle business, partnering with **Charley Hutton**, and jointly owned the Big Laramie Land & Cattle Improvement Company. Business was booming in 1885 when Charlie Trabing died at the age of forty. The brothers were en route to Omaha, Nebraska, accompanying seventy-two carloads of fat cattle divided into two trains.

At the whistle-stop in Sherman, Wyoming, Charlie entered one of the cars to save a downed steer in danger of being trampled. He rescued the steer but caught his finger on a random ragged edge of the stock car. He thought nothing of it for days, but the pain and swelling increased. Brother Gus was on a similar train just hours behind him. When they got to Omaha, Gus insisted that Charlie see a doctor for treatment, but his efforts were insufficient to save him. Nursing his brother overnight, Gus slept on a cot in Charlie's hotel room. The following day, Gus awoke to find Charlie dead. The newspapers reported that he had died either of blood poisoning or apoplexy from the pain.

By 1886, Gus Trabing was president of a new corporation, the Trabing Commercial Company, and he opened up a large store occupying an entire city block in downtown Laramie. His handsome twin stone stores eventually were the architectural gems of downtown Laramie. His *Boomerang* advertisements (naming Trabing Commercial as successors to the Trabing Brothers) featured for sale canned and bottled goods of every description, full weights and measures, and free delivery on railroad orders. The next day, the advertisement had expanded to a quarter page. They offered for sale wood- and willowware (carload lots of furniture), Budweiser, Anheuser Busch, and Schlitz beer, eight brands of champagne (including Mumms), eight brands of claret, eight brands of Rhine wine, seven brands of whiskey, hams and side meats, six kinds of cheese, eight brands of flour, as well as animal feed, both grains and hay. Customers could also buy a cord of wood. Trabing published a 345-page catalog of goods he offered for sale. His advertising stated:

> *You can get everything needed at Trabings, and at prices lower than the lowest.*

By the time Wyoming became a state, Augustus Trabing had served twice as Laramie's mayor and one term in the Territorial Legislative Council. His signature legislative acts allowed the governor to appoint the attorney general and marshal instead of proscribing their popular election. The year after statehood was attained, Trabing became president of the Laramie branch of the Columbia Building & Loan Association out of Denver, Colorado. He made the loans and built the buildings. His public admiration got him elected Wyoming senator in 1895, succeeding J.W. Carey.

~~~~~~~~~~~~~~~~

Trabing and his circle of friends (Holliday, Collins, Ingersoll, Caldwell, Cooper, and McKenna) engaged in multiple business concerns. As men with some capital, they formed the Wyoming Central Land Investment Company (WCLIC) to buy up UPRR land along the railroad right-of-way. As an incentive to build the transcontinental railroad, the government had given the UP Corporation every other section of land in the twenty-mile swath along the 1,200-mile right-of-way. Anticipating an influx of settlers after the railroad was complete, the government funded several survey expeditions to explore the far West.

One of these was led by John Wesley Powell. A one-armed Civil War hero, he courageously embarked on a fact-finding expedition to explore the Colorado River in three open, wooden boats. Powell rode the train to present-day Green River, Wyoming, at the time just a collection of tents at the time. He and his men disembarked and set up camp on what is now called Expedition Island. There, they prepared for one of the most daring expeditions ever attempted in the American West: the passage down the mighty Colorado River.

After enduring mountainous rapids and near starvation, Powell survived his journey and reported back to Washington. He recommended that the Homestead Act of 1863 be amended to grant 2,460 acres per applicant (instead of 160 acres) for patents west of the one-hundredth meridian, approximately Cozad, Nebraska. "Proving up" on a land patent had a specific meaning. Settlers had to build a house and live there for five years. Then, they got to buy the land for about a dollar-and-a-quarter an acre. Alternatively, they could pay $1,800 upfront, which works out to eleven-and-a-quarter dollars an acre.
~~~~~~~~~~~~~~~~

Back East, say near Washington DC, the number of acres necessary to support a single cow is a single acre or less. In the green pastures of Virginia, the grass grows back even as it is eaten by livestock. It must have been difficult for legislators to believe it would take forty acres to feed a single cow/calf unit. In the West, once a cow has taken her mouthful of grass from a plant, that plant will likely no longer be able to produce enough biomass for another bite. It is done for the year, dependent upon other means of reproduction besides seed production. If the plant has already produced seeds, the cow does the plant a favor by transporting them elsewhere and depositing them, well-fertilized, in another location. That is why allowing grasses to head out before grazing the pasture is vital. However, members of Congress had no appreciation of that fact, and they also had no appreciation for how different the climatic conditions were west of the one-hundredth meridian.

Congress stuck with the 1862 number, 160 acres per patent, about what was necessary to scratch a living on heavily forested, well-watered, deep-soiled Iowa land. They had never been to Wyoming and refused to heed John Powell's wise advice; their lobbyist friends from the railroad supported the idea. Many people tried, but very few managed to prove up legally in Wyoming. It was almost impossible as mandated. Later, in 1883, Powell famously warned Congress:

> *Gentlemen, you are piling up a heritage of conflict & litigation over water rights, for there is not sufficient water to supply the land.*

Land development companies began springing up like weeds when western lands became available for sale, and Wyoming was no exception. The WCLIC bought up 200,000 acres of land within Albany County that had been granted by the government to the UPRR, with no money down, no interest, and no payment required until they sold it. The consortium cleared $375,000, and the UPRR received $107,000 of much-needed income (worth $1.7 million today). This is how the Oxford Ranch gained ownership of its intervening railroad sections.

The consortium made money in two ways. They might roll over a title, retaining the water rights on bottomlands, an asset potentially more valuable than the land. Or they might promise to bring irrigation water to arid land, which they had divided into lots. They invested significantly in large irrigation ditch companies, including the Pioneer Canal. The WCLIC promised to bring water to dry uplands near Laramie. The consortium would loan money prospective clients at six percent interest to buy lots adjacent to their ditch. Implicit in the deal was that the ditch was capable of delivering water for croplands. Front page news in the *Boomerang* on May 30, 1885, announced the near completion of the canal, and an eight-page advertisement called for the attention of interested buyers; the WCLIC had land for sale.

Other irrigation projects were not so successful. I have crossed the Loback Ditch, or, should I say, I have crossed what remains of it. Above the North Fork of the Little Laramie, there is a long and arduously constructed ditch. It is deep, at least six feet. Large, round boulders from the last ice age litter the surrounding landscape. It must have taken thousands of man-hours to construct. It is bone-dry today and has always been. The vagaries of weather and underlying geology took their toll on that particular investment.

The WCLIC beat homesteader Peter Johnson to the courthouse and filed on the senior water right to the Harney Creek watershed on what was to become the Oxford Ranch. Why is this important to me? Because, as the holder of the junior water right, when water becomes scarce, my right to use the water that runs through my land might just dry up.

Water has always been key to Western development, and access to water also governs wildlife populations. Conservationists know that the key to big game management is contiguous habitat. Most large ungulates are highly migratory, but Man has altered this instinct. We decided to put the ranch in a conservation easement to preserve a contiguous route for large ungulate migration over the Laramie Range and onto the Great Plains. Before we could protect the Oxford Ranch from future development, we had to hire a geologist to ensure no commercially viable limestone deposits existed. Even the Nature Conservancy cannot stop the UPRR from selling "its" mineral deposits and demanding the right to deface our property. No matter how stringent the reclamation laws are in the state, no one can restore what is destroyed by hard rock surface mining.

~ ~ ~ ~ ~ ~ ~ ~ ~ ~ ~ ~ ~ ~

Late afternoon, 1996, finds me snacking at the very top of my new land, dangling my legs over a 100-foot drop of a sheer sandstone cliff face. From here, I can see the entire watershed. A cloud of dust catches my attention as the sun dips towards the glistening white Snowy Range summit. I hear noises echoing off the rock face — barking, whistling, and bawling calves in the distance. Finally, I spot a few cows cresting the ridge over to Sawmill Gulch. Gradually, more cows appear, calling to their calves who are dashing about, tails flagpole-high, bellowing back and forth, reassuring each other:

*Maaaaa-m* they call, I *am here. Where are you?*

The placid mother cows follow the narrow trail down the slope to the salt lick. It is a group of perhaps thirty coal-black cows, thirty half-grown black calves, and one enormous bull that must belong to my neighbor to the south. With my binoculars, I can pick out his "Rafter 4" brand emblazoned on the bull's side. The bull is long and black, and his heavily muscled sides are sleek with sweat. He thrashes his massive head, snorting to clear his oxygen-starved lungs of blood and mucus. He is worn out from breeding and certainly does not want to haul all 2,000 pounds of him over the hill, even to join his harem.

A lone cowboy on horseback is forcing him, swinging his lariat loop but never throwing it. A cowboy would be no match for even an exhausted bull. The pair plods slowly down to the stock water tank at the foot of my escarpment. The cows are still milling about, waiting. Those who have located their offspring stand, allowing the persistent calves to nurse. The cowboy pushes the herd up the narrow, sagebrush-filled gulch, whistling to his dog.

The cries fade away as the small herd moves up the darkening gulch. I have recognized my eastern neighbor by his white hat, paint mare, and black-and-white speckled dog. I am aware he has not seen me watching him cross my land uninvited, land that he had to sell to us to buy the larger ranch. Although I am a novice at this ranching thing, it is abundantly clear he is up to no good. He does not run cattle, so this herd could not be his. I am unarmed, and he may not be; open carry is the law in Wyoming, so I remain hidden. I watch him disappear.

Packing up my things, I pick my way down, around the steep, rocky ridge, to the stock tank. The sweet smell of fresh sagebrush, trampled by passing hooves, fills the evening air, masking the stink of fresh cow manure. The scent is almost sticky as I inspect the broken twigs along the dry stream bed. The cattle have left deep footprints in the soft soil, so I follow the trail. About a quarter-mile up, the tracks enter a narrowing gully. My property line bisects that gully. The topographic map tells me this was the old stagecoach trail between Laramie and Cheyenne. As erosion carved the ruts deeper, the route became unusable, so other routes crisscrossed the area. A labyrinth of old trails and cutoffs laces the entire eastern aspect of the watershed.

Following him, I find a hidden ravine branching off steeply to the east just before the property line. Inside the impossibly narrow, cool, tunnel-like gully, the trees overhead melt into a dark ceiling. Halfway through, where the fence runs, the wires are down, lying flat on the ground, half-buried in the soft soil underfoot. I might never suspect that, in addition to the cattle, a mounted man and his dog just passed through; until I notice that the fence is cut.

The sun was setting, so I hurried on, taking one of the winding old trails towards Laramie. This trail happened to pass by the little red arch, which was positively glowing in the setting sun. My little Crimson Arch has seen many such stories unfold. I continued on my way, mulling over what exactly I had just witnessed. Rustling does not happen anymore, does it? I make a mental note to call my neighbor about his bull.

In the West, many rules and regulations govern the movement of livestock. A rancher can haul livestock across state lines only with an official inspection in hand. The local livestock inspector, probably your neighbor, is the only person who can issue the paperwork. They take their task very seriously and inspect every single cow for evidence of branding. Not having a brand is no longer punished with confiscation, but the long-established ritual of stock inspection continues today.

Brand inspectors are the first line of defense against rustlers, so as soon as I arrived at the ranch house, I called Clay Lilley to report what I had observed. The next day, we set out to look for them. The topography in the area was very rough, filled with steep box canyons crowded with tall ponderosa pines and underbrush. The horseback search took many days. Eventually, twenty-nine cows were located and pushed back across the fence to their home pasture. A month passed, and finally, the last heifer materialized in another neighbor's corral, twenty miles to the south.

The bull, a pedigreed Angus, was never seen again. Indeed, in that market, cows can be worth upwards of $1,000 apiece, bulls $3,000. The price has since gone up to $2,200 per cow and $3,800 per bull. Cattle rustling, it appears, is alive and well in the West. No matter how tight your fences, someone with mal-intent can get through. As a rule in the West, good fences make good neighbors. This is true in today's Wyoming, as in Robert Frost's time.

~ ~ ~ ~ ~ ~ ~ ~ ~ ~ ~ ~ ~ ~

Meanwhile, back to Augustus **Trabing**, mayor, future senator, and businessman. His successful mercantile business occupied an entire city block in downtown Laramie. During the Panic of 1893, Trabing was forced to close his credit accounts and downsize his store by half. When the buildings burned down in 1895, it was front-page news. The entire city turned out to fight the fire, unsuccessfully. The disaster prompted the citizens of Laramie to improve their firefighting capabilities. Trabing's loss was calculated at $50,000, and he did not rebuild. He continued investing in the Laramie area, but eventually retired to a ranch in Sybille Canyon, thirty-five miles north of Laramie.

Gus Trabing's grand legacy ends with his suit against the US government. In 1892, Trabing filed for compensation for the burned trading post he and Charlie had established in North Platte, Nebraska, back in 1868. The 1891 Indian Depredations Act entitled him to reimbursement. His claim was denied because he was not a citizen at the time of the loss. Gus Trabing had entered the United States at the age of eleven; Charlie was three years younger. Their father had not completed the paperwork necessary to claim citizenship before Gus's eighteenth birthday.

He litigated for ten years, all the way to the Supreme Court. Unfortunately, Augustus Trabing died in 1906 before the successful ruling was handed down. Caught in a snowstorm between his ranch and the King Brother's place, Gus was forced to spend the night huddled beneath his wagon. He developed pneumonia but continued with his many business activities. He finally succumbed to the disease on November 28, 1906, at age 65. He was buried at the entrance of Laramie's Greenhill Cemetery near his brother Charles.

# *Chapter Twenty*
# TRAVIS/TANNER - '92
## *& the Transformation into Paradise*

E.J. TRAVIS / ETTA TANNER, 1892.
(PHOTO BY K. MCGUIRE)

The names **Travis/Tanner** are carefully spelled out, one over the other, on the eastern panel of the Crimson Arch. As far as I can tell from the census records, E.J. Travis was a cowboy, working on many of the spreads throughout the Laramie Basin. I am guessing that Etta Tanner must have been his girlfriend. The Kuster House employed an E. **Tanner** as a waitress; I suspect she was Belle Kuster's friend. E.J. and Etta represented two of the many regular people who populated the town during its heyday. Laramie had gone from a corrupt railroad town to a bustling community in twenty short years.

Most of Laramie's early development occurred in the first four years after the railroad's arrival. By 1872, the UPRR employed 330 men in Laramie City and had constructed a roundhouse, a machine shop, rolling mills, a foundry, a blacksmith shop, a railroad tie treatment plant, and a hospital. This commerce attracted more population as well as other businesses. Among these were a brick factory, a soda bottling company, several breweries, a flour mill, a gypsum plant, a cigar factory, a woolen mill, a glass factory, a tannery, a coal company, a chemical works, and an oil refinery. A highly successful plaster of Paris mine was located just south of town near the Oxford Ranch. Add a bustling Fort Sanders and the Territorial Prison construction project to this scene, and life in Laramie was good.

Emigrant families, such as the Baths from New York, were securely grounded in the entertainment, cattle, and construction businesses. They continued to thrive, as did their direct descendants, who still live along the rivers that crisscross the Laramie Basin. Eventually, most railroad facilities burned to the ground, and many private businesses failed or burned. But, on the whole, the agricultural community prospered until the Great Die-up of 1886. That winter put many ranchers out of business when constant blizzards and extreme cold killed ninety percent of the livestock in Wyoming.

In 1869, the territorial prison was sited on the high ground across the Laramie River from Laramie City. In a grand political compromise, Laramie was awarded federal funding for the University of Wyoming and the Territorial Prison, while Cheyenne became the new capital. Laramie's **M.C. Brown** was selected to oversee the construction of the new prison. He solicited several proposals for the project and eventually accepted Laramie banker Edward Ivinson's bid for $36,000.

Unfortunately, the flooding Laramie River had washed out the bridge and any easy access to the construction site. Many local cowboys joined the construction crews, including Mr. **Travis**. Local red sandstone blocks were quarried out of the canyon to the east, hauled into town, and ferried across the river. The outer walls were two feet thick, and the structure was dedicated in 1872 after three years of construction. In the first two years of operation, the Territorial Prison housed forty-four prisoners; eleven managed to escape.

WYOMING'S TERRITORIAL PRISON, 1872 (WIKIPEDIA)

The prison was overcrowded by 1877, but three years later, there were only three prisoners. That did not prevent the territory from spending money to enlarge the facility, adding a second cell block, complete with five cells designed to house women inmates. After remodeling in 1880, it featured three floors of cell blocks; each block held two rows of seven cells. The cells were six feet wide, eight feet deep, and eight feet tall. None had windows or shared an exterior wall. All twelve exterior windows in the main block were thirteen feet tall but only thirteen inches wide. The black mesh of iron bars still guards against escape.

By 1890, the city fathers had figured out that it was cheaper to ship federal inmates to Illinois for detention than maintain them in Laramie; it cost one dollar a day in Laramie and only twenty-five cents in Joliet Prison. After Wyoming achieved statehood, the Territorial Prison closed, and the building became the Wyoming State Penitentiary. During its life as a prison, the building hosted just over 1,000 men and women. However, the State Pen was an economic black hole. Attempts to fund its operating expenses included an inmate-staffed brick factory, a broom factory, an ice factory, and a limestone quarry. All failed economically, and besides, it made escaping too easy.

The most famous inmate ever to be incarcerated was Robert Leroy Parker, better known as Butch Cassidy. He lived in the main cell block from 1894 to 1896 alongside local cowboy Louis Bath, who was serving time for selling butchered Swan Company calves. Cassidy was a big-time horse thief whose gang, the Wild Bunch, made their headquarters in the badlands of central Wyoming, a place called Hole-in-the-Wall. Laramie law enforcement captured him after he reportedly stole a horse and locked him up after a very brief trial to serve a sentence of eighteen months. Butch was released for good behavior after fifteen months, promising never to steal horses in Wyoming again. He did not, however, indemnify the trains.

In a robbery sensationalized in *Butch Cassidy & the Sundance Kid*, Butch and his gang robbed the mail train as it ran north, thirty miles from Laramie. The gang blew up poor Mr. Woodcock's railroad car and sent thousands of dollars worth of gold and unsigned bank promissory notes into the sky. The seven bandits gathered as much gold as they could find, grabbed a bundle of singed banknotes, and rode for the hills.

The Wilcox telegraph operator issued an alarm when the train failed to turn up as scheduled. US Marshal Joe LeFors and some Pinkerton agents departed the Laramie Depot on a special train to pursue the robbers. It arrived at the scene an hour later, but the gang was long gone, back to their Hole-in-the-Wall. Federal Marshal Joe LeFors never gave up pursuing them after the Wilcox train robbery, chasing Cassidy across two continents.

Over the next twelve years, the Pinkerton men systematically tracked down the perpetrators by monitoring the serial numbers of the partially burnt bank drafts stolen by the gang. After the drafts were exchanged for cash, the serial numbers took about three months to reach the Pinkerton Office. Once identified, Pinkerton sent men to search for the bandits, and eventually, they found them.

US law enforcement likes to brag that all seven of the Wild Bunch died by gunfire. It took some years, but the Pinkerton men finally tracked Butch Cassidy as far as Argentina. Spooked out of his comfortable ranch at the foot of the Andes, Cassidy reunited with the Kid and robbed a payroll train in Bolivia. Officially, the Bolivian army killed both.

However, Leroy Parker's youngest sister attests that he visited the family home in Circleville, Utah, in 1925. Leroy enjoyed a piece of his mother's blueberry pie before moving on in his Model T Ford. Friends in Baggs, Wyoming, also reported a visit from Parker, as did J. David Love's doctor in Lander, Wyoming. Parker's face had been altered surgically in Paris, but the bullet wounds that the doc had patched up years ago remained the same. Parker's little sister had been too young to remember him, but his mother did not need her aging eyes to identify her son.

When the new State Penitentiary was finished in Rawlins, Wyoming, the old territorial prison building reverted to the University of Wyoming. They converted it into a sheep barn. Luckily, when the cell blocks were removed, they were carefully preserved. When I first saw the place, I wondered why a sheep barn would have barred windows. It remains one of the oldest and best-preserved buildings in Wyoming. In the 1980s, the prison grounds were beautifully restored as a tourist attraction that is well worth visiting. The summertime tours are wonderfully informative and accurate.

The University of Wyoming opened with much fanfare in 1886, welcoming forty-two male and female students and five faculty members. It had taken twelve years to complete. Its handsome Old Main building sat alone on the empty prairie east of town. The University remained cloistered, employing only six professors and a president until the 1920s. With a county board of commissioners' nomination, tuition was free for in-state students. Otherwise, tuition was five dollars, and room and board was twenty-five dollars. The library charged a fee of two dollars fifty for the right to peruse the scant collection of donated books, so the students also turned to Albany County Library's collection. When he decided to move to Boise City, Idaho, Jon Finfrock, the popular local doctor, donated his books to the Albany County Library.

Eventually, Laramie's library was endowed by the Carnegie Foundation, one of 2,000+ libraries begun between 1883 and 1929, 1,689 of which were located in the United States. That is half of the libraries built in America before 1930. Albany County Library was one of sixteen built in Wyoming with the $250,000 (about $7.5 million today) in Carnegie grants allocated to the state. Ten of these buildings are still standing, and five are still libraries. Laramie's Carnegie Library is now an attractive office building for the city.

The University of Wyoming persevered, although the campus has changed since 1886. Dr. Grace Raymond Hebard, the first UW librarian, described the campus as:

> *... a vacant lot, more actually speaking, with a single, isolated, substantial building surrounded by the perpetually snowcapped mountains of the Medicine Bow Range. The campus was without walks, or trees, shrubs, lawn, grass, or evidence of flowers during the past season. The library was a room without table, chair, desk, shelves, book-case, blackboard, curtain, and only three stacks of US government books piled in a pyramid in the center of the floor* (wyohistory.org).

THE UNIVERSITY OF WYOMING, CIRCA 1920. (WIKIPEDIA)

~~~~~~~~~~~~~~~

By 1879, with the Indian Wars over, Wyoming's economic focus shifted to Cheyenne, the gateway to South Dakota's goldfields. A new railroad spur marched north from Cheyenne, the emerging first city of Wyoming, to Deadwood, South Dakota. Fort Laramie closed, and Fort D.A. Russell (near Cheyenne) took up the mantle of protecting westward-bound travelers and territorial residents. The cavalry horse barns built during that era are remarkable. Three cavalry regiments were based there, each occupying one gigantic brick barn. The famous Buffalo Soldiers were, on occasion, stationed there.

In 1882, Fort Sanders closed, and its remaining nine square miles of land were sold off. Then, when the harsh winter of 1886-87 wiped out most of the livestock on the Laramie Plains, the economic situation did not look good. By 1902, the UPRR was virtually bankrupt, and Laramie became an
~~~~~~~~~~~~~~~

afterthought. Newly married, Mr. and Mss. **Travis** packed up and left the county for California, never to return.

Laramie weathered the Roaring Twenties and the Great Depression with barely a change in the population. When the men left to fight World War II, the remaining residents grew Victory Gardens and bought Freedom Bonds. Supported by agriculture and the university, the town stayed at 17,000 inhabitants throughout the 1960s.

When the newly constructed Interstate 80 arrived, it brought an economic resurgence reminiscent of the railroad's arrival a hundred years before. Truck stops and hotels popped up at the interchanges, and work was had for the asking. The best thing was that the downtown buildings were substantial and survived the art-deco era that disguised the handsome, gilded-age exteriors. Today, building owners keep it simple, stripping off the cheesy façades and exposing the original bricks and arching windows. Organic restaurants, public art, climbing shops, and microbreweries now dominate the downtown business community. It is a fun place to pass the time.

Called "Laradise" by the local Chamber of Commerce, a more diverse cross-section of Americana populates Laramie than the rest of the state. The presence of the University of Wyoming's student body and professors see to that. Additionally, the expanding population along Colorado's Front Range has caused many progressive-minded folks to move in, inclement weather notwithstanding. The Wild West mindset that spurred Laramie's initial development somehow remains, allowing a modicum of freedom that many crowded cities to the south do not enjoy.

The small ranchers, who still consider themselves Albany County's lifeblood, proudly post billboards announcing the agricultural production the county has achieved. The tagline, "Beef - It's What's for Dinner," is blazoned across the roadsigns, and these families probably eat beef daily. However, the rest of the world is out of sync with the mantra that the cowboys continue to embrace. Their livelihoods are slowly eroding due to climate change, vegetable substitutions, laboratory-grown meat, changing dietary preferences, and Chinese tariffs. China used to be an export market for beef, but western cattlemen act like they do not notice.

~~~~~~~~~~~~~~~

## *Chapter Twenty-one*
# MEP '95 - Mary Powell
### & *High Plains Justice*

M E P. The top two bars are eroded.
(Photo by K. McGuire)

There are at least two women in Wyoming's history with bizarre stories, Eva Langhoff and Mary Powell. They both were rustlers living north and east of Laramie; Eva in the Sybille Canyon area, and Mary on Horse Creek in the Iron Mountain area. Eva, a large, exotically beautiful woman, was married to a diminutive man named Fred Langhoff. Short and rotund, Mary was married to Fred Powell, who had come into the country working for the railroad in 1868. He was a brakeman, one of the more dangerous occupations available on the run between Cheyenne and Laramie. When necessary, Fred would dance along the tops of slippery Pullman cars or freight cars to turn the jackscrew that applied the brakes. Powell retired from the railroad after he lost his left arm in a fall from a moving train.

As he recovered at the hospital tent in downtown Laramie, he fell in love with Mary, a cook for the railroad. She was kind to him, and they eventually married. Fully recovered, albeit less one arm, but still strong and able, Fred staked out a homestead up on Horse Creek where the lush grasses fill the narrow valleys. This summertime oasis in the Laramie Range is just south of Sybille Canyon, where Eva lived. Sybille is a lovely canyon, but there is country nearby that could, in places, be mistaken for the moon's surface. Not to be denied the US government's promise of almost free land, both Freds put their patent stakes down.
~~~~~~~~~~~~~~~

Fred and Mary built a cabin on Horse Creek, moving in to try to scrape out a living, running a few head of cattle. It was he who pursued the last buffalo seen in the Laramie Basin. The old bull ran past a sheep camp early one morning in August 1880 with one-armed Fred Powell in hot pursuit. He had tracked him all the way from Iron Mountain. The sheepherders joined the chase, and the bull was run to ground and killed. They dressed the meat quickly and loaded it into a wagon bound for Laramie, twenty-seven miles away. It spoiled before they got there.

Fred Langhoff, on the other hand, was a German-born immigrant who came into the country in 1878, landing a job with rancher and rock signatory **Charley Hutton**. He worked for Charley for a couple of years and then tried his hand at homesteading over on the upper reaches of Dale Creek, very near the Crimson Arch. He met and married the beautiful Eva Farrell, Louis Bath's neighbor, and tried homesteading again in Sybille Canyon, thirty-five miles north of Laramie.  Fred and Eva produced three children, Anne, Louis, and Douglas. Anne and Louis regularly made the honor roll at their little one-room schoolhouse. The family group was rounded out by Fred's half-brother, Henry Langhoff, who homesteaded nearby.  Both newcomers immediately came in conflict with Swan Land & Cattle, the largest cattle producer in the area.

~~~~~~~~~~~~~~~

Meanwhile, back in Cheyenne, members of the Social Club held an emergency meeting. The winter weather was taking a toll, affecting their bottom lines. Feed was scarce everywhere, but especially near the home ranch headquarters. Home ranch meadows were continuously grazed to the nub during a long winter. Free summer pasture (like that up on Iron Mountain) was the margin that made the big ranchers. Until people like Langhoff, Powell, and their neighbors William Lewis and Bill Rogers showed up, summer pasture was not a problem. The increasing number of grangers coming into the area was concerning to the Swan Company. There was only one easy way to solve this problem, so the Cheyenne Social Club voted to hire a stock detective to do their dirty work. A former Pinkerton man seemed right for the job.

Tom Horn first appeared in the Cheyenne area as an employee of White Cap John Cobel sometime between 1891 and 1892. Ostensibly a law enforcement officer, Horn led a solitary life roaming the hills of southeastern Wyoming, watching things. He would watch his employers' cattle as they grazed on granger-owned land on the Horse Creek watershed. Tom would watch the grangers as they emerged from their crude cabins. He would watch
~~~~~~~~~~~~~~~

their sheep as they swarmed across the range. He tracked how many cows were out on a person's pastures. Tom Horn was a secretive and solitary man.

According to the Laramie *Boomerang*, only four major sheepmen occupied the Horse Creek area: E.P. Baker, H.D. Richardson, and the King Brothers. They shipped out 16,000 to 18,000 pounds of wool each in June 1892. That is a lot of sheep. When these men began receiving threatening notes, the *Boomerang* postulated:

> *...that they should be exercised over the Ku Klux notices that have greeted their eyes in numerous places on the open range, and they scarcely know what action to take in the matter. They are satisfied of one thing, however, and that is if Salt Peter gets in his work there will be a great many dead sheep on the range before long. As it is, the sheepmen are at a loss what to do to prevent the execution of the threat implied in the notice* (Laramie *Boomerang*, 1893).

The notes were Tom Horn's way of putting pressure on the grangers. "Salt Peter" is an ingredient of explosives, and the comment probably meant that sheep, perhaps even sheepmen, would be shot. That they were fighting among themselves did not concern Horn; it gave him cover.

On August 14, 1892, the "Langhoff Gang" (Louis Bath, Thomas Boucher, and Fred and Mary Langhoff) were arraigned before the court for stealing twenty-six horses from J.C. Cobel. The month before, those horses, combined with others stolen from Henry G. Hay (along the Laramie River north of Cheyenne), the Powder River Cattle Company (beyond Crazy Woman Creek), and the Hereford Association, filled three rail cars at the nearby Cheyenne stockyards. Fred Langhoff accompanied the stolen horses to Kentucky, where they sold for sixteen dollars each. Langhoff had papers for each of them; the problem was that their brands had been altered.

Once alerted of the thefts, Laramie County Sheriff Kelley pursued Langhoff across the country. He was gone for two weeks, tracking the shipment of horses. Kelley finally arrested Langhoff while he was visiting relatives in Wisconsin. The plaintiffs claimed that the gang had been stealing horses for years and celebrated his arrest.

The frontpage headlines announcing Langhoff's return to Cheyenne in handcuffs competed for column space with coverage of the twenty-six White Caps arrested during the Johnson County Invasion. Langhoff's arrest also coincided with his half-brother Henry's death; he was found hanging by his belt in his brother's shed. The degree of Henry's involvement in the escapade was as unclear as his cause of death. A month later, an article in the *Boomerang* joked about Henry having died of "pizen weed" poisoning. Pizen weed refers to death camas (*Toxicoscordion venenosum*), a highly poisonous plant that looks, smells, and tastes like a green onion. Faced with a slow death by poison or a quick one by hanging, Henry might have made his choice. The question remains: who would have poisoned him?

Fred had much to do after he was released on bond. He had to deal with his brother's suicide and was behind on his taxes. The ranch chores and the timber cultivation patent needed attention. While awaiting trial, he filed for divorce because his wife Eva had taken up with the ranch hand, Louis Bath. The Cheyenne *Daily Leader* reported six months after the fact that Swan Land & Cattle tried to make a deal with Langhoff. They would arrange to drop the charges if Langhoff turned over the deed to his land and left the country. He refused their offer.

This is not the end of the Langhoff saga, however. Al Bowie, the Swan manager at the Two Bar Ranch in Sybille Canyon, deputized Tom Horn and set him to work watching the Langhoffs again. Horn's sources indicated that Eva had delivered some butchered calves to Laramie two weeks previously and had promised to deliver more. On November 16, 1893, Tom Horn arrested five people for cattle theft: Eva Langhoff, Louis Bath, ranch hand Bill Taylor, and neighbors Bill and Nellie Cleve. They were all charged with butchering calves belonging to Swan. The charges against Taylor and the Cleves were dropped, but during the trial, Louis Bath confessed, swearing that Eva had nothing to do with the plan. She was acquitted, but Bath was convicted and sentenced to eighteen months in the Territorial Prison. He served almost a year before being pardoned by Wyoming Governor John Osbourne, a Democrat. Louis Bath and Leroy "Butch Cassidy" Parker were two of twenty-four prisoners that summer.

Fred tried to hang on to the Sybille ranch, but in March 1895, he failed to comply with his timber culture patent. In danger of losing his provisional patent title, Langhoff sold the Sybille Canyon ranch to the Hoffman Brothers the following year and left the country for New Mexico; his Wyoming property eventually fell into the hands of the Swan Company.

Eva Langhoff then left Louis Bath (who was serving time), and moved to North Park, Colorado. By 1902, Mss. Langhoff was a well-established resident and visited Laramie frequently; her presence always announced in the *Boomerang*. In 1909, her son Douglas, also of North Park, was arrested for stealing horses. He had been gathering the stolen ponies for some time, ranging far afield to collect the best specimens he could find. He sequestered them near Tie Siding, Wyoming, in a cleverly concealed grassy ravine. When he had a good bunch, he drove them to Fort Collins, Colorado, to sell. They were identified as stolen after one of them kicked his new owner to death in Loveland, Colorado, a week later. The local sheriff took a good look at the brand and decided it was one of three horses reported stolen in North Park the year before. Douglas was arrested and confessed on the way to jail in Fort Collins. He spent the next six years in Cañon City Penitentiary, Colorado. I could find no record of any Langhoff family member interred anywhere in Wyoming, Wisconsin, New Mexico, or Colorado.

~~~~~~~~~~~~~~

# Rustling 101

To claim a calf, the rustler might slit its tongue soon after birth, impairing its ability to nurse. After a few days, a mother's udder will swell painfully with milk. As the hungry calf tries in vain to suckle, he will bump his head, sometimes quite violently, right into her milk bag, hoping to release the milk. The resultant pain causes the cow to avoid the calf, perhaps even abandoning it. The gang would then claim the half-starved infant as an "orphan." Alternatively, they might shoot a cow as she crossed a swollen stream or river. The current would carry her body away, and there would be another orphan to rescue.

Rustlers employed various techniques to avoid being caught with "neat" cattle, branded cattle that belonged to someone else. If the hide of a branded cow ever turned up at a granger's cabin, that alone proved guilt. Remember that the skin of a cow takes a very long time to rot. It can be buried for years and still be identifiable. The rustler could not tan the hide to sell it either. Some Wyoming brands are oversized to minimize the chance that a branded hide might be marketable. Unbranded calves were a much easier target for a rustler.
~~~~~~~~~~~~~~

~~~~~~~~~~~~~~~

By 1892, Fred Powell's life was getting harder. Snowstorms ravaged the area all winter, and feed was scarce. He and Mary had divorced, but she and their son Will continued to live with him or Mary's sister, who had homesteaded an adjoining parcel. In June 1893, Horse Creek area granger William "Bill" Lewis, a neighbor of Fred Powell, was arrested for stealing calves from Swan Land & Cattle. Thus began a longrunning feud. By 1895, the Horse Creek Wars ascended to a higher level. No longer did burning each other's haystacks and killing livestock suffice for the good people of Iron Mountain. One morning, an unknown assailant shot and killed Bill Lewis as he loaded a skinned steer into his wagon. Removing the hide also removed the identifying brand, a sure sign of a rustler.

Lewis's 5,000 sheep habitually ran all over the upper reaches of the Iron Mountains on public land. In the good old days, that land would have been summer grazing for the Swan Land & Cattle Company. The cattlemen insisted that sheep damage the range by uprooting all the grasses as they grazed. Any good sheepman knows that sheep prefer to eat weeds and flowers and should co-exist with cattle on a well-managed range. This inability to appreciate a problem (that the range was overgrazed) provoked violence throughout southeastern Wyoming. Many accounts of sheep and sheepmen being slaughtered by vigilante cattlemen exist as far south as the Virginia Dale area.

Like Lewis, Powell also had a running feud with a neighbor, Etherton P. Baker. Mr. Baker was a large sheepman, but he also ran cattle. He suspected Fred of stealing a horse and burning his haystack. Fred was arrested and charged with two counts: one count for horse theft and one for arson. The horse theft charges were dropped, but he served four months in jail on the arson charges. Powell's release from prison occurred after Lewis was murdered. Arriving home, he found neatly written but unsigned notices left on his door for three days running. Each had the same message:

*mend your ways & practices, leave the country or be killed.*

He opted to leave the countryside. When haying season approached, Fred returned to harvest the hay. He worked for ten days and was almost done when a single shot fired from a distance away killed him in the field. The crime went uninvestigated, as had Lewis' death. The only clue linking the two killings was that both bodies were found with their heads resting upon a flat rock.

Mary Powell then became the definition of a tough lady. Claiming that Fred's will left the ranch to her, she and their eight-year-old son, William,
~~~~~~~~~~~~~~~

returned, intending to run it alone. She finished bringing in the hay and hunkered down for the winter. She was soon bound over to district court in a forgery suit brought by her brother-in-law. He claimed she had forged Fred's will, but the suit was dropped. So, she continued to live and work the ranch. She was still a member of the Horse Creek School Board and the Laramie County Elections Board. That brought in some hard cash; thirty-five dollars a year for the school board and six for being an election official.

As the winter wore on and the new year arrived, her nephew received a threatening letter in the Keane box at the Summit Post Office. It read:

> *Charley Kane [sic] if you do not leave this country within three days your life will be taken same as Powell's* (Laramie *Boomerang*, 1896).

He left, but Mary stayed on.

Two years after the murder of her husband, a series of events occurred that got Mary arrested at least ten more times. In 1902, **Mary Powell** was charged with shoplifting curtains, quilts, and wine glasses. After a few hours, the jury returned a verdict of not guilty. Two years later, Mary charged her neighbor, George Chapman, with horse theft. The case was dismissed. Then, a fire at Mary's ranch caused $850 in damage.

Nevertheless, Mary continued to be listed on the society page when she attended a full-dress Masonic Lodge gala. In 1905, Mss. Powell was charged twice with the possession of stolen cattle thought to be from the Oxford Ranch. She and her son stood trial in May, but the outcome is unclear. Later that year, Mary and Will turned themselves in after being charged with rustling seven of Dr. Stevens' cattle. The cattle were found on her ranch one year after going missing, their brands altered. Mary requested a change of venue but was denied. When the jury deadlocked, Mary was granted a new trial. She pled *nolo contendere* at the new trial and was sentenced to three months in jail.

In June 1908, Mary's son Will eloped with seventeen-year-old Dora Lewis, the daughter of the neighbor who was killed on Horse Creek, Bill Lewis. Mary was incensed. Will had a good job as a brakeman for the railroad, just like his father, and she expected more from him. He threatened to go to Oregon and never return, but they eventually came back. Not surprisingly, Mary and Dora never got along, and in January 1910, her daughter-in-law charged Mary with assault and battery. Dora had just given birth to a baby boy when Mary showed up at the house. Dora would not let her in. Through the locked door, Mary shouted:

> *Get your grave clothes on because I am gonna shoot you both.*
> (Laramie *Boomerang*).

Mary was arrested and released on $500 bail. The baby died soon after, and Mary was sentenced to thirty days in jail for disturbing the peace. Dora sued for divorce, citing cruelty, as her husband had sided with his mother. Later that year, Mary was again charged with disturbing the peace for fist fighting in the streets of Laramie. That charge was thrown out.

Still later in 1910, Mary was charged with arson by her neighbor Mss. Richardson and jailed when she could not post the $2,500 bond. Mary said she was camping in the area looking for a missing steer and left after an unfruitful search. She theorized that her campfire must have flared up and accidentally burned Mss. Richardson's hay and Joe Tietze's barn. The trial resulted in a hung jury. With **Judge Brown** as her lawyer, the sworn statements of eighty-five ladies, each stating various reasons why Mary should not be re-tried, were presented to the court. Mary was acquitted the second time.

In 1911, Mary was charged with stealing three colts from Mr. Davis. She had stolen the colts the year before and had placed her brand upon them. She was still at it two years later when she was again accused of rustling cattle, this time by her neighbor, Lord Charles Kennedy.

As I scrolled through ancient pages of the Laramie *Boomerang*, Mary's saga unfurled like a soiled banner. Between 1913 and 1920, Mary was arrested four times for shoplifting and brawling in the street over a stolen horse. In the fall of 1913, Mary was wounded in the arm when her son Will's new stepson fired shots at him in a dispute over the Saturday night bath. Will was killed.

Mary finally retired to her remote cabin, sometimes working as a cook for the Swan Company until she died in 1941. She is buried at the Greenhill Cemetery in Laramie next to her husband, Fred. Their son and the grandson, who died in 1910, were also buried there. Only Fred's headstone remains today.

~~~~~~~~~~~~~~~

One of Mary's neighbors was the Nickell family. They were involved in a blood feud with a neighbor, fellow granger Jim Miller. A feud that began over water rights escalated when Miller blamed Kels Nickell for the death of his oldest son, Frank (then fourteen years old), and the severe wounding of his daughter, Maude. Miller had driven his wagon into town, leaving his children to play in the back. When Nickell appeared unexpectedly on the street, Miller went for the shotgun he always carried under the seat. It accidentally discharged, striking the boy in the head and blowing off half of the little girl's face. In Miller's opinion, the shotgun would not have been loaded had Nickell not been such a threat. The truth was that Miller accidentally pulled the trigger in a fit of rage and he could not forgive himself.
~~~~~~~~~~~~~~~

A year later, Kels Nickells' next oldest son, Willie, was found dead less than a mile from the homestead on the North Fork of Chugwater Creek. As Willie opened the gate that foggy morning, his father postulated that two of three bullets fired from a long rifle struck him. He staggered twenty-two paces back towards home and collapsed. His body was not discovered until the next day. Muddy footprints surrounded the corpse, and his shirt had been torn open to expose the wounds, presumably by the killer. The overnight rain made collecting evidence difficult. A rock ring now marks the spot where he died; in the center of the ring is a particularly flat rock.

Suspicion immediately fell upon Tom Horn because of the flat rock under the head. To the Stock Grower's Association, this was proof that he earned the $600 a head they paid him to eliminate troublesome grangers. Many concluded that Tom Horn shot Willie, although Tom typically restricted his killings to cattle rustlers, certainly not boys.

Kels Nickell came under fire from unknown assailants a few days later. Hit in both arms and a leg by three of five shots aimed his way, he was hospitalized but survived. When he returned to Iron Mountain, he found that between sixty and eighty of his sheep had been shot or clubbed to death. Very soon afterward, Kels sold out to the Swan Land & Cattle Company and moved to Cheyenne. Eventually, the Miller boys, Victor and James, came to own the Nickell ranch.

The local federal marshal, Joe LeFors, was determined to nail Horn, so he devised a plan. He forwarded some letters to Horn's known residence in Bosler, Wyoming, ostensibly from a Miles City, Montana, rancher. The Montanan expressed a need for a stock inspector. In reality, this was a ruse to lure Horn into his office. Horn soon showed up in LeFors' Cheyenne office wanting a railroad pass so he could travel to Montana for an interview. He stayed, probably overnight, drinking, bragging, and shooting the breeze with LeFors.

Secretly, LeFors had hidden his deputy and a scribe in the next room, altering the lock so they could peek through the door. As LeFors plied Horn with liquor, he asked him leading questions about how good a shot he was. In reply to Le Force's question, from how far away had Horn fired the shot that killed Willie Nickell, Horn replied:

> *About 300 yards. That would have been the best shot I ever made and the dirtiest trick I ever done. I thought at one time he would get away.* (Carlson, 2001).

Those words, witnessed by the hidden deputy and recorded by the scribe, convicted Horn of a crime he probably did not commit.

During the trial, Horn had a formidable defense team. One member, Judge T. Blake Kennedy, took it upon himself to visit the crime scene. The following is an excerpt from Chip Carlson's excellent book entitled *Tom Horn, Blood on the Moon:*

> *I visited the place where the killing occurred and the entire surrounding country, and came to the conclusion that the boy was killed by a shot from a clump of rocks that was perhaps 30 yards from the gate which the boy was attempting to open at the time he was killed. Horn in his alleged confession to LeFors, in bragging about the shot, said that he had killed the boy from the head of a draw 300 yards away. As a matter of fact there was no head of a draw 300 yards away from which the gate could be observed.* (Carlson, 2001)

But then Horn effectively negated Otto Plaga's exonerating testimony. Plaga testified that he had seen Horn on his horse about twenty-five miles away from the killing that morning. Asked whether or not a person could have made that rough ride in the time allotted, Tom Horn sealed his fate. According to Judge Kennedy in Chip Carlson's book:

> *It would have been [valuable exonerating evidence] except that Horn, when testifying himself upon the trial, [was] not willing to subdue his passion for 'braggadocio' [and] responded to a question that he supposed it would not be impossible for a man who was a good rider and knew the country to cover the ground between where the killing took place and where Plaga had testified he saw him.* (Carlson, 2001)

Horn's shoes, confiscated the day he was arrested, remained in the sheriff's evidence locker. They might have proven that the water-logged footprints found near Willie's body were sizes too small to be his, but they were never presented in court. What the jury took to heart was Tom's statement to LeFors,

> *Killing men is my specialty. I look upon it as a business proposition, and I think I have a corner on this market* (Carlson, 2001).

Governor Fenimore Chatterton declined to stay the execution even though there were whispers that Miller's oldest son, Victor, was the one who had killed Willie Nickell. A signed affidavit from schoolteacher Glendolene Kimmell surfaced, attesting that she had overheard Victor and his brother James discussing the killing before Willie's body had been discovered. But the governor ignored that evidence. There were plenty of other unsolved murders that Horn probably did commit, enough to hang him, anyway. And they did just that on November 20, 1903, two years after Willie Nickell died.

The question remains: why did Horn's employer and friend, John Cobel, an influential stockman, allow Horn to be prosecuted, let alone convicted? Cobel paid for Horn's defense team, but they did little to defend him. They called no character witnesses, they did not try to establish an alternative motive, and they called not one of the White Caps to testify about anything. On the other hand, Horn said outrageous things on the witness stand, almost as if he were trying to be convicted. Chip Carlson (2001) proposes that the cattlemen were concerned that any testimony on their part would implicate themselves in the plot, so they kept quiet. Horn must have believed his employers would come through in the end and pardon him. They did not.

Governor Chatterton had also declined to intervene in the trial of the 1890 Johnson County war defendants, allowing them to be released. In Horn's case, Chatterton worried that if he commuted Horn's sentence to life, his friends would attack the train en route to the penitentiary and free him. The Cheyenne *Daily Leader* banner headlined a dubious story that Horn's friends had already been foiled once in a break-out plot. Independently, Horn had escaped once, only to be quickly recaptured when he was unable to fire the pistol he took from the overpowered guard. It had a safety latch on the trigger, and Horn had no idea how to disengage it.

Three men were lynched in Laramie in 1868 when the good citizens took justice into their own hands and cleaned up the main street. Wyoming legally hung seven men prior to statehood in 1890; all were convicted of murder. "Cattle Kate" and her husband plus three others were lynched in Johnson County in 1890 for the crime of cattle rustling. The last lynching occurred at Sheriff Nathaniel Boswell's ranch on the Big Laramie, also for cattle rustling. After statehood, eighteen men were executed by hanging in Wyoming, all for the crime of murder.

~ ~ ~ ~ ~ ~ ~ ~ ~ ~ ~ ~ ~ ~

# Tom Horn Found Innocent

In 1993, there was a movement by Tom Horn followers to retry him for the murder of Willie Nickell. The trial was a publicity stunt to convince Wyoming Governor Mike Sullivan to pardon Tom Horn posthumously. The facts of the case were well-known. The enmity between the Nickell and Miller families was well-established. The only real evidence in the case was the placement of a flat rock beneath the dying youth's head, Tom's inability to come up with an alibi, and Tom Horn's own words.

A jury was convened in the Cheyenne courthouse to retry the case. Although they had no force of jurisdiction, the participants took their roles very seriously. The mock defender called Joe LeFors' testimony "highly questionable." The prosecutor declared, "You cannot imagine the political pressure on the prosecutor at the time not to implicate the big landowners. No big ranchers were ever called as witnesses."

When it came to light during the modern defense that Joe LeFors had attempted to bribe Mr. Miller to leave the country, the scale of justice tipped. After all the evidence was presented, the jury deliberated. After a few hours, they found Tom Horn not guilty. Too late for Tom, in any case. He had already been hanged, and his body was amoldering in the grave.

## Chapter Twenty-two
# EM '95 - ESTHER MORRIS
### & the Equality State

I vote at the local fairgrounds, a collection of well-kept, seasonally empty barns on the outskirts of Laramie. There is never a line, and a neatly matched set of friendly volunteers, mostly ranch women dressed in jeans, long-sleeved shirts, and boots, always greeted me. The women of certain families have been election board officials for generations. The pay has always been sparse; in 1894, election officials such as **Mary Powell** received six dollars. Usually, the wind howls outside in November, so huge overhead heaters moderated the temperature inside. I take voting for granted. I do not work nine to five; a Tuesday is the same as a Sunday, only the bank might be closed. Voting is uncomplicated and quick. After all, Wyoming was the Equality State, a seemingly well-deserved moniker.

After voting, we always head into town for lunch, where there are several excellent brew-pubs. From my window seat at Altitude, visible across the street is a small park that rose like a phoenix from the remains of a burned-down business several years ago. Instead of replacing the retail space, donors built a history house to honor Wyoming women. A life-sized bronze statue in a full-length gingham dress and bonnet seems ready to step into the busy street. She is 72 year-old Louisa Swain, one of the first Wyoming women to cast a vote along with ninety-three others, in the general election of 1870. Inside is information about Estelle Reel of Cheyenne, Wyoming, who in 1894 became the first woman ever to break the glass ceiling and be elected to state office in Wyoming. In 1924, Nellie Ross of Wyoming became the first woman governor of any American state when she won the special election to succeed her late husband. She was not re-elected in the next election cycle, but a dormitory building on the University of Wyoming campus is named in her honor. Wyoming suffrage, it appeared, resulted from the labor of many people, both men and women.

~ ~ ~ ~ ~ ~ ~ ~ ~ ~ ~ ~ ~ ~

**Esther Hobart Morris** was a fifty-nine-year-old resident of South Pass City, Wyoming. She stood six feet tall and weighed 180 pounds. Born in New York, orphaned at eleven, and widowed as a single mother at thirty-one, Esther married a merchant many years her senior, John Morris. Soon to be the mother of twins, she followed him to South Pass City, Wyoming, in 1868, taking the train halfway across the continent with kids in tow. Most of the town's population of miners lived in Salt Lake City from December through March; the climate in South Pass was just too wicked. Mss. Morris and her family declined to retire to warmer climes during the winter, as did her neighbor William Bright. The Morris family lived in little more than a dug-out cave covered with a sod roof.

After Wyoming became a territory, the political landscape was as stark as its topographical one. On the one hand, Democrats controlled both houses of the assembly. On the other, Republican appointee John Allen Campbell was the territorial governor. In the wake of the Civil War, Republicans were busy advocating for the Fifteenth Amendment to the Constitution (which would allow black men to vote).

Nationally, the Grand Old Party considered women's suffrage not worth the time and effort to pursue. The hot debate in Congress concerned Negro suffrage. There were no women's suffragette marches in the capital's streets, yet; that would not come for another decade. The fight animated Wyoming Democrats; they were virulently anti-Negro, but some were also pro-woman. They had suffered together with their wives in the savage cold and wind of Wyoming territory enough to measure a woman's worth.

To negate the expected enfranchisement of the few African Americans in the state, Democrats concentrated on empowering their women. First, they passed a resolution that allowed women to sit in the hall where the assembly met. Then, they passed a resolution guaranteeing that teachers would have equal pay, male or female. Given that the vast majority of teachers in Wyoming were (and are) women, it was unclear if the schoolmarms got a pay raise or the schoolmasters a pay cut. Finally, they passed a bill guaranteeing that married women could be assigned property ownership rights on par with and separate from their husbands. The gallery erupted in applause.

There were many driving forces behind Wyoming suffrage. Recently, the neighboring Dakota Territorial Legislature had come within a single vote of passing women's equality laws, and naturally, Wyoming wanted to be first. Some say the Wyoming legislature just wanted a public splash to attract more women to the state; at the time, there were six men for every woman. Another possible reason Democrats wanted to pass a suffrage bill was to force Governor

Campbell into vetoing it. Caught between Negro suffrage and women's suffrage, Democrats hoped the conundrum would embarrass the governor. Finally, they figured they could get more mileage out of their grandstanding if they temporarily championed their women. In the private smoking lounges, it was only a cruel joke; Democrats never thought suffrage would survive their political maneuvering. Publicly, local newspaper coverage exploded in a frenzy, arguing over the question. A Cheyenne columnist ran the following quote from an unnamed legislator:

> *if you are going to let the n——rs [Negros] & pigtails [Chinese] vote, we will ring in the women too.*

After the Council passed the suffrage bill, the House attempted to amend it to make it even more unacceptable to the governor. One amendment proposed to extend the vote to "squaws" and women of color. That one did not pass. The only amendment that survived raised the voting age from eighteen to twenty-one. The House passed the bill (seven votes to four with one abstention), as did the Council (six votes to two). After several days of deliberation, Governor Campbell unexpectedly signed the bill into law on December 10, 1869. To everyone's surprise, Wyoming became the *Equality Territory.* Nationally, Negros were allowed to vote the following year when the Fifteenth Amendment to the Bill of Rights was ratified.

Laramie's sheriff, Nathaniel K. Boswell, took up the mantle of women's equality. The county commissioners summoned all of Laramie's respectable women and men for jury duty for the term running from March 1870 until late 1871. Calling them in order, some upstanding women such as Mss. Ivinson (the banker's wife) refused her civic duty, believing it to be un-ladylike, but most did not. Chief Territorial Supreme Court Justice John H. Howe empaneled the first co-ed jury in March 1870. Justice Howe, addressing the jury pool, said he had:

> *...long seen that woman was a victim to the vices, crimes and immoralities of man, with no power to protect and defend herself from these evils.* Howe continued, saying *it seems to me to be eminently proper for women to sit upon grand juries, which will give them the best possible opportunities to aid in suppressing the dens of infamy which curse the country.*

Crime dropped significantly as these bold women meted out real frontier justice. Unlike the local large stock growers who believed cattle rustling to be a crime more serious than murder, the women convicted cattle rustlers and murderers alike. The female jurists also enjoyed a degree of immunity from physical reprisal. After all, they were ladies and commanded a modicum of respect amongst polite company, even on the western frontier. Suddenly, male jurors ceased drinking alcohol during jury breaks.

In the first district petit jury in which women populated the jury pool, **M.C. Brown** was co-counsel to W.W. Corlett, defending a man accused of murder. When the first potential woman juror was called, prosecuting attorney Stephen Downey's challenge was overruled by Judge Howe. Brown then passed a note to the judge asserting that he had overheard the potential juror saying she "thought the defendant was most assuredly guilty." Howe allowed her dismissal. Brown similarly challenged the next woman, so Judge Howe disallowed the remaining peremptory challenges. The petit jury was soon seated, complete with some women as jurors. The defendant was indicted.

Judge Howe stepped down from the bench in 1871 after overseeing numerous trials in which women were empaneled as jurors. His successor chose to revert to the legislative rules passed three days before the suffrage act, allowing only male jurors. Members of the fairer sex would not again serve as jurors until 1948, when the arcane rules were overturned. In the interim, they continued to vote in all local, state, and federal elections and hold real property.

Meanwhile, back in South Pass, **Morris** was the only qualified candidate who lived year-round in that painfully remote South Pass City. So upon William Bright's recommendation, District Court Judge John W. Kingman appointed her Justice of the Peace. With that appointment, **Esther Morris** became the first woman in the West to serve as a judge of men.

Ironically, the Democrats realized too late that most of the women would unexpectedly vote Republican. This turn of events was so repugnant to the Democrats that they attempted to abolish the suffrage act during the following year's assembly meeting. Governor Campbell vetoed it immediately. Even though the House overrode the veto, the Council failed to do so. The anti-suffrage act failed by a single vote.

After that, there was one more attempt to take women's voting rights away. When J.W. Carey introduced the draft constitution at the 1889 Constitutional Convention, some members attempted to remove the suffrage act from the proposed state constitution. But their efforts were defeated, again, by a single vote. But women's rights as full citizens continued to be quietly curtailed by both social and cultural norms. Laramie's pioneer women had succeeded in carving out their place in history, and they continued to fight for their rights, sometimes to the dismay of their husbands. Indeed, any woman who could survive the depredations meted out by hostiles, nature, and society had to be, by definition, tough as nails.

~~~~~~~~~~~~~~

Women's suffrage aside, Wyoming wanted to become a state. Standing in their way was that they did not meet the minimum population requirement. This fact was unlikely to change soon, and they knew it. Despite this obvious impediment, two Wyoming residents dedicated to statehood began haunting the Willard Hotel's lobby on Pennsylvania Avenue in Washington, DC. Dr. Hiram Latham (the US Army Surgeon General posted at Fort Sanders) and J.M. Carey (Social Club member) lived in Washington for the next eight years. Carey argued for Wyoming's statehood before Congress, while Latham lobbied the social scene. The term "lobbyist" was first used to describe such men who would hang out in the Willard's lobby. There, they had a chance to waylay congressmen who usually stayed there when Congress was in session.

In long and eloquent speeches, Carey presented Wyoming's case describing a "robust" economy, the "ten to fifteen million acres" of arable land just waiting to be farmed, and most importantly, the growing population estimated between 110,000 and 125,000 citizens. They managed to persuade Congress that Wyoming would soon support a population of 130,000 people, the threshold required for statehood. Wyoming did not achieve that milestone until fifty years later. Today, Wyoming has trouble maintaining more than 500,000 people at any one time; the population of the entire state is approximately that of Denver, Colorado.

When chided in Washington for Wyoming Territory's embrace of women's suffrage, Carey was widely quoted as telling Congress that:

*Wyoming would wait one hundred years longer for statehood rather than join without the right to women's suffrage.*

The seeds of national suffrage were thriving.

The 1890 census, conducted after statehood was granted, counted only 62,555 people, including ninety-four Confederate veterans, 1,171 Union veterans, 1,850 Indians (down from 45,000 plus in 1850), 474 Chinese, and 200 Negros. Since the politically disenfranchised were being actively discouraged from remaining in the state, the correct figure would put the American citizen population at about 60,000 souls. This figure is a far cry from the 110,000 estimated by lobbyist Carey. The official census papers in Washington were "temporarily misplaced" shortly after J.W. Carey was seated as a freshly minted Wyoming senator. A fire in 1921 destroyed most of the national 1890 census, including that of Wyoming.

Then the state went to work on polishing its image. Despite their historically adversarial nature, every small Native American band was forcibly relocated
~~~~~~~~~~~~~~

to the Wind River Indian Reservation in central Wyoming. To the whites, an Indian was an Indian. To a Shoshone, an Arapaho was an enemy. Wyoming was ethnically cleansing itself. When the Bureau of Indian Affairs realized it had ceded some of Wyoming's very best hay meadows to the tribes, they moved to reclaim some of it. The reservation was effectively downsized by allowing white ranchers to take over the vast meadows near present-day Riverton, Wyoming. The instrument used to "free" reservation lands for white ownership was the allotment system. If, after each tribal family was assigned 160 acres, there was still land left over, white settlers were allowed to either purchase or homestead that land. The same thing happened in Oklahoma. Today, Frémont County harvests more grass hay than any other Wyoming county from mostly white-owned ranches.

As for the Chinese, they were also considered sub-human. There are many conflicting stories about how the Chinese district near Rock Springs was burned in 1887 by angry, striking coal miners. The fact is that fifty-seven Chinese scab coal miners and their families died. It seems that the white miners had gone on strike against the Union Pacific Coal Company, UPRR's wholly-owned subsidiary. In a strikebreaking move, the UP shipped hundreds of Chinese workers in from San Francisco to replace them. Incensed, the white miners attacked and burned the makeshift miner's camp. Chinese families perished as they huddled in their tar paper shacks, unwilling to leave the family treasures and cash buried under their dirt floors.

The African American population was simply expected to move on; there was nothing for them in Wyoming. The one exception was that of Bronco Sam. He lived around Laramie and worked on most of the big ranches at one time or another, including the Oxford Horse Ranch. Mostly, he worked for Thomas Alsop; he was eternally grateful after Sam plunged into the Laramie River to save Alsop's drowning son.

~ ~ ~ ~ ~ ~ ~ ~ ~ ~ ~ ~ ~ ~ ~

**Esther Morris** served with distinction as Justice of the Peace in South Pass City for nine months. She was a vocal supporter of the suffragette movement as it swept the East and regularly corresponded with Isabella Beecher Hooker. Although she loathed train travel, she attended rallies in San Francisco, Philadelphia, and Cleveland. In a letter read at the 1902 Suffrage Convention in Washington and reprinted in the Laramie *Daily Sentinel*, Morris wrote:

> *Circumstances have transpired to make my position as a Justice of the Peace a test of woman's ability to hold public office. I feel that my work has been satisfactory.*

She went on to list her daily responsibilities: she assisted in choosing jury members, she ran the elections, looked after the ballot box, and canvassed the votes after the election. She said of her duties:

*I do not know as I have neglected my family any more than in ordinary shopping.*

Her first official action was to arrest her predecessor, who refused to turn over the court docket to someone he judged as unqualified. Her second official action was to recuse herself from the prosecution. Esther presided over twenty-six cases during her tenure, none of which were overturned. When Wyoming finally became a state two decades after her retirement, seventy-five-year-old **Esther Morris** participated in the ceremonies with much fanfare. By then, she had retired to Cheyenne, happily leaving the rigors of living in South Pass with an abusive, intoxicated husband behind. Morris presented a neatly folded Wyoming flag to Territorial Governor F. E. Warren. Stepping to the podium, she spoke in a voice that could be heard clearly at the back of the crowd. She thanked Governor Warren:

*...on behalf of the women of Wyoming, and in grateful recognition of the high privilege of citizenship that has been conferred upon us* (Rea, 2014).

Morris spent the rest of her days in Cheyenne, living with her son, occasionally traveling to Laramie to lecture at the University of Wyoming; she always preferred to travel by coach. On one of those excursions, I would like to think that she stopped by the little Crimson Arch to shallowly inscribe her initials, **E M '95**. Unfortunately, hers is one signaure that has yielded to erosion and is gone forever.

Morris died in 1902 at the age of eighty-seven. She never witnessed the ultimate success of the suffragette movement, but she was among the first to stand up and demand to be counted. She is not well remembered in the era's history and is only mentioned peripherally by male historians. As the first woman judge, she deserves to be ranked alongside Estelle Reel (the first woman elected to state office and the first woman confirmed by the Senate to hold federal office), and Jeanette Rankin (the first woman member of Congress), or even Sandra Day O'Connor (the first woman Supreme Court member). She paved the way and proved that women could perform civic duties in what was, and still is, a man's world. She is buried in Cheyenne, Wyoming.

In 1963, a statue of "Mother Morris" was erected in front of the capitol building in Cheyenne. It has since been moved to the basement. A similar statue is one of two that the state has chosen to represent Wyoming in the

Washington DC Capitol Rotunda's statuary hall. Each state is entitled to two, and today, they crowd the hall. There are only nine statues of women in that hall. As in life, she is surrounded by men.

~ ~ ~ ~ ~ ~ ~ ~ ~ ~ ~ ~ ~ ~

ESTHER HOBART
MORRIS, 1814-1902

## Bronco Sam

Sam Stewart was a mixed-blood (British/ Negress) enslaved person from Texas. After "Juneteenth," he dropped his cotton hoe and headed north. He is famous for riding a giant longhorn steer through the streets of Cheyenne during the early Frontier Days parades. But his greatest love was bronco riding at the annual summer roundup in Laramie.

Bronco Sam was the best of them all. Called a "horse whisperer," after roping a wild bronc, he immobilized, stroked, and spoke to it in his deep baritone voice. Afterward, Sam could throw on a saddle, mount up, and ride calmly away. The crazy Swedes preferred other methods. They would rope a horse, blindfold it, saddle it, mount up, and hold on for dear life.

Sam came to an untimely end when he caught his new Spanish wife with another man. An expert shot, he killed them both with a single bullet and then turned the gun on himself. Shot through the breast, Sam lingered before dying. His friends came to see him every day, hoping he would recover. They asked him why he had found it necessary to kill himself as they would have surely gotten him off.

## *Epilogue*
# THE O/X - COMING FULL CIRCLE
### *The Oxford Horse & Cattle Ranch*

Like **John Iliff**, Dr. Whitehouse, and the Swan Company, early Wyoming ranchers overstocked their land. They knew about vast herds of buffalo and figured that if that many large ungulates could survive on the Laramie Plains, so could that many cattle. Absent any scientific calculation method, there was no way to know how many animals the range would support. Remember, in the arid West, carrying capacities are drastically less than in Kentucky. The science of range management was invented in 1930 with the passage of the Taylor Grazing Act. That act created the forerunner to the Bureau of Land Management (BLM). Today, it is up to the BLM and the Forest Service to dictate how many AUMs can be legally grazed on public lands.

Buffalo naturally practiced a management technique today called the Savory Method. This technique deliberately overgrazes large tracts of land and then rests them, allowing the grass species to recover. In the 1960s, a wildlife biologist named Allan Savory studied African migration routes and designed the method that bears his name. Not surprisingly, North America's large, wild ungulates "managed" their range similarly. Before being systematically wiped out by white hunters, the buffalo matriarch instinctively followed different routes across the Great Plains every year. Not only did she know where to go, but she deliberately avoided other groups. Because their passage devastated the available forage, it would be disadvantageous for other groups to tailgate another herd.

The mighty herds would not pass that way again for years; there was that much open prairie. Left ungrazed for a season or two, the trampled range recovered, essentially undamaged, even stimulated, by the passing buffalo. This phenomenon should not be surprising because the Great Plains' dominant grass species evolved with the buffalo.

Unlike buffalo, cattle are not instinctively migratory. Because they are private property, cows and sheep are necessarily confined either by fencing or by active herding. Seeking the abundant grasses on what was primarily public land, livestock used to roam freely in high numbers. Intent upon maximizing their incomes, early ranchers allowed them to consume all of the range forage every season. This practice would not be allowed today, but between 1880 and 1890, at least one positive result was associated with overgrazing the Grand Teton watershed in northwest Wyoming. Accidentally, the decades-long trampling of the high-altitude stream banks destroyed the nesting habitat for the Rocky Mountain locust. As illustrated in books such as *Little House on the Prairie,* the hordes of destructive insects that plagued the Great Plains were effectively exterminated (Lockwood, 2004).

Besides exterminating the beaver, the most harmful collateral damage caused by early whites, was the elimination of predators. Domestic cattle, sheep, and horses are easy prey for the top predators (grizzlies, wolves, and mountain lions), so ranchers made it their business to eliminate these species, driving them to the brink of extinction. Wildlife biologists have only recently correlated the elimination of top predators with watershed damage. Without predators lurking near the water source, domestic livestock lose their fear of remaining along the stream bank to feed. Those areas became overgrazed, the stream banks trampled, and the water fouled. With the reintroduction of predators, the favored hunting spots have recovered first. In Yellowstone, wildlife managers have documented the remarkable recovery of riparian ecosystems. Biologists now have new data points to describe predator/prey interactions.

The government-intiated grazing allotment plan helps manage the vast areas of public lands west of the Mississippi. Usually awarded to adjacent ranches, grazing allotments monetized the use of public resources otherwise reserved for wildlife. The right to access other public resources, such as timber, minerals, and fossil fuels, can be similarly leased out to interested parties. This way, there would be an income source to compensate the taxpayers for maintaining public lands.

In a perfect world, this multi-use approach is an acceptable arrangement. However, the archaic rules favor a handful of ranchers; there is no way to prioritize competing interests. Recently, the BLM has added conservation as a potential "use" for public land. This proposal caused a massive uproar as ranchers demanded continued, unfettered, and unregulated use of public land for themselves. The BLM has prevailed, so far. The Freedom Caucus-led legislature is literally throwing a fit.

Unlike the ranches near national forest land, the Oxford Ranch had only one section of public land to augment its privately held grazing resources.

Over the years, even that has been whittled away to a mere 230 acres. Given the low carrying capacity, the ranch can support only about 100 mother cows in its present configuration.

When I was ranch manager, we were diversified. We had outside income from the Laramie environmental business and a herd of 1,000 cashmere goats. We had on-demand labor in the form of three capable children. We hired foreign ranch help using a special US government visa program. This program allowed them to work agricultural jobs that American workers would not take. The government dictates the maximum wage and oversees the working conditions. Many of the large sheep ranchers in the West use this program today to hire mostly Peruvian herders to shepherd their sheep, either in the national forests or out on the windswept BLM lands. From April through November, the Peruvians live in sheep wagons parked in remote places. They are resupplied monthly but they are mostly alone with their dogs, a horse or two, and thousands of sheep. Luckily, a thousand dollars a month goes a long way back in Peru.

When it came time to retire from ranching, we had little hope of continuing the ranch as a ranch. We had sold off two of the front bull pastures to pay off our mortgage, which took much of our pasturing flexibility away. The kids had graduated from high school and were away to college without a stated intention to return. The cashmere goat venture ended when the dehairing machines necessary to process commercial quantities of fiber moved to China. We considered selling out but sold only the ranch headquarters and the state lease.

That was a sad day in my life, but economics required the move. The buyer immediately turned the property into an ugly mobile home park and let the place fall back into dis- or misuse. Old cars, downed cottonwood branches, and trash littered the barnyard once again. Weeds took over the overgrazed uplands and the parched meadow. We could only watch from the other side of the fence and shake our heads. He did not harm the barn, although it broke my heart to see it standing there unused and unloved.

In the ensuing years, we rested the remaining land, about 3,000 acres, and placed it in trust with the Nature Conservancy. All around us, land was being divided into thirty-five-acre parcels and sold for rural housing developments. We were determined to preserve at least some contiguous habitat for the elk, deer, and antelope. Finding a buyer for restricted land was difficult enough, and the recession further depressed buyer interest. We held on.

When our son and his wife decided they would like to try to make a go of ranching, we had just the ticket. They were both graduates of Indiana

University and had traveled in Central America before settling down. They figured they could make it with a minimal herd, if the old tractors could still harvest the hay. Their idea to start a side business, an Internet-based company akin to Facebook, was, at the time, radical. After earning more degrees at the school of hard knocks, the Internet business failed. Then bad weather and economics intervened, as they often do in agriculture. They eventually gave up the idea of ranching without an outside income to fill in the gaps. Moving closer to Denver, they each used their invaluable experience to assume professional jobs. Happily, they have been able to buy a home and start a family. Their kids have next-door neighbors and a school around the corner. However, we were left with an empty, lonely ranch.

Then, unexpectedly, Kelly, the baby of the family, stepped up and presented a diversified business plan that included boutique beef production, a bed and breakfast, a livery stable, a riding arena, an events venue, and the potential for more ideas. As in nature, diversity is the key. The barn was looking so forlorn; we just had to do something. So the Oxford Horse & Cattle Ranch began to rise phoenix-like out of the ghostly remains of the Old Oxford Horse Ranch.

We were still carrying the mortgage from the 1998 land sale, and there had not been much value appreciation in the intervening fifteen years. Plus, the owner was about to close his tax preparation business and move back to Torrington. So we jumped back into the fray and bought the Oxford Ranch headquarters for a second time. Like Dr. Whitehouse, Kelly had a dream and good credit with the family as her bank.

With Kelly's ideas and enthusiasm, we sunk another $300 grand into completing the renovations begun in the 1990s. The derelict mobile homes were sold, burned, or hauled to the dump. Fifteen years of horse manure came out of the barn and onto the hay meadows. Ditches and weirs were repaired and employed. The old corrals that no longer served their purpose were replaced with sturdy post and pole corrals. The sheep dip, located very near the hand-dug well, was removed. A new riding arena has taken the place of Dr. Whitehouse's foaling sheds. The barn was repainted (using a color appropriately named "Barn Red"), and the old cement chinking (dating from 1885) was replaced with modern polymerized caulking. The stallion stalls that once lined the corridor inside are slowly being rebuilt. The vast hayloft could someday become a music venue, if only it had a dance floor and a million dollars.

The best improvement was the rebirth of the ranch manager's house. Since the mansion house burned in 1914, the old two-story log house had done little but go downhill. The greenhouse attached to the east side to accommodate Dr. Lembke's horticultural hobby has become a cozy apartment. Following Kelly's vision, the cheap walnut paneling came down in the main house, and the straight-grain beechwood floors were exposed and refinished. The old windows were replaced. The asbestos shingles were stripped, and the rubble buried where it could do no harm. The transformation from a marginally livable dump to a sumptuous accommodation has been eye-popping.

The return of the ranch to its former glory has been one of the most fulfilling and satisfying projects I have ever undertaken. That people can once again experience the magnificence of an era long past is thrilling. I hope the new Oxford Horse & Cattle Ranch guests can return in a hundred years and find their ancestors' signatures in the Oxford Ranch guest register. For more information on the activities of the Oxford Horse & Cattle Ranch, go to www. oxfordranchwyoming.com.

By then, the signatures on the Crimson Arch will be gone, and the arch itself toppled by the relentless Wyoming wind. Standing in the barnyard and looking east, the view is almost the same as 150 years ago. Visitors do not have to close their eyes to be transported back to a simpler time. Walking through the barn, ghostly hoofbeats of magnificent horses echo against the wooden stalls. It was a heady time, back in the 1880s, an era that can now be revisited and savored like a fine bottle of wine.

~~~~~~~~~~~~~~~

THE LIVING ROOM AT THE OXFORD HORSE & CATTLE RANCH BED & BREAKFAST.
(PHOTO BY K. McGUIRE)

THE ARISTOCRAT - A SUITE CHOICE AT THE BED & BREAKFAST.
(PHOTO BY K. McGUIRE)
~~~~~~~~~~~~~~~

# OBITUARIES OF PROTAGONISTS

In my research, it became clear that many of the people mentioned within these pages are buried in the local cemetery. Using an online resource called Find-a-Grave.org, I have below reprinted the obituaries of those protagonists featured in Meanwhile, Back at the Ranch. They are listed alphabetically primarily and, secondarily within family groups. Other interesting obituaries can also be found on the website.

## Henry Bath

Birth: 25 Nov 1832 Germany

Death: 1 Jan 1917 (aged 84) Laramie, Albany County, Wyoming, USA

Burial: Greenhill Cemetery, Laramie, Albany County, Wyoming, USA

Plot: Row I-GAR Lot 29 Space 4

Bio: Henry Bath, 84 years of age, father of Lou Bath, chairman of the Democratic County Committee, and one of the pioneers of Albany County and Wyoming died last night at 8:30 at the Sydenham hospital, following an illness of four weeks. Death was due to old age and gangrene. Mr. Bath probably was better known in Albany County than any other person. He came to Laramie in the Spring of 1868 from Boone, Iowa. He drove from Cheyenne to Laramie with an ox cart. He has made Laramie his home ever since with the exception of a few years that he spent in San Diego, Cal. Henry Bath was born in Germany in November, 1846. He was educated in the old country and came to America when 16 years of age. He lived in New York for some years during which time he conducted a livery stable. He married in New York and when the Civil war broke out he joined the forty fifth New York Infantry as a private. Twenty-one months of the time he served in the Civil War, Mr. Bath was a prisoner of war in Libby prison. At the close of the war Mr. Bath was mustered out of the service as a first lieutenant and he & his wife moved west to Boone, Ia., where they conducted a hotel. They remained in Boone for a couple of years and then listened to the call of the wild and came to Wyoming. After remaining in Cheyenne for a few weeks Mr. Bath & his wife came to Laramie where Mr. Bath erected & conducted for a number of years the Globe Hotel on First Street. Mr. Bath became interested in the surrounding country and soon went into the ranch business and has been ranching ever since. Thirteen years ago Mr. Bath went to San Diego, Cal., and left his children here to run the ranch. Last year he was taken ill and brought back to Laramie. About the first of December he became seriously ill and later was moved to the Sydenham hospital where his condition gradually became worse. Mr. Bath is survived by five children, Phillip H. Bath, Fred C. Bath, Louis Bath, Emma Rogers & Kate Greaser. He is also survived by some 40 or 50 grandchildren & several great-grandchildren. Funeral arrangements have not been completed.© Semi-Weekly Boomerang no.1 January 02, 1917, page 1.


## Magdalene Bath*

Birth: 6 Nov 1806

Death: 19 Sep 1883 (aged 76)

Burial: Greenhill Cemetery, Laramie, Albany County, Wyoming, USA

Plot: Row IOOF, Lot 22, Space 7

*Hanna Bath was Belle Kuster's grandmother for whom she and Gus were looking when they signed the Crimson Arch.


## Herman Bath

Birth: 3 Feb 1878 Albany County, Wyoming, USA

Death: 21 Jul 1896 (aged 18) Larimer County, Colorado, USA

Burial: Greenhill Cemetery, Laramie, Albany County, Wyoming, USA

Plot: Row I-GAR Lot 29 Space 2

Bio: Herman Bath Killed Struck by Lightning This Morning Near Fort Collins. The following dispatch was received in this city this afternoon: Fort Collins, Colo., July 23, 1896. M.H. Murphy. Laramie, Wyo. Our readers understand that Herman accompanied his brother Fred, Tom Carrol & Bert Nottage on their recent trip south with a herd of horses which they hoped to dispose of down in Oklahoma. The trip was abandoned in the vicinity of Pueblo, owing to the drought prevailing in Colorado, as the horses could not be fed and properly watered. They were on their return trip when Herman was struck by lightning & killed. The accident probably occurred this morning, and it is presumed that the remains will be brought here by rail tomorrow. It is a most sad feature to the trip. The deceased was the son of Henry Bath on the Little Laramie and was 18 years of age. His many friends in this city and this section of country will receive the sad news of his untimely death with sorrow. © Daily Boomerang no. 110 July 23, 1896, page 2.


## Judge Melville Cox Brown

Birth: 16 Aug 1835 Kennebec County, Maine, USA

Death: 9 Apr 1928 (aged 92) Laramie, Albany County, Wyoming, USA

Burial: Greenhill Cemetery, Laramie, Albany County, Wyoming, USA

Plot: Row I Lot 34 Space 2

## Sir George Vincent Hamilton Gordon*

Birth: unknown Oxford, City of Oxford, Oxfordshire, England

Death: 14 Sep 1887

Burial: Greenhill Cemetery, Laramie, Albany County, Wyoming, USA

Plot: Row D Lot 6 Space 6

* Gordon was accidentally shot & killed by his best friend, Arthur Whitehouse.


## Charles Hutton

Birth: unknown

Death: 29 Oct 1899

Burial: Greenhill Cemetery, Laramie, Albany County, Wyoming, USA Plot: Row I Lot 92 Space 1

Bio: PASSING OF A PIONEER, Charles H. Hutton Dies at his Fort Sanders Home Sunday was a Morning - Came to Laramie in 1866 - Was Among the First Successful Ranchmen on the Plains - Generous &

Public Spirited - Helped to Establish Communication Between East and Pacific Coast - Charles H. Hunton, a pioneer in Wyoming and one of the first settlers on the Wyoming Plains, died at his home at Old Fort

Sanders Sunday morning. He will be buried on Wednesday, at 10:30 a.m. at the city cemetery. Mr. Hutton was a native of New York. He was among those who crossed the continent long before the railroads had penetrated the Rocky Mountain region and wintered in Laramie in 1886, when it had not yet become even a city of tents. He was at that time engaged in distributing wire for the telegraph line that was to connect the east with the Pacific coast, but being favorably impressed with the country here and has continued his residence in Laramie from that date until the time of his death. He engaged extensively in the ranch business and in stock raising, in which he was eminently successful. There were very few in the early days who knew better the value of the nutritious grasses of this region and how to make the most out of a herd of horses or cattle, when the range was still open, than did Mr. Hutton. He prospered, and he deserved to. He founded the Pacific Market and conducted it for years. He was public spirited and charitable, and when at one he was esteemed as wealthy he was the same whole-souled, big-hearted Charley Hutton the he was a third of a century ago. Mr. Hutton had been failing in health for some time and a week ago had a stroke of paralysis. It was evident at the time that he would not live for many days and in fact his time was numbered by hours as he became unconscious and continued in that condition up to the time of his death. He was but 66 years of age, yet, while he had not reached the allotted age of three score and ten years, he had probably crowded into his life as much of usefulness as can be credited to any man. Obituary added by editor.

## John Wesley Iliff

Birth: 18 Dec 1831 McLuney, Perry County, Ohio, USA

Death: 9 Feb 1878 (aged 46) Denver, Denver County, Colorado, USA

Burial: Fairmount Cemetery, Denver, Denver County, Colorado, USA Plot: 63

Bio: Colorado Pioneer and Cattle Baron. Attended Ohio Wesleyan University and then turned down an offer from his father for an interest in an Ohio farm and headed west. Initially in Kansas where he helped organize Ohio City Town Company in 1857 and built the first store there. Sold the store in 1859 and moved to Aurora (now Denver), Kansas Territory, with a wagon load of goods. He opened a successful general merchandise store; about 1861 sold the store and bought cattle weakened after the long trek across Plains. Nursed & fattened the cattle, then sold them for substantial profit to mining camps, Denver butchers, Army posts. Acquired about 25,000 head of cattle and 7,908 acres of land. Imported shorthorn bulls from Ohio to improve his stock. By 1866 he was listed in a Denver business directory as a "Stock Dealer." In 1868 moved to Cheyenne, Wyoming to better manage his operations selling beef to railroads there. Estate probate records show he owned 15,500 acres in 54 sections always near water throughout Colorado. In later years he returned to Denver where he had successfully invested in Denver real estate and banks, as well as shares of Chicago's Union Stockyards. After Iliff's death, wife Elizabeth sold his ranch holdings, invested the proceeds and donated $100,000 to endow Iliff School of Theology. Originally interred in Riverside Cemetery (where the family still owns the center circle plot). In 1920 his daughter, Louise, had his remains and the 65-ton monument moved to Fairmount Cemetery. Cause of death: obstructive jaundice.


## Isabelle "Belle" Gorie Mueller*

Birth: unknown

Death: 20 Mar 1919 Los Angeles, Los Angeles County, California, USA

Burial: Greenhill Cemetery, Laramie, Albany County, Wyoming, USA

Plot: Row IOOF Lot 54 Space 3

Bio: Peter Smart this afternoon received a telegram from the daughter, Vera, telling him of the death of her mother, Mrs. Belle Mueller, this morning at Los Angeles, from complication following an attack of influenza. Mrs. Mueller's brother, Charles Kuster, had started for Los Angeles and as soon as he arrived would take charge of arrangements, probably bringing the body to Laramie for burial. Mrs. Mueller is a daughter of the late Charles Kuster, and was for many years a resident of Laramie, the Kuster family being among the pioneers here. Her husband, a switchman, was killed in the yards here Decoration day a number of years ago. Peter Smart this morning received a telegram from Charles Kuster, the brother of Mrs. Belle Mueller, whose death occurred Thursday morning at Los Angeles. Mr. Kuster wired that the relatives had decided to place the body in a vault in that city and hold the funeral at Laramie at a later date. Mr. Kuster's telegram did not contain any details as to the date.© Laramie *Republican* March 22, 1919.

* Belle & her husband-to-be Gustave Mueller signed the rock in 1883.

## Gustave H. "Gus" Mueller

Birth: Apr 1861 Illinois, USA

Death: 30 May 1906 (aged 45) Laramie, Albany County, Wyoming, USA

Burial: Greenhill Cemetery, Laramie, Albany County, Wyoming, USA

Plot: Row IOOF Lot 54 Space 2

Bio: One of the saddest accidents in the annals of railroading in the state occurred Wednesday evening, at 6:45, in the yards near the rolling mills, resulting in the instant death of G.A. Mueller and the death about four hours later of Charles Van Dayton, each leaving a family and each being mourned by the whole city as good citizens and enterprising workmen. Coroner Robinson held the inquest today, his jury consisting of R.G. Fitch, John R. Cordiner, & Sam Wallis, with Harry Hunt as the stenographer. Messrs. Mueller & Dayton were members of a switch crew working in the yards here, the engine being in charge of Engineer James King & Fireman Matthews. They had attached their engine to a caboose on an incoming freight train, known as the second section of No. 52, and were in the act of taking that caboose and a damaged box car from the train, that the damaged car might be repaired here and that the caboose of the conductor to take the train to Cheyenne might be put in the place of the one arriving from the west. The whole end of the box car had been damaged, and it was necessary to chain it to the caboose to remove it from the train. Mr. Mueller, from the evidence adduced at the inquest, was stooping over between the two cars, adjusting the chain, Mr. Dayton standing up between the cars. The crossing at Fremont Street had been cut when the train arrived, and when the new engine was attached to the front of the train the crossing was closed. The forward part of the train bumped against the rearward part, driving it a few feet against the end of the caboose, catching the men between the two cars. Mr. Mueller was killed instantly. Mrs. Mueller & daughter, Miss Vera, were at Brooklyn, N.Y. at the time of the death of Mr. Mueller, but were telegraphed to by Charles F. Kuster, the brother of Mrs. Mueller, and are probably now on their way west. The son, Arthur Mueller, was at work at the electric light plant at the time, only a short distance from the scene of the accident, and hurried to his father's side. Later he was sent home in the care of friends. His heart was almost broken, other relatives have been telegraphed the sad news of the death of Mr. Mueller. The switchmen had been working during the day and in a few minutes would have been off duty. The cutting out of the caboose and the damaged car and putting on of the new caboose was the last act of the crew for the day. Ten minutes would have seen them relieved and on their way home. The other members of the crew was not injured. © Laramie Republican no. 246 May 31, 1906, page 1. Daughter Vera married Otto Steele in Denver in 1910.


## Esther Hobart McQuigg Morris

Birth: 18 Aug 1814 Spencer, Tioga County, New York, USA

Death: 2 Apr 1902 (aged 87) Cheyenne, Laramie County, Wyoming, USA

Burial: Lakeview Cemetery, Cheyenne, Laramie County, Wyoming, USA

Bio: Suffragist. Born in Tioga County, New York, she was orphaned at eleven, she was then apprenticed to a seamstress, and eventually started a successful millinery business. She married Artemus Slack in 1841, and was widowed three years later. She moved to Peru, Illinois with her infant son, to settle the property held there by her late husband's estate. Eventually, she married a local merchant, John Morris. In 1868, her husband & son, Archibald Slack, moved to a boom town in Wyoming Territory. A year later, she & her twin sons followed, and settled in at South Pass City. Esther promoted the idea of granting women the vote in Wyoming Territory, and the Wyoming Territory's enfranchisement of women came in 1869, along with laws giving married women control of their own property, and providing equal pay for female teachers. District Court Judge John W. Kingman appointed her justice of the peace & the Sweetwater County Board of Commissioners in a vote of two to one approved her application on February 14, 1870. Her first act was to arrest her predecessor, who refused to hand over his court docket. Eventually, she dismissed her own case, ruling that she, as an interested party, could not arrest the former justice and recused herself. She was the first woman to hold judicial office in the United States. She served for nine months and handled 26 cases, none of which were overturned on appeal. In February 1872, she participated in the American Woman Suffrage Association Convention in San Francisco. The following year, she was nominated by the Woman's Party of Wyoming as a candidate to the Wyoming Territorial Legislature, but she declined the honor. In July 1876, she addressed the National Suffrage Convention in Philadelphia and in July 1890, presented the new Wyoming state flag to Governor Warren during the Wyoming statehood celebration where she was honored as a suffrage pioneer. In 1895, she was elected a delegate to the National Suffrage Convention in Cleveland, Ohio. She died in Cheyenne at 87. In 1960, the Cheyenne State House & Statutory Hall in Washington, DC installed sculptures of her, honoring her role in the suffrage movement.

## *Fredrick Upsher "Fred" Powell*

Birth: unknown

Death: 12 Sep 1895

Burial: Greenhill Cemetery, Laramie, Albany County, Wyoming, USA

Plot: Row D Lot 37 Space 4

*Fred was shot & killed in a Tom Horn-style killing, but it may have been his neighbor, E.P. Baker, who pulled the trigger.

## Mary Ellen (Keane) Powell*

Birth: unknown

Death: 13 Jan 1941

Burial: Greenhill Cemetery, Laramie, Albany County, Wyoming, USA

Plot: Row D Lot 37 Space 3

*After Mary was widowed, she joined the Langhoff gang and was involved with cattle rustling.

**Charles A. Trabing**

Birth: 17 Dec 1844 Baden, Landkreis Verden, Lower Saxony

(Niedersachsen), Germany

Death: 24 May 1885 (aged 40)

Burial: Greenhill Cemetery, Laramie, Albany County, Wyoming, USA

Plot: Row A Lot 48 Space 6 1/2

Bio: Charles A. Trabing, of the firm Trabing Brothers, Laramie City, died in Omaha last Sunday of blood poisoning. Mr. Trabing was one of the pioneer residents of Wyoming. He was also the first man to open a store and trading post in this county, and a post office on the Wyoming stage line named after him.


**Augustus Trabing**

Birth: 2 Jul 1841

Death: 28 Nov 1906 (aged 65)

Burial: Greenhill Cemetery, Laramie, Albany County, Wyoming, USA Plot: Row A Lot 1 Space 4

# Places to Visit

## Wyoming:

- **American Heritage Center.** 2111 East Willett Drive, Laramie Wyoming. Open 8 am M - F. Educational center with programming & a vast library of historic documents, manuscripts & archives.

- **Greenhill Cemetery.** Corner of Willett & Fifteenth Street, Laramie, Wyoming. Open 24 hours. Final resting place of many.

- **Ivinson Mansion Museum.** Corner of Sixth & Ivinson Ave, Laramie.

- **University of Wyoming.** Corner of Ninth & University.

- **The Wyoming Territorial Prison.** 975 Snowy Range Road, Laramie, Wyoming. A beautifully designed tourist attraction.

- **Fort Sanders**. Historic Marker located three miles south of Laramie on US Highway 287. Ruins of the guard house & armory remain.

- **Vedauwoo Campground & Recreation Area.** Twenty minutes east of Laramie off I-80. Unique geological shapes.

- **Tree Rock Point of Interest.** Past Vedauwoo towards Cheyenne. Located in the median of I-80. Features an old limber pine growing out of some rocks.

- **Fort Laramie.** Two hours northeast of Laramie on State Highway 26, near Lingle, Wyoming. A well preserved tourist attraction well worth the visit.

- **Fort Fetterman Historic Site.** 752 Wy-93, Douglas, Wyoming. Two Hours North of Laramie. Open 9 am Tuesday - Saturday. Routing by way of the Fetterman Road reveals typical Iron Mountain ranch land.

- **Fort D.A. Russell.** Warren Air Force Base, Cheyenne Wyoming. One hour east of Laramie. Wellpreserved 1868 cavalry base.

- **Lake Marie.** 40 miles west of Laramie on Highway 130. High altitude lake with gorgeous views.

## Nebraska:

- **Fort Robinson**. Soldier Creek Road & US Highway 20, Crawford, Nebraska. Three hours northeast of Laramie. A well-preserved historic site. Crazy Horse is buried here.

# National Historic Places Nearby the Oxford Ranch:

| | | |
|---|---|---|
| Ames Monument | Cooper Mansion | St. Matthews Cathedral |
| Gurnsey State Park | Dale Creek Crossing | St.Paul's Kirche Luth. Church |
| Fort Steele | East Side High School | Union Pacific Athletic Club. |
| Hanna Basin Museum | Flying Horseshoe Ranch | (AKA Grey's Gables) |
| Como Bluffs | Vee Bar Ranch | Wood's Landing Dance Hall |
| Bath Ranch | Laramie Downtown | Charles E. Blair House |
| Libby Lodge | Centennial Depot | N.K. Boswell Ranch |
| Mountain View Hotel | Richardson's Overland Ranch | |
| Brooklyn Lodge | Old Main at the University of Wyoming | |

~~~~~~~~~~~~~~

# BIBLIOGRAPHY

## Books

Adams, Gerald M. *The Post Near Cheyenne: A History of Fort D.A. Russell 1867-1930*. Cheyenne, Wyoming: High Flyer Publications, Wyoming, 1997.

Allen, John L. *North American Exploration. Volume 3*. Lincoln, Nebraska: University of Nebraska Press, 1997.

Alter, J. Cecil. *Jim Bridger*. Norman, Oklahoma: University of Oklahoma Press, 1986.

Ambrose, Stephen E. *Nothing Like it in the World: The Men who Built the Transcontinental Railroad, 1863-1869*. New York: Simon & Schuster Paperbacks, New York, 2005.

Ambrose, Stephen E. *Undaunted Courage: Meriwether Lewis, Thomas Jefferson & the Opening of the* West. New York: Simon & Schuster, 2013.

Anthony, Ross O. *History of Fort Laramie*. Thesis (M.A.). Los Angeles, California: University of Southern California Press.

Bagley, Jerry. *Daniel Trotter Potts, Rocky Mountain Explorer, Chronicler of the fur trade & the first known man in Yellowstone Park: Also, Two Additional Eye-witness Reports, Beaver Dick Leigh & White Man's Sickness 1858-1876, The Slaughter of the Buffalo 1871-1878*. Rigby, Idaho: Old Faithful Eye-witness Publishing, 2000.

Bartlett, Ichabod S. *History of Wyoming* (3 volumes). Chicago, Illinois: S.J. Clark Publishing. 1918.

Beach, Cora. *Women of Wyoming*. Casper, Wyoming: S.S. Boyer Company, 1927.

Beckwourth, James P. & Thomas D. Bonner. *The Life & Adventures of James P. Beckwourth*. Norman, Oklahoma: University of Nebraska Press, 1972.
~~~~~~~~~~~~~~

Benton, Thomas H. *Thrilling Sketch of the Life of Colonel J.C. Frémont (United States Army); With an Account of his Expedition to Oregon & California, & the Discovery of the Great Gold Mines.* London, England: J. Field, 1850.

Berry, Don A. *A Majority of Scoundrels: An Informal History of the Rocky Mountain Fur Company.* New York: Harer Publishing, 1961.

Bond, R. *The Original Northwestern: David Thompson & the Native Tribes of North America.* Spokane, Washington: Spokane House Enterprises, 1972.

Bowles, Samuel. *Across the Continent: A Summer's Journey to the Rocky Mountains, the Mormons, & the Pacific States, with Speaker Colfax.* New York: Hurd & Houghton, 1865.

Brackenridge, Henry M. *Journal of a Voyage up the Missouri Performed in Eighteen Hundred & Eleven.* London, England: Coale & Maxwell, Pomeroy & Troy, Printers, 1816.

Breed, Noel J. *The Fur Trade in Wyoming.* Thesis (M.A.) Los Angeles, California: University of California Press, 1925.

Brown, Dee. *Bury My Heart at Wounded Knee.* New York: Holt, 1970.

Burns, Robert H., Andrew S. Gillespie & Willing G. Richardson. *Wyoming's Pioneer Ranches.* Laramie, Wyoming: Top-of-the-World Press, 1955.

Caesar, Gene. *King of the Mountain Men: The Life of Jim Bridger.* New York: Dutton Publishing, 1961.

Carlson, Chip. *Tom Horn Blood on the Moon: Dark History of the Murderous Cattle Detective.* Glendo, Wyoming: High Country Press, 2001.

Chatwin, B. *In Patagonia.* London, England: Jonathan Cape Publishing, 1977.

Chittenden, Hiram M. *The American Fur Trade of the Far West: A History of Pioneer Trading Posts & Early Fur Companies of the Missouri Valley & Rocky Mountains & of the Overland Commerce with Santa Fe.* 2nd Edition. Clifton, New Jersey: A.M. Kelley Press, 1976.

Chisholm, James & Lola M. Homsher (ed). *South Pass, 1868: James Chisholm's Journal of the Wyoming Gold Rush.* Lincoln, Nebraska: University of Nebraska Press, 1960.

Clyman, James, L. M. Hasselstrom & W. Blevins. *The Journal of a Mountain Man: James Clyman's Own Story.* Missoula, Montana: Mountain Press Publishing Company, 2013.

Coyner, David H. *The Lost Trappers; A Collection of Interesting Scenes & Events in the Rocky Mountains; Together with a Short Description of California: Also, Some Accounts of the Fur Trade, Especially as Carried on About the Sources of Missouri, Yellow Stone, & on the Waters of the Columbia.* Cincinnati, Ohio: James Publishing, 1847.

Coutant, C. G. & Ichabod S. Bartlett. *The History of Wyoming.* New York: Chaplin, Spafford & Mathison, 1899.

Cozzens, P. T*he Earth is Weeping: The Epic Story of the Indian Wars for the American West.* New York: Atlantic Books, 2018.

Crutchfield, James A. *A Primer of the North American Fur Trade.* St. Paul, Minnesota: Pioneer Press, 1986.

Dahlquist, Laura. *Meet Jim Bridger; A Brief History of Bridger & his Trading House on Black's Fork.* Torrington, Wyoming: Private Press, 1948.

David, Robert B. *Finn Burnett, Frontiersman: The Life & Adventures of an Indian Fighter, Mail Coach Driver, Miner, Pioneer Cattleman, Participant in the Powder River Expedition, Survivor of the Hay Field Fight, Associate of Jim Bridger & Chief Washakie.* Glendale, California: Arthur H. Clark Company, 1937.

Dobler, Lavinia G. & Loren Jost. *Rendezvous on the Wind: Plenty of Trade, Whiskey & White Women.* Riverton, Wyoming: Big Bend Press, 1990.

Dodge, Grenville M. *Biographical sketch of James Bridger, Mountaineer, Trapper & Guide.* New York: Unz & Company, 1905.

Douglas, Walter B. & Abraham P. Nasatir. *Manuel Lisa.* New York: Argosy-Antiquarian, 1964.

Fergus, Jim. *One Thousand White Women: The Journals of May Dodd.* New York: St. Martin's Griffin, 2017. (fiction)

Fetter, Richard L. *Mountain Men of Wyoming.* Boulder, Colorado: Johnson Books, 1982.

Finfrock, Jon W. *Diary, 1864.* Laramie, Wyoming: University of Wyoming Press, 1902.

Flannery, L.G. *John Hunton's Diary.* Cheyenne, Wyoming: Apex Press, 1967.

Fowler, Jacob. *The Journal of Jacob Fowler.* Lincoln, Nebraska: University of Nebraska Press, 1970.

Frémont, John C. *The Journals of John C. Frémont.* St. Louis, Missouri:

Frémont, John C. *Memoirs of My Life.* New York: Cooper Square Press, 2001.

Frémont, Jessie B. *The Letters of Jessie Benton Frémont.* Urbana, Illinois: University of Illinois Press, 1993.

Gates, Charles M. *Five Fur Traders of the Northwest: Being the Narrative of Peter Pond & the Diaries of John MacDonnell, Archibald N. McLeod, Hugh Faries, & Thomas Conner ... With an Introduction by Grace Lee Nute.* Minneapolis, Minnesota: University of Minnesota Press, 1933.

Ghent, William J. *The Early Far West.* London, England: Tudor Press, 1936.

Gilbert, E.W. *The Exploration of Western America, 1800-1850: A Historical Geography.* Cambridge England: Cambridge Press, 1933.

Gowans, Fred R. *Fort Bridger, Island in the Wilderness.* Provo, Utah: Brigham Young University Press, 1975.

Gowans, Fred R. *Rocky Mountain Rendezvous.* Layton, Utah: Gibbs Smith, 2005.

Gwynne, S C. *Empire of the Summer Moon.* London, England: Constable Press, 2011.

Hafen, Leroy R. & F.M. Young. *Fort Laramie & the Pageant of the West, 1834-1890. Lincoln, Nebraska:* University of Nebraska Press, 1984.

Herr, Pamela. *Jessie Benton Frémont: A Biography.* New York: F. Watts, 1987.

Herriot, James. *All Creatures Great & Small.* London, England: St. Martin's Griffin, 2014 (fiction)

Henry, Alexander & B.M. Gough. *The Journal of Alexander Henry the Younger, 1799-1814.* New York: Champlain Society, 1992.

Hill, S., Wilson, J. L. & J. Bradbury. (1916). *John Bradbury.* St. Louis, Missouri: Missouri Historical Society, 1916.

Holmes, Reuben. *The Five Scalps. St.* Louis, Missouri: Missouri Historical Society, 1938.

Holmes, Kenneth L. *Ewing Young, Master Trapper.* New York: Binfords & Mort Publishing for the Binford Foundation, 1967.

Homsher, Lola M. *The History of Albany County, Wyoming, to 1880.* Thesis (M.A.) Laramie, Wyoming: University of Wyoming, 1965.

Honig, Louis O. *James Bridger, the Pathfinder of the West.* Kansas City, Missouri: Brown-WhiteLowell Press, 1951.

Hufsmith, George W. T*he Wyoming Lynching of Cattle Kate.* Glendo, Wyoming: High Plains Press, 1993.

Hunt, Lester C. *Wyoming: A Guide to its History, Highways, & People.* Lincoln, Nebraska: University of Nebraska Press, 1981.

Hunton, John L. *Bridger's Recollections of Jacques laRamie.* Laramie, Wyoming: Laramie Printing, 1920.

Hunton, John L. *The Grattan Massacre.* Laramie, Wyoming: Laramie Printing, 1920.

Irving, Washington. *Astoria.* New York: G.P. Putnam's Sons, 1895. (fiction)

Irving, Washington. *The Adventures of Captain Bonneville.* New York: Twayne Press, 1899. (fiction)

Jackson, *William E. & J.Orin Oliphant. William Emsley Jackson's Diary of a Cattle Drive from La Grande, Oregon to Cheyenne, Wyoming in 1876.* Fairfield, Washington: Ye Galleon Press, 1984.

James, Thomas & Milo Quaife, (ed). *Three Years Among the Indians & Mexicans.* Chicago, Illinois: R.R. Donnelley & Sons Company, 1953.

Jordan, T. *Riding the White Horse Home: A Western Family Album.* New York: Vintage Books, 1994.

Kelly, Charles & Dale L. Morgan. *Old Greenwood; The Story of Caleb Greenwood: Trapper, Pathfinder, & Early Pioneer.* Georgetown, California: Talisman Press, 1965.

Kendall, George W. & Milo Quaife (ed), *Narrative of the Texan Santa Expedition.* Chicago, Illinois: Lakeside Press, R.R. Donnelley & Sons, 1929.

Kherdian, D. *Bridger: The Story of a Mountain Man.* New York: Greenwillow Books, 1987.

Kissling, Herbert H. *The Evolution of the British North American Fur Trade 1700-1821.* Thesis (M.A.) Laramie, Wyoming: University of Wyoming, 1952.

Krakauer, John. *Under the Banner of Heaven.* New York: Anchor Books, 2003.

Lageson, David R. & Darwin R. Spearing. *Roadside Geology of Wyoming.* Missoula, Montana: Mountain Press. 1988.

Lamb, Peter O. *The Sign of the Buffalo Skull; The Story of Jim Bridger, Frontier Scout.* New York: Frederick A. Stokes, 1932.

Larpenteur, Charles & Milo Quaife (ed) *Forty Years a Fur Trader on the Upper Missouri: Personal Narrative, 1832-1872.* Lincoln, Nebraska: University of Nebraska Press, 1962.

Larson, Taft A. *History of Wyoming.* Lincoln, Nebraska: University of Nebraska Press, 1965.

Lavendar, David. *Wyoming History.* Lincoln, Nebraska: University of Nebraska Press, 1938.

Lockwood, Jeffry A. Locust: *The Devastating Rise & Mysterious Disappearance of the Insect that Shaped the American Frontier.* Laramie, Wyoming: Basic Books. 2004.

Love, Ethel W. & John D. Love. *Life on Muskrat Creek; A Homestead Family in Wyoming.* Bethlehem, Pennsylvania: Lehigh University Press, 2018.

Luttig, John C. *Journal of a Fur-trading Expedition on the Upper Missouri 1812-1813.* St. Louis, Missouri: St. Louis, Missouri, Historical Society, 1920.

Mackey, Mike. *The Equality State: Essays on Intolerance & Inequality in Wyoming.* Casper, Wyoming:Western History Publications, 1999.

Mason, Mary K. *Laramie, Gem City of the Plains.* Dallas, Texas: Curtis Media, 1987.

Mattes, Merrill J. *Jackson Hole, Crossroads of the Western Fur Trade.* Jackson, Wyoming: Jackson Hole Museum & Teton County Historical Society, 1994.

McLoughlin, John & Burt Barker (ed). *The Letters of John McLoughlin; Being the Record of his Estate and of his Proprietary Accounts with the North West Company (1811-1821) and the Hudson's Bay Company (1821-1868).* Iola, Wisconsin: Kraus Publishing, 1968.

McPhee, John A. *Rising from the Plains.* New York: Noonday Press Farrar, Straus & Giroux, 2000.

Michener, John A. & J. Fisher *Centennial.* Norwalk, Connecticut: Easton Press, 1988. (fiction)

Miller, A.J. *Braves & Buffalo: Plains Indian Life in 1837. Water-colours of Alfred J. Miller, with Descriptive Notes by the Artist.* Toronto, Canada: University of Toronto Press, 1973.

Miner, Charles & A. Hubley. *History of Wyoming: In a Series of Letters from Charles Miner to his Son William Penn Miner.* Philadelphia, Pennsylvania: J. Crissy Publisher, 1981.

Mullins, Reuben B. & J. Roush, *Pulling Leather: Being the Early Recollections of a Cowboy on the Wyoming Range, 1884-1889.* Glendo, Wyoming: High Plains Press, 1988.

Oglesby, Richard E. *Vision of Empire: Manuel Lisa & the Opening of the Missouri Fur Trade.* Thesis (PhD), Chicago, Illinois: Northwestern University, 1962.

Pinkerton, Joan T. *Knights of the Broadax: The Story of the Wyoming Tie Hacks.* Laramie, Wyoming: Pronghorn Press, 2017.

Powell, John W. *The Exploration of the Colorado River & its Canyons.* New York: Dover Publications, 1961.

Rand, Ken. *Tales of the Lucky Nickel Saloon: Second Ave., Laramie, Wyoming, US of* A. Laramie, Wyoming: Yard Dog Press, 2002.

Rauzi, E. *The Fur Men on the Missouri & its Tributaries 1822.* Thesis (M.A.) Laramie, Wyoming: University of Wyoming, 1934.

Reavis, L.U. *The Life & Military Services of General William Selby Harney.* St. Louis, Missouri: Bryan, Brand & Company, 1878.

Reynolds, Karen D. *Alfred Jacob Miller: An Artist on the Oregon Trail.* Forth Worth, Texas: Amon Carter Museum, 1982.

Revere, Ray. *A History of Fort Sanders, Wyoming.* Thesis (M.A.) Laramie, Wyoming: University of Wyoming, 1960.

Robbins, E. *My Life in the Mountains.* New York: Rosen Publishing, n.d.

Sabin, Edwin L. *"Old" Jim Bridger on the Moccasin Trail; A Tale of the Beaver West & of the Men who Opened the Mountains.* New York: Thomas Y. Crowell, 1928.

Sandoz, Mari. *The Beaver Men.* Lincoln, Nebraska: University of Nebraska Press, 1982.

Sandoz, Mari. *The Cattlemen.* Lincoln, Nebraska: University of Nebraska Press, 1966.

Sides, Hampton. *Blood and Thunder: The Epic Story of Kit Carson and the Conquest of the American West.* New York: Doubleday, 2006.

Smith, M.R. *Koo-koo-sint: David Thompson in Western Canada.* Red Deer, Alberta, Canada: Red Deer College Press, 1976.

Speck, Gordon. *Breeds & Half-breeds. C. N. Potter;* New York: Crown Publishing, 1969.

Spencer, Charles F. *Wyoming Homestead Heritage: Memoirs.* Hicksville, New York: Exposition Press, 1975.

Stansbury, Howard. *Exploration and Survey of the Valley of the Great Salt Lake of Utah, Including a Reconnaissance of a New Route through the Rocky Mountains.* Washington DC: Smithsonian Institution Press, 1852.

Starr, Eileen. *Architecture in the Cowboy State, 1849 - 1940. A Guide.* Glendo, Wyoming: High Plains Press, 1992.

Stegmaier, Mark J. James F. Mulligan: His Journal of Frémont's Fifth Expedition, 1853-1854, His Adventurous Life on Land & Sea. Glendale, California: A.H. Clark Company, 1988.

Stegner, Wallace. *Beyond the Hundredth Meridian: John Wesley Powell & the Second Opening of the West.* New York: Penguin Books, 1992.

Storti, Craig. *Incident at Bitter Creek: The Story of the Rock Springs Chinese Massacre.* Ames, Iowa: Iowa State University Press, 1931.

Strahorn, Robert E. *The Handbook of Wyoming and Guide to the Black Hills for Citizen Emigrant & Tourist.* Cheyenne, Wyoming: Knight & Leonard, 1877.

Stuart, Robert & P.A. Rollins. *The Discovery of the Oregon Trail, Robert Stuart's Narratives of his Overland Trip Eastward from Astoria in 1812-13, from the Original Manuscripts in the Collection of William Robertson Coe, Esq.; Which is Added an Account of the Tonquin's Voyage & of Events at Fort Astoria (1811-12) & Wilson Price Hunt's Diary of his Overland Trip Westward to Astoria in 1811-12,* translated from Nouvelles annales des voyages, Paris, 1821. New York: Scribner, 1935.

Talbot, Theodore. *The Journals of Theodore Talbot, 1843 & 1849-52, With the Frémont Expedition of 1843 & With the First Military Company in Oregon Territory, 1849-1852,* Portland, Oregon: Metropolitan Press, 1931.

Thrapp, Dan L. *Encyclopedia of Frontier Biography.* Cleveland, Ohio: A.H. Clark Publishing, 1994.

Thwaites, Reuben G. *A Brief History of Rocky Mountain Exploration: With Especial Reference to the Expedition of Lewis & Clark.*, New York: D. Appleton & Company, 1904.

Thwaites, Reuben G. *Early Western Travels, 1748-1846: A Series of Annotated Reprints of some of the Best & Rarest Contemporary Volumes of Travel.* Cleveland, Ohio:A.H. Clark, 1904.

Togstad, Gary & Carla Togstad, *Camp Devin-Bradley Expedition 1878: Little Missouri River, Wyoming Territory.* Laramie, Wyoming: Sand Creek Printing, 1986.

Trenholm, Virginia C. *Footprints on the Frontier: Saga of the Laramie Region of Wyoming.* Douglas, Georgia: Douglas Enterprise, 1945.

Twain, Mark. *Roughing It.* Los Angeles, California: University of California Press, 1972.

Unruh, J.D. *The Plains Across: The Overland Emigrants & the Trans-Mississippi West, 1840-60.* Champagne, Illinois: University of Illinois Press, 1979.

Utley, R.M. *Frontier Regulars the United States Army & the Indian, 1866-1891.* New York: Macmillan Publishing Company, 1973.

Vestal, Stanley. *Jim Bridger, Mountain Man; A Biography.* Lincoln, Nebraska: University of Nebraska Press, 1970.

Victor, Francis F. *The River of the West: Life & Adventure in the Rocky Mountains & Oregon, Embracing Events in the Life-time of a Mountain-Man & Pioneer, with the Early History of the North-western Slope, Including an Account of the Fur Traders ... Also, a Description of the Country.* Hartford, Connecticut: R.W. Bliss & Company, 1870.

Viner, Kim. M.C. *Brown: Wyoming Jurist.* Laramie, Wyoming: Albany County Women's League, 2010.

Wagner, Henry R. & Charles L. Camp. *Plains & the Rockies: A Bibliography of Original Narratives of Travel & Adventure, 1800-1865.* (classic reprint). London, England: Forgotten Books, 2015.

Walls, J. *Half-broke Horses: A True-life Novel.* Stuttgart, Germany: Klett Sprachen, 2014.

Warner, Robert C. *The Fort Laramie of Alfred Jacob Miller: A Catalogue of All Known Illustrations of the First Fort Laramie.* Laramie Wyoming: University of Wyoming Publications. 1979.

Wilder, Laura I. *Little House on the Prairie.* New York: Harper Collins Publishers, 2017. (fiction)

Wood, W.R. *Early Fur Trade on the Northern Plains: Canadian Traders Among the Mandan & Hidatsa Indians, 1738-1818: The Narratives of John MacDonell, Davis Thompson, Francois-Antoine Larocque, & Charles Mackenzie.* Norman, Oklahoma: University of Oklahoma Press, 1985.

## Newspaper & Periodical References

Abbott, Frank. "Over the Oregon Trail with Cattle in Laramie." *Wyoming Stock Growers Collection.* University of Wyoming Archive, 1941.

Anonymous. "Trabing Commercial Company: Reminisces of Early Days in Laramie III." WPA Subject 864, Laramie, *Wyoming Early Citizens.* n.d.

Anonymous. "Internal Commerce of US Assessed Valuation of Property in Wyoming Territory for 1870-1880 by Counties." Washington: *House Executive document* First Session, 51st Congress, 1889, Volume 23, page 834-5.

Anonymous. "Laramie City: Review of Laramie City for 1868-69." *Laramie Weekly Sentinel* May 5, 1883. Reprinted in the Annals of Wyoming 15:4:391-402, October 1943.

Anonymous. "The Search for Jacques Laramee: A Study in Frustration." *Annals of Wyoming.* 1964 36 (2) pp.169-174.

Anonymous. "Jacques Laramie? Laramie Named After Ill-Fated Trapper." *In Wyoming. March-April 1975.*

Foster, Jack. "The Colorado Question Box; Strongbox recalls Jack Slade stagecoach robbery near Virginia Dale." *Rocky Mountain News.* 1952, January 27, Page 15A.

Frost, Donald M. "Notes on General Ashley, the Overland Trail & South Pass." *Proceedings of the American Antiquarian Society* (V.54, p. [161] - 312). 1945.

DeCalesta, David S. 1976. "Predator Control: History and Policies." *Oregon State Extension Service, Extension Circular 710-B.* Corvallis, Oregon: Oregon State Extension Service.

Goodell, G. B. "A Wyoming Blizzard - Cheyenne & Niobrara." *Breeders Gazette,* pp. 1183-1184. December 30, 1903.

Hebard, Grace R. "Jacques LaRamie." *Midwest Review,* Volume 7, Number 3, pp. 32-70. March, 1926.

Jackson, W. Turrentine. "The Wyoming Stock Growers' Association: Its Years of Temporary Decline, 1886-1890." *Agricultural History* 22, no. 4 (1948): 260-70. http://www.jstor.org/ stable/3739523.

Killough, Harry. "Redeeming the Desert West." Chicago: *Breeders Gazette,* p. 1189. December 4, 1907.

Langhoff, Dever B. & Murray L. Carroll. "Tom Horn & the Langhoff Gang of Wyoming." Annals of Wyoming, Spring 1992.

Larson, Alfred. "The Winter of 1886-87 in Wyoming." *Annals of Wyoming,* pp 5-17, January, 1942.

Mueller, E. C., E. L. Frye, & L.R. Maki. "Laramie City: Review of Laramie City 1868-69." *Laramie Weekly Sentinel,* pp. 391-402. May 5, 1883.

Peck, Daniel. "Major Andrew Henry; The first white man to see the Bighorn Basin." *The Lovell Chronicle,* p. 4A. June 27, 1991.

Thompson, John. C. "In Old Wyoming." *Wyoming State Tribune,* pp. 1-3. May 6, 1942.

Whitehouse, Arthur & Axel Palmer. "Making Bulls for the Range." Chicago: *Breeders Gazette*, p. 879, November 20, 1901.


# Internet Sources

Access Genealogy. "Indian Wars, Their Cost and Civil Expenditures." *Access geneology.com,* https://accessgeneology.com/indian_wars,_their_ cost_and_civil_expenditures. Last updatedOctober 27, 2012.

Albany County Public Library. "Laramie Boomerang Digital Collections." *newspapers.wyoming.gov.* https://Newspapers.wyoming.gov/ laramie_*boomerang.*

Canadian Agricultural Partnership. "Predation Compensation." *SCIC.ca.* https://SCIC/ predation_compensation.

Carlson, Chip. "Tom Horn: Wyoming Enigma." *WyoHistory.org,* https:// WyoHistory.org/tom_horn. Last updated November 8, 2014.

Chapman, Fred. "Medicine Wheel/Medicine Mountain:Celebrated and Controversial Landmark." *WyoHistory.org.* https://WyoHistory.

org/medicine_wheel/medicine_mountain. Last updated April 10, 2019.

Davis, John W. "The Johnson County War: 1892 Invasion of Northern Wyoming." *WyoHistory.org,* https:WyoHistory.org/the_johnson_county_war.

Department of the Interior. "Livestock Grazing." *DOI:BLM.gov,* https://DOI:BLM:livestock _grazing. Last updated February3, 2016.

Dobson, G.B. "Wyoming Tales and Trails." *WyomingTalesandTrails. com.*

Graves, Malcolm. "There Will Be Scandal: An Oil Stain on the Jazz Age." *NewYorkTimes.org.* https://TheNewYorkTimes.org/there_will_be_a_scandal. Last updated February 13, 2008.

Herman, Marguerite. "Albany County, Wyoming." *WyoHistory.org,* https://WyoHistory.org/ albany_county. Last updated November 8, 2014.

New York Times. "Once Guilty Now Innocent But Still Dead." *NewYorkTimes. org.* https:// TheNewYorkTimes/once_guilty_now_innocent. Last Updated September 20, 1993.

New York Times. "Overlooked No More: She Followed a Trail to Wyoming. Then She Blazed One." *NewYorkTimes.org.* https:// TheNewYorkTimes.org/she_followed_a_trail_to_Wyoming. Last Updated May 23, 2018.

Rea, Tom. "Right Choice Wrong Reasons: Wyoming Women Win the Right to Vote." *WyoHistory.org,* https://WyoHistory.org/right_choice_wrong_reasons. Last updated November 8, 2014.

Tanner, Russel. "Leasing the Public Range: The Taylor Grazing Act and the BLM." *WyoHistory.org,* https://WyoHistory.org/leasing_the_public_range. Last updated August 30, 2015.

Viner, Kim. "Edward Ivinson, Laramie Banker and Philanthropist." *WyoHistory.org.* https::// WyoHistory.org/edward_ivinson. Last Updated November 8, 2014.

Viner, Kim. "Wyoming Lawyer Melville C. Brown: A Man for his Time." *WyoHistory.org,* https:// WyoHistory.org/wyoming_lawyer_melville_c._brown. Last updated May 31, 2015.

Western, Daniel. "The Mineral Leasing Act of 1920: The Law that Changed Wyoming's Destiny." *WyoHistory.org.* https://WyoHistory.org/the_mineral_leasing_act_of_1920. Last updated November 8, 2014.

Walsh, Dave. "The Cheyenne-Deadwood Trail." *Wonders of Wyoming.org.* https://The_wonders_of_Wyoming/The_Cheyenne_Deadwood_Trail. Last Updated April 2, 2013.

Weed, James A. "Vital Statistics in the United States." NCHS.gov, https://NCHS.gov/ Vital_statistics._Winter_1995. Office of Population Research, Princeton, University.

White, Deborah. "What is Gun Ownership by State." *Thought.co,* https://Thought.com/ what_is_gun_ownership_by_state.

Wikipedia contributors, "Ames Monument," Wikipedia, The Free Encyclopedia, https:// en.wikipedia.org/w/index.php?title=Ames_Monument&oldid=897568106 (accessed August 25, 2019).

Wikipedia contributors, "Catecholamine," Wikipedia, The Free Encyclopedia, https:// en.wikipedia.org/w/index. php?title=Catecholamine&oldid=892828436 (accessed August 25, 2019).

Wikipedia contributors, "Cherokee Trail," *Wikipedia, The Free Encyclopedia,* https:// en.wikipedia.org/w/index.php?title=Cherokee_Trail&oldid=849999772 (accessed August 25, 2019).

Wikipedia contributors, "Claude Dallas," *Wikipedia, The Free Encyclopedia,* https:// en.wikipedia.org/w/index.php?title=Claude_Dallas&oldid=906674207 (accessed August 25, 2019).

Wikipedia contributors, "Coyote," *Wikipedia, The Free Encyclopedia,* https:// en.wikipedia.org/w/ index.php?title=Coyote&oldid=912379630 (accessed August 25, 2019).

Wikipedia contributors, "Dale Creek Crossing," *Wikipedia, The Free Encyclopedia,* https:// en.wikipedia.org/w/index.php?title=Dale_Creek_Crossing&oldid=906287200 (accessed August 25, 2019).

Wikipedia contributors, "Desert Land Act," *Wikipedia, The Free Encyclopedia,* https:// en.wikipedia.org/w/index.php?title=Desert_Land_Act&oldid=851046915 (accessed August 25, 2019).

Wikipedia contributors, "Fort D. A. Russell (Texas)," *Wikipedia, The Free Encyclopedia,* https:// en.wikipedia.org/w/index. php?title=Fort_D._A._Russell_(Texas)&oldid=877678836 (accessed August 24, 2019).

Wikipedia contributors, "Fort Lewis," *Wikipedia, The Free Encyclopedia,* https://en.wikipedia.org/w/index.php?title=Fort_

Lewis&oldid=903512034 (accessed August 24, 2019).Genocide of Indigenous Peoples - Wikipedia.

Wikipedia contributors, "Genocide of indigenous peoples," *Wikipedia, The Free Encyclopedia,* https://en.wikipedia.org/w/index.php?title=Genocide_of_indigenous_peoples&oldid=910917593 (accessed August 25, 2019).

Wikipedia contributors, "Goodnight–Loving Trail," *Wikipedia, The Free Encyclopedia,* https:// en.wikipedia.org/w/index.php?title=Goodnight%E2%80%93Loving_Trail&oldid=906615857 (accessed August 24, 2019).

Wikipedia contributors, "Immigration Act of 1924," *Wikipedia, The Free Encyclopedia,* https:// en.wikipedia.org/w/index.php?title=Immigration_Act_of_1924&oldid=907628727 (accessed August 24, 2019).

Wikipedia contributors, "Indian agent," *Wikipedia, The Free Encyclopedia,* https://en.wikipedia.org/ w/index.php?title=Indian_agent&oldid=910858670 (accessed August 24, 2019).

Wikipedia contributors, "Indian Removal Act," *Wikipedia, The Free Encyclopedia,* https:// en.wikipedia.org/w/index.php?title=Indian_Removal_Act&oldid=911996780 (accessed August 24, 2019).

Wikipedia contributors, "John Wesley Powell," *Wikipedia, The Free Encyclopedia,* https:// en.wikipedia.org/w/index.php?title=John_Wesley_Powell&oldid=911320340 (accessed August 24, 2019).

Wikipedia contributors, "Land-grant university," *Wikipedia, The Free Encyclopedia,* https:// en.wikipedia.org/w/index.php?title=Land-grant_university&oldid=903379269 (accessed August 24, 2019).

Wikipedia contributors, "Pacific Railroad Acts," *Wikipedia, The Free Encyclopedia,* https://en.wikipedia.org/w/index.php?title=Pacific_Railroad_Acts&oldid=912203871 (accessed August 24, 2019).

Wikipedia contributors, "Sagebrush Rebellion," *Wikipedia, The Free Encyclopedia,* https:// en.wikipedia.org/w/index.php?title=Sagebrush_Rebellion&oldid=910068192 (accessed August 24, 2019).

Wikipedia contributors, "Timeline of glaciation," *Wikipedia, The Free Encyclopedia,* https:// en.wikipedia.org/w/index.php?title=Timeline_of_glaciation&oldid=909658207 (accessed August 24, 2019).

Wikipedia contributors, "Watershed Management," *Wikipedia, The Free Encyclopedia,* https:// en.wikipedia.org/w/index. php?title=Watershed_management&oldid=906057576 (accessed August 24, 2019).

Wikipedia contributors, "Wyoming Territorial Prison State Historic Site," *Wikipedia, The Free Encyclopedia,* https://en.wikipedia.org/w/index.php? title=Wyoming_Territorial_Prison_State_Historic_Site&oldid=869356761 (accessed August 24, 2019).

World Ocean Review. "Living in Coastal Areas- A Report on the state of the World's Oceans." *World Ocean review.com,* https://world_ocean_review.com/living_in_coastal_areas.

## Other Sources

Personal communication, Amy Lawrence, Laramie, Wyoming. August, 2004.

Personal communication, Craig Kling, Bellevue, Colorado. August, 2020.

~~~~~~~~~~~~~~
~~~~~~~~~~~~~~

~~~~~~~~~~~~~~

*A person who will not read
has no advantage*

*Over one who cannot read.*

*Mark Twain*

*The true mission of a
journalist is to expose the
truth, not to play the part
of a literary showman.*

*Mark Twain*

~~~~~~~~~~~~~~